Michael Nayak

SENTIENT

THE ICE PLAGUE WARS, BOOK II

ANGRY ROBOT
An imprint of Watkins Media Ltd

Unit 11, Shepperton House
89-93 Shepperton Road
London N1 3DF
UK

angryrobotbooks.com
A cold day in hell.

An Angry Robot paperback original, 2026

Edited by Simon Spanton Walker and Dan Hanks
Cover by Sneha Alexander
Set in Meridien

ISBN 978 1 91599 844 6
Ebook ISBN 978 1 91599 845 3

Printed and bound in the United Kingdom by CPI Group (UK) Ltd, Croydon CR0 4YY

The manufacturer's authorised representative in the EU for product safety is eucomply OÜ - Pärnu mnt 139b-14, 11317 Tallinn, Estonia, hello@eucompliancepartner.com; www.eucompliancepartner.com

9 8 7 6 5 4 3 2 1

For
DARPA,
where I've learned how the world behind the world really works.

And for all of DARPA's Program Managers, past and present.
I'm proud to have been one of you.

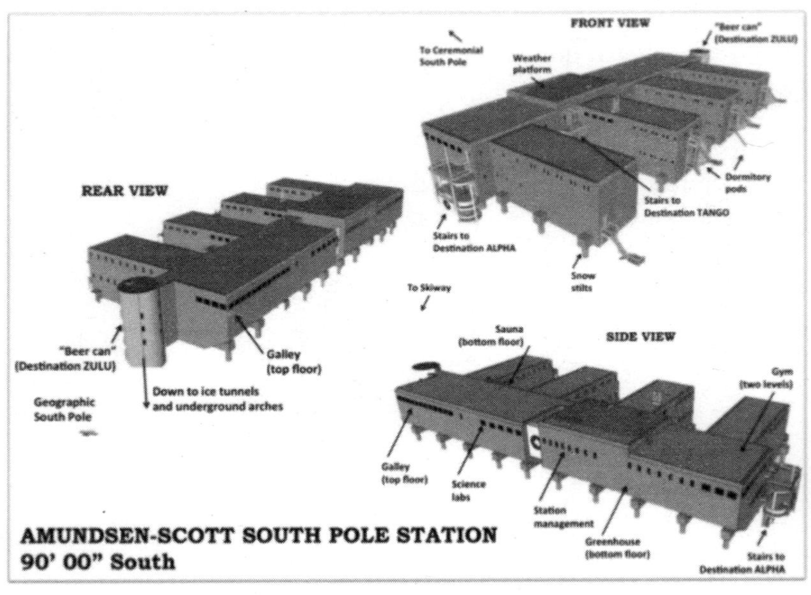
FRONT VIEW
To Ceremonial South Pole
Weather platform
"Beer can" (Destination ZULU)
Dormitory pods
Stairs to Destination TANGO
Stairs to Destination ALPHA
Snow stilts
REAR VIEW
"Beer can" (Destination ZULU)
Galley (top floor)
Down to ice tunnels and underground arches
Geographic South Pole
To Skiway
SIDE VIEW
Sauna (bottom floor)
Gym (two levels)
Galley (top floor)
Science labs
Station management
Greenhouse (bottom floor)
Stairs to Destination ALPHA
AMUNDSEN-SCOTT SOUTH POLE STATION
90' 00" South

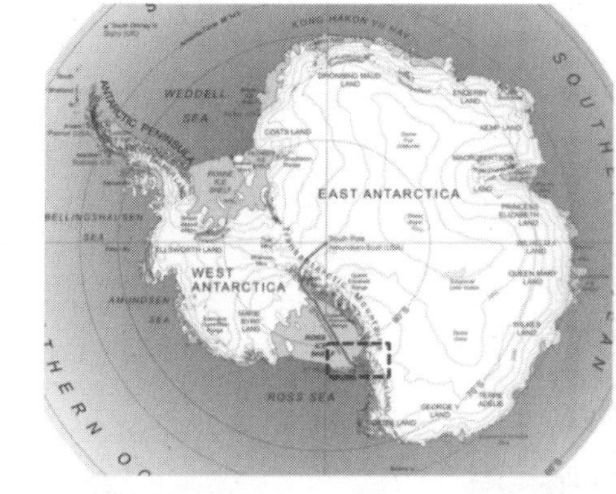

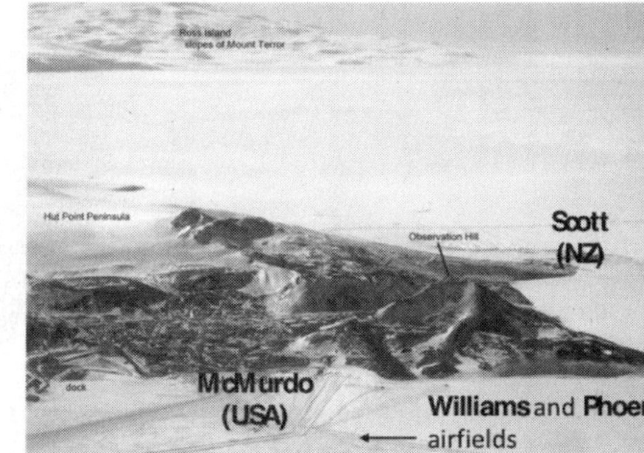

Credit: Coolantarctica.com/Bases/McMurdo/hut-point-peninsula.jpg

McMurdo Station, Ross Island, Antarctica

Image credit Peter Somers, archdaily.com/

Mac Helipor
Movement Control Center
Crary Science Lab
Cafeteria
Southern Exposure bar
Church of the Snows
Dormitory buildings
Air Nat'l Guard warehouse
NSF Chalet
McMurdo Station (summer view)

AMUNDSEN-SCOTT SOUTH POLE STATION

SURVIVORS, WINTER-OVER CREW, 2028

Starting Total: 41 (29 support, 12 science staff; 31 male, 10 female)
Deceased: 35 (27 support, 8 science staff; 27 male, 8 female).

Survivors:

1. Dr. Rajan Chariya, Major, US Air Force. Long-duration Antarctic Night & Daytime Imaging Telescope (LANDIT) Science Lead.
2. Siri Monthan. Heavy Equipment Operator, Cargo team.
3. Keyon Geerts. Foreman, Facilities team.
4. Jonah Mitchell. Atmospheric Research Observatory (ARO) caretaker.
5. Dr. Bethany Hamidani. South Pole Telescope (SPT) caretaker.
6. Greg "Lucky" Penny. Ice Cube Laboratory (ICL) caretaker.

McMURDO (MAC) STATION KEY CREW MEMBERS, WINFLY CREW, 2028

Winter-over total: 191 (140 support, 51 science staff; 145 male, 46 female)
Win-fly total: 426 (360 support, 66 science staff; 328 male, 98 female)

Station Manager	Winston Pele
Deputy Station Manager and Special US Deputy Marshal	Anne Pabon

Medical: Physician	Caitlin Morris
Medical: Lead Nurse Practitioner	Michael Frazer
Writers and Artists Program Fellow	Mariana Egan
Meteorology Team	Pasch Evans, Justin Voithofer
Historic Conservation Team	Ricardo D'Souza, Ramon Garcia
Williams Airfield Ground Crew	Sam Eske; Ryan Barbosa
Fire Technician	Heather Heigele
Mobility Technicians	Gisela Childers, Michelle Ajuria
Electrician Lead	Wayne Weiss
Pastor, Chapel of the Snows	Taylor Kwanje, LCDR, US Navy
Production Cook	Aaron Bateman
Fuelie	Stuart Crowe

RESCUE CREW

Team Lead:	Jackie Colson.
HAVE VIKING Project Scientists:	Dr. Richard Mason (CIA) and Dr. Jon Kim (DARPA).
Fire team:	Sal (operations lead); Kaushik (medic); Barham (sniper); Mackie (breacher/spotter); Lansdown (comms); LoNigro (logistics).
Basler Aircrew:	Tristan Hyatt (pilot); "Maui" Hathaway (co-pilot).

BOOK ONE

Patient and Hidden

AUGUST 2 – SEPTEMBER 23

For all the day long have I been plagued.
When I thought to know this, it was too painful for me;
Until I went into the sanctuary of God;
Then understood I their end.

Psalm 73:3 – 17

PROLOGUE

2028, the second year of the Pacific Rim War. A stalemate, the pundits and generals on both the Chinese and American sides say, but there is no forgiveness in war. Only patience until an advantage reveals itself.

Like a stage ninja in the wings, Russia lurks on the sidelines. Not involved in the war, not yet, but providing assistance to China, as the Americans had to Britain during the early days of World War II. Waiting, military analysts think, for the right moment of weakness in which to pounce.

The Antarctic plain stretches in every direction, unending, starting to brighten more with every passing day. Nothing but white in the snow ahead, and the white of the Trans-Antarctic Mountains behind. The sky is still tinged with the winter dark, but is retreating by the day. Some day soon, and then for months thereafter, it will be daytime all the time.

The cold wind surges into our raw throat and against our peeling face, but we don't feel it anymore. We heal faster now; we feel nothing. There is nothing left for us at South Pole, except the journey to *more*.

Ben Jacobs walks.

We walk.

We keep walking, a speck on a vast untamed snowy desert. Toward the sun, now, heading north to warmer climes.

Chapter One

COMMUNIQUE: TRANSCRIPT OF ENCRYPTED COMMUNICATION

LOCATION: ████████████████████, JUNE 27, 2028

(TS/HCS/SAP-HV) Identity of Subject: ████████ ████████. Subject is ████████ ████ (career field specialty code ████ ████████) assigned to the ████████ ████. Subject was recruited by Case Officer ████████████████. Subject was presented with funding], selection as ████████ ████, in return for limited support to HAVE VIKING Phase II operations.

(*ops-desk*) Please identify.

(*Subject*) ████████████████ / not much time / summary follows.

(*ops-desk*) Report status of visitors?

(*Subject*) 13 crew dead from initial contact with extremophile microbe of unknown origin / ████

████████████████████████████. 7

add'l dead since initial contact / station mgr compromised / request evac asap

(*ops-desk*) Say nature of mutation?

(*ops-desk*) Symptoms?

(*Subject*) Confirm medical evac as soon as wx permits.

(*ops-desk*) More information needed. Do you have a report with details?

(*Subject*) You're not fucking listening.

(*ops-desk*) Evac confirmed asap wx.

(*ops-desk*) Say nature of microbe mutation, upload report?

(*Subject*) Fuck you. Details available on evac so better hope we make it. Persons touching down must have Level A Hazmat gear. Aircraft must have USAF Transport Isolation System or equiv.

(*ops-desk*) Can you say symptoms, possible mitigation?

(*Subject*) Consider all survivors infected until tested negative.

--

August 2, 2028. Chicago, Illinois, USA

Jane Bradshaw, Editor of the *Chicago Tribune*, takes off her glasses and chews on the stem. It's a bad habit she's had since her days as a young reporter running the financial beat, but it's either that or chain-smoking, so she's given up trying to change it. In her hand she holds a printout of the redacted communique Mariana has received from a source deep in the intelligence community.

"Okay," Bradshaw says, and now her eyes focus on Mariana Egan, sitting across the conference table from her. One of her best investigative journalists. "Take me through it."

Mariana sits forward, and gestures to the date of June 27 on the redacted printout. "That is from just over a month ago," she says. "First of all, nothing but crickets on that from my Pentagon sources."

"Well..." Bradshaw doesn't say the name *General Rason*, but to Mariana, her little shrug says it anyway.

"Yeah, okay, I'm not exactly welcome over there. Yet... no one still talking to me will comment on `HAVE VIKING`" – she motions toward the report – "which tells me it's an unacknowledged operation. Black money funded." Mariana tucks a stray curl of greying hair behind her ear and points to the classification sticker at the top. "See that, 'TS/HCS'? That's 'Top Secret, Human Intelligence Control System.' Human intelligence – or HUMINT – is almost always CIA."

Bradshaw doesn't say anything, so Mariana keeps going. "Okay, first. Amundsen-Scott South Pole station went offline right around the time of that transmission. No internet pings, no radio, nothing. I've talked with several families of crewmembers deployed down there. Their partners have missed every communications window for the last month. When the families reached out to the National Science Foundation, they got stonewalled. Total silence."

"I'm sorry, why NSF?"

"Ah, yes. By statute, NSF runs all US operations in the Antarctic," Mariana says. "The idea goes back to the Antarctic Treaty of 1959, which states that Antarctica is a global common for research and scientific activity only. Air Force planes supply cargo and people, but the stations are NSF-run, and no other military operations are allowed."

"So, NSF is in charge of all things Antarctica. Got it. I assume you poked them for a formal explanation?"

"The official reason I got was that a charged particle event has taken down satellite communications. Problem is, when I talked to some scientists down the road at Northwestern, they can't find any record of such an event. Never happened, they say."

"Could be they just don't have the data."

"So I asked the NSF to confirm: are they, or are they not, in contact with South Pole Station? I told them I was researching a story about thirty days of no-contact with one of our most remote scientific stations, and a freak solar storm no one can find. This time I got a call from their legal counsel."

Bradshaw raises an interested eyebrow. "Touched a nerve, then."

"Big time. On the call, they said they *are* in contact with South Pole Station."

"Despite the satellite being down?"

"In the old days, before satellite, they kept in touch via over-the-horizon HF radio. They said the long-range HF antennas are still active. The bandwidth is low, so they can't spare it for family hellos. But apparently everyone at Pole is fine, to the best of the NSF's knowledge."

"Great. What's the problem?"

"I think they're lying," Mariana says flatly. "I reached out to the Antarctican Society. It's this old-guy alumni club. People who have spent time in Antarctica before. The President of the Society put me in touch with the folks who built the long-range HF transmitters at South Pole back in the day. Those people swore they also *dis*assembled those antennas as soon as the NSF got overhead satellite working. That's why I think that communique in your hand is referring to South Pole. Dead crewmembers, a compromised Station Manager, and some type of serious infection. That's what I think the NSF is trying to cover up."

Bradshaw is starting to look attentive.

"Now let's talk about Kunlun Station, located on top of Dome Argus, or Dome-A," Mariana presses on. "This is a Chinese Antarctic station, and it has *also* gone completely dark recently." She reaches into a file and pulls out a series of papers. "I've been working with our cyber team to comb the dark web, and here's a sampling of what I've found."

Bradshaw leans forward, puts her glasses back on.

"There are rumors of deaths at Dome-A. Families have lost contact with their loved ones. No formal answers from the Chinese government, but a flood of black-hat traffic targeting people making these posts. Someone is throttling these rumors."

"That isn't particularly surprising. China's at war with us. They'll throttle any rumor."

"I know someone on crew at Dome-A this winter." Mariana starts talking faster. "Lingling Mei, Professor of Glaciology. I met her when I was posted to Nanjing before the Pacific Rim war. She and her husband Xi Lin are both down at Dome-A. I was getting regular messages relayed via HF radio transmission from her, and then suddenly… nothing." Mariana knows that it won't be hard for Bradshaw to tell, from her tone of voice, that this is what had gotten her started on this investigation. "Her brother Jiuyin Mei works for the Chinese government. We go way back, so I asked him about his sister's station going dark. He said he also stopped hearing from her around mid-May."

Mariana pulls out a map of Antarctica, and lays it on the table between them. She points at Dome-A. "Mid-May, offline." Then she points to South Pole, in the very center of the map. "Mid-June, offline." She taps the censored communique in Bradshaw's hand, which references a contagious infection. "And there's the connection between the two."

Next to the map, she lays a grainy printout: a picture from an overhead satellite, marked TOP SECRET // TALENT KEYHOLE. "I got this from the same source as that communique. Taken by a spy satellite, one of ours."

The picture is black and white, and shows mostly ice. But in the center of the image are two snow vehicles. Their tracks visible behind them.

"This was taken on June 10. Right after Dome-A going silent, but before South Pole going silent. These two vehicles are 300 miles from Dome-A, moving south-west. And the only thing in that direction… is South Pole Station."

She sits back. Stays silent as Bradshaw again chews on the stem of her glasses and studies the information in front of her.

"You think there's a story here."

Mariana's heart sinks at her editor's phrasing, but the determination in her voice rings as clearly as a church bell. "This is the age of overhead satellite connectivity, Jane. Two stations don't just drop offline, even at the bottom of the world. And every spidey sense I've picked up across my career is telling me these two stations, being associated with the two major players in the Pacific Rim war, can't be a coincidence."

"I get that. And I get what this is hinting," Bradshaw gestures to the redacted communique. "But we can't publish it. It's unsubstantiated and there's no way the CIA will validate it. Take that away, and here's what I see: the Chinese are censoring Chinese people posting about the Chinese station. Is that really surprising? Half of China doesn't even know we bombed their capital city and took out Zhongnanhai. And yes, NSF is maybe lying about HF comms with South Pole, but in a time of war, even pure science agencies have to be careful what information they give out. They'll say we just need to wait until the Antarctic winter is over to check on our station's people. I'm not seeing the investigative angle here, Mariana."

Mariana hesitates over the last document in her folder. She almost takes it out, then closes it and nods. "All right, Jane."

Bradshaw bites on her glasses. "Just because we can't publish yet doesn't mean there isn't something here, though. Find me a source who will talk to us on the record and validate your suspicions, or validate this CIA communique, and we'll go to press. But without that, this will just be labeled as fake news and quickly disregarded."

Mariana nods, lips thin and pale. "Understood."

Back at her desk, Mariana Egan pulls out the item she had chosen not to show her editor: a letter from the NSF; a response to a seemingly unlinked application she'd made in her personal capacity.

`Congratulations! You have been selected as part of the National Science Foundation's Writers and Artists Program. Your proposal to document separation resilience via photography and a series of written articles has been accepted.`

`We are unable to grant your proposed location of South Pole Station (90° S 0° E). However, the committee felt your project could be fully accommodated at McMurdo Station (77° S 166° E).`

`We cannot guarantee your requested date of 15 October. Please report to Antarctic training as laid out below. Manifest priority will be determined based on trained crewmember backlog and mission factors once you are on the ground in Christchurch, New Zealand.`

Mariana puts her head in her hands and takes a deep breath. *There's always a moment,* she thinks.

She has covered wars on three continents, and even deep into a twenty-year career as a war correspondent, there's always a moment when she has to ask herself whether she will run toward the gunfire, or away from it. Every time, she's not sure which she'll choose.

The electric chill of adrenalin courses up from the pit of her stomach and flushes her cheeks.

Every time, she has chosen to run toward the gunfire.

She types jerkily, but every stroke is sure. She doesn't hesitate before hitting send.

Hi Jane. Taking a leave of absence to do some freelance work. I'll be back in February 2029.

Mariana Egan goes home, packs her bags, asks her sister to water her plants every so often, and gets on a flight to Denver, Colorado. Three weeks later, after training with the Antarctic Services Corporation, she is on a flight down south to Christchurch, New Zealand, the logistics launch point for the US mission in Antarctica.

She does not know that she will never see Chicago again.

Chapter Two

February 22, 2028. Just over six months ago.

At 0220 local time, callsign Borak 27 lifted off from Runway 02 in Christchurch, New Zealand. There were six people on the Basler airplane, but the official manifest showed only two pilots aboard. Two hundred miles south of Invercargill, its transponder turned off.

Eight hours later, Borak 27 overflew McMurdo Station on the coast of Antarctica.

At 77 degrees South, the sun was a fading red and orange glow barely lighting the horizon. Flights to South Pole had closed down nine days ago for the isolated winter. But Williams airfield had one more crew to refuel before they were done.

Two hours later the Basler was airborne once more, flying deeper into the continent.

Thirty minutes out from the scheduled drop time, Dr. Richard Mason walked up the narrow aisle to the cockpit. Tristan Hyatt was in the left seat; a young but experienced civilian Antarctic pilot. The co-pilot's last name was Hathaway, callsign "Maui". He was an Air Force test pilot and C-17 Special Operations Low Level graduate with special-access security clearances.

Dr. Mason tapped Maui on the shoulder and made a phone call hand-gesture.

Maui dialed up an encrypted UHF frequency reserved for military use. In the HAVE VIKING mission room at Langley, someone would be checking video surveillance feed from the sixteen surreptitiously installed cameras at the Chinese Dome-A Station. The Basler carried four hours of extra fuel if they needed to linger until the Dome-A crew was asleep.

They didn't want anyone awake and looking up at the sunlit sky.

The response came back. "Condition green confirmed."

"Cleared to drop," Dr. Mason said, and went back to his seat.

The two burly loadmasters behind him began to inspect the unmarked airdrop container on rails by the tail door. The unmarked cargo had three small explosive charges.

The first would consume the parachute.

The second would propel the containment sphere fifty yards downrange and destroy the cargo container.

The third charge was so tiny it would barely take off a fingernail, triggered by a double-thermocouple. Once temperatures dropped to under minus 75 degrees, a small vial of acid would shatter, and the containment sphere would begin beeping loudly for attention. The acid would start eating through a copper diaphragm, calibrated to the micro-inch. It would burn through in twenty-four hours, triggering the second thermocouple.

And a tiny explosive charge that would fracture the sphere along pre-drilled facets.

Nature would take its course from there.

Four months later. June 21, 2028.

Dr. Richard Mason was scared, and he didn't want anyone to see it in his eyes.

The computer screen with the yellow TOP SECRET//SAP-HV/TK *banner was subdivided into sixteen video screens. All sixteen screens were still. Nothing moved, except the wind sweeping through the half-open door on Screen 8. The pant leg on the man lying face down in an archipelago of dark bloody icicles tugged just a little farther up every day. But, as always, Mason's eyes came back to Screen 12, where Dr. Lingling Mei lay with her head in the sink.*

On the dining table behind Lingling was Dr. Mason's unmarked clear containment sphere, fractured like a peeled flower. The screens, beaming relayed feeds from covertly emplaced cameras, were soundless, but he knew it was beeping softly and insistently.

Casualties had always been in the projections.

The violence and scale of the microbial outgrowth once in its native environment, however, had been entirely unexpected.

Screen 2, a man tumbled at the foot of his bed, a kitchen knife buried in his back.

Screen 6, a scientist with no shirt on, sprawled wide in the snow like a scarecrow blown over in the night.

Screen 15, a heap of ice that no longer resembled a human corpse.

In the ultraviolet frequencies, every single dead body was positively squirming with activity. The woman slumped over the sink had moved two inches since dying five weeks ago. The level of virulent, almost hostile growth had blown the fancy DARPA models right out of the window.

So far out that just thinking about it made the fear tickle in his throat again.

Dr. Mason stood. After the satellite pass, it would be time to go home, but Screen 12 would stay with him, behind his eyes. Especially when he looked at his wife.

Tingzhi Mason looked a little like Lingling Mei.

The CIA scientist strode out of his office to the vault at the end of the bland grey hallway. An LED screen scrolled with text: TOP SECRET // SPECIAL ACCESS REQUIRED. *Dr. Mason pressed his badge against the reader and keyed in an eight-digit pin.*

He hardened his face. His eyes went blank.

He entered.

The satellite control center was dark. The large screens against the far wall had not yet lit up with live imagery.

"Mason." CIA Deputy Director for Operations Bill Stone emerged smoothly from the shadows.

As DDO, Stone held the national authority to be the single focal point for execution of US clandestine operations. Not just for the CIA, as in the old days, but for all seventeen organizations in the US intelligence community. Everyone called him "Evil Bill" behind his back, because his job was to handle the dirty work. He was exceptionally good at it, the way only someone who enjoyed their work could be.

"HAVE VIKING is turning into a cluster fuck," Evil Bill said, his voice like boots crunching through glass.

"There's still useful data to be gathered from South Pole Station." Dr. Mason's voice emerged cool and collected.

"We wired Dome-A for data," Evil Bill hissed in his ear. "And I had no American deaths to explain to Director Navarro. You want to tell me how you plan to extract useful data from a station where you have no eyes and no spectral analysis?"

The large screens dissolved into a vast expanse of snow. Dancing aurorae hovered over the edge of the planet, visible from space. A speck of a station was in the middle of it all, at the South Pole of the planet.

Scorch marks on the snow by the food arches were immediately evident. There was a hole into which massive amounts of ice and snow had fallen. The satellite view skittered, then tracked over the snow. A naked body was dusted over with snow, a picture eerily like the one from Dome-A. Another lay on a plastic sheet, pixelated face staring upward.

"It's spreading," Evil Bill whispered.

The only video feeds they had access to at South Pole Station began blinking in. Reels of digital video from the cameras on every corner of the ARO building, a quarter-mile from the main Station, were downlinked for later analysis.

"Dr. Jon Kim. You remember him, right?"

"Program Manager at DARPA Biological Technologies Office." Dr. Mason was careful to let no dislike trickle into his voice. "Former Harvard professor. His DARPA program created the microbes I airdropped over Dome-A."

"He just sent me a rather interesting presentation," Evil Bill said. "Dr. Kim remains convinced that our little extremophiles will undergo a forced evolution once they are brought out of a closed ecosystem."

"He's as wrong now as I said he was before. We saw no such evolution at Dome-A."

"Ah, but he says the takeover at Dome-A was too quick. The microbes didn't need to evolve, because they overcame every nutrient source in a matter of days. South Pole is a bigger station. More population diversity. More time needed for the microbes to overwhelm them."

"Dr. Kim would nuke a nursery to study what radiation did to baby carcasses," Mason said evenly. "He fundamentally doesn't care about the dangers of uncontrolled evolution."

"But should the microbes evolve to tolerate a less extreme environment, that would be a unique weapon to send Russia crashing out of the war the second they enter it. You underestimate how interesting I would find that," Evil Bill replied. "So interesting that I'd give the gold star to whoever brought me that data. I'd hate to think my best scientist wasn't up to the job."

Dr. Mason's face didn't change, but he didn't go home after the satellite pass, either. He spent the next two hours on the phone with Antarctic Logistics, LLC, negotiating another Basler aircraft flight as soon as the weather would allow.

He fell asleep in his office and dreamt of his wife lying dead over the sink.

Chapter Three

August 31, 2028. 77° South, 166° East.

McMurdo ("Mac") Station, Antarctica.
1,400 kilometers north of South Pole.

To older veterans of McMurdo Station, the Southern Exposure bar means debauchery, obscenities, all-nighters, and in general, an environment more like a raunchy college dive bar than an Antarctic research Station. But on this last day of August, Southern Exposure houses fewer than 20 of the station's 191 winter-over crewmembers. The acoustics of the large room muffle the dull music into little more than thudded bass notes. There's only one bartender from the Facilities group on duty, and she is playing solitaire at the far edge of the bar.

It has been dark for four straight months.

Against an arcade machine that looks old enough to have children of its own, two people sit at a weather-warped table by themselves. Between them sits a rare prize in Antarctica: a twenty-year Macallan single malt Scotch whisky.

"See this?" Winston Pele grunts as he gestures around the empty bar. "This is what rationing gets you."

"You say that like this place being empty is a bad thing." Marshal Anne Pabon reaches for her glass, swirls the dark liquid around. "Last winter, I had to ban nine people from this bar in one season. *Nine*. That's not even counting Gallagher's."

Winston grunts at the mention of McMurdo's other and smaller bar. "People are gonna do what people are gonna do," he replies. "I just worry about them doing it where we can't tell 'em to knock it off."

Winston Pele has been the Station Manager for McMurdo – known to its inhabitants as Mac or Mactown – for five winters running. He's somewhere between Mayor, Sheriff and Antarctic legend. He's a wide man, with a bulldog-like face and sloping forehead framed with flecks of curly white hair. He sports a long, carefully-groomed white handlebar mustache and low-slung cowboy hat.

Marshal Anne, on the other hand, is the actual arm of the law. She's Winston's deputy manager, but she's also an officer with the US Marshals, badged as responsible for law enforcement at all US stations and field camps in Antarctica. In the summer, that can mean almost twenty different locations around the continent.

Anne and Winston are very different personalities. When he talks it's in a low gravelly tone, almost never with eye contact; the canonical man of few words. Anne talks fast and loudly, her face jumping into a variety of expressions. But when she goes quiet, and her pixie-like face falls still, her beauty sharpens into something unsettling, a live sparking wire held in high tension, and people know it's time to do whatever comes out of her mouth next.

They've worked together for three of the last five years, and have grown into a quiet companionship. Both are effective, divorced, in their fifties, and at the bottom of the world to get the hell away from everyone else.

Marshal Anne raises her glass. "It's been a good winter season."

"And now it's time for it to all get fucked for the summer." Winston sighs as he clinks his glass to hers. "I hate Winfly."

Winfly is the start of Operation Deep Freeze: an early cluster of logistics flights just a few days after the first sunrise cleaves the four months of darkness at Mac. The pre-operation brings the cargo and workforce needed to prepare Mac's facilities for the heavy traffic of the Antarctic summer. The Station is a cluster of logistics and scientific buildings huddled together on Ross Island, on the eastern tip of the Antarctic peninsula, overlooking large ice floes that haven't parted to show the ocean underneath in months.

"Mac's population is about to double in number. My head always feels like it's going to pop off with that many new people at once."

"And in January, when we're at thirteen hundred, or even more?" Winston dampens his mustache with his tongue, then runs his palms across it. "The only faces I'll learn are the damn troublemakers. It makes me cranky."

"So, um. That's why I wanted to talk to you before the first Winfly lands tomorrow."

Marshal Anne looks around, discreetly. Southern Exposure isn't private, but most people are out of their alcohol ration by the last day of the month, and it's late enough into the winter that the cliques are firmly formed. There are no more social butterflies. They will be left alone unless they go out of their way to be otherwise.

She looks back at Winston and her face has changed. "South Pole," she says.

"What about it?"

"I've been catching some uneasiness from the NSF folks in Denver. It's almost like they don't believe their own story."

"Which one of their stories? That a whole station just decides to stop answering the internet because of a freak storm, or that they all got some new strain of COVID?" Winston says dryly.

Marshal Anne rolls her glass between her callused palms. "And now there's more. That Winfly flight tomorrow will have a special team on it. Waived customs inspections on their gear. Manifested with top priority."

Winston straightens. "This is the first I'm hearing of it."

"Yeah, I don't think I'm supposed to give you a heads up about it. But I got a call directly from Rob McHenry."

"Who's that?"

"His official title is the Associate Director for Operations, but don't let that bland title turn your head one bit." Marshal Anne's lips twist. "He's the ops boss for the *entire* US Marshals Service. McHenry is top of the chain for Witness Protection, Intelligence Operations, Dignitary Protection. Winny, I've been a Marshal for twenty-two years and I've heard of him the way you might hear about the Mayor if you shine shoes outside

City Hall. And yet, yesterday, when I called in for a regular tag up with my Division Chief, he was on the line."

"McHenry was there?"

"To talk to me. To talk at me, I should say."

Winston rubs his mustache, listening.

"That special team," she says slowly, "are the only ones who will be heading to Pole."

Winston snaps forward. "Wait, what? We've been working a response plan ever since–"

"I know. I know, Winny. But believe me when I say that Rob fucking McHenry doesn't come down from the ivory tower to give suggestions."

"So come tomorrow, we get a bunch of trigger-happy badges swarming off the very first plane." Winston shakes his head like he wants to spit into his glass, and readjusts his Stetson hat. "Just another reason to hate Winfly."

Both of them sip their drinks in silence for several long moments. The good thing about wintering over – and therefore the bad thing about the abrupt transition that Winfly brings – is the time and space to be alone with your thoughts.

Winston makes a noise through his teeth. "Some shit must have really hit the fan down there at Pole."

Anne nods. "June 25. That's the last time anyone heard from them. Two months is a long time to be offline in one of the harshest places on Earth." She takes a quick gulp of her drink, then says it aloud: "What if they're all dead?"

Winston looks like he's weighing something, then clears his throat. "I talked to Pasch about this freak solar storm that supposedly caused SATCOM degradation at Pole."

This surprises her; he'd hardly mentioned that he'd been thinking about South Pole Station. Anne, on the other hand, has thought about little else. She squints at him.

"And?"

Winston shrugs, an answer and not an answer. "He couldn't figure how such a storm could disrupt Pole but not us. Because our internet has been working just fine."

"Why are you telling me this? You're not a conspiracy guy."

"I'm just saying be careful, Anne. That's all."

September 1, 2028. Winfly Day 1.

At just after 9:30 in the morning, the sun sluggishly rises and squats fat and red on the horizon, where it stays until it dips away less than six hours later. The day is bitter cold, with a high of negative 18 degrees Fahrenheit.

Mac has three snowy airfields, but this early in the season all traffic flows through Williams Field. Known colloquially as Willy, it is underpinned by ten-foot-thick blue ice, meant primarily for ski-equipped aircraft like the LC-130s and Baslers. It is seven miles away from the main Ross Island stations of McMurdo and Scott.

Half a mile from Willy, a small line of weathered cargo-container-based support structures dot the horizon. One container is the air traffic control tower. Another is the Transponder Landing System, or TLS, to throw precision guidance up to the incoming airplane. The shanty town hosts fuel lines to pipe Jet-A gas over from Mac's depots, a weather station, the crew that maintains the runways, and isolated scientific experiments. There is a small cafeteria with military-style MRE food, and an eight-bed dormitory. Winston has, in the past, used the remote billeting at Willy as a threat to help ensure good behavior at Mactown.

The sun is up, but the light spilling over the horizon is soggy, not enough to punch through the ice fog hugging the ground. Winston and Marshal Anne stay in the warm confines of their SnoCat as an orange-tailed LC-130 dips its wing and makes an approach from the east. The first Winfly plane to land will mark the start of the next ice season.

It's impressive to watch the LC-130 land. From far away, its large skis make it seem almost toy-like. But when it's right overhead, it's like suddenly being engulfed in the shadow of a moving mountain. The LC-130 can carry almost 15,000 pounds of cargo over a nine-hour one-way trek from New Zealand. It touches down, and kicks up a plume of snow that's almost two miles long by the time it comes to a stop. The propellers keep spinning, their flat drone carrying through the quiet air. It's too cold to let the engines stop. The Mactown fuelies will pump its tanks full, crews will unload the Winfly cargo and first passengers of the new season, and before the precipitous cold of nightfall, the aircraft will be airborne again, headed back to New Zealand.

It's even colder, and still dark twenty-four hours a day, down at South Pole.

Winston and Marshal Anne clump through the cold air to the small cargo container, elevated on stumpy stilts, that serves as the terminal building. Winston notices Anne unbutton her Antarctic-issue jacket, despite the cold – to free up her gun holster and better display the badge beside it.

She is, after all, the only cop on this continent.

They wait on the steps, faces slowly turning numb. The first man to come over from the LC-130 is swallowed by a red Canada Goose jacket just like theirs. Issued to every traveler to the ice, with fifteen pounds of insulation within, the jackets are lovingly referred to as Big Reds. The man walks up, rubbing his hands together, then catches sight of Anne's gun and badge.

"You must be the Marshal!" he shouts, above the noise of the propellers. His breath clusters in a thick cloud by his face.

"I am," Anne says.

He grins, a different kind of friendly sparking in his eyes. "Real pretty to be a Marshal."

"Bullet hurts the same whether a pretty girl shoots it or not, pal."

Something flickers in his eyes, like he realizes he's made a faux pas. Winston steps forward. "What's your name?"

"Jon. Uh, Dr. Kim."

"Come on inside, Dr. Kim. Let's get warm while we wait for the others."

Inside, Winston experiences a tickle of déjà vu while looking at Kim stomp the snow off his Antarctic-issue bunny white boots. "Hey, I know you, don't I?"

"Yeah? I deployed out of here for two field seasons at Lake Byrd." The man's face is leaking as the snot caked around his lower face starts to thaw. "I, uh, used to be a Harvard professor. I think you were the deputy manager then."

"Now I remember. You were with the glacial drills. What brings you back?"

Dr. Kim busies himself with a tissue. "Uh, consulting."

"Consulting, huh?" Winston keeps his friendly smile on. "Consulting on what?"

"Oh, just to figure out what this pandemic at Pole might be. I brought a few students along for the ride too."

Winston decides not to probe that too much. Not yet. "Well, there's coffee in that corner. Can't say much for it except that it's hot."

Dr. Kim is just taking his first sip when the door splits open again, and this time four people enter with Marshal Anne. One woman, three men. They are all tall, muscular, dressed in black except for their Big Red. Two of them have long duffel bags that drop to the floor with loud metallic clanks.

Kim waves, saying something, but Winston is already thinking: *Grad students my ass.*

Marshal Anne catches his eye. "Boss, we've got four more hombres out by the plane unloading gear, but apparently they don't talk much. These other four are the ringleaders."

The tallest of the group steps forward. He pulls his beanie off to reveal a finely shaven head, flushed cheeks and piercing blue eyes. "You the Station Manager?"

"That's me," Winston says. "Fifth year running this little beach oasis called McMurdo Station by no one who lives here. We call it Mac, and people call me either Winston or Boss."

"My name is Dr. Mason," the man says. "Tall, ugly-looking dude at the end is Doc Kaushik, our medic. Next to him, looking like he swallowed something poisonous but won't spit it out, that's Sal, our operations lead. You already met Dr. Kim. And finally, this is Colson. She's who you actually want to talk to."

Colson is the shortest of the four, but she exudes toughness, with a rawboned face and eyes of singular intensity. Based on the white flecks in her neatly scooped-back hair, she's also the oldest of the group. Winston shakes her hand. Colson is wearing a gun openly on her hip, and a badge. Winston doesn't know enough about cop badges, but it's not a Marshal's badge like Anne's.

Colson's voice is short, feminine, clipped. "I don't want any mistakes, so having you and Marshal Anne here helps us get the ROE straight right at the opening move. You know what I mean when I say ROE?"

"Rules of engagement," Winston says. "I used to be a Marine."

"Oo-rah, Winston. I'm former Navy myself. You operate any?"

"Two tours during the early days in Iraq were enough for me."

"I can accept that. Just like any desert you and I have been to for Uncle Sam, Winston, I have a job to do here, and I plan to get it done quickly and efficiently." Colson's gaze flits between Winston and Marshal Anne. "Here's my ROE. My team and I will be taking operational control of anything at McMurdo – excuse me, Mac – that has to do with the South Pole. Comms, flight manifests, equipment, anything. That also means we won't need help. No status updates, no info sharing, no questions. I don't mean to offend, but I don't want any misunderstandings either."

In the back of the small metal room, Dr. Kim looks embarrassed, as if he'd expected her to lean into the paper-thin cover story a little more.

"Now I can see how that might be a tough little pill to swallow," Colson says. "We're making no moves for the next 24 hours except figuring out which way is chow, so you've got that long to call up your overlords at NSF and verify that I have the authority I've just said I have." She turns to Anne. "Marshal, I presume you and I understand each other?"

"We do," Marshal Anne says. She's slipped into the same clipped speak that Colson uses.

"Excellent. Let's you and I have a few more words about what's next, yeah?"

Dr. Mason watches the Marshal and Colson leave, then turns back to Winston.

"She's a bit of a blunt instrument," Mason says. He's not apologizing, simply acknowledging a fact.

"Former Navy, I guess that figures. It's Mason, right?"

"That's right."

"That a first or a last, or all you folks have only one name?"

A flicker of a dimple surfaces in the man's cheek. "Just Mason is fine for now, Winston. Now we've got a Basler aircraft that's enroute with more of our gear. Talk to me about who needs to know that aircraft is coming?"

Chapter Four

Three days later. September 4.

Lieutenant Colonel Jiuyin Mei, People's Liberation Army, stands alone on the aft deck of the *MV Xue Long 2*. The Chinese Ministry of State Security officer thrusts his face into the chilly wind, hands deep in his jacket pockets. His mind is far away. His pale face is immobile in the cold, a mask carved from frozen wood, but underneath frozen eyelashes his dark eyes are lit lamps of focus.

Around him, the crack of the sea ice is a constant threatening rumble as the icebreaker ship bores forward. The groan of metal against ice thrums through the superstructure and up into Jiuyin's chest. It's an awe-inspiring sight: to be surrounded by nothing but hostile nature and frozen ice, but be powering forward anyway. Pushing straight into dense pack-ice that has the consistency of poured concrete.

From his vantage point, Jiuyin can also see behind the ship. A few miles out, the channel of watery ice they have carved has resolidified, as if their passage has meant nothing. This is how the Russian tanker *Renda* had gotten trapped out here a decade ago. Even with the nuclear-powered might of their ship, it's a risk to be running this deep into the Antarctic ice so early in the season. Ice reformation can kill them if they don't make it to Zhongshan Station.

But his journey will only be beginning at Zhongshan, China's second permanent Antarctic station. From there, it will be a brutal overland trek to Kunlun Station at Dome-A. 1,260 kilometers. Three weeks in good weather. China doesn't have an airlift in Antarctica, so their icebreaker ship carries a fleet of vehicles to help their crew make that journey by land. Plus Ground Penetrating Radar to find deadly crevasses in the ice, drones to scout ahead, and fuel – lots and lots of fuel.

If the weather holds, they can make it to Dome-A by September 30 – one week before the Americans find their footing for the season and begin full-scale air operations out of McMurdo Station to anywhere on the continent. That's all this early push will buy their task group: a short window for a pre-empt, if one is needed. Nothing belongs to anyone, per the Antarctic Treaty, except by presence. An empty station could be reoccupied by someone else and legally claimed.

But Jiuyin Mei has another mission.

He thinks back to the call from Mariana Egan, about his sister. He and Lingling lived very different lives. She was in the academic realm, openly publishing, working on scientific expeditions. He was deep in the shadows, playing cat-and-mouse with the West.

But if his sister is in trouble, he has to answer the call. A month ago, Jiuyin had hung up with Mariana and, immediately after, called Colonel Fong Li.

When Jiuyin had been a young spy under his command, Fong Li's name had been spoken only in whispers. The famed spymaster had been pushed out by Minister of State Security Wang Jun, head of the Chinese CIA, after failing the nation on a critical operation against the Americans. But he had spent a career developing personal relationships and cultivating disciples. If anyone could set him on a path toward Dome-A, it would be Fong Li.

Fong owned a dacha in Yunnan province, where he had set up an international hostel after his forced retirement. There weren't many tourists passing through Lijiang City in these days of war. In a quiet lounge that would otherwise have been full of foreign travelers, Fong had said, "This is an interesting time for a Chinese station to go offline."

Jiuyin frowned, suddenly afraid. "Interesting how, Colonel?"

"The Americans cannot attack us further because that might draw Russia in on our side. But a lot of our combat forces are spent from the assault and partisan war in Taiwan. Imagine if, instead of consolidating our forces, China had to dedicate resources to defending its interests in Antarctica."

"Are you saying," Jiuyin said slowly, like a child just told Santa Claus wasn't real, "that America may have something to do with my sister's station going offline?"

"I'm saying I agree a man like you should be down there," Fong Li had said.

And just like that, Jiuyin Mei had found himself appointed deputy of a task action group headed to Dome-A to investigate why the Station had gone offline.

Jiuyin makes his way down icy ladders and into the ship's belly. He lies on his small bunk, listening to the vibrations thrumming through the ship as it crunches slowly forward. The sick anticipation of what he might find at the end of the long journey ahead makes him feel like he's drowning every moment he's awake.

He plugs his headphones into his laptop. For perhaps the hundredth time, he listens to the recordings received over HF radio from the Dome-A Station commander, a man named Jiang Cheng. Cheng's recordings talk about an epidemic. People getting sick, feverish, then violent. Multiple casualties. It's clear, just listening to Cheng's voice, that watching an epidemic claim the lives of crewmembers he was responsible for was eating away at him.

Cheng's final transmission: continuing at Dome-A Station had become untenable. The survivors were planning to evacuate, despite the 24-hour darkness. Cheng did not think they could make it alive, over unstable ice, back to Zhongshan. They would instead push the 900 kilometers to South Pole.

To seek shelter and safety with the Americans.

Cheng does not name any casualties. Jiuyin does not know if his sister went with Cheng, or died at Dome-A.

A terrible deep sorrow draws over him every time he thinks of Lingling, always the idealist. She might be already dead. And if that has happened, it happened several weeks ago, too late to do anything about it.

Jiuyin Mei stares up at the pipes in the ceiling, the ice melting from his eyelashes indistinguishable from tears, dark emotions flitting across his cold skin.

I will avenge you, sister, he thinks. *If the Americans had something to do with your fate, I will not stop until I kill every last one of them.*

Chapter Five

Three days later. September 7.

Seven thousand feet above McMurdo Station, Antarctica, the voice of insanity bursts into Dr. Richard Mason's ear. "Red light!"

He looks up, every muscle in his stomach tightening.

"Green light. Door!"

Ahead of him, Sal pulls up the jump door in the side of the Basler BT-67 aircraft. The sound of the air whooshing by sweeps into his ears. Dr. Mason is instantly chilled to the bone, even as adrenaline lights his skin aflame.

Sal sticks his head into the airflow, holding his oxygen tube with one hand to keep it untangled, checking the position of the aircraft with respect to their landing zone. Then he gives the other six men in the plane a thumbs up.

"Exit!"

One by one, the CIA team shuffles forward. Each of them grips a pilot chute, already out of its sheath and ready to toss into the air. Their gloves are too thick to risk fumbling at the base of their parachutes for the release mechanism, and even the smallest exposure of skin to the air will result in instant frostbite.

One by one, with a loud swoosh, the CIA paratroopers disappear out of the plane. A dull rushing pressure builds inside Dr. Mason's chest, an unstoppable current bearing him toward the airplane door. His panting breath fogs up his oxygen mask. Individual ice crystals race up from his neck to cover the inside of the mask. It has been a long time since he has done tactical jumping, but this is the only advantage he has over Dr. Kim.

Jonny fucking Kim.

Dr. Mason jumps blind.

The wind rips his legs up and over his neck. Everything flaps and beats his frozen skin. He lifts his broad shoulders, trying to squint through the ice now thick on the inside of his mask. It pinches the sides of his nose with cold, restricting his breathing. Five, six…

Throw.

Mason hurls his pilot chute away from him; feels his body roll as he does. The thin air catches the drogue and inflates it, pulling his parachute out. He's yanked up and immediately wrenched around, the risers crossing behind his neck, pinning his chin to his chest. He reaches up, drawing a short gasp of a breath. A line twist malfunction. *Shit.*

He hangs there limply for a moment, then gets to work. He reaches back and pulls the risers apart just above his neck. He cartwheels his lower body, kicking his legs like he's riding a bicycle. It spins him around, and the risers come loose in his hand, releasing his head. He looks up toward his parachute, but he can't see anything.

The ice inside his mask is too thick.

His eyes dart around like a trapped dog. There's a small hole of clear visor by one eye. He reaches behind him to pull on his left riser. Slowly he starts to move to the left, carving the world through that single tiny hole. Waiting… waiting…

Come on.

Then he sees another white-clad figure, below and ahead of him, under parachute. Mason stops pulling the risers, adjusts his weight in the harness. He can't see his navigation equipment, can't do his post-opening parachute checks, but he can follow this person to the ground. Keeping them in his sights, Dr. Mason runs his hands blindly over the gun slung around his chest, and the other gear strapped to him. Every member of the team is a former military special operator. They don't go into anything unprepared.

His audible altimeter beeps to tell him he's within a thousand feet of the ground. Mason reaches to his side and pulls a handle to release his gear pack on a long lanyard. It doesn't release, frozen solid.

Fuck, will nothing go right?

The one hole in his visor has closed, trapping him in a claustrophobic sheath of ice. The ground is getting close. He pulls again, jackknifing his body as he does. Nothing. He uses his leg to kick up as he tugs a third time. Finally, the big gear pack under his butt separates from the parachute, ripping his back to the side as it falls to dangle beneath him.

Sweat dots his brow. The parachute has toggles, but he can't guarantee that he will feel for the right thing. He decides he will land with the brakes only half-on. He grips the risers and waits.

He is blind.

Drifting toward the ground on an unknown heading.

Then he feels it – the equipment pack slamming into the snow beneath him. Immediately he pivots forward, like he's on the end of an anchor. Adrenalin surges through his body. He draws a sharp breath, snaps his legs together and pulls hard on the back risers.

It's barely enough to slow him before he slams into the ice. His legs contact first and he rolls over them. The parachute tangles, trying to wrap around him, but he keeps rolling; thighs, then hips, then he leverages that momentum to stand up to his knees, feeling himself sink into the soft snow. He feels so jacked on adrenalin that it's practically shooting out of his eyeballs.

He made it. He's alive.

And this is fifty degrees less cold than it'll be during the real thing at South Pole.

Dr. Mason draws a shaky breath, his lungs flat as popped inner tubes. He tries to claw his skydive helmet up. It's frozen solid. He feels a stab of panic. He uses his gloved finger as a saw, manages to crack the mask, then wrenches it up by force, spilling ice shards down his snowsuit. The wind stings the exposed skin below his goggles but he lets it be, breathing hard, Adam's apple bobbing like a pogo stick.

His eyelashes are frozen. His lungs are straining for oxygen that isn't there. And yet, there's something strangely beautiful about the landscape, blending into the pale sky, as white and brittle as a skin of ice. So much nothing. So much space.

It's like being on another planet, completely untethered to the Earth of his memory.

Dr. Mason turns toward the rumble of an approaching SnoCat. He feels a raw flush of victory looking at Dr. Kim, huddled in the cab beside Colson. The DARPA scientist isn't a parajumper; he'll be anchored on the ground at Mac, while Mason himself forges forward to Pole.

Ever since three Chinese survivors had fled Dome-A and unwittingly brought his microbe infection to South Pole, it has been a constant struggle between Dr. Mason and Dr. Kim for control of what should come next. Camera feeds from the ARO building at Pole had captured Ben Jacobs, one of the building caretakers, stripping down to his bare skin and chasing down a breakfast cook with what could only be described as inhuman speed. The video is proof that the microbes have undergone a new evolution, as Dr. Kim had predicted. So DARPA is now along for the ride, and how Dr. Mason feels about that doesn't matter. His experiment has been to prove the Antarctic microbes could be useful in cold Russia and northern China, and that goal has been successful. He just needs to get on the ground and find out exactly how it happened, and he doesn't trust Dr. Kim not to push the boundaries farther than is safe. They are dealing with a completely new lifeform with virulent potential.

This is how we end the world, he has often thought, *and that's different than winning the war.*

Colson opens the door of the SnoCat. She stands on the running board. "How was it?"

Dr. Mason's throat feels swollen from the cold as he replies. "There's an O-ring in the breathing system that's failing. I had to jump blind, with my mask iced up. If we get something like a horseshoe malfunction on the Pole jump, and need to look at our parachutes to fix it… it's gonna be a bad day."

Colson sighs. "We've just never jumped this cold. Not even in the Arctic. The gear isn't built for it."

Mason hates to admit this, especially with Dr. Kim right there. But no matter when the jump happens, he has the advantage. "The first sunrise at South Pole isn't for another two weeks. Can the Agency get a fix to us on a Winfly flight by then?"

The explosive infection of South Pole Station, and death of several dozen American citizens, necessitates a cover-up of epic proportions. That's Colson's specialty, which is why she has tactical lead down here. She is one of only three women to ever complete the Navy's grueling Special Warfare Combatant-Craft Crewmen course; the only woman to ever successfully compete for a position within DEVGRU, known to the world as SEAL Team Six. She's smarter than the average operator. She knows how to consider multiple points of view, and Mason has all the subject matter expertise.

"We know there are survivors down there," Colson says. "Right?"

"Right. Infrared satellite recon picked up a snow vehicle moving around as recently as a week ago."

"Then we've got to hit the ground ready to deal with them," she replies. "We'll stand down, and see how quickly the Agency can turn around some equipment fixes."

Chapter Six

Two weeks later. September 23, 2028.

88 days after the fight for South Pole.
2 days after local sunrise.
South Pole Station Population: 5 (Deceased: 39).

The sun is just a scar on the horizon, scattering the clouds into pink and red and orange wisps. Siri Monthan and Rajan Chariya stand on the roof of Amundsen-Scott South Pole Station, wrapped in their Big Reds. This far south, sunlight comes later, more reluctantly. It's still cold, in the low negative fifties. It has been getting lighter in the sky for two weeks now, but this morning, it is definitely morning.

Rajan looks at the sun, barely peeking above the shiny ice. "I honestly didn't think I'd see the sun again."

Without much to do after burning down his own telescope–

(*with three people inside*)

– Rajan has spent most of the last three months thinking and building theories.

Any country could "inspect" another country's station in the name of Antarctic treaty compliance. If the CIA had in fact seeded the microbes into Dome-A, as he suspects, they could then observe the Chinese investigation under the auspices of the Treaty. Someone like him, who'd just spent a winter at the South Pole doing legitimate civilian science, would look unconnected to Langley.

Rajan strongly suspects that this is why the CIA had paid for his telescope experiment at South Pole. Would they have told him how to protect himself from the microbes, or kept him in the dark for plausible deniability? He doesn't care to dwell on that too much, but Dr. Richard Mason better pray not to meet him in a dark alley.

"I still dream about it," Rajan says, very softly. "The deaths of our crewmates are burned onto the backs of my eyelids."

"I know," Siri says. "You cry in your sleep."

He looks away. "So do you."

"Fucking CIA," she says. "Fucking assholes."

"That's why we can't let them find any of the symbiotes. Their mutation created a legitimate bioweapon."

The initial black-generation microbes, unwittingly carried to them by the Chinese Dome-A scientists, had undergone a mutation at South Pole, into what they called the grey-generation. The black-generation clustered on the skin and could be killed by heat treatment, in the Station's sauna. But the grey-generation were hosted inside the body, in a symbiotic relationship with their human host. Creating a hive mind that allowed them to communicate with and sense each other. From the outside, it was impossible to tell who was infected and who was not.

"The CIA might intend for the microbes to be used only in Russia or northern China," Rajan continues, "but like Summer Kerce used to say… life finds a way."

Siri looks behind her. The scorch marks of over two dozen cremated bodies on the roof of the Station have almost been swallowed up by new snow. Over the last two months of darkness, they have found and burned all the dead symbiotes – their former crewmates – with two exceptions. "We'll find Ben Jacobs and TC's bodies. There's a whisper every time it gets cold."

Something tickles in Rajan's mind – an instinctual feeling that one of the two might be long gone – but he nods gravely. "How's Keyon doing?"

She looks away. "It's… going to be a while before he feels like himself again, and even that might not be good enough." She chuckles a little. "Penny, on the other hand…"

Rajan rolls his eyes at the mention of Greg Penny, the somewhat vacuous former caretaker of the IceCube Neutrino

Laboratory. "He tried to convince me to stop locking up Bethany. Apparently, she didn't *mean* to try to kill us."

In the last scramble against their microbe-infected crewmates, Bethany Hamidani and Jonah Mitchell had locked up South Pole Station, refusing to let anyone else in, infected or otherwise. Tensions over that betrayal were still hot. They had decided to confine Bethany to the upper gym and Jonah to the lower gym, both of which have been converted into makeshift prison cells.

Siri puts her hand out and smiles at Rajan. "Let's go see what the sunrise looks like from your bedroom, Raj. While we still have the South Pole to ourselves."

They don't have the South Pole quite to themselves.

Invisible to the facility on the horizon, Dr. Richard Mason scans South Pole Station with his binoculars from the Basler flying just below the clouds, under the callsign of Borak 12. Back at the controls is Tristan Hyatt, who has been promised three years' salary for one flight that ends with them parachuted down five miles from South Pole Station. In the co-pilot seat is "Maui" Hathaway, who had flown the initial drop of the microbe payload into Dome-A. SOLL pilots like him have supported clandestine airdrops over enemy territory for decades.

As expected, the survivors have not cleared the snow runway at South Pole, so the Basler cannot land. But as soon as the parachute mods get to Mac, Dr. Mason and the six Arctic-trained Special Operators crowded into Borak 12 will get Pole Station to themselves nevertheless.

"Dr. Mason?" he hears Maui Hathaway's voice in his headset. "Take a listen to this."

Mason crouches and hop-walks up to the cockpit. The co-pilot shows him where to plug in. "What am I listening to?" he asks.

"Short-range radio," Maui replies. "Probably good only to fifty miles from the source. Picked it up with the spectrum analyzer. It's an old military frequency, not used since they got satellite internet down there. Some kind of recording, it just loops over and over."

Dr. Mason listens. A scratch, a hiss, and then a voice.

"Our internet is being blocked here at South Pole Station. Turn on the internet, and we will plow the runway and allow you to land. Pass this on to whoever is running the `HAVE VIKING` program at Langley."

Mason listens to the message three times, by which time he's fairly certain he's listening to Major Rajan Chariya's voice. The man he'd recruited to be his canary in the coalmine. Now he was a survivor; an understandably bitter one.

He'll have to be one of the first to go, when they clean this op up.

Dr. Mason heads back to his seat. The Basler banks into the sun. He touches his glove to the little dark speck on the ice, so small it could have been dirt on the window.

"See you soon," he whispers.

Over a thousand kilometers away, Ben Jacobs walks.

An unending daze. A constant nightmare. Blood in his shoes. Burying himself in the snow because even though our microbes loved the cold and protected him, our human body could only take so much. Struggling to dig us out, feebly poking at the snow that had piled on top of us. We have been walking for a long time.

Past pain.

Past protest.

Deep into a towering galaxy of multi-colored hurt we – neither man nor microbe nor the *us* that merges the two – have never suspected could exist.

Something deep within us acknowledges a swelling despair as we stumble across miles and more miles of this terrible cold wasteland. A purgatory of both body and soul.

But we are also stronger than either of us have suspected. Every day, we find the will to claw back out of the snow and power north.

Always north.

We are almost where we need to be, we tell ourselves. And when we arrive, *ohhhhh*, we will *feast*.

We have been hungry for so long.

Siri climbs down the ladder from the roof of South Pole Station, careful to chain the hatch closed behind her. Rajan smiles, then impulsively scoops her up in his arms and kisses her. Siri

Monthan is a voice of sanity in his fiery, twanging, over-tired brain. Theirs has been a slow burning romance, finally kindled by coming so close to losing each other.

Siri is a pixie-small Scandinavian, just four feet and ten inches tall, her spiky blond hair now growing out into flowing tufts that frame a heart-shaped face. Rajan is a tall powerful man of Indian origin, with densely curly grey hair, generous lips, and clusters of worry lines around his eyes and forehead. They are a study in contrast as a couple, but one layer down, they share a suppressed urgency that underlies every movement they make.

They are survivors. Constantly with one eye over their shoulders.

Rajan puts Siri down and turns to see Keyon, the third and final member of their clique. He resembles a grizzly bear poked awake from hibernation: unshaven, matted kinky hair, puffy reddened eyes that are panicked ovals in his dark face.

"We've got a problem," Keyon says.

"Most people don't know this system exists," Keyon says, jerkily, "but as a facilities foreman, I was one of the few people qualified to repair it."

"What are we looking at here?" Rajan asks.

Keyon points at an oscilloscope-like screen. "This is the readout from a Transponder Landing System, or TLS. The runways on the ice move every year, so the TLS calculates a synthetic approach for an incoming plane."

The screen on the computer next to the oscilloscope blinks, showing them an overhead map view of South Pole Station. Beside it are lines for where South Pole runway used to be stamped into the snow.

"The TLS is fully self-contained in a standard twenty-foot shipping container out there in the ice. Wrapped up in that package is precision approach radiolocation, an Instrument Landing System, but also…" Keyon hits a few buttons. "A military-grade surveillance radar. Easy to miss."

The screen lights up with a yellow track. It's dashed, at first, then draws in faster.

Circles and circles, drawing densely over themselves.

Rajan's throat goes dry. "Is that what I think it is?"

Keyon's anxiety radiates palpably from him. He nods. "There's a plane circling above us right now."

"Holy shit," Siri whispers. "They're here. The CIA is here."

The tracks disappear, to be replaced by a single dot, moving in a circular track just above the Station. 185 knots. Altitude 16,000 feet above ground level.

"Just high enough that we can't see them or hear them," Rajan murmurs.

"If it weren't for you, Keyon!" Siri grips his shoulder.

"Are they close enough to get our radio recording?" Rajan asks.

"Definitely," Keyon nods.

As they watch, the aircraft climbs up, but it doesn't fly away. It sets up an orbit around another spot, maybe five miles grid-west of the far-flung IceCube building.

"Hey look!" Siri yells. "They're diving!"

The radar display paints the aircraft as rapidly descending out of 16,000 feet AGL. 13,000, now 10,000...

Keyon gasps, strangled. "Oh God, here they come."

"No, look," Rajan says, and he feels the relief in the room. "They're leveling out."

They watch the airplane repeat this pattern three times. Circle one mile grid-west of IceCube at 16,000 feet, dive down to 8,000 feet, fly a straight line for three miles, then climb back up. At last, the aircraft appears to head away... back toward McMurdo Station.

None of the three survivors let out an easy breath until the Basler leaves radar range. "Holy shit, man," Keyon runs a hand through the sparse hair atop his head. "The fucking CIA. Out here doing CIA shit. Spying on us."

Rajan is scrunched into a chair, chewing on his knuckles, anxiously thinking. When he looks up, his eyes are bleak.

"I think they were doing a dry-run for a tac-assault." The military officer's face is tight. "They aren't trying to land. They're planning to parachute out the side. Low enough that you land within a mile of your target regardless of what the wind is doing." His muscles twitch under his jaw like a distressed horse. "The altitude profile is right. The location is right, too... out beyond IceCube, where there's no one to see you land."

"They're getting ready to storm this place, just like that?" Keyon's voice is pleading. "No negotiation?"

Rajan wants to lie, even to himself, but he can't. "Yeah. Yeah, I think so."

Siri and Keyon look at each other. Underneath that look, something grey and secretive passes between them, like a poisonous mushroom.

"Maybe you're right," Keyon says, in response to seemingly nothing. "Maybe it is time to put him on the microbe net."

Rajan looks up. "The microbe net? What is that?"

Siri kneels in front of Rajan. The air around them shimmers with 200-degree heat. Her hand gently cups his chin and lifts his head until she can meet his eyes. "Hey," she says. Her voice is very gentle. "Are you okay?"

Rajan sits on the stiff hot bench of the South Pole sauna, chest rising and falling rapidly. His fingers grasp the wooden bench like it's a railing on a slippery ship deck. Muscles twitch in discordant sequences, like the rattling of the sauna coils as they bristle with heat. His body is streaming with sweat and the black dust of dead microbes.

"Dear God, that was *so* much worse than I thought." His voice is strangled. His eyes are red-rimmed.

"Sit back, man," Keyon says, and his voice is also gentle. Both of them have been through what he just has. "Catch your breath. The blood infection can be pretty bad."

Normally, the black-generation microbes pass by touch, multiplying on skin. Months ago, however, Siri and Keyon had caught the infection by blood. And the blood infection has left them with a strange kind of telepathy.

A new way of sentient communication that doesn't need spoken language.

Doc Wei, their now-deceased Station doctor, had suspected that such a mechanism had evolved to allow the microbes to communicate across their primordial home of sub-ice deep Antarctic lakes. To summon each other to a nutrient source when one was found. Wei had taken meticulous samples from infected crewmembers. Siri and Keyon have just put Wei's slides to use to dose Rajan with a blood infection like theirs.

Rajan rubs his cheekbone. There's a still-fresh bruise on it, with a bloody cut at its center. Black dust drips out of the cut, tumbling to the floor of the sauna.

They sit together, in a circle, while the heat stays at 200 degrees F. They'll be in here for another twenty minutes, just to make sure the heat kills every last microbe they have just infected Rajan with.

"Neither of us wanted you to have to go through that, Rajan," Keyon says softly. "But the microbe net is how Siri and I survived what happened here in June, and if the CIA is coming… shit, we need an ace up our sleeves to come out of this alive."

The three of them sit quietly for several moments, thinking their own thoughts. Or, in the case of Siri and Keyon, thinking each other's thoughts. Rajan catches drifts he can't quite decipher every few seconds, like leaves in a fast-moving river. He tries to focus on it, and feels a lancing pain in his forehead.

Siri looks up at him. Her lips don't move, but he hears her voice clearly. *Between* his ears.

(*don't force it it'll come to you*)

(*holy shit is that you in my head*)

"I remember being next to Keyon in the breakfast line. Months ago; right after we first put our whole crew in the sauna to kill the black-generation," Siri muses. "And we… somehow had a whole conversation without opening our mouths."

"Can you imagine if the CIA knew *this* was possible? Microbe telepathy for their spies?"

Keyon nods. "They'd bury our bodies deep to keep that secret."

"Should we bring Penny in on this? Or…" Rajan feels a spike of betrayal. "Even Bethany and Jonah?"

Rajan *feels* the anger that frissons through Keyon at the thought. Feels it like it's his. He's jerked out of his aching body by its stabbing, bright intent.

"I don't think we can trust Bethany and Jonah," Keyon says flatly.

"But the microbe net means we hear each other's thoughts, right? It's the ultimate in trust."

"Let me put it another way." Keyon looks up. "I don't *want* to trust Bethany and Jonah."

Siri winces, sensing what he's about to say, but it takes Keyon a few moments to collect himself enough to voice it in words.

In the last days of the microbe infection, Keyon had been forced to set Katie, his girlfriend of several Antarctic seasons, on fire. Killing her as she tried to turn him into a grey-generation symbiote. And then–

When he speaks, his face is twisted like a tree stump struck by lightning. "I had to *burn* Katie, man. And when I got to the door of this station, I thought, fuck, at least I did it for something, you know? Bethany and Jonah took that away from me when they locked us out. I'm happy it all worked out. I am. But in that moment..." His eyes are hollow. "In that moment, if I'd had a gun, I would have shot myself. I still think about killing myself. You know." He says this to Siri. Then he looks up at Rajan. "You will."

Siri puts her hand on his leg. Rajan feels a spike of jealousy for the intimacy of their connection. He tries to remind himself that Siri has trusted him *without* being able to read his mind.

"God knows I've done some things that would be hard to forgive. I've been a bad guy in my past, and I'm trying real hard to be better," Keyon continues in a low guttural groan. "But I can never forgive Bethany and Jonah for what they did to us. This is an intimate connection, Rajan. I don't want to share that with someone who was okay with me dying."

"And Penny?" Rajan says.

Keyon closes his eyes, as if marshaling his inner strength. "Do either of you remember what I told you at LANDIT, before the symbiotes surrounded us?"

Rajan nods soberly. "Let's kill our monsters."

"We've all killed our monsters."

Suddenly, clearly, Keyon is speaking, but his lips don't move.

(*Katie Khaled Joe Gaudin Baia Tanzhou Tim Rob*
killed them all I killed them all)

Siri bows her head, tears welling up in her eyes. Rajan thinks it's for Keyon, but then he hears her voice, too.

(*Bret Clint Andrea I killed them Bret Clint Andrea*)

The rawness of this shared mental moment spills over Rajan like the radiance of the sun. He hesitates, then closes his eyes and tries to think outward.

(*Allen McKenzie I killed him I drowned him*)

Keyon looks up. "That's right," he says quietly. "We've all killed our monsters. But not Penny. No, Penny was at IceCube the whole time. And hey, I'd rather be him than me, any day. But we killed. And we might have to use this fucking microbe net to kill again." He pauses, emotional.

(*we share the same*)

"We share the same demons now. If it's got to be to the death – then I want it to be with you, and not with someone who doesn't understand what that feels like."

"It's the soldier's burden." Rajan's face goes hollow and gray, remembering his past with the military. South Pole wasn't the first time he'd been forced to kill. "I'm sorry you have to know what that is, Keyon. I'm sorry any of us do."

"And let's be real," Siri says. "If we make it out of this, you know Penny will be the type of guy who'd post on Instagram that he's got telepathy."

The other two chuckle.

"Penny's the type of guy who'd use telepathy to get a girl's number… and then just text her *hey girl sup,*" Rajan says, and they break up laughing.

It's a nice moment between the sauna three.

It's not so nice for Penny, who is listening outside. His eyes flicker grey, angrily.

His time will come.

He just has to be patient, and stay hidden.

The chessboard is moving, and his time will come.

Chapter Seven

Later that same day, Rajan stands on the lower floor of South Pole Station. He hesitates, arm raised.

Then he bangs his fist on the door of the gym.

"You know the drill, Jonah!" he calls.

Jonah Mitchell's bearded face appears in the porthole of the gym door. Then he backs up, within view of the porthole, until he stands on the far end of the basketball court.

Rajan unlocks the chains on the door and removes the metal bar that blocks the handles from swinging open. He holds the bar by his side, like a baseball bat, as he enters.

Three months ago, Jonah had locked up South Pole Station in a similar way, leaving Siri, Keyon and him to be consumed at the hands of their symbiote crewmates. They had retaken the Station, but a peaceful coexistence without locked doors between them was not in the cards anymore.

The gym spans both floors of the Station. The ground level is a basketball court, where Polie social events had once been held. Today, it's a prison in which Jonah lives, shits, and sleeps. Upstairs and overlooking it through a wide pane of glass, accessible only from the second floor, is a workout room with a narrow view of the ice outside; that one is Bethany Hamidani's prison. Upstairs, Bethany is framed in the window, screaming silently down at him. She makes her feelings clear by thrusting two very aggressive middle fingers toward him.

"Nice to see you too, you fucking psycho," he mutters.

Jonah looks disheveled, because they haven't given the old man something sharp to keep himself looking neat with. His white beard is curled and frizzing at the edges. His long hair is a bowl around a jowled face, set with hard, laser-like eyes that flit over everything, calculating. Rajan feels Jonah's attention on him, sharp as a switchblade, and he finds himself at a loss for what to say.

Much of what Rajan has learned about how to navigate life on the ice has come from Jonah, who has spent twenty-three long winters in Antarctica. He'd been one of Rajan's closest friends on crew. And yet, Rajan had come very close to dying – or worse, becoming one of the symbiote hive – because of choices Jonah had made, without pity, or consideration for their friendship.

"So, if I'm keeping track of time correctly," Jonah says, "Mac is opening up for Winfly."

Rajan nods.

"So we'll have company soon."

As always, Jonah has gotten right to the heart of the issue.

"That's right." Rajan feels a large upwelling of anger. Now that he has seen a glimpse of the pain that Keyon carries with him, it has reinforced the wound of Jonah's betrayal. "And I'm going to make sure you see charges for attempted murder."

"It was self-defense." Jonah's voice is quiet. He's not angry; he simply states it as a fact. "Even right now, the grey-generation could be dormant inside you. I simply don't know."

"You're a son of a bitch, you know that?"

Jonah keeps his voice level. "What would you have done?"

"This! I would have done this!" Rajan is trying not to get agitated, but it's not working. "I would have knocked you out and locked you up and let you live!"

"That's a chance you say you were willing to take because you never had to," Jonah's composure is immaculate. "But you're not here because of that."

"What?"

"You're too good a jailer." Jonah closes his eyes. "Keyon just tosses the food in, grabs the shit bucket and leaves. He can't even look at me. Siri and I have had long talks. We've beaten the bushes, she and I. And Penny? Well…" Jonah lifts his eyes to the upper gym. "I've probably seen too much of Penny."

Then his eyes return to Rajan.

"But not you. You're always by the book. Same two questions. 'Is it too cold in here? You need anything more to read?' Then you're off, see you in three days. But today, you're in here to talk. So… what's going on, my jailer?"

Rajan hesitates, then says, "The CIA is coming."

Jonah is silent for a long moment, then he just says, "Ah."

"Do you know what that means?"

Jonah's eyes flicker. "It means you probably won't get your day in court to point the finger at me."

"No, because we'll both be dead. Murdered here, then dumped at the bottom of the Antarctic ocean."

"I know. I understand."

"So then why…" He trails off.

"Look, Rajan," Jonah says. "You keep wanting an apology or something. An acknowledgment of guilt. You're not going to get one. I'd do what I did again."

Rajan turns fiery eyes to him, but Jonah looks back at him steadily.

"You and Siri and Keyon took care of our crewmates who were infected," Jonah says. "I know what that takes, because I had to kill two of our crewmates as well, remember? Friends of mine." For the first time there's discernible emotion in his voice; a hitch that hints at the hurt he carries deep inside him. "Morals are fine to have on a piece of paper. But when it gets down to it, it's all about survival, and *when it got down to it,* you killed, same as I did. What you're obsessing over is storytelling, and congratulations. That's a luxury you have. That doesn't mean what I did was wrong. It just means you get to pretend like it was."

Jonah draws a deep breath.

"So, if you've got trouble coming, you'd better stomach that. Get nice and comfortable with it. Because it's still all about survival. Just against the CIA now, instead of the symbiotes."

Rajan whirls away. An emotion raw and ugly washes over him; makes him shudder. He wants to reject any similarity with Jonah, with every fiber of his being.

Jonah looks after him. "You need my help, Rajan. If the CIA really is coming to cover their tracks, you need my help."

Chapter Eight

Blizzards. Almost a month of blizzards.

A total of six LC-130 flights get in to McMurdo's Willy Airfield, disgorging 152 new people. An expanded Facilities crew preps 11,000 feet of compressed snow at Phoenix Airfield for the first wheeled C-17, but before the cargo workhorse can get to the ice, carrying the cold-weather jump equipment fixes for the CIA team, a system of snowstorms sweep across Ross Island, delaying Winfly and the start of the summer season. Nothing but bad weather luck plagues the rest of September and early October.

Marshal Anne manages to get the plane of shame away and headed back to the mainland before the blizzards roll in, which she considers her primary win. Also known as 'Con Air,' the passengers aboard are winter-overs who have misbehaved in some way, and have to leave the ice early. There were some sons-of-bitches on that plane, and two sets of formal charges to be filed in the District Court of Hawaii.

The first two weeks of Winfly are mostly alcohol patrol: making sure that previous residents of Mactown understand the NSF has implemented a new rationing system. They can't just show up to Gallaghers or Southern Exposure or the Coffee House, lay down money and get drunk. Mac has never been known for a culture of cohesion; some of the old-timers choose to take the alcohol limitation poorly. One of them actually picks a fight with Marshal Anne over it, and she puts that man on the Con Air flight, cutting his season brutally short. Just to let the message get around town.

It's hectic enough that Winston almost forgets about the CIA invasion of his station.

Almost.

Unlike the other arriving crewmembers, the CIA team doesn't have science or logistics tasks to do. They are stuck in limbo; new jump gear is just waiting, in New Zealand, for the weather to clear.

Dr. Kim befriends some of the scientists, known colloquially as "beakers"; they have dinner every night in the central blue building that contains the cafeteria. As it pounds sheets of thick snow outside, Sal and the five other CIA shooters – Barham, Doc Kaushik, Lansdown, LoNigro and Mackie – do what special operators do when on mission and without orders: they get drunk and compete in silly acts of strength or agility.

"When they run out of ration tickets, I hope they realize I won't go to Winston to get them more," Colson says sourly to Dr. Mason one night in the cafeteria, as the six commandos leave dinner to head to Southern Exposure for the second time in less than twenty-four hours.

"I probably shouldn't say this," Mason replies with a bemused smile, "but there's an underground network for ration tickets and they've already tapped into it. Beakers who don't drink, or want a little extra cash, trading with the loggies who want to drink down a long day. I doubt they'll need you."

Colson rolls her eyes and stands up to leave. Dr. Mason watches her sign out a radio and disappear into the cold, heading up toward Observation Hill. Colson has started going on long runs anytime it's not snowing hard enough to restrict visibility. Thursdays are American nights at Scott Base, home of the New Zealand Antarctic Program and a brisk eight-mile jog away. Colson can get her exercise, and get herself drunk at the Kiwi Station, without being seen by her men.

Dr. Mason isn't pleased that he's not in charge down here, but if it had to be someone, Colson had been a good choice. She holds the bone-deep confidence of a leader who has achieved, against the grind of her detractors, what she has always believed herself capable of. And she is implacably effective. In a situation that could spiral out of control at any moment, that's what matters most.

After dinner, Dr. Mason walks the down-covered path to the Chapel of the Snows. It's snowing lightly over the sea ice that marks the end of land and the start of frozen ocean. The sky and the ground blend together in whiteness.

The only Church in Antarctica is simple. Neat pews, well-arranged hymnals, not a speck of dust or snow anywhere. Mason's boyhood pastor would have been proud of the operation that Pastor Taylor Kwanje is leading at the bottom of the world.

Mason walks by stained glass that depicts the Antarctic continent, and a memorabilia case with key relics from the previous Mac church, burned to the ground by industrial fire in 1978. Coming here has become a new routine for him over the past few weeks.

The church puts his frantic hamster-wheel brain to rest. When he sits down in a pew, he can feel time slipping through his fingers. Like some exquisite silk, cool and relieving against his tense brain.

He doesn't mean to, but he dozes off while sitting upright.

Screen 12: Lingling, laying with her head in the sink. The microbes are eating into her dead flesh, multiplying, shifting her body on a river of slime. Then she twitches.

Slips, slides, then straightens. Looks back at the camera.

Her face is that of his wife. Her skin gray, peppered with blistered craters of infection.

Her eyes accusing.

He starts awake from the dream, and Pastor Kwanje waves at him from a pew over. Dr. Mason clears his throat. "Pastor."

Taylor Kwanje is a stout man with brown eyes and clusters of curly hair trimmed short against his skull. He is a Lieutenant Colonel in the Chaplain Corps of the US Navy. Mason is a man of the shadows, Pastor Kwanje is a man of God, but they both serve the US Government. There's something comforting in that commonality.

They talk about nothing at all, for a long time. Mason has grown to enjoy these rambling, pleasant conversations. At the end, when Pastor Kwanje has to move on to the rest of his duties, he says, as he always does: "There's something on your mind, Richard. Would you like to lay that burden down with God?"

"No," Dr. Mason says. His guilt over the Antarctic deaths is rotting at his subconscious, but that is his burden to carry. "But I appreciate the talk."

"God is always listening if you want to speak to Him yourself."

A dark rasp floods his voice; a twisted knife aimed directly at himself. "Is He? Seems like God has been allowing some evil things to happen lately."

(*evil things like what I did*)

"War has always been a rending of the soul," the pastor says, sorrow in his voice.

Dr. Mason's chin quivers. The guilt dammed behind his brain suddenly seems to weigh more than his skull can carry.

"But it's never too late to make the world a better place," Pastor Kwanje says with a gentle smile. "The only thing to fear, my dear Richard, is not caring enough to try."

The next day is October 9. At breakfast, Colson fills him in. "The weather looks good enough tomorrow to send the C-17 from New Zealand. Lots of people, lots of gear. The crew has been instructed to airdrop our gear even if they can't land. Sure you want to head to South Pole and jump, Dr. Mason?"

Mason stuffs a roll into his mouth. It's still his only ace in the hole against Dr. Kim. "Yup."

"Couldn't come soon enough. I'm tired of sitting on my ass in this damn place."

"Just another desert, Colson."

She flashes him a rare grin. "Just another desert, Mason."

When Dr. Mason gets back to his room, he inserts a token card into a USB reader. The front of the card is blank except for a bald eagle with a red and blue shield, clutching a silver key in its talons.

The logo of an intelligence agency.

```
ssh keygen -t rsa -C richard.mason.11@cia.ic.gov
– sha512
> 12 packets transmitted, 12 packets held, RSA key
```

He types a sixteen letter-and-digit password, followed by numbers from an RSA fob small enough to fit on a keychain. The numbers on the fob, generated by a cryptographic scheme, change regularly.

```
> Connection successful.
restorecon -R -v /root/.ssh dirops.cia.ic.gov/
cobra
request encryptlevel=TS—SI—TK—HCS—SAP:HAVE-VIKING
> Access granted.
```

There is a single message waiting for him. A classified communique.

```
(TS//TK) CHINESE TRAVERSE FROM ZHONGSHAN ALSO
SLOWED BY BLIZZARD WX. EXPECTED TO REACH DOME-A
KUNLUN STATION TOMORROW 10 OCT.
```

Soon, they will see my handiwork, he thinks. *And the questions will follow.*

When Dr. Mason falls asleep, he dreams of his beautiful Tingzhi lying over the sink at Dome-A.

Her lipless mouth opens soundlessly, but he knows what she's saying.

You did this to me, Richard. You let this happen to me.

Chapter Nine

October 9, 2028.

Christchurch, New Zealand.

Mariana Egan waits in an alcove of the International Antarctic Centre. Across the street, she can see the tail of a C-17 sticking above the gate surrounding Christchurch airport. The jet is rumored to be leaving the next day for McMurdo Station.

She needs to get on that plane.

A shadow emerges: a Major in a US Air Force flight suit. He has removed his Velcro nametag from his chest.

"Mariana?"

"Austin, hi. Thanks so much for seeing me."

"Listen, I don't know if I can."

"Please. Please try." She steps toward the Major, trying not to sound too desperate. "The NSF won't manifest me on a plane until January, and that's just too late for what I need to investigate. I'm really hoping you can help me out."

Major Austin Baker, part-time C-17 pilot with the New York National Guard, and risk analyst for a wealth consolidation firm, hesitates. "Were you really embedded with General Rason at Kunsan?" he asks, in an almost awed voice. "The night we hit the Chinese White House?"

She starts to respond, then reaches into her bag and extends him a folded file. It contains a series of articles published in the *Chicago Tribune* under her byline, but also printouts of her notes. Mariana has long kept a thorough diary. She has toyed with the idea of assembling it into a book one day, reporting on the early days of the Pacific Rim war.

"I was right beside General Rason the night they hit Zhongnanhai," she says. "There are details in there that aren't public yet."

Austin's eyes widen as he devours the file. "Damn! You know, my brother Royce was on that sortie." His lips twist. "He was playing decoy, though. He wasn't part of the strike group."

"That's a good thing. For your brother, I mean. Not many of the strike group made it back."

"Yeah, but that strike was history, man. Immortality. Damn sight better than this ass-end of nowhere." Austin sounds insulted, a wet cat. "I should be flying the second island chain, fighting the good fight."

Mariana stays silent. Waiting.

He looks up from the file. "I need to know, Miss Egan. You're absolutely sure you can get me assigned back to active duty? Last time I tried…" A shadow crosses his face. "There were issues with my record."

"Yes." Mariana nods. "You punched out a superior officer."

"He was sleeping with my wife. The record leaves that out."

"You were lucky to keep your commission."

Austin starts to reply, but Mariana puts her hand up. "Major Baker. I've already made the calls. Your record of insubordination will not be a problem. Active-duty orders will be headed your way in a few weeks if I make one more call to Colonel Potter at the Pentagon. He owes me a favor. A big one."

Austin sighs and closes the file. "Fuck it. Why not? It's not like I'm taking you into a war zone."

She lets a relieved smile split her face. "Thank you. With all the weather delays, it's hard to get manifested this early–"

"You know the right people, Ms. Egan. You have your Antarctic gear?"

"Yes."

"Be at the deployment center at 4:00 AM tomorrow, and ask for me. I'll bring you to the pilot lounge, and give you a flight suit. Sit in the jumpseat, put your headset on, look busy, and don't leave the cockpit until we are wheels down on the ice. Got it?"

"Got it."

"And make that call to Colonel Potter before we leave, please."

October 10.

"Winfly 07, come in. This is Mac weather."

Austin Baker's fingers twitch on the throttles of the US Air Force C-17 jet. He'd been suspecting that this one would go right down to the wire. And now, as if right on cue, comes a call from the weather post.

"The blizzard is moving off as forecasted, but the wind at the field is still high." The disambiguated voice comes in over the radio. "Gusts up to thirty-eight knots. Visibility at Phoenix Airfield just dropped below half a mile. How far out are you now?"

His co-pilot, Major Jess Marsh, checks the GPS display and responds. "Sixty miles off the Antarctic coast." Off the radio, she looks at Austin. "What do you think?"

It's the second week of October, and that's late in the season for the first C-17. Theirs is the first big transport of the 2029 season. They are loaded to the gills with 75 tons of cargo and 102 passengers; vanguard of the extraordinary logistics train of Winfly that will expand McMurdo from its relatively small winter-over population into a bustling summer town.

"Is the TLS up?" Austin says. With Mariana seated behind them in the cockpit, he has a strong reason to get this bird down on the ice.

Jess pushes buttons; nods. "I've got good needle deflection."

"Let's take it down to minimums and see what we see."

"What about airdrop?"

The two pilots are under strict instructions to airdrop a subset of gear down to the surface if they cannot land. But the drag from putting the tail ramp down will restrict the number of times they can try an approach before needing to bug out on the long six-hour flight back.

"No more than two tries. Then we airdrop and boomerang back to Christchurch."

"Copy that." Jess turns over her shoulder, past the woman in the jumpseat, to the loadmaster. "Chief, let's get passengers buttoned up, please. Final checks."

Austin looks out of his window. He can see flecks of ocean, but more and more, his view is taken up by massive floes and bergs of blue-tinged ice. In places where there's an edge of thawed water, the ice is black-flecked: hundreds of penguins crammed together, squeezing on to shove each other into the frigid water. He watches them for a moment, a wedge of a smile on his face. He's getting divorced this year – this is going to be the year, damn it – but he wishes his kids could see the penguins before that happens. The Ross Ice Shelf is thick with them, like clumsy cute teddy bears in tuxedos, flapping about, oddly unafraid of humans.

Seeing a penguin's open beak last year had been an interestingly weird experience for Austin. Penguins didn't have teeth. They had serrated needle-like spines called papillae lining their mouth and tongue. Sharp and angled backward to send fish toward their throat, the inside of a penguin's mouth had looked like a cave filled with crooked stalactites. He'd found them adorable. Especially the baby penguins, hopping about in the snow, generally making a mess of themselves until they were in the water and swimming gracefully.

The heavy jet crosses over the last cracks of ocean onto white, featureless ice. As Austin guides them beneath ten-thousand feet, the snow picks up, blowing over his heated windshield, instantly degrading visibility.

"It's almost a whiteout down there," he mutters.

"Wind is zero-niner-zero, gusting forty knots."

"Oof. That's a lot of snow being picked up."

Landing in Antarctica is hard on a good day. There's no sensory input of approaching terrain to the pilot. Everything is flat and white. The ice can surprise you.

Austin banks around in a large semi-circle, setting up an arced approach, then stabilizes the aircraft on its final heading. The wind creates swirling eddies everywhere. He keeps his eyes locked straight ahead, staring through the whiteout.

"Five hundred feet to minimums," Jess says. "Speed looks good. Gear is down, you are cleared to land if you can see the field."

A brief smile flickers across Austin's face at the idea of a 'field.' Everything is white. The sky is white with blowing snow. The ground is white with ice and snow. The only splash of color is the grey of the nose, straining to find someplace to land.

"Two hundred to minimums."

Austin tenses. There's something ahead. He can see color. A horizon?

He lets the big jet, almost a million pounds heavy, settle toward the ground. This is going to be close–

The wind-tossed snow clears, and dead ahead, in the very center of the ice runway, is a man.

(a man?)

In a bright red Antarctic issue jacket.

Not moving.

"Who the shit–" Jess is shouting. "Go around, go around–"

Austin snaps the throttles forward, all the way to the stop. The big jet responds, lurching for the sky immediately. His wrist tightens on the controls. Dipping the wings around, sweeping a large circle, looking back. Jess is shouting into the radio. "Hey, Phoenix ground crew! There's somebody down there! Some asshole is right in the middle of the ice r–"

The wind buffets the edges of Austin's peripheral vision, kicking up massive curtains of snow, but he keeps his eyes centered out his side window. Just three hundred feet below him, the man looks back up, head moving to track the circling aircraft.

"I swear he sees me," Austin murmurs. "Who the hell are you, buddy?"

He's too high up to read the nametag on the man's Big Red jacket, but it reads: BEN JACOBS.

Ben Jacobs has made it to McMurdo Station.

BOOK TWO

QUARANTINE

October 10 – October 14

I have cut off nations;
Their battlements are in ruins;
I have laid waste their streets
so that no one walks in them;
Their cities have been made desolate,
without people, without inhabitants.

Zephaniah 3:6

Chapter Ten

EXCERPT from *In the Wake of War: A First-hand Account of Humanity's Deadliest Struggle,*
Winner of the Pulitzer Prize for Explanatory Reporting (posthumously awarded)
Assembled from the diaries of Mariana Egan, War Correspondent, *Chicago Tribune*

As presented at the Fifth Global Conference for Armament Limitation, Geneva, 2043 AD.
Edited by Jane Bradshaw.

While embedded at PACOM headquarters, first in Honolulu and then forward-deployed to Kunsan, I had the chance to chat frequently with General Rason, the Supreme Commander of America's combat forces in the Pacific Rim War. Mostly late at night, when he would come down to the bar and have a drink with his young staff officers.

When Russia began offering military aid to China, the pace of the war ground to an abrupt halt. Russia had to be kept on the sidelines, which meant drawing back hostilities against a limping China. There was nothing to do but dig in and look for a way out of stalemate.

One of our late-night conversations changed my life. It was the week before Christmas, 2027. Rason hadn't seen his family in a year and had just gotten a call from the President of the United States - a man who held no love for the Chinese, but also had many hazy ties to Russia.

"What did the President want?" I asked the General. I knew, even then, what he might say. 2028 was an election year, after all. And the President was term-limited. Perhaps it was inevitable.

Rason stared into his whisky glass. Rotated it slightly, casting the light of the lamp behind him against it. "What men in power always want," he said. "A way to keep it."

"What are you worried about, General?"

I could see him weigh his words. Decide if they might drag him down if he cast them into the air between us.

"I'm worried that Russia will win this war from Washington DC, because they have a man in the White House," he said. And then, much softer: "I'm wondering what I'm willing to do about that."

But he was wrong, of course. The war was lost in a place far away, a place so far south Rason hadn't even thought about it.

A place, and a horror, which I would soon see with my own eyes.

Chapter Eleven

October 10.

Between Antarctica, and her regular life of flying around in bush planes in remote Alaska, Mactown doctor Caitlin Morris knows how winter weather can ravage the human body. Doc Cait has seen ice crystals growing out of amputated arms; lungs on frozen corpses so ravaged that they look like Styrofoam. But when Ben Jacobs is rushed into her clinic, Doc Cait doesn't understand how he is anything but stone-cold dead.

She stares at Sam Eske and Ryan Barbosa, the ground crewmen who have brought him in, her heart pounding with adrenalin. "How the hell did this happen?"

"No fuckin' idea, Doc. Dude was in the middle of the runway at Phoenix, just walking," Eske says, bewildered. "He collapsed as we came up to him, so we brought him straight here."

She snaps on gloves and places a stethoscope against Ben's shriveled chest. His breathing is incredibly shallow. She can't feel a pulse in his throat or his wrists. He is a desiccated shell of a man, somehow clinging onto life, but that could change at any moment.

She looks at the nametag on his Big Red jacket. "Ben Jacobs," she says. "I don't recognize that name."

Eske and Barbosa shake their heads also. "Maybe a Winfly add?" her physician assistant Michael Frazer offers, in his annoying nasal voice.

She strips away the jacket and the fleece underneath, exposing his caved-in ribs. Her small face screws up into a painful knot. "No way," she says. "Look at his skin. This guy has been out in the cold for a *while*."

Ben's skin is flayed so raw that it looks almost transparent. There's a blue tinge suffusing his skin, like an underglow, but almost everywhere, she sees patches of black. Dead tissue, from lack of blood flow. Massive, deeply purple cold blisters are on every finger, his mangled nose, his ears. He is one nosebleed away from a life-ending haemorrhage.

"Doc," Barbosa groans. "Doc Cait, look at his throat."

She can see great gouts of frozen blood. His Adam's apple has been sheared off. There's almost no thyroid or cricoid cartilage left. His jaw seems to be hanging on by nothing but blue-tinged ice-pitted skin, frozen in place. Just touching it, she can feel cold through her gloves. His throat is basically nothing but frozen jerky.

"My God, how is he *alive*?" Frazer breathes, in a voice like glass.

Eske and Barbosa are white as sheets. Her hands are steady as she cuts Ben's windpants away, but her mind is experiencing something similar. It's a sinking feeling, rooted in the most basic of primal fears – the fear of death. Being this close to a breathing carcass has put them all on edge; like they can sense the last of his life draining from his body as they watch.

The skin of Ben's thighs looks like a gangrenous warzone. In places, his skin has split open, bled, and then frozen back together through the sinew of his muscles.

She steps back, takes a deep breath.

"Let's get some IVs on him," she says. "Saline fluid and morphine. Tissue plasminogen activator for thrombolysis, twenty-four hours only. Titrate a bag of iloprost for me, Frazer, get that in him as well. He'll need debridement surgery, if he survives the night."

Frazer stands there for too long a minute, frozen in inaction or dread, she can't tell. Doc Cait has to resist snapping her fingers in his face. "Questions, Frazer?" she says impatiently.

"Dosage on the iloprost?"

Okay, that's a fair question. "Max it out. Two nanograms per kilogram per minute. He's got bigger problems than hypotension." She runs her gloved fingers over Ben's, feeling the stiff, board-like constituency. "If he starts to bleed out from the tissue plasminogen activator, we might have to amputate." Her head suddenly hurts. It'll be a race to save any of his limbs, but shock from blood loss during the amputation could kill him.

A hundred things could kill him.

"Get him wired up, Frazer," she says. "*Quickly.*"

Doc Cait turns her attention to Eske and Barbosa. "Either of you recognize this man?"

"Been thinking about that, Doc," Barbosa says. "I know faces, and I've been working out at the runway for all the Winfly flights. I don't know this dude. Then again, he looks like he got in a fight with the ice and lost, so could be I just don't recognize him in this state."

It's a fair point. Ben's face is swollen and decimated, caved in on one side, jaw displaced. Massive cold blisters decorate his cheekbones and nose like an obscene Christmas tree. He could be someone she'd met face-to-face, and she might not recognize him like this.

She looks up. "Can one of you call the Boss?"

Winston Pele comes in fifteen minutes later, mustache stiff with ice. "Heard what happened," the Station Manager says, getting right to the point. Doc Cait does the same.

"I don't think this guy is one of ours, Boss."

She sees something change in Winston's face as his eyes cut over to Ben: a tightening of the jaw, a sharp intake of breath. His body instinctively angles away from Ben's. It's a common response when non-medically trained people see another human being in obvious physical distress. As if the other person's suffering might be contagious.

Then a look sets into Winston's face. He stares at Ben openly now.

"Just… give me a minute." Winston hesitates, then steps away. "I'll be back, okay?"

Between the outer and inner door of the hospital, Winston pulls out his radio and dials up Anne Pabon's private radio channel.

"Marshal." He uses her formal title.

"Boss." She does the same.

"Meet me at the Chalet. I'd like you to check me on something."

The so-called NSF Chalet is the main administration building for McMurdo, situated next to a historic memorial to Rear Admiral Richard Byrd. Byrd's expeditions in the 1920s and 30s had included the first aerial explorations of the South Pole, and today, airlift was integral to Antarctic life. Winston pauses, as he often does, by Byrd's statue.

To all who follow in Admiral Byrd's footsteps, this monument is dedicated, the plaque says.

The words never fail to stir him. Life is harsh down here. No matter how much time you've spent on the ice, nothing is ever routine.

Today, however, a different inscription on the memorial draws his eye as he mounts the wooden stairs to the Chalet's back entrance. Another quote, attributed to Byrd:

I am hopeful that Antarctica, in its symbolic robe of white, will shine forth as a continent of peace.

Winston thinks about the mercenary types lurking about his station. His lips twist under his mustache.

"Continent of peace, huh?" he mutters to himself.

The twelve flags of the original Antarctic Treaty nations flap placidly in the background.

On the second floor of the Chalet, with the door to his office closed, Winston logs into the NSF manifest system. Every person who has flown on a US Antarctic plane is within these records. Winston sorts by this season and South Pole, and finds who he's looking for immediately.

Benjamin Jacobs. Lieutenant, NOAA Commissioned Officer Corps. Ben is bland-faced, clear-skinned and chubby. Wispy blonde hair falls over one eye.

There's a knock on his door, and Marshal Anne enters. She comes to stand behind him.

"We picked a guy off the runway at Phoenix. He was just wandering around, almost dead from the cold. No one saw him beforehand. The tag on his Big Red says Ben Jacobs." He gestures to the photo. "Ben Jacobs is a winter-over… from South Pole Station."

Marshal Anne's eyebrows climb. "You got *this guy* in the clinic?"

"If you took about half the weight off him, yeah."

"I'd be ravaged too if I'd squeezed myself into a snow vehicle and driven all the way from Pole," Anne says. "We didn't find a vehicle, though, right?"

"No. But it's not like he *walked*. That would be impossible." Winston shudders, despite himself.

Both of them are experienced veterans of Antarctica. They each carry a primordial respect for the brutal cold they are here to survive against. They are at the edge of the world, holding on by technology. If that were stripped away, they would wither in the face of the unforgiving elements. The elements are stronger, always.

"I don't know how the hell he made it here, even with a vehicle, but he's got answers," Anne says. "He knows what happened at Pole."

"But he's got frostbite, just... everywhere. His throat is ripped out. I'm no doc, but I doubt he'll ever talk again without major reconstructive surgery."

"Still. Colson is gonna want to know about this."

"Colson and her goons." Winston thinks of the words of Admiral Byrd. "She doesn't need to know right away, right?"

Marshal Anne considers him with lidded eyes. "What are you suggesting?"

"Let's at least confirm he is who we think he is. Make sure he doesn't disappear into a hole."

Anne casts her eyes to the floor. Thinking.

"I have an old-school ink fingerprinting kit in my office next door," she says. "And I've got everyone's fingerprints on record from their NSF background check. I'm no analyst, but I know how to match the twelve basic points."

"Yeah, great." Winston's mind is elsewhere. "We've got to keep our eyes open. It's too easy to lose what this place is, with people like Colson and Dr. Mason running around."

Chapter Twelve

Marshal Anne Pabon walks from the Chalet to Building 142, an uphill walk that takes her just over five minutes. Inside her jacket, she has a fingerprint kit, and paper print cards.

Building 142, the McMurdo General Hospital, is a corrugated steel building with a red-painted roof and doors that have faded to pink. She steps through two sets of doors into the entrance area, facing down a wall of medical relics, neatly shelved and collecting dust. There are old beakers, material safety data sheet binders, military first aid kits from the 1950s, aged oscilloscopes, and even a rickety reception desk and rusty metal chair in the lobby.

Mac is an industrial town, with construction and exploration at its core. The hospital is equipped to support the inevitable industrial accidents. She walks by a fully-stocked medical supply room and a hyperbaric chamber that supports Antarctic diving operations. There's also a dental room, pharmacy, digital X-ray lab, and a physical therapy room.

Marshal Anne follows yellow arrows painted onto the floor to point out the direction of flow for triaging a mass casualty incident. The hospital has six hospital beds and four trauma bays, and one of the bays has its motion-activated lights on. She opens the door, expecting to find the Mactown doctor inside.

What she finds is Colson.

Doc Cait is standing in the corner of her own trauma bay, arms crossed underneath her small frame, looking royally pissed off. Michael Frazer stands next to her, a frozen expression on his large sloping face. Colson stands in front of them, legs spread, jacket thrust to the side. Anne notices, immediately, that she has a pistol strapped to her waist, and one of her hands rests on it.

"Marshal," Colson says, her voice hard. "We are not going to have a good relationship if you start holding out on me."

Marshal Anne's uneasiness spikes. "I'm not holding anything," she says. "I just found out about this myself." She looks sideways, at the human form under a hospital blanket on a narrow examination table. Multiple IVs run into Ben Jacobs, and he's hooked up to a heart monitor that shows a dangerously low heart rate. Barely beating.

"What's that in your jacket? Take it out. Slowly."

There's no mistaking her tone. Anne's body floods with the sick anticipation of a fight, even as her palms close with an effort to remain measured. She removes the fingerprint kit, being careful to hold it by its edges. She wishes, quickly and brightly, that she had her gun with her. She almost never carries it around. But that mentality is a luxury, reserved for when everyone is part of the same crew.

Colson and her men are not on her crew. They are their own crew, with their own agenda.

"What's that for?" Colson says. Still clipped.

"To confirm his identity."

"It's right there on his jacket."

"Could be someone else's jacket."

"There's no way you're touching him," Colson says.

"She stopped me from working on my patient with the same line," Doc Cait says from the corner. Then she pushes off the counter and walks around, headed toward Ben.

"Marshal, if you would please inform whoever this is, that–"

Colson snaps her gun out of its holster and points it right at Cait.

"If you take one more step toward that man – *look at me, doctor* – one single step closer, I will put you down." Colson's voice is deadly and quiet.

Doc Cait opens her mouth, her body leaning toward Colson, and Marshal Anne feels a horrible sense of cold shock. The doctor doesn't understand: Colson is not bluffing. Special operators like her don't bluff. Doc Cait is upset by Colson's unannounced entrance, and is drawing too much confidence from the US Marshal being present. She's about to try Colson. Doc Cait is an energetic Tasmanian devil in a petite five-foot-two package; fun to see in jello wrestling, but right now, a character trait that's going to get her killed.

"Doc Cait. *Doctor Caitlin*!" Marshal Anne's voice rises to a shout, until the doctor turns her head and makes eye contact with her.

"Not now, Cait," Anne says. "Just do what she says."

"Anne, this is *my* hospital, and–"

"Caitlin." Marshal Anne firms up her voice. This is a tone the rest of the Station has come to know well. "Close your mouth. Step back into the corner."

Doc Cait looks shocked, and more than a little hurt. She'd been expecting her fellow winter-over crewmate to back her.

Sorry, doc, Anne thinks. *This is to save your life.*

One heartbeat, two, then the small doctor subsides back into the corner of the trauma bay. Frazer hasn't moved at all, face frozen in anxiety.

Colson turns her body, drawing her gun back against her hip. Still ready to shoot. With her other hand she removes a radio clipped to her belt.

"Sal," she says into it.

Silence, then the radio sparks. "Sal here."

"Find Doc Kaushik and meet me at the hospital. Come hot."

"Come hot, aye Chief."

Colson puts the radio down, then holsters the gun. Her voice is calm; without the undertone of someone about to be in a firefight. Marshal Anne feels a brief stab of admiration. *Fuck*, she's tough.

"No one touches Ben Jacobs," Colson says. "No one lays a finger on him. Put your hands down, Marshal, I'm not going to shoot you."

Anne lowers her hands. "I recommend you tell me what I need to know right now."

"In a minute." Colson turns to Doc Cait. "Doctor, I need precise answers to my questions. Who brought Ben Jacobs in to this facility?"

"Sam Eske and Ryan Barbosa."

"Who are they?"

"Facilities guys. They're on the runway crew this month."

"Anyone else bring him in, or come near him?"

"Just Winston. We're not running our full-up summer operation here yet."

"Did Winston touch Ben? Have any physical contact with him at all?"

"No."

"You can't be sure of that, though."

"Actually, I can." Doc Cait explains her observation about Winston's body posture. "I'm confident he didn't make any physical contact. Wouldn't have wanted to."

"Thank you, doctor. Follow me out of this room."

Colson points them into the neighboring trauma bay. After they enter, she steps back, keeping Marshal Anne in the hallway with her. Her eyes are filled with urgency.

"Marshal, I'm invoking station emergency lockdown protocol. You're familiar with it?"

Anne feels a bright stab of alarm. "Yes."

"Good. You asked me to catch you up on what you needed to know? Here it is." Colson's eyes are shot black with focus. Every word thrums from her like beats from a drum. "That man back there, Ben Jacobs, was part of the crew at South Pole. He could be a carrier for a microbe which disabled that station over the winter. This is a possible infection situation, but with fifteen times as many possible victims as South Pole. So I need you to start being part of the team. You with me?"

From the moment she'd first heard NSF float the idea that Pole had been victim of some mysterious pandemic, Marshal Anne had been skeptical of that explanation. Standing here now, facing Colson's high-voltage certainty, it's hard to summon that same skepticism.

And she'd been willing to shoot Cait to prevent her from touching Ben.

Anne nods.

"I'm with you. Tell me what you need."

"I need Eske, Barbosa, and anyone they may have been in contact with in here. I do mean *anyone*, Marshal. This infection passes by touch. And time is of the essence. The longer Eske and Barbosa are out there, the more people they touch."

The swinging doors at the end of the hallway smash open. Anne looks up to see Sal and Doc Kaushik running toward them. Both men are in their Level A bio-hazmat suits – head-to-toe white, fully enclosed and positively pressurized, with oxygen cylinders on their backs inside the suits. Both have submachine guns, 9mm Heckler and Koch MP5Ns, cradled in their arms. Slung across his back, Sal also carries an M4A1 with an M203 grenade launcher strapped to it. So that's what had been in their diplomatic no-inspection cases.

She's no longer the only armed person on the continent.

They look ready to mow down a field of civilians, she thinks with dismay.

"Kaushik – make sure no one leaves this building," Colson says. "There's a doc and her PA in this room, and a patient in that room who should not be touched under any circumstances. This hospital will be ground zero for quarantine. We're going to round up some possibles and bring them to you." She looks at Marshal Anne. "Can I trust you to manage the emergency broadcast?"

"Winston can do that." Anne points at her radio. "I'll help you find Eske and Barbosa. I'll get my gun and meet you outside the cafeteria."

Colson bares a shark-like grin at her. "You won't need your gun, Marshal. We've got your back."

Chapter Thirteen

Colson, Sal and Marshal Anne step down the hospital's corrugated metal stairs, covered by slushy snow. The sun is dipping toward the horizon. It's 9:30 PM, maybe an hour before sunset.

"This is Station Management." Winston's voice goes out across every loudspeaker, strangely echoing and Doppler-displaced. "McMurdo Station is now in an emergency lockdown. All personnel outdoors, secure yourselves in the closest building. No foot traffic around McMurdo is authorized. This is not a drill."

A pause, then his voice repeats, on an endless loop that will keep playing for the next hour.

Marshal Anne looks down the emptying streets of McMurdo. "The problem with this station," she says, "is that people don't all live in one building like Pole. There are dozens of active buildings. Hundreds of crewmembers."

"I know, Marshal." Colson nods grimly. "Four hundred and twenty-six souls."

Two of Colson's men run up to them. Both in hazmat suits, guns slung around them.

"Barham, Mackie," she greets them. "We're looking for men who need to be brought directly back to the hospital and locked down. Together with anyone in their vicinity who even *might* have been in physical contact with them. Clear?"

"Aye, Chief."

"Eske, first name Sam. Marshal, you said he'll most likely be at the bar?"

Anne nods. "He drinks like a man with a talent for it," she says. "If you don't find him at Gallagher's, try the Coffee House. Some of the old-timers hang out upstairs and drink their personal supply. I assume you boys are familiar with both?" A little smile comes to her mouth.

"You know it, Marshal."

"Bring anyone within spitting distance of Eske," Colson says. "Tell them this is by order of Marshal Anne. If you meet any resistance... *put it down.*"

"Yes, ma'am!" The two men take off at a run, despite the heavy Hazmat suits.

Colson turns to her. "Now, Barbosa. The dorms?"

"Most likely." She points. "He's assigned to that one, building 155."

They jog up Main Street. Ahead of them loom six dull brown three-story buildings, each on tall stilts to stand it out of the snow, every window speckled with spidery ice. The dorms are not connected, and for that, Anne is quietly thankful.

"How many doors, Marshal?"

"Three. North, West and South. We're looking at the south door."

Like a distended ghost voice, Winston's voice floats over to them. *McMurdo Station is now in an emergency lockdown. All personnel outdoors, secure yourselves...*

"Sal, go cover the north door. No one in, no one out." Colson snaps her radio up. "Dr. Mason, Dr. Kim, where are you?"

One by one, the replies come in.

"This is Kim, I'm in the Crary Science Lab. Third floor."

"Mason is at Chapel of the Snows. I see you." Colson looks to her left, and sees Dr. Mason's tall frame centered within the door to the church.

"We've got a containment situation. Dr. Kim, don't leave, lock yourself in. Dr. Mason – get to LoNigro up at the mobility center. Get him to unlock crates two and four, and arm up. Haz suits on. Bring my suit, and meet me right here. Make it as fast as humanly possible."

Dr. Mason starts running. His tall, lanky frame moves surprisingly fast. Up the hill sits the Movement Control Center, the building that all inbound luggage comes through; Antarctica's equivalent of an airport baggage claim.

Colson and Anne look at each other, breath frosting in front of them. Once again, Marshal Anne finds herself feeling admiration, and a small tinge of jealousy, for Colson's command aura. She's collected and fucking *on*, and her men are responding to that.

"Are we in time?" Marshal Anne asks.

"There's a chance we're early enough to contain this." The creases on Colson's face deepen until they look almost carved. "There's also a chance that we miss one person who starts a cascading infection that gets everyone else."

"Is that what happened at Pole?"

Colson takes a long time to answer. "Yes."

"What is this infection?"

Her eyes darken with some unknown weight. "Nothing you want to catch."

Then her head snaps up.

Marshal Anne looks behind her to see a Ford van, with tires removed and snow tracks on, *National Science Foundation* printed along the side, rumbling down a side street.

"Use that badge. Go!"

It's Anne's turn to run. The cold immediately bites into her lungs. She keeps her eyes focused on the red van uphill. She skids onto the street, then runs alongside it, banging on the door.

The van comes to a stop and the window cranks down.

"Marshal?"

It's one of the fire techs, Heather Heigele. "Don't you hear the announcements, Heather?" she says, trying not to gasp too hard.

"Well, uh, Marshal, I kinda–"

"Get out of the van." She pulls the door open.

Heather shrugs and steps down. The average workweek at Mac is ten hours a day, six days a week. Most of the loggies will, rather sensibly, take the lockdown as a reason to cut down on their working hours for the day.

The Facilities, Engineering, Maintenance and Construction building, or FEMC, is just up the road. The trade shops inside keep Mac ticking, but more importantly, there'll be enough people there to keep Heather in all the trouble she could want. She points at it.

"Pick up your feet and run, Heather."

Colson is squinting up the hill toward the Movement Center, as if she can make Dr. Mason move faster just by staring in his direction. "We're going to need volunteers to enforce the lockdown," she says, as Anne jogs back toward her. "People here seem to have no discipline."

"I wouldn't say that," Anne says. "The Mac culture is to follow authority… except where it doesn't make sense."

"Go on, explain," Colson turns toward the dormitory door. "We've got a minute."

"This station has changed over the last ten years. A series of previous managers have, at the NSF's direction, tried to impose excessive discipline. To take away any fun outlets that Mactowners have." Her breath fogs at her lips as she speaks. "Being here is work, work, work. But it's also *just enough* like a real town – by that I mean people you don't know, round-the-clock internet, and yes, the collective grunge that a thousand people in one place leave behind – that it's easy to lose perspective on one simple thing: you're still in Antarctica. At Pole, you look outside the window, and the edge of civilization is evident. You're filled with a sense of place." Anne turns in place, and Colson follows her with her eyes. "When I look out here, I don't get that sense. I see industrial buildings and shacks and vehicles and messy noisy people. I could just as easily be in a mining town in North Dakota."

"I sense a big *but* coming."

"But… we still have the problems of Antarctica here. There's hot water, but the shower shocks you with a zap of electricity every so often. There's round-the-clock internet, but it's dial-up speed. Mac can be a rotating cesspool of low-grade suck, enough to strip away all the romance of being in Antarctica… with just enough hints of real-world living that you forget it takes a village out here, and that village includes you."

"Tell me about these fun outlets you mentioned. Or is that just a euphemism for drinking?"

Marshal Anne guesses she's asking for a reason. Perhaps thinking about how she'll administer the people here, if it comes to that.

Has it come to that?

"There are morale activities we try not to notice in management," Anne replies. "Jello wrestling, for example. A huge waste of airlifted Jello is one way to look at it, but no one ever eats the fucking Jello, so until they stop sending it, if it provides an outlet for five hundred people who are missing home and want to create a tradition, then why not?" She sighs. "Ten years ago, this ex-Navy guy was appointed as the Station Manager, and he decided there would be no more Jello wrestling. What would the world think, if it came to light? There was almost a revolt from the crew, but NSF management loved it. They've been slowly stripping all that culture-building away. Turning this into just another place to work. In return, now the crew thinks before they obey an order, because who knows? That order could be the last time a Mac tradition survives."

"Jello wrestling, huh?" Colson flashes a quick grin.

"Fully clothed, I might add. Just in case you're thinking I'm not doing my job."

Motion, in the corner of her eye. Both women turn to see the door to the Movement Center up the hill fly open.

"I have no reason to think that, Anne." Colson shrugs. "It's the same thing on a combat deployment. It's a thin line between entertainment while bored, and being mission ready at the drop of a hat. The only people who fuck it up are the by-the-book officers, and the sexist Neanderthals."

"Bad leaders."

They can make out Mason now, in his Haz suit, running toward them.

"Is Winston a bad leader?"

"Oh God, no," Anne says. "Most of Mac respects the hell out of him."

"But what I should take away," Colson says carefully, "is that the Station has an attitude problem. I'm going to deal with a lot of rebels who think they know better."

"That's as good a description of McMurdo as any."

Dr. Mason chuffs to a stop beside them. He looks red and hot inside his suit, but he's armed. Colson wriggles into her suit, in full view of every south-facing dormitory window. Mason helps her run integrity checks. Her mask fogs up, then clears. Colson puts up a thumb and two fingers. *Good to go*. She looks at Marshal Anne. Her now-metallic voice comes from speakers mounted on the outside of the suit.

"Sorry, Marshal. If we make it through this, I'll get you a spare suit and some training."

If? Anne feels a flicker of alarm. "Uh, thanks, I guess."

Colson holds her pistol awkwardly in front of her, having no holster for it. "Dr. Mason, secure the west door. No one in or out. Marshal, you and I are going in the south door."

As they march up the flat steps, sized to large ice boots, the door opens and a dark-haired woman steps out, looking like she's in a hurry. Her eyes snap to Colson and her Hazmat getup.

Marshal Anne recognizes the woman. She wasn't supposed to be on today's flight. She had talked herself into the jumpseat on the C-17.

"I know you heard the announcement," Marshal Anne says in her cop voice, and Mariana Egan disappears back into the dormitory without a further word.

They walk into the quiet hallway of the dormitory. Marshal Anne leads the way up the stairs. They round the corner to the next level, on the third floor now, and Colson pauses by a printed sign, poorly laminated in plastic and taped to the inside of the door. It says:

> Residents of 155:
> You know what would be amazing? If you didn't slam or push your door closed like an asinine human being.
> I don't know if you know this, but sound travels and no one wants to hear the noise of a slamming door. So please refrain from slamming your door and use common sense.

Colson studies the sign with her jaw set. Then she moves her chin at Anne, who continues walking down the hallway.

She stops and points at a door. "Barbosa is in this room."

Colson sizes up the door. "Just him?"

Marshal Anne lets out a short laugh. "Everyone at Mac has a roommate. Barbosa has two."

She reaches for the door handle.

"No!" Colson barks, and she snatches her hand back. "Don't touch anything Barbosa might have touched. If you so much as brush sleeves with him, I'm quarantining you also."

Anne knocks her boot firmly against the door. "Mactown Marshal," she says, loudly.

A curious head pokes out of a room down the hall. "Stay in your room," Colson barks.

Marshal Anne kicks the door – hard. "Barbosa. Open up right now!"

The door jerks open. The man in the doorway looks sleepy, his hair disheveled. "What the hell, Anne?"

"Luethi and Pasch in there with you, Ryan?"

"Pasch is. Man, I just fell asleep."

"I need both of you to come with us," Marshal Anne says.

He opens his mouth and Colson steps up next to her. Barbosa's eyes catch sight of her gun, then he disappears back into the dark room.

When Barbosa reappears in the door, dressed in his Big Red, Colson puts up a hand. "Between leaving the hospital and walking into this door, who did you talk to?"

"Talk to?" Barbosa scoffs. "Fuckin' nobody. Management don't want us talking to anybody; why you think they're cutting back on the drinking and social stuff?"

"Who did you pass in the halls on your way here?" Colson presses.

"Uh… I don't know." He scratches his head. "Ricardo from the conservation team was coming in same time I was, I guess."

"Ricardo is on the second floor," Marshal Anne says.

"I'll get him, and his roommates," Colson says. "Barbosa, one last question. Who drove the van with Ben Jacobs? From the airfield."

His brow crinkles up. "Gisela, I guess? She's probably back at Phoenix by now."

"Last name?"

"Childers."

Colson snaps up her radio, talking to her last two men. "Lansdown, LoNigro. Suit up, get a van and hustle out to Phoenix Airfield. I need you to track down a Gisela Childers, van driver, and anyone she's been around. Bring them all to the hospital."

* * *

Over the next hour, the group in the hospital grows. Ten men and two women who were in Gallagher's bar at the same time as Sam Eske, including the bartender. Gisela Childers and the six people she'd been playing cards with in one of the Phoenix berthing rooms. Barbosa and his roommate Pasch; Ricardo D'Souza and his roommate Justin Voithofer. And, of course, the now-apoplectic Doc Cait and her hapless PA Michael Frazer. Twenty-six people, spread amongst the trauma bays of McMurdo General Hospital, all under the watchful eye of the haz-suited, gun-toting SEAL Doc Kaushik.

Colson heads to the Chalet. She waits for a comms satellite to come over the horizon, then makes a sat-phone call to a Langley operations room dedicated to `HAVE VIKING` support.

"Kill Mac's internet," she tells them. "No one gets through but our team."

Winston coordinates his FEMC leads to pair up in teams of two. They will roam the streets of McMurdo, starting up at Observation Hill, and all the way down to the sea ice, each with a radio and flashlight. They will ensure no one leaves, while taking a census of who's in which building. There are twenty-four active buildings, most brought online since Winfly.

By the time the sun sets, at 10:40 PM, the streets of McMurdo Station are deserted. In the slowly-falling dark, stretched like translucent dusky paper over the hard bones of the Antarctic sky, the sea ice glimmers mysteriously. The message on the speakers now is that the Station will be on lockdown for forty-eight hours. The teams conducting the census will document access to food, and Winston puts together a plan with the cafeteria team to supply anyone who needs it.

Colson's men rally up outside the hospital for their next orders. Dr. Mason and Dr. Kim, Colson and Sal, Barham and Mackie, Lansdown and LoNigro, with Doc Kaushik inside. All of them are in haz gear now. The men have unpacked a cleanroom tent in the Movement Control Center to top up their oxygen. They'll be living in the suits until they know more.

Behind them, a team of two, wearing distinctive green bandannas on their arms, push up the hill toward the fire station, starting the census.

Colson looks around at her men and lets out a short, harsh laugh. "Holy shit, that was close," she says. "Twenty-six people quarantined is nothing. Manageable, even."

"Assuming we didn't miss someone," Dr. Kim cautions.

"Agreed. The census teams are spreading the word to be on the lookout for unexplained rage, violent behavior and fever. We'll quarantine any building where we get such a report. Limiting mobility in the streets should help us control any spread to the rest of the population."

She looks at Dr. Kim and Dr. Mason. "Am I correct to think," she says slowly, "that the man in that building, Ben Jacobs, is exactly what we came to Antarctica for? A living specimen?"

"If he's the shirtless Ben Jacobs from the ARO video," Dr. Kim nods vigorously, head bobbing inside his suit, "then he's *exactly* what I'm here for."

Colson laughs. "And he just came to us. Nearly a thousand fucking miles from Pole."

"To drive all that way in a SnoCat is the only way you could make it. I mean, the conditions are brutal out there."

Dr. Mason has been experiencing a mounting sense of unease, and Colson's mirth brings it to the forefront for him. "Yes, but *why*? That's what concerns me. Why is Ben Jacobs at McMurdo, when he should be at South Pole? And what did he leave behind there?"

"Who cares?" Dr. Kim rolls his eyes.

"You don't think he came a thousand miles for a reason?"

"I think the man can barely breathe. We get Doc Kaushik to run him an IV of something sleepy, put him on a plane, and it's mission accomplished."

"That's a mile-high ethical leap," Dr. Mason says, tension enveloping his face like the tightening of bridge cables. "This is a pandemic situation, and he's the source."

Dr. Kim responds at once. "Ben is everything I need to prove my theories–"

"Taking him off the ice could put thousands of people at risk–"

"–is that what's really bugging you, Mason?"

"What if Ben Jacobs didn't just so happen to walk into our arms?" Dr. Mason snaps. "What if he meant for us to find him and put him on a plane? Just as you're suggesting."

Dr. Kim rolls his eyes. "I can't believe this. We might not need to do a risky skydive at South Pole, might not need to look for a needle in a haystack in an infected station, and all you can think of is that this might be *too* easy?" He looks at Colson as if to say, come on.

Dr. Mason also looks at her. Silence falls, both men waiting for her to weigh in.

"We still need to go down to Pole," Colson says at last. "If we have all we need from Ben Jacobs, then we need to do a deep clean on that Station."

Sal grins wolfishly. "My specialty," the big man says. There's ice in his voice.

Killing anyone left alive at Pole will finish the cover-up, and with it, Dr. Mason's career. He'd planned to leapfrog Dr. Kim by being part of the team parachuting down to Pole, but now Kim, by the luck of the devil, has been handed his golden goose. All the data on symbiotic evolution the DARPA scientist needs.

Dr. Mason is about to become irrelevant, unless he can find other answers at Pole.

"Wait a moment," he says.

Now even Colson's face shines with ire.

"Look, you saw Ben in there," Dr. Mason talks quickly. "He's in bad shape. Kim will get medical samples from him, but what we really need to make this microbe *operational* is to learn *how* the microbes we sent to Antarctica mutated. We're still missing that piece of the puzzle."

"You're saying the survivors at Pole still have mission utility?" Colson's voice is flat.

"It's possible."

"You want to chase that thread, I'm okay with that," she says. "Sal, pick two men."

"Lansdown and LoNigro."

"Okay. If we don't see a microbe breakout by morning, then you three and Dr. Mason will fly down to Pole, and round up any survivors. Make them talk, put them down and get a runway carved out, otherwise we can't land our Basler and exfil you. Kim?"

Dr. Kim laughs, happily. Like he can't believe his luck, the fucker. "I've got all I need right in there."

"Mackie and Barham, you'll stay here," Colson says. "We enforce the quarantine, look for suspicious fevers, and contain any spread."

"Got it, Chief."

"One other thing." Colson looks at Sal. "Langley intel reports a traverse from Zhongshan Station will arrive at Dome-A sometime today. That means China is about to lay eyes on Dr. Mason's little snuff show. The questions won't be far behind. Make sure you scrub Pole for any trace of the Chinese scientists from Dome-A. If the Chinese come looking for their compadres, I don't want them finding so much as a hair. As far as they know, their people dropped into a crevasse somewhere far from us."

"Roger that," Sal nods.

Dr. Mason clears his throat. "Colson. I just want to reiterate my concern. Think about how COVID-19 spread around the world. The risk of an outbreak becomes exponential the second we airlift Ben Jacobs back to civilization."

Dr. Kim interjects at once. "That's my department, Mason."

"Then what's your response to Dr. Mason's concern?" Colson asks.

To his credit, Dr. Kim answers thoughtfully. "I'll start running tests on Ben Jacobs here, in an environment we control. That will help quantify the risk. But, ultimately, the whole point of `HAVE VIKING` was to get an infected person – especially an evolved microbe host like Ben – back to the lab for further study. That's the only way to figure out how to weaponize this thing against Russia, and there's absolutely a way to do it safely. If we figured out safe transport for Ebola, we can here too, for heaven's sake."

"Mason?"

Dr. Mason can see from Colson's expression that Kim has hit exactly the right note. He puts on a brittle smile. "Fair enough. But until we're sure we don't have another outbreak on our hands, can we at least suspend incoming flights to Mac? The population of this station will double in the next week if the NSF has its way."

Colson nods. "As soon as you take off for Pole, I'll shut the airfields down." To Dr. Kim: "You don't make a move to examine Ben Jacobs without Doc Kaushik standing right next to you, understand? I want his thumb on a tall syringe of knockout drugs, ready to push it like a trigger if Ben so much as twitches."

Colson looks around at her men. "You've done well, boys. We've moved decisively, and it's given us an advantage. Let's make sure we hold it."

Chapter Fourteen

October 10.

Mariana Egan looks out of her dorm room window for the thousandth time.

The men in white Hazmat suits and guns have withdrawn from the snowy streets, replaced by pairs of two in Big Red jackets like hers. If she had a cameraman with her, the two of them would be able to roam the streets freely. But by herself, she's limited in her ability to investigate.

Mariana hears footsteps outside. She opens her door, and steps into the dull corridor.

Follows the Mactowner walking down the hall.

The common room at the very end of her floor holds just a vending machine, a sink and a ratty looking couch, but the room is full. People playing cards, talking, opinionating. The closest to a town square she's seen yet.

No one asks her to introduce herself; Winfly is a time of change for Mac Station. Some new faces are staying for the season; others are waiting to head onward to field camps. She listens for a while. *It's always something at Mac,* the dominant sentiment seems to be. *Better to be in here than working out there in the cold.*

Mariana decides this is as good a place as any to start canvassing people.

"Hi," she says to the tall pimply man sitting on the cheap plastic counter. "What have you heard about what happened at South Pole Station?"

Chapter Fifteen

Chinese Dome-A (Kunlun) Station. 80° South, 77° East.

October 10.

STOP!

It's the first word on the note, prominently taped to the door of the main building at the Dome-A Station.

Dressed in head-to-toe Hazmat gear, Jiuyin Mei studies that word for a long moment, slashed in bold Mandarin script, as if lost in it. A tremor runs up his arm, then shivers across his whole body.

STOP!

There is a contagious environmental poison of unknown origins that has claimed the lives of 11 of 15 residents of this Station.

This pathogen could be airborne or in the walls of the Station.

DO NOT ENTER without protective gear.

The four residents Jiang Cheng, Qu Tanzhou, Chin Xiaofeng and Liu Nengye have decided to evacuate this site and attempt to shelter in a new environment: South Pole Station.

Signed,
Jiang Cheng
Commander, Dome-A Kunlun Expedition 40
June 07, 2028

His sister's name is not on the list of evacuees.

Facing the reality of what that means, in black and white, is like a burning crown of coals slipping down his skull to clamp over his throat. Suddenly, Jiuyin wants to be anywhere but here.

Colonel Su Zhou, commander of the task force, reads the same sign beside him. The two men stand ahead of a bedraggled column of vehicles and snow-crusted travelers. It has been a long journey from Zhongshan; a brutal month of sleeping in the cramped confines of Sno-Cats and several days of blizzard conditions. But they can't rest. Not yet.

Jiuyin firms up his jaw. Tells himself that it will be a relief to know. To put his sister to rest with some dignity.

"Pardon me, Colonel. May I go first?"

He opens the door without waiting for the answer.

The corridor is dark; the lights all off. Even through his Hazmat suit, he can hear the wind howling in through a door or window that has been left open.

Jiuyin turns on the headlamps on his suit, and freezes in his tracks.

A man lies face down in one of the doorways, outstretched arm reaching toward the bed inside the room. A kitchen knife is buried to the hilt in his back, high up between his shoulder blades. Dark blood has seeped out and frozen in a pool of small icicles, staining the handle of the knife.

Jiuyin carefully steps around the congealed blood. A peculiar vibration begins in his belly and starts to resonate. It's as if his insides are strings and they are being plucked with an intensity that increases with each step toward the end of the hallway. Jiuyin recognizes it as innately as he would a fall wind, or the sound of trumpets.

His sister is close by.

He steps into what would have been the common room and kitchen.

He experiences a falling feeling. Plummeting down, down, down into an infinite void.

Past the table, draped over the sink, lies his younger sister.

He would recognize Lingling's long tresses of rich, dark hair anywhere.

She is sloped almost haphazardly against the counter, one arm dangling into the sink, the other flung outward, as if pointing away from herself. *Look away, brother.*

Her face is frozen in something like a grimace, her soft upper lip turned up against her nostril. Her eyes are closed, but not all the way, pupils peeking out of the bottoms like a dreaming dog. *Are you there, Jiuyin? Can you see what killed me?*

His body breaks out in chicken-skin, and he turns over his shoulder. On the table behind Lingling, an unmarked clear containment sphere is fractured along several facets like a peeled flower. When he holds his breath and stops rasping into his oxygen mask, he can hear a low and drawn out beep. Like the battery it runs on is almost empty.

Can you see what killed me, brother?

Lingling's legs are planted and she appears to be at an angle. Jiuyin steps closer. A soft gelatinous substance, like a smear, seeps out of her mouth and across the counter, draping into the sink. Like she's been dragged, or moved, and left a trail.

His eyes are paper-dry from the oxygenated suit, but he wants to cry. In death, his sister is frozen like marble. Something is missing from her features, taken away like a punishment.

He extends his hand toward her face, to close her eyes all the way.

Lingling's face *slides*, like a reflection in a lake, sideways toward him.

Something gluey and transparent reaches off her face.

Jiuyin freezes his hand in place, jaw frozen in shock.

Her face keeps pulling. Closer and closer to him. Her features mirrored in the moving glue.

He takes three quick steps back. Loss, fear and loathing flood through him as a series of escalating full-body slaps. The anger, when it finally comes, is a relief. It is clean, hot, scouring through him and purging everything else before it.

He stares at the back of his sister's head as he speaks into his radio. "There is definitely a biological contagion inside, Colonel," he says. "I recommend we make camp at least half a mile away. We will need samples, and a safe site to scrub and detox."

As he hears people start to give and acknowledge orders on the radio, Jiuyin looks at the open g lass container on the main table, still beeping intermittently.

"What are *you*," Jiuyin murmurs, "and where did you come from?"

Chapter Sixteen

October 10.

South Pole Station.

Greg Penny, nicknamed "Lucky," and Bethany Hamidani, are lying wedged together on the only two workout benches in the upstairs gym of South Pole Station. Both of them are breathing hard, and the tiny room smells exactly like what they've been doing. Penny knows where the keys to her gym cell are, and they have fallen into the routine of starting a workout together – it seems ludicrous to put on weight while having nowhere to go except a gym, after all – then getting partially naked and having a quickie. Just enough to get the blood going. They finish their workout, then they finish each other off. Leave no endorphin unstimulated. *A girl has to make her own entertainment when she's forced to live and fuck and shit in a damn gym,* Bethany thinks.

"All right, cover up," Bethany says. Penny obediently throws his muscular arm over his eyes.

She walks across the gym, and squats over the orange construction bucket in the far corner, staring at Penny to make sure he doesn't peek. Just because he gets to fuck her doesn't mean he gets to watch her relieve herself like an animal.

She puts her tanktop and tights on, then comes over to lie beside him, perching her bony hips on the edge of the workout bench. It's either the bench or the suspiciously grey carpet, and who knows what's been there.

"God," she says, half to herself. "I would kill for a toke right now."

In a time not even that long ago, one of her two boyfriends at South Pole had a hookup with the breakfast cook, TC. Plant growth and soil not native to Antarctica was forbidden, according to the Antarctic Treaty, but TC had been secretly growing hydroponic marijuana. They'd made the best brownies to get high with.

Except now, TC and both her boyfriends were dead. Infected, then died.

Antarctica really sucked all the fun out of itself.

"I wouldn't say no to a toke." Penny's laugh rumbles deep in his chest. "A few months ago, I got a little something from Clint, but it was barely two blunts. Gone like a heartbeat."

"Gone like a heartbeat? What are you, a fucking poet now?"

"Always, baby." He grins his easy grin at her. "What we just did was poetry."

She rolls her eyes, but her dry lips crack in a smile.

She puts her head back on his chest. She waits until his heart rate slows down, then throws the question. "So, how did talking to Rajan go?"

His heartbeat picks up immediately. But his voice comes out relaxed. "Yeah, um, I had a chat with him yesterday about letting you out of here. Got in his face about it all. I mean, when there's so few of us left, it's crazy–"

"Penny." Her voice is sharp. She can't help it. It's been part of her nature since she was a child. When her parents were getting divorced, they had separately tried to snow her with rainbow flavors of bullshit. She'd had to learn to see through it quickly.

"It's a no-go, babe," Penny admits. "But I think they're coming around. Rajan and Siri and Keyon are real busy out there. I think other people are coming soon. That's when things are gonna change, I bet."

"Yeah?" Her voice is casual, although her eyes are anything but. "You know who's coming?"

"People." Penny yawns. "I didn't ask specifically, but Winfly has gotta be happening right now. Gotta be Mac people, right?"

His eyes are drooping closed, so he doesn't see the absolute contempt that etches itself into every nerve of her beautiful, icy face. *Men*, she thinks contemptuously. Where the hell would she be if she had to depend on them?

She doesn't share with her lover that Rajan had come to see her, right after being down there with Jonah. She's locked in here, and yet, she knows more than this meathead wandering the halls freely.

Rajan had told her the CIA was coming. Their negotiation tactic of internet for runway hadn't worked.

Rajan hadn't told Penny. Probably because Penny hadn't asked, but honestly, why would he bother? Lucky Penny always ended up on top of the wave and not crushed by it. Back when they – yes, even fucking Rajan and Siri – had been battling for their survival, Penny had been getting high at IceCube half a kilometer away. Totally fucking clueless that other members of their crew were killing, and dying.

For an evanescent moment, Bethany feels a deep loathing for letting Penny touch any part of her. Sure, you had to be a realist in a man's world, but *God*. A shudder runs through her body as she looks down at him.

She's a survivor, if nothing else. She told Rajan what he wanted to hear. Yeah, of course she'd work with him; work with him real good. Whatever he needed.

Maybe he believed her, maybe he didn't.

Either way, a girl always has to make her own luck.

She rouses Penny before he falls asleep in her prison. The privilege of the jailer napping in the cell makes her shudder all over again. "Just leave the door unlocked for me again, baby," she tells him. "And you hustle on back here before 9:00 AM and lock it back up properly."

An indecisive look flits across his beach bum face, and she feels his heart rate amplify again. "You know, with all the activity picking up, I wonder if–"

She stands up, and lifts her shirt off.

Penny stops talking.

She strips her tights back off, and keeps him quiet.

Right after she brings him to a head, she hustles him out of the gym. Whatever objection he'd been cooking up has been lost to the ether. He leaves the chain loosely looped through the door handles, with no lock on it.

Bethany sits with her back to the door, and waits.

All her thoughts are dark thoughts.

You're a survivor, she reminds herself.

You survived Afghanistan as a child. You'll survive this. Your capacity to eat shit and wait for your moment exceeds theirs.

And so she waits.

There's no clock in the gym. The small window set high in the wall shows constant sunlight, but the others tend to sleep in. Not much to do, after all, is there? Everyone is fucking dead. All their crewmates and friends and lovers – dead.

She waits, gnawing on her fingernails.

She's hoping Rajan and Siri and Keyon are tired from whatever they've been doing. Enough that, perhaps, she'll be able to create a different result than any other time she's been outside her cell.

Bethany faces the gym double doors. She ties her long dark hair back in a ponytail, out of her eyes. She tugs sharply on the door.

The chains slink through the handle on the other side, and rush to a pile on the floor.

Good boy, Penny, Bethany thinks. *You'd march right off a cliff as long as I'm there to massage your balls while you walk, wouldn't you?*

Bethany Hamidani pads, in her socks, down the upstairs hallway of South Pole Station. Quickly, quickly. She ducks into the science lab on the right. The lab is dark, windows covered by cardboard. Tall shelves loom like scarecrows.

She passes the desk of Mike McCafferty, formerly one of the research assistants, now fucking dead. Her footsteps slow as her eyes focus on a shadowy piece of cardboard, still taped to the side of the desk. *Will science 4 flight 2 Pole. Plz Help.* An inside joke, for how long McCafferty had waited for a slot to South Pole.

Only to be killed by microbe attack.

Bethany feels a sudden slam of sadness. Like a diamond, dead is forever. What a shitty ending to his story.

She's played it back a million times, during her weeks and months locked up with nothing but kettlebells to swing at her rage. Yes, it's true: she and Jonah had barricaded Siri, Keyon and Rajan out of the Station. But without a way to detect the grey-generation microbes inside her, the alternative would have been to go to sleep every night unsure if she would awaken human, or a symbiote. To be consumed by something inhuman, from the inside out, was a fate worse than death. She'd had no choice. No choice at all.

Which means what she has to do next isn't a choice at all either.

Bethany reaches into McCafferty's unlocked top drawer. Her fingers curl around a sharp kitchen knife. She's left it there from previous quiet expeditions.

She runs a finger across its sharp edge. Razor sharp.

Bethany slides down the gloomy hallway to Berthing Block A. She pushes the sliding door open as quietly as she can.

The sunlight spilling through the window highlights the second-to-last blue door, and the lone piece of duct tape on it. DR. RAJAN CHARIYA.

Bethany lifts the knife up by her face, holds her breath, and gently turns the door handle.

It turns – none of the doors at Pole lock – but the door doesn't budge.

Rajan's door is still barricaded, something heavy pushed against the door. The smart thing to do, really, when you've got two prisoners in a careless jail. She considers just throwing her shoulder against the door and forcing her way in, but in a one-on-one fight with the military guy, the element of surprise is her only true weapon.

She's never killed anyone before. But after being locked up for a hundred days and threatened with attempted murder charges?

Murder itself doesn't seem that much of a fucking leap.

Siri's room is empty. She's probably bunking with Rajan.

Keyon's room is empty. Bethany has no idea where he sleeps these days.

She checks every corner before she moves. The fact that she can get out of her prison is the only ace up her sleeve. And with the CIA coming soon, the stakes have never been higher.

Bethany's socked feet whisper into the sunlit cafeteria. Penny, of course, has told her where her jailers keep the keys. Then, like a dark wraith, she's gone, down the mid-hallway stairs. She pauses in the shadows outside the double doors by Destination Alpha, the front entrance to the elevated station.

There are chains on the door. Bethany softly undoes the lock with the keys she has taken.

Pushes open the door to the lower gym.

She stands there, knife raised. "Jonah," she whispers. "Come out where I can see you."

A long, dark moment passes; then Jonah emerges from the shadows by the door, silently.

"I was wondering when you'd stop by to see me on your little jaunts," he says, voice low.

She follows him into the lower gym. At first, she's jealous of how much room he has. But there's nothing in the cavernous space. A few yoga pads in the corner, where he sleeps; a basketball he could use to exercise, but not a whole lot else.

His shit bucket is farther from where he sleeps, though.

After a hundred days, things like that start to matter.

Once, Jonah hadn't been the only repository of all secret knowledge about Pole. But the person who had tied his record for winter-over seasons is now dead, just like everyone else. Dead, the fuck-you that keeps on fucking you.

"Do you know," she asks, "where Siri or Keyon sleeps?"

"Why do you ask?"

"Reasons," she says, with a flat and unsmiling bite.

He pauses for a long moment. Then shakes his head. "I don't. I'm sorry."

Bethany hesitates, then presses on. "Penny would be with us."

"There's an us?"

"If there's no us, tell me now. I'll leave you right where I found you."

"I'm not saying that."

"Then it's three on three."

Jonah's face tightens into something that's like a smile, but isn't. "Penny would fight?"

"Okay, well. He'd look the other way after it was all done." Bethany rolls her eyes. "But first I need your help. I'm thinking Rajan told you what he told me."

"The CIA is coming. We're all expendable."

"Unless we give them something they want."

"They want the infection."

She nods. "And I think I know where TC would have gone to die."

Tommy Chapman's underground marijuana hustle had ended up an unfortunate gift, because the symbiote takeover would not have been possible without it. The THC in the marijuana had catalyzed the symbiotic grey-generation microbes' ability to bind to human endocannabinoid systems. Without TC's curse, the black-generation microbes would have been little more than fleas, waiting to be burned off the skin or boiled out of the blood. But with it, they could drive up a six-lane highway directly into the central nervous system, and control the human mind.

Ben Jacobs, the first symbiote, had become obsessed with finding TC's grow source. Enough to convert the other crewmembers into his symbiotes.

More dangerous. More infectious. More powerful.

"Dave Atkins and I used to buy from TC," Bethany says, referring to one of her two former boyfriends. "The three of us used to get high together. Our own little secret club. When TC was half-burned from the fire? I think that's where he would have gone to die. One of the old junkers at the End-of-the-World."

"Interesting," Jonah murmurs, with a quickening of interest. End-of-the-World is a collection of containers from previous seasons; obsolete equipment and cargo not worth flying back off the ice. It's like an island of lost toys. Half the cold walk to End-of-the-World could be done via the ice tunnels underneath the Station.

Where TC had last been seen. Setting a fire, to try and lure half the Station outside in the form of a firefighter team.

"That body is our chance to survive," Bethany says. "If we give the CIA its location once we're free and clear..."

Jonah's eyes flick up, sharp as a hook. "And you think this is a good idea? Giving them the blueprint to reverse-engineer microbial warfare by symbiote?"

Bethany starts to respond, but it's too late. Every wrinkle on Jonah's face is now held smooth by scorn. His expression tells her that he has read the truth on her face: she hasn't thought about right or wrong at all. Doesn't give a fuck about it, in fact.

"Look–" she starts.

"I don't agree with Rajan on many things," Jonah says quietly. "But you've seen what the microbes did to our friends."

He sounds disbelieving now. "After all we've been through… your plan is to *find* the solution to give it to the CIA?"

"I don't need to convince you of anything," she says, angrily. "I'll tell them myself. And I'll be the only one left alive."

"But TC's body is a two-man job. At least, if you don't want to be infected. Isn't that why you're here?"

"I'll do it by myself if I have to," she says, and her voice is lined with steel.

An amused look casts across Jonah's face. "I believe you would. You don't give a fuck about anybody else, do you?"

"Do they give a fuck about me?" she responds angrily. "Or you?"

Jonah puts his hands half-up, as if ceding her point. Then he sighs and rubs his forehead. "I guess… let's go find a dead symbiote."

Chapter Seventeen

Penny stands by the window of an upstairs berthing room looking out through a porthole window.

They are covered up from head to toe in winter gear, but he recognizes the gait of Jonah and Bethany as they leave. Jonah walks stiffly, like someone who hasn't been in the cold in a while. And Penny could pick out the way Bethany's body moves in the middle of Times Square.

"Oh sure, Bethany," he murmurs. If he knows he's talking aloud, he makes no indication of it. "You think you're working me. But I've worked you, baby. I've worked *you*."

His eyes blink grey, then black. "Ah, fuck, it hurts," he groans.

It hurts more often these days.

He looks at himself in the mirror mounted on the back of his dresser. His face looks lean and tight, bones starting to extrude through his skin, because the grey-generation is eating him up.

Patience, something whispers to him. So quietly that it could be in the noise of his head.

Patience. All things will come to us.

He is the last compatible symbiote host. The grey-generation's last chance for survival. In some primal way, Penny knows what the wafer-thin strand hiding away inside of him wants. It wants to *spread*. It's hungry to spread. But it understands that there's nowhere to spread to. They have no catalyst. No THC. So until something changes, the microbes are self-regulating inside him. Killing older cells as the newer ones grow. Not multiplying. But the newborns still have to eat.

It's why he looks so lean, so fit. He is being eaten alive from the inside.

Bethany and Jonah have almost disappeared into the bright sunlit horizon. He puts his finger up and blots Bethany out.

He laughs. It could have been a snarl.

"One," he says aloud. "Then two, then three. Then all of you fuckers."

There are hundreds of cargo containers at End-of-the-World, but Bethany moves with the confidence of someone who has thought about exactly where to go. Jonah follows her between broken-down snow vehicles, rusted scaffolding and ancient piles of frozen equipment. Deep in the snowy maze, she comes to a stop in front of a half-collapsed astronomical dome.

A shiny lock on the door latch stands out like seaglass on a dull beach, but it lies open.

The door is cracked.

Bethany's voice is a disbelieving chuff bubbling from her lips. "There he is..."

Through the crack in the door, behind a tall snow drift piled up the steps, they can see a human arm. Bent backward at an unnatural angle. Jonah sucks in his breath.

They stand still, watching for any signs of movement, but all that stirs is the wind, pushing grains of snow between their legs like sand skimming up a shoreline. Bethany turns to him, her eyes glinting like hard diamonds. "Shovels," she says. "We need to dig him out."

"You know where to find one around here?" Jonah opens his arms as if to indicate the hundreds of places one could be.

"Oh yeah," she says.

"I'll wait here."

Bethany rolls her eyes, then walks away, disappearing into the maze of hulking ice toys.

Jonah walks up the steps, carefully. He doesn't want to touch anything, but he kicks against the door with his booted foot. It doesn't budge; there's too much snow piled against it, driven through the crack in the door by the wind. He can see, however, that the body on the other side of the door is indeed TC. Despite his half-burned face, Jonah recognizes his former crewmate.

He turns, eyes moving rapidly, casting out across End-of-the-World. He has spent nearly thirty seasons in Antarctica. He recognizes most of the neglected equipment here: from when it had been an active science experiment, or a once-popular implement, or even a part of the old dome station now sunk in fractionated pieces beneath the ice.

His eyes narrow as he spots the edge of an observation tower he recognizes. It had once lived near his facility of ARO; hosted a massive diesel generator to power a radar. The primary fuel tank would have been drained, but they might have missed the backup tank welded to the bottom of the structure. It had been an afterthought, to keep the instruments running while the primary tank was being refilled; an old design that wouldn't have passed modern safety regulations. Old diesel doesn't go bad like gasoline does. And the foam around the secondary tank would flash heat.

He looks over his shoulder. No sign of Bethany.

He walks quickly toward the tower.

Chapter Eighteen

October 11.

Sal crouches down onto one knee. "Bring it in, fellas," he shouts, over the aircraft engines. His oxygen mask is up, but they can hear him on their tactical radio net.

Dr. Mason huddles closer on the Basler airplane's bench seat. LoNigro and Lansdown kneel in the aisle between the seats. Their airplane feels as dangerous as a pressure cooker clamped under a sealed lid.

They are about to jump out of a goddamn plane at the South Pole.

And hopefully not freeze to death.

Sal's narrow eyes blaze with an intensity so hot it feels like a physical slap. "All right, you fuckers," he growls. "It's almost go time."

"Hooyah!" LoNigro and Lansdown bay like wolves, which makes Dr. Mason's radio shriek, but it puts the same wild look on his face.

"This is going to be a gnarly jump, boys. It's minus 54 degrees Fahrenheit on the ground. When I open that door, it'll be minus two-fucking-hundred degrees with wind chill. No one has *ever* skydived this cold." Sal hefts the gun dangling around his neck. "But fuck it. We signed up to do the shit no one else can do, yeah?"

"Hooyah!" LoNigro and Lansdown yell again, and this time Dr. Mason joins them.

"We're exiting at 8,000 feet above ground level. Chutes open by 5,000. If the chute doesn't feel right and you can't see it, cut it the fuck away and go to reserve. Don't hesitate. We'll rendezvous at the IceCube building, clear it, and push from there. You boys ready?"

Dr. Mason puts his whole body into shouting through his jitters. "Hooyah!"

"That's what I like to fucking hear. Pair off. Check each other for *any* exposed skin. If it's out there, you'll lose it. Get ready to be colder than you've ever been. This is gonna be a great story when we get back to Langley!"

Behind them, two military jumpmasters ready the cargo that will be shoved out of the Basler after them. Two crates full of spare weapons, Hazmat suits, and the cleanroom tent they will be living out of until they can clear enough runway for their Basler to land at South Pole. Every surface and every person at 90 South must be assumed contaminated.

Above the narrow side door, in the back of the plane, a jerry-rigged red light goes on.

"Here we go!" Sal shouts. "Giddy up, you lazy fucks!"

He braces by the door, then throws it open. The wind howls in and Dr. Mason can't believe how quickly the temperature drops. The cold is like a *wall.* He feels a deep chill in his stomach, inside his ice boots.

Nothing is enough when it's this cold.

"Fuck," Dr. Mason moans, just under the sound of the wind. He's scared. Negative 200 fucking degrees? He can barely think, and he has to jump out of an airplane. Hell yeah, he's scared. *"Fuuuck."*

There's no sticking a head out into the wind to check that they are in the right place for the drop; Sal stays huddled in the back of the plane with them. It's all white down there, an unrelenting expanse with no distinguishing features. They extract each other's pilot chutes from the bottom of the parachute container. Roll them tightly, clutch them in one hand, then wait.

Abruptly the plane bunts, nosing over. The four men brace against the seats. Their ears pop, then pop again, and suddenly the green light over the door is on.

"Let's go!" Sal screams into their ears. And with no hesitation, he rises to a crouch, snaps his gun down to his chest, and bombs out of the back door.

Gone with a swoosh that Dr. Mason imagines, but can't hear, because everything is so loud.

Mason is next. He shuffles awkwardly, protecting the pin on the back of his container from prematurely opening. Then he's in the door, and it's so cold that every single thought is wiped out of his head.

He puts his chin on his chest and tumbles out.

The propeller roar drops away quickly. Dr. Mason feels himself going head low almost immediately. The air *feels* thinner here. He flails, trying to find some air to grab stability from, but he just goes steeper and steeper.

His body feels like it's been cut in half. He can't feel anything beneath his waist.

Steeper and steeper.

A shrill cacophony shrieks directly into his ear. What the hell is that? What does it mean?

Oh, shit. That's his dead alarm.

Parachute open now or you're dead.

Dr. Mason's arm is frozen in place. He peels his fingers back, and each one feels like it's snapping off the digit. Abruptly the line catches. Something whizzes through his frozen palm. And then, so suddenly it unzips his neck and back, he's yanked upright. A thud, then the world goes quiet.

Quiet as just after a first snowfall.

Mason looks up, dazed, hypoxic, and sees his white parachute gently fluttering above him.

Then he hears something. Thread sawing through air. A rapid unwinding, like a tortured spool. He swallows and his hearing pops back. There are voices on his radio. Panicked voices.

"Ah, fuck, goddamn lineover, it's cutting through my canopy!"

"Go to reserve!" Sal is shouting on top of him. "LoNigro, cutaway. Cutaway!"

"I can't find – where the fuck is it–"

Dr. Mason twists in his harness and he *sees* LoNigro. LoNigro had exited after him but is below him now, rapidly corkscrewing toward the snow. Fast. Too fast. LoNigro's canopy is bowed in half, like butterfly wings.

With a cold certainty that wraps around his heart, he knows LoNigro is trying to find his cutaway handle, normally lodged just under and in front of the left armpit, but he can't feel his hands.

He doesn't know what he's grabbing.

He might not be grabbing anything at all.

The canopy abruptly goes from spiraling toward the ground to seemingly floating. Dr. Mason cranes his head. He sees LoNigro's tumbling frame for a moment, then a streamer of a pilot chute appears.

A reserve parachute begins to blossom–

Then LoNigro goes into the ground. The snow swallows him whole.

"He went in." Dr. Mason recognizes his own voice. The thin wavering tones of an old man. "He's right below me."

"Mason, you stick with him." Sal's voice is tight. "You got a good chute?"

Dr. Mason tugs on his right riser, bringing his parachute around in a low flat turn. He can't see LoNigro anymore, but he keeps his eye on where he saw him go in. He starts to spiral down.

He's cold, so cold, but adrenalin is flooding through him now, baking him from the skin inward.

"Dr. Mason!"

"Yeah, I got a good chute," he replies, breathlessly. Still spiraling down, eyes fixed. "I'm going to get to the ground and ping his beacon."

"Radio when you have something. Lansdown, rejoin on me. We'll clear IceCube."

The ground is flat, dazzlingly white. So white that Dr. Mason doesn't realize how low he is until the horizon abruptly jumps above his eyeline. "Fuck!" he screams, and yanks as hard as he can on his opposite riser. Trying to cancel the diving turn.

It barely works. The canopy draws above his head… and then Mason slams into the ice. Feet, knees, face. Instantly buried in the neck-deep snow.

Instantly, *claustrophobically*, buried. It's like falling into a tree well while skiing.

He screams into his full-face helmet. The wind tugs on the parachute, pulling hard, rolling and yanking him sideways, carving a human-sized canal. It's always windy at the South Pole. There's no mountain or terrain to stop the wind for hundreds of miles. Snow spills down his neck, into his helmet. The ice on his faceshield thickens as he panic-pants into it.

Dr. Mason gasps, fumbling for his cutaway handle, then his mind returns to him in a cold clear rush. He feels his way up to his risers and pulls as hard as he can.

The canopy twitches around, into the wind, turning it into a sail. Mason feels a force pulling upward now, upward toward the light. He crests the snow. The force of the wind in the canopy drags him upright.

He holds a riser down with one hand, willing his frozen body to cooperate. With the other hand he fumbles at his chest for his navigation kit. Inside a battery-powered warm box is a grid-controlled GPS system.

He can't see another living being. Every direction looks the same out here. He's never felt so alone in his life, and now, he has to go find a teammate who may be no more than a dead body.

"Okay," he mutters, grimly, aloud. His hands and feet are clammy underneath his clothes. "Come on, beacon. Okay, there we go. Let's go that way."

Dr. Mason angles the canopy, and it takes off like a windsail. He points his toes, and suddenly he's parasailing over the light snow, boots kicking up a trail behind him. His gear drags behind him, attached by a long tether. LoNigro is about half a klick away.

Despite the GPS, Mason misses him. Dressed in white camouflage, flying a white parachute, LoNigro is just another bump in the flat light amongst endless undulating hills of deep snow. The wind is too strong for Dr. Mason to tack upwind, so when the GPS tells him he has shot by, he cuts the parachute away from his shoulders. It's gone shockingly quickly, a white kite, blending into the environment.

He feels drained, as if he has just been in a firefight. The cold is sapping his strength. He raises the hood of his jacket against the wind, and sets off walking.

His legs sink in almost to his hips. The landscape is nothing but blown snow, not compacted except by time. Every step is a struggle. The altitude is already starting to get to him. "I'm within a hundred meters of LoNigro," he gasps into his radio. "Still looking."

"Copy," Sal responds. "Lansdown and I are about the same distance from IceCube."

It takes Dr. Mason almost twenty minutes to find him. LoNigro is buried, only his gear pack floating on the surface. Mason digs him out, huffing in tortured gasps. LoNigro's eyes are open, face frozen in a grimace.

His neck is broken. His face is already starting to turn blue behind his visor.

"I'm sorry," Mason whispers. He doesn't even know the man's first name. "It could have been me. It could have been any of us."

Dr. Mason plants a flag on him. It flaps viciously in the wind. They will come back for him later, together with the cargo pallets out there somewhere in the snow.

The buttons on his nav unit are big enough to be mashed even with mittens on. The GPS draws him a course to IceCube. 1.2 miles away, grid northeast. The prevailing wind at South Pole is east to west, so the wind will be in his face. Resisting him with every step.

Dr. Mason unstraps his weapon, checks it with shaking fingers, then returns it to its front resting position around his neck.

He sets his face into the wind and starts on his long, cold walk.

Dr. Mason uses the edge of his pack to nudge the back door of IceCube open, careful not to touch anything. Inside, he feels waves of heat, and moans aloud in relief.

He dumps out his gear on the warm floor – where there are unlikely to be microbes – and methodically steps into his crinkly white Hazmat suit. He resists the urge to hurry, or to break into shivers. He will be living in this suit for the next several days, and he cannot leave any gap by which to pick up something.

Something he could take home to his wife.

Once his suit is pressurized, Dr. Mason steps out into the central area of IceCube. Three stories up, latent sunlight spills in through the ceiling dome. Above him, metal walkways looking over the central area lead into other rooms. Sal and Lansdown stand next to a splintered table and fake potted plants lying on the floor.

"What did you find?" Dr. Mason asks.

"Place is empty." Sal gestures to the broken table. "Some signs of a struggle. Blood in the server room upstairs."

"Any snow vehicles?"

"Probably parked in the climate-controlled arches underneath the main station. Lansdown, you keep an eye out. We'll have to tow the para-dropped gear back with it."

"And LoNigro."

Sal's lips tighten, and he nods. "And LoNigro, yes."

"I'm sorry about him," Dr. Mason offers.

"Part of the deal we all signed, brother." Sal's face is so blank that it might not have been alive at all, but there's no mistaking the fury seething in his voice. "But if these survivors fuck with me, they aren't going to find me wanting."

Amundsen-Scott South Pole Station looms on the horizon, a single building elevated on stilts that looks half-buried in snow already. Large mounds of clustered ice-pack create a bowl-like depression inside which the Station lives. Their Hazmat suits are snow-white; the bulky Antarctic jackets underneath them also white. Even their guns, loaded with tranquilizer dart ammunition, are white.

They slide down the blown snow hill into the shadows underneath the building. The Station's stilts are large, each as wide as a car. They move toward Destination Tango, an entrance to the Station on the second floor. But a ladder nailed into the side of the building leads higher.

On top of the Station, Mason sees at least two dozen char marks on the roof. "Holy shit." Lansdown bends over and scrapes his glove at some clumpy residue. "I think these were bodies."

"The survivors aren't stupid," Dr. Mason says. "These were likely infected crewmates."

"Any intel value in these?" Sal asks.

Dr. Mason shakes his head. "Anything we could use would have burned up."

The men advance to the hatch in the roof. A dull beacon glows beside it, highlighting that the Station still has power.

The hatch is locked from the inside.

Dr. Mason draws his weapon while Lansdown assembles a blowtorch from his pack.

Sal rocks back on his heels. "I'll take LoNigro's sector on the lower floor," he says. "Mason, Lansdown, sweep the upstairs level. Don't go into the ice tunnels without me."

Then he disappears, through the hole in the hatch.

Even though it has power, the Station is dark. Not even the hallway lights are on. The polar sun spills through distant windows, creating interspersed columns of light that highlight lazily dancing dust motes. Dr. Mason finds it difficult to hear over the rasp of oxygen in his suit. When he holds his breath, it's as silent as the grave outside.

The Station is just one long hallway, with doors on either side. Mason steps carefully, sweeping his gun from side to side. It's deserted.

They're here somewhere, he thinks. *At least Rajan is.*

"I got something," he whispers into his throat mike. "I'm at the upper gym. The door is chained shut. There's someone locked inside."

"I see the same on the lower floor," Sal replies. "Sweep the rest of the rooms and we'll come back to those."

The Destination Alpha door is warped with fire stains and buckled in the center. A makeshift plastic and reinforced tarpaulin barrier is taped around it. The berthing rooms he pokes into are empty, almost disused. No dorms here like Mac; each resident gets their own room. The lonely pool of light from the end of his gun roves over a greenhouse, an art room, a laundry room. Now a ghost town.

"Contact two!" Lansdown. "Upper floor, cafeteria!"

"Mason, get there," Sal grates.

"Moving!"

Dr. Mason accelerates down the hallway, flashlight bouncing erratically off the walls. He rounds the corner into the cafeteria, gun stiff-armed in front of him. Tall windows look out onto the Ceremonial South Pole; sunlight spills through them, highlighting neatly-arranged long tables and chairs.

Lansdown is in the center of the room, gun pointed. As soon as Mason enters, he moves to his left, disappearing into the pantry.

Dr. Mason's gun sweeps across a man and a woman with a half-hearted game of cribbage in front of them. He recognizes the dark-skinned man immediately – it's Rajan Chariya. The woman is short, with badly-cut blonde hair growing past her shoulders. He's looked through the roster many times; her name will come to him in a moment.

"Contact one!" It's Sal, on the radio. "Found another, sleeping in the berthing area."

Rajan is squinting, trying to look past the flashlight at the end of Dr. Mason's gun, then he stands. Mason sees a knife in his hand, held down by his side.

"Easy. You don't want to come near me with that pressure suit on," Rajan says. "Just one little poke, and you'll –"

Dr. Mason shoots him.

With a nasty little *whap*, a fully loaded chempoule dart slams into Rajan's chest.

He weaves unsteadily, looking down in confusion. He collapses back toward his chair, misses, and smashes unpleasantly into the floor.

Siri – that's her name, Siri Monthan – cries out and springs to her feet.

Dr. Mason shines his flashlight right in her face. Gun centered.

"Easy way or hard way?" His voice comes out of the suit speakers in a rasp.

Slowly, keeping her eyes on him, Siri puts her hands up.

"Good choice. Put your butt back in that chair."

She fumbles for it, sits down. "What did you do to him?" she asks.

Off to his left, Dr. Mason senses Lansdown's return. "I shot him with a tranq dart, Siri."

Her eyes narrow on hearing her name.

Sal enters the cafeteria, a man stumbling in front of him. Dr. Mason takes a step back, making sure to keep his gun on Siri, who looks ready to spring at him if given half a chance. The newcomer has a full head of wavy surfer-blonde hair, looking like he's done nothing but lift weights all winter, an expression of fright on his well-etched face.

Dr. Mason runs through his mental rolodex.

Greg, he thinks. *This is Greg Penny.*

"Penny. Sit down over there next to her."

Sal gestures to Rajan, on the floor, and raises an eyebrow. Dr. Mason shrugs. "Dumb fuck brought a knife to a gunfight."

Sal smirks. "Lansdown, check out the locked gym rooms. One by one."

"Aye, chief." He disappears.

Sal reaches into his gear bag. Tosses handcuffs at Siri and Penny. "Put those on."

Siri bares her teeth. "Come over here and make me."

Sal sighs, and lifts his gun.

"All right! All right." She picks up the handcuffs.

"That's good," Sal says. "The sooner we establish who's in charge, the less gabbing and *wah-wah*ing I have to listen to." He pulls out an ampoule from his kit and tosses it to Penny. "There's a syringe in there, surfer guy."

"Greg Penny," Dr. Mason interjects.

"There's a syringe in there, Penny. Give your stupid friend on the ground there a jab so he can wake up and talk to us."

Lansdown reappears with an old man, hunched over, a ragged beard growing past his neck. Jonah Mitchell. A few minutes later, Lansdown returns with Bethany Hamidani. She looks more put together, long hair swept up into a high ponytail that exposes her prominent cheekbones and thin, slash-like lips. Her eyes flit between the three of them, as if trying to evaluate who's boss.

By this time, Rajan is stirring. He makes a sound like a plunger in a clogged sink, then rubs his chest. He struggles up to a sitting position, clutching his head.

"Yeah." Sal smirks. "It's a hell of a hangover. Don't recommend any of you try it."

Rajan looks up, now seeing Dr. Mason without a light in his face. The recognition is immediate. His features stretch and squeeze into a rich amalgam of hatred and unmistakable anger.

"Richard Mason," he growls. The unmistakable tone of a man facing down his nemesis. "You fucking son of a bitch."

Chapter Nineteen

Sixteen months ago.

They always met in a major chain hotel, a Marriott or a Hilton or a Wyndham. Always the hotel room closest to the stairwell.

Dr. Richard Mason leaned forward. Studied the tall man in front of him.

"Three unsuccessful attempts, Major Chariya," he said, in a composed but regretful voice. "You've been foiled, each time, by the policy paper-pushers in the State Department. Turns out they really don't want a military guy to be part of an Antarctic crew."

"There's plenty of military in Antarctica." Rajan's voice carried an undertone of stubbornness and frustration; a mix Mason has been fostering for a while. "The Navy has gone down hundreds of times. The Air Force flies the airplanes."

"Ah, but that's just keeping the place running and ticking and fucking. Nobody believes a military guy with a security clearance is out there trying to do science with a telescope." He shook his head sorrowfully. "Why do you want it so bad?"

Rajan debated not answering, then decided why the fuck not. "I want to be an astronaut one day," he said. The lack of emotion in his voice cried out with how much he cared. "It's been my dream since I was a kid. Since I'm not a fucking test pilot, and I don't work at mission control kissing astronaut ass, a winter-over in Antarctica is as close to a meaningful resume as I can get."

Dr. Mason let the silence fall. Let it linger. Then he dropped his bait: "What if I told you I could make sure you went?"

Rajan looked up.

"And not just any season. This season. Four months from now."

"I've already been turned down by the NSF this season." Rajan sounded dejected.

"Let's assume I know people. What would you say?"

Rajan sat forward, steepled his fingers under his chin. "Dr. Mason, I've been around the military long enough to know what type of shadow comes knocking with offers that sound too good to be true. Who do you work for?"

Dr. Mason grinned wolfishly at him. "You know who I work for."

"But I want you to confirm it."

"I work for the Agency."

"You're an actual blue-badge employee of the Central Intelligence Agency."

"That's right. Twenty years now."

"And you're aware that since the NSF hasn't funded my telescope, you would have to?"

"That's part of the offer," Dr. Mason said. "I'd like to read you into a program called HAVE VIKING. *The NSF will suddenly get a million dollars to pay for your telescope, and they'll agree to put you on crew. You keep an eye on things at South Pole, and after your season is over, you'll go to another station for me. You'll tell me everything you see and find down there. And this conversation will have never happened."*

Chapter Twenty

October 11.

The CIA men lock the survivors in the lower gym, and interrogate them three at a time. Three on three: Dr. Mason in the cafeteria, Sal in the science lab, Lansdown in the arts and crafts room.

"I have information for you," Bethany says. She's handcuffed with her arms behind her. "If you don't kill me."

"I'm not here to kill you." Dr. Mason straddles a chair turned backwards, gun slung over one shoulder. "I'm here to find out why this station went offline."

"That's horseshit and we both know it. I'm telling you. I can give you the microbe."

He can read the desperation coming off of her in noisome waves. "I already have the microbe."

"I can show you a body. The one they couldn't find."

"What would I do with a body?"

Uncertainty flickers across her face. "I don't know. Study it. Isn't that why you're here? To figure out how the microbe evolved to be symbiotic with us?"

"Bethany. Do you know Ben Jacobs?"

"Yeah, I know Ben." Her jaw tightens.

"I've got *his* body."

Shock falls across her face. "Where the hell did you find Ben?"

"Doesn't matter," Dr. Mason says. "I'm telling you that just so we can skip past the part where you think you can deal your way out. Answer me truthfully, and you'll be just fine."

"How do I know you'll keep that promise?"

"You don't, Bethany. But you have no cards to play. So, you might as well try, right?"

Her face crumples.

"Look. The CIA in the real world isn't like the CIA in the movies, okay?" Dr. Mason rolls his eyes a little. "It's actually a lot of paperwork to kill someone. I want answers, not paperwork."

She wants to believe him, he can tell. She wants to believe him so badly that helpless tears fill her eyes. "Okay." She sniffles.

"Tell me about this body. Who is it?"

"His name was Tommy Chapman. He was one of the cooks." Something trips inside her, and she bursts out wailing. "It's burned," she sobs. "We found his body and I swear I was going to give him to you guys so you could learn whatever you wanted but Jonah started a fire without telling me and, and… and *he's all burned up now.*"

Lansdown, interviewing Siri in the arts and crafts room.

"Tell me about these notebooks you mentioned."

"They're Doc Wei's." Siri's voice is barely audible even in the small room. "Wei was the Station doctor. Before the last wave of symbiote infections got him, he was studying the microbes' evolution. He took slides, detailed medical notes… everything you boys could want."

"And where are they?"

Her lip curls. "I'm not telling you that."

"You want to make a deal for the notebooks, then. Is that right?"

"Yeah, I want to make a deal."

"Too bad." Lansdown flashes his teeth in a predatory grin; the grin of a hunter that would swallow you whole without even spitting out the bones. "One of our team died trying to get down here. I'm fresh out of deals."

"You might want to check with your boss first. I'm pretty sure that's why he came."

"Yeah, and who's my boss?"

She looks at him. "Richard Mason."

Lansdown showcases two rows of perfect Chiclet teeth. "Mason's just a ride-along."

Siri's eyes smolder at him. "You might want to check. Just saying."

"I'll get right on that, partner," he smirks. "Now you were the... equipment mover on crew. That right?"

"Yeah."

"Well now I gotta do your fucking job. Carve out a runway so nobody else has to jump into that bitch of a cold sky. Tell me about the snowmovers."

"Sure. I put the batteries and keys for all of them right where I put the notebooks."

Lansdown's shark-smile turns into a brittle frown. "The fuck you say?"

Siri looks up at him and now her voice is perfectly clear. "Good luck shoveling, partner. Go make me a deal and don't come back until you do."

Lansdown kicks aside the small table between them. "How about I start pulling your fingernails out?" he snarls.

"Good luck in that suit."

"You know what, maybe I just start with your eye."

"Sure, except if you want to get on an airplane and get away from this place, you're gonna need me." She looks right into his eyes. "And let me tell you something. I hold grudges. Take one of my eyes, and you can be damn sure I'll want *both* of yours before I help you."

Sal and Rajan, in the Science Lab.

"Yeah?" Sal cocks an eyebrow. "And why am I gonna need you?"

"Because you're not gonna find either the batteries for the snow movers, or the med data Mason wants, unless you keep us alive."

"Shit deal," Sal laughs. "Here's a new deal. I'll hurt her."

"Who?"

"Your little blonde girlfriend. Oh yeah, I've seen the way you look at her." Sal leans forward. The vertical creases in his cheeks deepen until they look like cuts from a sharp knife. "And I bet… that when I get to peeling Siri's pretty face open like an orange, right in front of you? You'll talk real fast."

"If you touch her–"

"What?" Sal smirks. "You'll bring another knife to a gunfight?"

Rajan's face opens into a wide and malignant smile. "Keyon won't give you what you came for. He has it all, and he'll just burn it."

"Keyon?" Sal blinks. "Who the fuck is Keyon?"

Dr. Mason, and Bethany Hamidani, in the cafeteria.

"We couldn't tell who was infected and who wasn't," Bethany is explaining. "And after what I saw them do to Summer–"

"Bethany, shut up."

Dr. Mason listens intently to the voices in his radio, then his eyes pin on her. And this time there's no give in them.

"Answer me very clearly. How many survivors are left in this Station?"

Bethany looks confused. "Six. The five of us here and Keyon."

Mason takes a deep breath.

"Where is Keyon?"

"I don't know."

"Where is Keyon?"

"I've been locked up. How the hell would I know?"

"Because you've been sneaking out," Dr. Mason says, implacably. "The lock on your door wasn't closed. You could have gotten out anytime. And I bet you did. That's how you and Jonah found TC. Isn't that right?"

A sulky look comes over her face. "Yeah."

"Then tell me, Bethany, so I can clear a fucking runway. Where is Keyon?"

Chapter Twenty-One

Keyon is shrouded in the dark, and he likes it that way. These days, darkness is the only thing that lets him think.

Once, Keyon Geerts had been the Loki of the South Pole. Once, he'd made a game out of suffering and angst. He had enjoyed watching other people's anguish with a certain malign callousness. If you were older than ten and you still blew with the untidy wind of your own emotions, the old Keyon had no sympathy for you.

It meant life hadn't been hard enough on you.

The only way to learn, then, was exposure therapy.

Keyon had shut off his emotions a long time ago as a defense mechanism. At a hideously tender age, he'd seen the most brutal things human beings can do to each other. His parents survived multiple rounds of ethnic cleansing by the Janjaweed – Sudanese Arabs who wanted to drive Black residents of Darfur out – until they poisoned his father's well. His mother had been away, helping her sister give birth, and Keyon had been left alone in a dying village, trying to nurse his father back to health. His father had been thirsty, had cried out for water, but Keyon had no water to give him. No safe water, anyway.

His father died of thirst within reaching distance of a well he had dug with his own hands, and Keyon watched the life leave his eyes.

After that, there was not much more the world could do to him.

A year later, with his mother, he began a long and torturous voyage across the Saharan desert toward Europe. Dodging human trafficking gangs, robbed by roving miscreants, raped with the end of a walking stick by an old man in Morocco when they'd been out of money, luck and mercy. The old man did it just for a sense of power; he kept spitting at the child, telling him not to look at him.

After that, *surely*, there was not much more the world could do to him.

Then came the boat voyage across the choppy and cold English Channel. Keyon clung to the sides as waves spilled into the boat, as the smugglers screamed at them, and finally, as the boat capsized. They were overloaded, of course; too many people with not enough hope. His mother brought him that far, but it was her last voyage. She sank beneath the foam-capped waves of the Channel. Her body was never found.

Keyon was only ten years old.

That was the first time the *hard stripe voice* whispered to him. A friend in a lonely existence.

His education in the sharp knives of life came as part of the British foster child system. If you had anything – money, parents, security, even unaccented English – you had more than he did. And so, he had nothing to lose by trying to take it from you. He'd experienced so much pain and cruelty, and the world seemed hellbent on sending him more. Why should others miss out on the same opportunity?

Kids he knew were pickpockets, smash-and-grab thieves, even underground boxers. Anything for a few quid. But Keyon had a different skill.

He could go into a crowded place like Waterloo station, sit down, listen… and home in on a patsy. Someone carrying around too many feelings, ripe for a scam. They could be relieved of their money, phones, cards… sometimes their dignity came with it as well. Keyon took it all; bathed in it.

But when you're a professional egg-breaker, sometimes you break the wrong eggs.

The wrong egg was Penelope Russell.

He was nineteen, she was twenty-one. She wanted to take him in, show him the finer side of life, soothe away all his cares, if she could sit on his dick on her father's bed at his country manor.

He didn't realize that she wanted to be discovered.

He also didn't realize that her father was Lord Russell, the foreign secretary.

Lord Russell was a staunch conservative; one of the crusty white millionaires pushing for a more restrictive line on boats coming across the channel. He did not enjoy the visual that his daughter presented to him.

Lord Russell had Keyon arrested.

The charge was rape.

It was handled hush-hush, of course. All Keyon had to do was sign a confession, and the police would do him a favor and make sure he only served the minimum sentence.

Keyon had never enjoyed an encounter with luck. He had no reason to believe this would be the time that changed. But the hard-stripe voice stepped in and changed his life. It whispered to him that *he* was the one with an advantage.

"I'll take my day in court, lads," he told the Scotland Yard detectives with a wide grin on his Black face. "I can't wait to tell those fuckin' judges all about how Miss Penelope invited me to her family manor for the weekend. There might even be a few other details I haven't shared with you yet. Maybe Lord Russell asked her to do it. Maybe, once I go to court, it turns out he's the kind of man who likes to watch."

"You know we're recording you, right?" one of the detectives seethed. "That testimony will be instantly struck down."

He shrugged expansively. "Maybe. But it'll make so many nasty headlines when I take the stand. Nasty, nasty, nasty. Look at me. *I'll make sure it's nasty.*"

He was out of jail by dawn, and deported by the end of the day. Across the Channel to France, to await a decision by a magistrate about a safe third country he could be shipped off to. In Calais, Keyon shimmied out of a bathroom window in the halfway house where he was being held. He had his British passport in the bottom of his shoe. In those pre-Brexit days, that earned you the right to work across Europe and, later, a short path to immigration to America. Keyon found that he was quite resourceful at finding work, and then bending that work to his own benefit.

There was a rhythm to his life during the next few years. It was an unkind rhythm, no beat to shake a leg to, but one that kept him entertained. This was a world filled with tragedy of all flavors. Pain erased everything but pain. In America, there were so many people who had experienced no pain at all. But oh, they thought they had, and that made them like ripe fruits, pleading to be plucked.

The darkness of South Pole was the ultimate microcosm of human angst. Isolated from the world, so many sweet flavors of anguish lingered in the hallways. Hardened veterans who thought they understood loneliness found a new depth to drown in. At Pole, as everywhere before, Keyon had been a dry rock in the surf. Free to reach out with a casual word of malice or a pointed question, then step back and watch the puppets dance.

But Pole found a new depth to drown him in, as well.

South Pole made you forget. It untethered you from your old life. Away from the hustle-culture of the world, Keyon found himself softening. Falling in love. He could admit that now. He'd loved Katie Caberto.

He'd also set Katie on fire. Watched her burn to death.

His inner demon brought back memories of the waves closing over his mother. Of his father's swollen, parched lips mumbling incoherent syllables as his eyes glazed over. It was survival, the hard stripe voice tried to tell him.

But Keyon hadn't caused either of those deaths with his own hands.

Nothing lit his mind on fire like thinking about Katie's skin peeling off her face, from a match that he lit.

And Keyon decided he was tired of listening to the hard-stripe side of himself.

The voice started to change as Keyon's resolve stuck. It took the tack of old friends, just suffering from a small misunderstanding. Then it became wheedling and coaxing.

Don't you remember all the good times, Keyon? All the privileged people we've brought down together?

And when that failed to move Keyon, the voice became mocking. Cruel. *It's too late to be a warrior for justice,* it laughed. *Look at the morals you've built your life around. You may have loved Katie, but do you think she loved you? You think* anyone *could love you?*

You're a monster!

You're a monster.

You're a monster.

"I know," Keyon whispered back. "I know I am."

(*Katie Khaled Joe Gaudin Baia Tanzhou Tim Rob killed them all I killed them all*)

Keyon's churning emotions make him feel like a new recruit swept from the deck of a ship in a hurricane. Barely clinging to life, knowing there's nothing coming to save him. No salvation except the blackness of the deep sea.

Isn't this where it was always going, the hard stripe voice asks. *When the Chinese traverse showed up with a dead body, you wanted to see the corpse. Remember that, Keyon? You went into that truck and you stared into that dead guy's eyes and then* you licked the blood, you sick fuck. *You wanted to know what it tasted like.*

That's what got those microbes into your bloodstream.

You were always destined to be a murderer.

"No!" Keyon screams. "NO SHUT UP NO NO!"

His eyes snap open in the darkness of the crawl space. *Oh shit,* he thinks. *Oh shit shhhh–*

In the science lab, and in the arts and crafts room, Sal and Lansdown pause. Listening.

"Hey, did you hear that?" Sal says over the radio.

Lansdown swings his gun up, and pokes the ceiling tile with the tip.

It moves.

"There's a fucking crawl space above us," he snarls. "I think someone's in it."

Siri closes her eyes and thinks as hard as she can.

(*Keyon they heard you run run RUN*)

Keyon shoots up to his hands and knees and slams forward through the crawl space. The rooms are marked off, metal rivulets corresponding to the walls he's crossing on top of. His back brushes against the dusty ceiling, pulling out snarls of cables in his wake.

Shit. Shit, shit, shit.

He's their ace in the hole, and he has just outed himself.

Behind him, a ceiling tile knocks itself to one side. Keyon jerks around.

A flashlight stabs up into the darkness of the crawl space. Dazzling him with its brilliance. Then it points right at him.

(*Keyon JUMP NOW!*)

He doesn't hesitate. He rolls to the side, smashing through the ceiling tiles, right as *rat-a-tat* gunfire breaks out, incredibly loud in the confined space.

He falls downward, his back catches the edge of a table, then he bashes into the floor.

Above him, gunfire, then silence.

He scrambles to his feet, pain stabbing into his back. Keyon stumbles through a door, into the second-floor hallway. He looks wildly to one side, then the other.

(*here he comes here comes another*)

Keyon hastens into a run.

Behind him, the door to the Science Lab bursts outward. Sal shoots from the hip, but Keyon is already across the hall, smashing his shoulder through the swinging door to the berthing area.

(*go up Keyon go up if you can now*)

Siri and Rajan's voices are guiding him, in his head. He jumps up, boot striking a wall. He uses his momentum to push off and jump against the opposite wall in the narrow hallway. His arms lunge upward, craning, reaching–

His fingertips grab the edge of a ceiling tile, stabbing through to find a grip on the sharp metal rail behind it. He hangs by three fingers, gasping, his shoulder wrenching.

Come on Keyon, come on. You can't fail them, not now.

They are all you have left.

Somehow, he finds the strength to jerk his body up and find purchase with his other arm. A brute-force chin-up, until he can hoist an arm over the edge. He worms up into the crawl space as quickly as he can, then claws behind him desperately–

Slides the ceiling tile into place right as the door below him smashes open.

"Take the left, I got the right," Sal's voice says. "Sweep every room."

Keyon turns himself around in the narrow space slowly. Dust swirls into his nostrils and he struggles not to sneeze.

He inches forward. Then scuttles faster.

He takes a right, back above the main hallway of the Station. It won't take them to long to sweep the rooms and realize that he's double-backed on them.

(*I'm in the hallway*)

Siri's voice. He feels comfort run through his veins. She has been with him, in his head, from the beginning. She has looked into his darkness, before he knew how to hide it.

She has helped him survive before.

(*you're still clear*)

Keyon increases his speed, now moving at a loping pace. The crawl space comes to an end. He pushes aside a tile and pokes his head down.

Down the hallway, he sees Siri.

She's in a chair, arms handcuffed behind her back but hop-shuffling forward, dragging the chair with her.

Across to the berthing door. Blocking it.

(*thank you Siri*)

Keyon drops down to the floor. In front of him is Destination Zulu, the back entrance to the Station. Through the Zulu doors is the "beer can," a tall metal structure that wraps around the winding outdoor stairs. At the bottom of the beer can, steps drop into tunnels carved beneath the ice shelf.

He can get lost in the subterranean darkness down there.

The doors are locked, with chains and a lock that he has the key to. He fumbles in his pocket. He has seven keys on a ring.

He has just enough time to pray he knows which one is which–

Behind him, a *bang*, metal into metal. One of the CIA thugs trying to push back through the berthing doors, and running into Siri's chair.

(fast Keyon fast now)

Keyon slides the right key into the lock and turns it. The chains slip to the floor. He casts one last look over his shoulder, right as Siri is knocked over onto her side.

(*stay gone Keyon*)

He vanishes down the stairs.

Chapter Twenty-Two

October 12.

"I'll wring it out of these fuckers." Sal's face is red. His eyes glare fury out of dark hollows. "Watch me with a knife, Mason. They'll be singing before I'm halfway through tattooing them."

"Sal, listen," Dr. Mason says urgently. "Think. That couldn't have been an accident."

"The fuck do you mean?"

"We didn't know about the second-floor crawl spaces. If that was Keyon, he could have stayed hidden up there forever. Why, then, did he yell out his position? He literally *yelled* that he was up there."

Sal pauses, a frown descending onto his rugged face. "That's an interesting question."

"I think he did it on purpose."

Sal looks incredulous. "He almost got himself shot on purpose?"

Dr. Mason shakes his head. "He was announcing his position so we would know he was real. He's toying with us. Letting us know we're on his turf." Mason sighs. "We *need* those snowmover keys to get the hell out of here, and I need to learn what I can from the samples their doc collected. If we can't kill them all, we can't kill anyone. We have to negotiate."

Sal lets out a groan of pure frustration. "I'm already starting to hate this fucking place."

* * *

Keyon runs fast, down the ice tunnels. He is in utter darkness; his fingers brush along the ice wall. Every so often they dip into one of several "shrines" carved into the ice walls. Buzz Aldrin's tissue, jars of pineapple, inside jokes; a shelf-like cutout is left behind by each winter crew to commemorate their season. He counts shrines as he goes deeper and deeper.

At last, he stops, panting. He holds his breath.

Looks behind him and listens.

Nothing, except the sound of his exploding heartbeat.

(*can you guys hear me*)

He waits.

(*rajan siri can you hear me*)

Keyon Geerts sinks down to his knees, hugging himself. He starts to laugh in the darkness, a lonely, echoing sound. Alone, physically and in his head, for the first time in weeks.

"All right," Dr. Mason says. His face is stone. "Let's talk."

Dr. Mason and Sal face Rajan and Siri, who are no longer handcuffed. They stand across the cafeteria from each other, arms crossed. Outside, through the windows, blowing snow obscures the flapping flags surrounding the Ceremonial South Pole. The bottom of the world.

Rajan's proposed deal is simple – snowmover keys and batteries in exchange for seats on a plane to Mac, then off the ice to a neutral third-country. When they arrive, they will radio back the location of Wei's clinical notes and symbiote samples that will help the CIA understand how `HAVE VIKING` evolved.

"What a well-thought-out plan." Dr. Mason's mouth turns up in an expression that holds none of the warmth or amusement of a smile. "Would you like to hear my counter-offer?"

Sal leaves, and re-enters with Bethany, pulling her with one arm until she stands across from Rajan and Siri. Dr. Mason keeps staring at Siri and Rajan. "Bethany."

"Yes, Dr. Mason."

"Tell your friends here what I just told you."

Bethany stiffens her face up. Her voice comes out as brittle as sandstone. "I found TC's body. My only mistake was bringing Jonah. That fucker burned it before I could trade it for my freedom."

(*this devious little bitch i knew I KNEW she wasn't to be trusted*)

(*jonah came through though rajan*)

"Not that," Dr. Mason snaps. "The other thing. The thing *I* told *you*."

"Oh. Right," Bethany says. "You've got Ben Jacobs at McMurdo."

"That's right." Dr. Mason's smile widens. "I've got Ben Jacobs at McMurdo. Alive."

Siri turns grey. "What the *fuck*?" she gasps.

"So, you see, I really don't need your notes or samples or whatever you've collected..."

Suddenly Siri and Rajan's heads snap toward each other.

(*did you hear that*)

(*yes it's pulsing out of him he's AFRAID*)

The microbe net lets them read each other's thoughts clearly, but it is sensitive to thoughts in general. And Mason's worries are suddenly beating through him so hard they are *leaking out.*

(*he's terrified of losing control of this whole project*)

(*Kim who is Kim*)

"Are you two listening to me?" Dr. Mason barks.

Rajan turns back to Mason. His face wears the unnerving smile of a poker player who has just drawn the winning card.

"Dr. Mason, I think you're going to make us a deal."

The CIA man's smile falters. "The hell I will."

"Not only that. It's going to be a good deal. Because Kim has you by the balls if you don't."

(*the first name I can't tell can you hear it*)

(*it's Jon I think*)

"Jon Kim," Rajan drawls. "Yeah, Mason, you need us. You."

(*you personally*)

"You personally. Because you don't have Ben – Dr. Kim has Ben."

A tortured look, like smelling something disgusting, comes across Dr. Mason's face. His bony fingers clench at his sides like distended spiderwebs.

"We can help you."

Dr. Mason is still and silent. Turning the problem over. Calculating.

"We can help you, Dr. Mason," Siri says.

"I could make a deal," Dr. Mason says, at last. His mouth releases the word *deal* as if it's coated in grime. "But someone has to stay behind."

"What?"

"There's nothing to prevent all of you from disappearing into thin air once you leave Antarctica. There has to be a canary left in the coal mine. Once I get the samples I need, that last person gets off the ice. You tell me who that canary should be."

Rajan looks at Siri, and she sighs with capitulation. Dr. Mason grins; opens his arms.

"So tell me. Where are the snowmover keys and batteries?"

"We'll dig for it tomorrow," Siri sounds beat down. "It's been a long day."

"No, it's got to be now. Our clean room tent needs to be towed in," Sal interjects. "That's where we sleep. It's not safe out here. There could be killer microbes on anything. This table. That door handle."

Siri chuckles. "The microbes are completely inert at warmer temperatures. As long as you don't go outside, anything you pick up won't activate. And before you go out… well, South Pole Station comes fully equipped, gentlemen. A library, a greenhouse, and… a sauna."

"So that's how you beat it back," Dr. Mason murmurs.

"Yeah. Twenty minutes, at 200 degrees, kills any microbes on your skin. In other words, you don't have to walk around looking like astronauts."

Dr. Mason looks at Sal. "What do you think?"

"I could go for a sauna sesh and a nap, sure." Sal jerks his thumb across the room. "But we're locking these fuckers up."

Dr. Mason turns to them. "I have a feeling Jonah and Bethany will be somewhat vindicated to see them as fellow prisoners."

When the doors of the lower gym slam shut, Rajan closes his eyes. Ignoring the other three Polies.

(*we're ready*)

Siri comes up next to him. She puts her hand on his shoulder and squeezes. His headache lessens a little.

She amplifies his mental message, syncing up with him.

(*keyon we're ready*)

* * *

Deep in the ice tunnels, surrounded by darkness, Keyon hears a whisper. An echo.

He sits up. Turns on his flashlight and sweeps it up and down the tunnel.

Nothing.

Then it hits him suddenly.

(*we're ready keyon we're ready*)

Keyon scrambles to his feet and starts running. Back to the station.

Once their prisoners are locked away, the three CIA men remove their bulky Hazmat suits. "Thought I'd be living in this fucker," Sal says with a velvety sigh of relief.

"Don't get too comfortable," Dr. Mason warned. "There's still a symbiotic strain that the sauna may not kill, and any of the survivors could have that strain."

"But while those jagoffs are locked up?"

"Yeah, we should be fine to go suits off."

Dr. Mason and Sal decide to go into the sauna first. They leave Lansdown on armed watch right outside, with plans to swap immediately after. They step inside, drawing the door closed behind them. The two naked men look at each other and chuckle dryly.

"Don't make this awkward, Sal."

"Good thing we're both equally, massively endowed. Right?"

"Sounds right to me."

They sit across from each other, sweat already starting to glisten on their bodies in the dry heat. "So..." Sal says, hesitantly. "How do you know if... you know. There's a microbe on you?"

Dr. Mason considers the question. "I think it would be like an ant on your skin? If you crush it, but don't kill it, the ant digs in. It bites you in case the pain it's inducing can help it get away. I'm guessing the microbes might have a similar survival response?" He shrugs. "But... those are exactly the types of answers that we can't learn unless I play ball with these guys."

"At least for now."

"Exactly." Dr. Mason winks. "Until a better position presents itself."

Keyon whispers up the stairs to Destination Zulu, a ghost in a dark tunnel. He tugs on the door just enough to understand that they've done up the chain on the other side.

He pushes through the door of the beer can, into the cold sunlight of the exterior.

He walks under the Station until he arrives at Destination Tango, then climbs up the ladder in the side of the structure. Not too long ago, he had perched on this very roof in the winter darkness. Siri had thrown open the Tango doors and blasted the symbiotes trying to enter with fire. They'd turned to run… and Keyon had rained flames on them from above.

"Fuck you, Keyon," he says aloud. Abruptly, he punches himself in the face, so hard he feels a tooth dislodge in the back of his jaw. "Fuck you, you murderer, you piece of shit."

He crouches by the roof hatch. His suspicion is confirmed. There's a neat circle cut into it. It's how he would have entered the Station too.

Katie had used this entrance all the time. The weather equipment up here was once hers.

Keyon slips through the hole, down into the warm Station.

In the waiting room outside the sauna, Lansdown shrugs off his white Antarctic jacket. It's warm out here. He peeks in through the small window set in the sauna door.

"Stop fondling each other in there, you two," he says, laughing.

"Fuck you, Lansdown," comes the prompt reply.

"Don't make Daddy come in there and smack you–"

He breaks off and whirls, some unquantifiable instinct alerted. His gun comes up, but right behind him, Keyon's arm is already moving.

Splashing liquid onto his neck. It drips down his white sweater.

"Eat microbes and die, fuckhead!" Keyon yells, eyes maniacally wide. Then he ducks away.

Lansdown's fingers touch the damp spots on his neck, his chest, one of his ears. He lets out a shriek. "Fuck!"

He turns, and rips the door to the sauna open.

Steps inside and starts tugging off his clothes, as quickly as he can.

Sal turns his head. "The fuck are you doing, Lansdown?"

Dr. Mason looks up just in time to see Keyon's grin flashing at him from the window in the sauna door. He springs off his feet, past Lansdown, who is in a ball on the floor trying to tug his pants over his large boots. He slams his shoulder into the door–

It's made of firm, thick wood. Barricaded shut.

Keyon looks him right in the eye. Puts up a finger, as if to say, *hang on one second*.

He disappears for a moment.

Then reappears with a white machine gun in his hands. One of theirs.

Lansdown looks up. His face is blank from panic. "He got me. He got me with microbes. He threw them at me!"

Mason stares at the droplets on his neck, already starting to shimmer in the heat. "The microbes aren't liquid, you moron." He turns back, and sees Keyon doing a little dance with the gun. "*Fuck*!"

Keyon tries not to think anything, to keep it a surprise, but when he unlocks the doors to the gym, Rajan and Siri rush out and hug him, laughing already.

"You got 'em, Keyon!" Rajan pounds his back. "Well done!"

"You are one brave motherfucker, dude," Siri says.

"Eh." Keyon shrugs, but he flashes a grin. It's the first time he's felt happy in a long time. "It's easy when I've got you two in my head."

Abruptly he turns, shrugging one of the guns off his back. "Uh-uh," he says. Rajan turns to see Bethany, who had been about to exit the gym. "Not you. Don't think I've forgotten that you and Jonah tried to *kill us*. You two sit right back down where you belong."

"For fuck's sake, Keyon!" Bethany screams.

Keyon racks the gun. Lifts it to his shoulder.

"Come at me so I can say it was self-defense," he grates. "*Please*."

Bethany steps back. Her face is a twisted heap of hate.

"Hey man," Penny says. "Can I get out of here?"

"Penny, you piece of shit!" Bethany screeches. "You leave now and you'll never get to fuck me again!"

Keyon chuckles. "I think I'd be doing you a huge favor by getting you out of there, bud."

Penny hesitates. He looks over his shoulder. "Bethany, come on." He flashes her a grin, opens his arms wide, and at that, she springs at him, fingers extended and hooked into claws. Penny leaps backward, but not before she gouges four deep lines into his cheekbones, down to his mouth.

"Dammit, girl!" Penny stumbles backward, fingertips coming away with blood. Keyon lifts the gun, but Bethany sags to the floor, sobbing.

Past her, Jonah just stands in the darkness, saying nothing. Rajan hesitates, then steps forward.

"Jonah, I… I did want to thank you." The words drag out of his throat unwillingly. "For doing the right thing and burning TC's body. I won't forget it."

They make eye contact for a long moment, then Rajan steps back, and Keyon locks the doors to the gym.

"Damn!" Penny is muttering, over and over. He's examining his reflection in a commemorative display of South Pole markers. The location of the Pole itself moves, with the ice. Every year, the crew plants a new marker, designed by the crew, and adds the old one to this display. Now, all it reflects are bloody abrasions down Penny's face.

"Hey, y'all want to see something funny?" Keyon grins.

Back at the sauna, the three CIA men trapped inside are sweating freely. Dr. Mason is red as a lobster. All of them immediately send muffled shouts. *Hot,* they mime. *Turn down the temperature.*

"Should we let them out?" Keyon smirks.

"Nah," Siri speaks for all of them. "Let 'em get a tan."

Chapter Twenty-Three

October 12.

Siri speaks calmly, but as she tells the story of the symbiote infection at South Pole, the thread of pain rings clear in her voice. There are places where loss and sorrow and fear have taken chunks out of her. At her feet, the three CIA men are on the floor of the South Pole sauna, handcuffed to each other. Wrist to ankle, ankle to wrist, one shackled caterpillar. The sauna heat, mercifully, has been turned off.

"Ben Jacobs was patient zero down here." She pinches the bridge of her nose as if in pain. "And this is the guy you think you have contained at Mac."

"Look," Lansdown starts, "we don't–"

"Hey, hired gun," Siri snaps. "I'm talking to the brains of the operation. If I need to hear from a mercenary, I'll let you know."

The malevolence in her voice shuts him up.

"These microbes can evolve faster than any of us can respond, Dr. Mason," Rajan says flatly. "If Ben Jacobs gets off this continent, a lot more people are going to lose their lives."

"Kim and a SEAL doc are studying Ben Jacobs. He's completely out of it," Dr. Mason says. He is still the color of an overripe tomato. "Throat ripped out, barely more than human jerky. He hasn't said a word, or even regained consciousness."

"When was this?"

"Two days ago."

Siri and Rajan look at each other, horrified.

"You are really underestimating how powerful Ben is with this microbe in him."

Chapter Twenty-Four

McMurdo Station.

We open Ben's eyes.

Slowly, slowly, we inflate his lungs. The too-warm air sears his throat, his chest, his stomach.

But he's alive.

(*We. We are alive*)

Ben's eyes roll in his sockets, slowly, like creaking floorboards in a rotten house.

Oh yes. We are alive.

It takes us a very long time to collect our bearings. Ben Jacobs is in a dull yellow-painted room, lying on a medical cot. His arms are thick with wires, bags of fluid flowing into him – into us. We are choking with the hated warmth. We feel cataleptic. Something in one of these bags is robbing us of our extraordinary strength.

Some part of Ben's fatigued brain brings up that an ordinary man would be out, stone cold.

Ah. But we are no longer ordinary, are we?

No. He, Ben Jacobs, has the destiny of Adam. Father to a new generation of *us*. The long, cold, brutal trek has cut Ben's body in half, but we have made it to our promised land. Our new Eden.

Ben's body is tied to the bed. Covered with several thick blankets. It's as if his doctors are trying to hurt us, but oh, they have no idea how strong we are.

We hear a noise, and we quickly shutter Ben's eyes. A door swings open, with a short stir of tepid air, and we hear footsteps. We reach out, searching.

(*this could be the Nobel fucking Prize if I handle this right*)

Dr. Jon Kim, we think. His desires slough through his mind, off his skin to wash over us. We sense the ambition oozing from him.

There is another man in the room, but we focus on Dr. Kim. Focus on what else he will tell us about himself without meaning to. We hear the rasping of their Hazmat suits, the safe oxygen they are breathing, but we can wrench that off with one easy twist. Like uncorking a wine bottle.

We tighten Ben's fists under the restraints, a cobra ready to strike–

Then we relax his fingers.

It's okay. We are where we need to be.

A knife slides into Ben's side, rummages, scrapes. Draws a sample away with its sharp point. The pain brings Ben to the forefront of us, but we comfort him. We let him shout into us; we take the pain away. Our moment is almost here.

Chapter Twenty-Five

October 13.

McMurdo Station.

In the Chalet, Winston fills his lungs with righteous anger.

"Colson, it's been three days. Seventy-two hours of confinement for four-hundred people. People have to get to work to keep the Station functioning!"

Colson leans forward, and Winston steels himself.

"You're right, Winston."

Winston blinks.

"Didn't expect me to agree, did you?" She flashes him a quick grin. "Well, you're right." She looks over at Marshal Anne. "You're both right. We've sampled every person on this Station over a dozen times. No fevers. No outbursts of anger, except for that one from you just now." She looks at her watch. "I'll release the emergency lockdown tomorrow. But I have some conditions."

"Of course you do," Winston grumbles.

"I want at least another 72 hours of observation to make sure we didn't miss anything. The internet doesn't go back up until the observation period is over."

"Another 72 hours without internet won't kill anybody," Marshal Anne says.

"But we're sure gonna hear some Mac-class bitching about it," Winston says sourly. "All right, Colson. What else?"

"We should call an all-hands tomorrow, and provide an explanation. And…"

Winston rolls his eyes. "You need us to figurehead it up on stage."

Colson clicks her tongue and makes finger guns at him: *exactly*. "And finally, the hospital stays on lockdown. That's Ben Jacobs, but also the twenty-six people quarantining in there. Season's over for those folks. When my evac aircraft gets here, they'll all be on it, back to the mainland."

"Wait a minute. You've got our only doc, at least two of my key maintenance leads…"

Colson holds up a hand. "There will be replacement crew coming in on the evac aircraft. A one-for-one personnel swap, no loss to station ops. But until then, no one goes in or out of the hospital except my men."

"And me," Marshal Anne says.

Colson shakes her head. "No."

"I'm not asking," Anne says, her voice cold. "You're a ghost with a fake badge, Colson. *I'm* law enforcement on this continent. If I say you're not going to keep me out, you're not going to keep me out."

Colson's face is a cold mask of refusal, but Marshal Anne doesn't back down. The tense standoff swells. Fills the room.

At last, Colson sighs. "Fine," she says. "You, and only you, if you haz-suit up. The last thing I want after all this is a new strain of infection."

"How soon does this evac flight of yours arrive?"

"They have to retrofit a C-17 with a full medical quarantine system." Colson spreads her hands. "It's in work now. A week at the most."

The three of them look at each other, nothing more to argue about. Marshal Anne decides to stick one last iron in the fire. "How about Pole?" she asks. "Any word from the people you sent down there two days ago?"

A small smile flickers on Colson's face. "How'd you hear about that, Marshal?"

"It's my job to know these things."

"Sometimes," Colson murmurs, "I find myself curious about your background. What ops you've been a part of. What the hell brought you down here."

"That last one is easy," Anne comes right back. "Divorce. And the rest is just none of your business." But she says it with her head cocked. Short straight strands of dyed blonde hair fall across her glasses, a thousand-watt smile beaming through them, and it's completely disarming. In fact, her smile hits Colson in the gut like a formless prayer for help.

Chapter Twenty-Six

October 13.

South Pole Station.

"I think we have to do it," Rajan says.

"No. No freaking way, man," Keyon insists.

"Look. If we put Mason on the microbe net with us, we can live inside his head. He won't be able to double-cross us!"

"And if we do put him on the net, then he becomes aware of that ability. I don't need to be inside the head of a career CIA guy to know what he's gonna do with that information."

Rajan runs his hands through his messy, curly hair. He's with Siri and Keyon in the South Pole cafeteria. The three CIA guys are locked up in the sauna; Jonah and Bethany are locked up in the gym. Penny is off doing whatever it is that he does when he's not trying to get with Bethany. They don't like him enough to chase him down.

Keyon looks at Siri.

(*what do you really think about putting Mason on the net*)

Her eyes are grave. "Mac is the only gateway to the rest of the world, which is why I think Ben Jacobs went there. And can you *imagine* what would happen if Ben made it to the mainland?"

Keyon's face blanches.

"He could single-handedly cause more deaths *than the entire Pacific Rim War*. That's the real problem we need to address. And..."

(*we need the CIA on our side to stop him*)

"We need all the allies we can get to stop him," she finishes.

Rajan nods emphatically. "Keyon, no one wants to turn Mason's face into a bloody pulp more than me. But we *have* to risk it. There's no other way to ensure he's on our team."

Keyon shakes his head. "I think evil is evil whether you hear it or not. I vote no."

"I think I vote yes," Siri says, slowly.

"Well, there you have it." Keyon shrugs. "Two against one."

Rajan meets his eyes.

(*no – we do this together or not at all*)

Keyon sighs, then raises his arms and turns them upward. "Damn you, Rajan. You're appealing to this new good nature that I'm trying to cultivate."

"Thanks, Key." Rajan looks relieved. "I'm glad we have a plan."

"But."

The look on his face draws Rajan's attention like a wound: hard and dreadful.

"If the time comes that–"

(*mason even thinks about telling others that the microbes can create telepathy*)

"Then we all agree that we'll do what needs to be done."

Rajan hesitates, then nods.

"We'll do what needs to be done," he says.

"What the fuck what the *fuck*," Dr. Mason's eyes are red-rimmed, fixated on the medical slide Siri is holding. His throat pulses with suppressed fear.

There are thousands of black flecks of dormant microbes on the slide.

"It's gonna be okay," Siri says. "We're gonna kill them from you."

"Why put them on me in the first place?" An undercurrent of panic thrums in his throat. He knows what the microbes really are – a death sentence. He has seen it on the Dome-A cameras. "Come on, Rajan, you know how the classified game works! It was need to know!"

Rajan bends in front of him, and his gaze holds no pity. "That's why I'm going to take some satisfaction in this."

Rajan punches him in the nose.

Then again, harder.

Dr. Mason's nose starts to bleed.

"Consider us even," Rajan says. "Okay, let's dose him."

They wrestle Dr. Mason outside, into the face-numbing cold. Almost immediately, he starts to groan, choking with internal pressure, writhing in their arms as the microbes multiply greedily. Consuming him. After twenty minutes, they lock themselves in the sauna with him. Siri takes up a position by the back exit, blocking him from leaving. As the microbes feel their impending doom and dig in, all he will want is the refuge of the cold.

When the sauna temperature hits +100 F, Dr. Mason starts to scream. It drills into their ears like thin silver nails. Mason climbs the walls of his pain, pulsing and contorting on the wooden floor.

Then black dust begins to spill outward from the bleeding squashed strawberry of his nose. Scalding tears and snot flow with it. Like an invisible blowtorch crisping his nostrils and lower face.

From there, they wait. The heat continues to climb. Siri helps Dr. Mason up into a sitting position on the hot planks, where he tries to catch his breath.

"Dear God, that was the worst thing," he whispers. His jaw twitches like a humming tube of neon. "The worst thing."

Rajan takes him by the back of the neck and squeezes gently. "Take my hand," Rajan says. "Take Siri's hand. *Listen.*"

(*listen for the sound of my voice in your head*)

(*can you hear*)

Dr. Mason relaxes into Rajan's grip, like a tiger cub being held in the mouth of its mother.

(*can you hear*)

Dr. Mason's eyes flutter closed… and his mind blasts away, dissolving into theirs. Reliving the horror of their last few months at South Pole Station in terrible first-person high-definition.

* * *

It takes Dr. Mason a long time to recognize that the past has stopped playing. His heart gallops like he has just run a mile at high altitude. He did more than see their struggles. He'd *lived* them. Felt them.

"Mason. Dr. Mason."

The man's skittish eyes find Rajan's; focuses on them.

(*now you see why don't you*)

Mason nods jerkily. "Yes. My God. We can't let Dr. Kim take Ben Jacobs off-continent."

"That's right. This microbe cannot get off the continent. Not a vial, not a slide, and *definitely* not a symbiote. The CIA cannot learn how to turn the microbes they have into a weapon."

Suddenly Dr. Mason's mind fills with jarring noise. Roaring with indecision. Thoughts spin through his mind – and theirs – with rapid snapping. Top secret things, quickly thrust aside. Wartime priorities. Career choices. Somebody named Evil Bill. A woman, slumped over a sink. His eyes ping-pong in his sockets.

"Uhhh…" Mason says. Loudly, as if aware of his thoughts and trying to drown them out.

And then, for the first time, they hear his voice in their heads, instead of the other way around.

(*Ben has to be taken care of*)

Keyon nods.

(*taken care of yes*)

"Now we'll get to work on plowing the snow runway," Siri says. "You call your buddies at Mac and tell them to come get us. And remember, Dr. Mason–"

"I know, I know." He taps the side of his head. His fingers turn into a trigger, placed against his skull. Pow. "You live up here now."

"If you try any kind of double-cross, just know," Rajan says. "It'll be me who pulls the trigger, and I'll do it gladly. Look into my mind and see if I'm bluffing."

Dr. Mason blinks, then suddenly, his eyes widen.

Rajan nods. "That's right."

"But Rajan, try to understand." Dr. Mason pleads. "The woman Langley sent to handle this mess–"

(*colson*)

"–her hands are going to be tied if the story of the microbes comes out."

"You mean she can't let the CIA's role in this whole fuckaboo come out."

Dr. Mason gulps. (*exactly*). "If Pole survivors are flying back to Mac, there has got to be a reason that the rest of the crew is not with you."

Rajan smiles thinly. "On that, Mason, we agree. Come with me."

In the library, Rajan points Dr. Mason toward a shelf. Wedged between *Paradise Lost* and a dog-eared Stephen King thriller is an unmarked black notebook.

"Doc Wei left us a present from beyond the grave," Rajan says. "This is the diary of our former Station Manager, Bill Gaudin. The last few pages give you the point most directly."

Dr. Mason opens the notebook. He reads, and his eyebrows climb. "Whoa. Um, okay. I can work with this."

(*but one of you will still have to stay as leverage or she won't–*)

Mason completes his thought. "Colson won't buy it otherwise."

He looks up, biting his lip. Thinking. "Do you think we can get the runway prepped by tomorrow?"

After months being trapped, the thought of being able to leave South Pole Station drives all the survivors. For the first time in a long time, it's all hands on deck, together; even lackadaisical Penny works without complaint, grooming and shoveling and packing snow and driving caterpillar snowmovers. It's hard work, in unforgiving weather, and they only get seven-thousand feet compacted and cleared. But that is just enough for the tailwheel Basler BT-67 to put itself down.

Keyon, Rajan and Siri gather by Destination Alpha, looking out at the runway they have just stamped into the snow. Behind them, the fire-eaten entryway is a sober reminder of their winter battle against their own crewmates.

(*it seems obscene to ask this here*)

Keyon puts one burly hand each on Rajan and Siri's shoulders. He tries to smile.

(*it should be me*)

"It should be me," Keyon reinforces his thought with his voice. "I'll be Dr. Mason's canary. I'll be the one who stays behind."

"Bullshit," Siri says furiously. "Bethany and Jonah started this by barricading themselves in. Let one of them stay."

"Mason knows we won't hold our tongues for them," Keyon says gently. "If the CIA wants leverage to keep everyone quiet, it's got to be one of the three of us who stays behind."

(*and the hard stripe voice and I need to talk*)

Siri's eyes are filled with tears. "Keyon, I know you feel like you have some kind of penance to do–"

"It doesn't matter why, Siri." Keyon squeezes her shoulder.

(*but yes we need to be alone with no one else in my mind*)

Siri bursts toward him and hugs him fiercely. "I hope you find peace," she says into his chest. "I really hope you do."

"I think this is the only way I can," he whispers.

Rajan meets Keyon's eyes. "We'll be back for you," he says, his voice determined. "If we have to drag Mason behind us every step of the way, we'll be back for you."

Dr. Mason establishes an encrypted sat-phone link to Colson at Mac Station. His connection has the proper keys to be allowed through the firewall that has been thrown up around Antarctica. Rajan listens to him explain that the survivors are a treasure trove of information about the microbe, to include things that will help them better exploit Ben Jacobs in the future. He explains that Keyon will stay behind as leverage to ensure the survivors play their part, and goes through the diary of the former Pole Station manager, Bill Gaudin.

"The diary has some crazed ramblings in it, and the survivors will swear it was all Gaudin. No infection to speak of. You can sell that to Winston and Marshal Anne, and have them pass it on to everyone. Together, I think this is the formula for wrapping everything up," Dr. Mason finishes.

Colson is silent for a long time. Dr. Mason looks at Rajan, anxiously. He opens his mouth to say more, and Rajan throws up his hand.

(*wait wait*)

"I don't know what you said to turn them into such helpful little bees, but well done," Colson says into the silence.

Dr. Mason closes his eyes with relief. Colson's next words make his eyes fly open again.

"How do we know that they aren't infected with whatever killed the rest of South Pole?"

(*technically they are*)

(*technically i am too now*)

"Uh..." Mason's eyes ping-pong in their sockets. "I think they'd be dead by now too if that were the case, Colson."

Colson is silent for another long moment. When she speaks, she sounds matter-of-fact. "We'll have to take the risk and monitor for symptoms; Mac will revolt if I keep them locked down any longer. A blizzard warning just came through from the National Weather Service. One hell of a storm is kicking up at Mac day-after-tomorrow, but we'll have just enough time to get you back if the aircraft can do a hot turn down there. Will it be able to refuel?"

"Yes. The survivors are thawing out the fuel arches now."

(*when is Ben Jacobs due off the continent*)

Dr. Mason clears his throat. "And, ah, how are the quarantine mods to that C-17 going?"

"Closing nicely. The jet leaves the depot in two days. It'll be in Christchurch in four days ready to fly."

Dr. Mason looks at Rajan, who nods grimly. "Coming up soon, then."

"Not. Soon. Enough," she replies. "People are restless as hell down here. But the Pole survivors showing up might help. Nothing quiets a mob like a good death story."

(*nice gal this one*)

(*hey there's a reason the roman emperors built the coliseum*)

"Well done, Mason," Rajan says after he terminates the connection.

Dr. Mason looks up at him with haunted eyes. "I'm hearing things, Rajan. Murmurs." He jerks his thumb at the window outside. "From out there."

Rajan grimaces. "The microbes are on the microbe net too. And they're hungry."

Chapter Twenty-Seven

October 13.

Colson has accepted that she hates Antarctica. Hates the bitchy loggies, who are like a high-school clique constantly teeth-gnashing about how things used to be. Hates the whiny scientists, who seem to have little else for conversation except ripping ass about all the things they don't have and can't do.

It doesn't help that she's lost a good man – LoNigro – and she's stuck with Barham and Mackie. They're a great sniper-spotter team, but neither have any conflict-resolution skills to speak of. Which means they are of no use to her as she tries to balance the demands of an ice-bound frontier town. If not for Winston, Colson would have invoked Kabul rules by now. Shoot one bitching Mactowner in the leg, wait thirty seconds, shoot another in the leg.

See who grumbles then.

By virtue of decisive action, she has grasped a handle on this fuck-up. In a matter of days, she'll have herself a CIA commendation, a nice little gold-and-blue Antarctic medal, and it'll be on to cleaning the next fuck-up. Hopefully someplace warm. Addis Ababa doesn't sound so bad anymore.

By the time darkness falls, Barham and Mackie have already left for the empty bar, where the lack of adult supervision means they'll grunt and slur their way through enough alcohol to slay a small elephant. Doc Kaushik is essentially Dr. Kim's assigned shadow; despite her outer appearance of impartiality, Colson does not trust the shifty DARPA scientist one bit. Men like Jonny Kim had invented the nuclear bomb and sarin gas.

Men whose need to *know* is so overpowering that they don't care who gets wasted in the process.

It's the last night of quarantine, so Colson decides to enjoy one of the luxuries of being shadow station leadership. She commandeers one of the administration snowmobiles, and drives across the McMurdo Sound; eight miles to Scott Base.

At Scott, the bar is housed in one of several green container-like buildings on short stubby stilts. Scott Base houses 85 people; maybe half that number are crowded into the small bar. Music plays dissonantly from a cracked speaker; the majority of the noise comes from the crowd.

Colson claims one of the rigid chairs at the end of the small bar. Wedged into an awkward corner spot by a freezer, she can keep her back to a wall and watch the crowd. "Shot and a beer," she says to the weathered woman behind the bar. Her name is Patty. She's an oil and heating tech.

Patty reappears with a shot of something cloudy and a bottle of Tui. The shot is awful. She chases it with a gulp of beer, and lets out a deep sigh.

"That kinda day, huh, mate?" Patty says. Her five American-dollar bill disappears like a magic trick. Colson idly wonders how much of the money makes it into the till at the end of the night.

"That kinda life, honestly," Colson says, and the truth of it clubs her over the head a little.

She'd tried quitting twice: once after ten years in the Navy Special Warfare development group or DEVGRU; once again after four years as a grimy forward-deployed Agency contractor like Sal. She has fought *hard* – with her whole soul, really – to carve out her place as one of the single handful of women in special ops. To be not just one of the men, but leading the men. That siren call, and the danger, had drawn her back again and again. Regular life is just so mundane compared to that.

Still… what legacy can be left by someone whose job it is to go in and fix someone else's blunders? Operating at her best, the most she does is return things to normal.

An hour, maybe two, slide by like smooth ice. Two men drift over to talk her up, and she sends them packing with a swift efficiency born of practice. The different accents from the orange-jacketed Kiwis swirl and wash around her. Mac is a grimy mining town. Scott is more of a working scientific oasis. All the buildings match, painted a fresh green. The snow is swept while it still gleams white. The people seem nicer; more like a crew.

"Another," she tells Patty.

"Hardly any Americans over this week," Patty says in a gossipy tone. "Heard you lot have been locked down?"

Colson shrugs. "Some kind of COVID thing, I don't know. Just happy to be here."

"Some kind of COVID thing?" says a voice next to her. Colson turns, a little too sharply, into the half-smiling face of Mariana Egan. "Seems to me you could do better than that, Ms. Colson."

The snow melting on her jacket implies she has just walked in. There's ice frozen into her hair. She has somehow slipped the last of the lockdown and walked, all the way from Mac, eight miles on a somewhat-maintained flagged path around Ross Island. Not undoable, even in the cold; Colson has run it before. But impressive from someone who isn't a special operator.

There's no open seat next to Colson, so Mariana slides in between the seats, suddenly very close to her. She struggles out of her bulky Big Red. "Buy a girl a drink?"

"With American dollars, a girl can buy herself a drink."

Mariana leans over the bar, two twenty-dollar bills appearing between her fingers. Patty is suddenly standing close enough to touch.

"What's the nicest whisky you've got?"

"Got a few pours of Thomson. Personal allowance."

"Two doubles."

"I'll be back," Patty says, and vanishes from behind the bar.

Mariana turns toward Colson. "They're both for me, I'm afraid. It's been a long walk."

Colson finds herself grinning. "I would have bought you the five-dollar shot and beer if I'd known it was an investment in a good-whisky future."

"That's the thing about gambling, Ms. Colson. You have to play to win."

What the hell, she thinks.

"Jackie," she says. "My first name is Jackie."

Mariana ends up giving Jackie Colson half a slug of Thomson, and she buys her a drink in return. They play a game of pool, at the other end of the bar; Colson starts by going easy on Mariana, and Mariana takes the small window to run the table and smoke her, so pointedly that one of the Kiwis nearby pats Colson on the back and murmurs, "I hurt for you, mate." She challenges her to double or nothing, and Mariana grins at her.

"The other thing about gambling, Jackie Colson, is that you have to quit while you're ahead."

The music has increased in volume. It's just a few people swaying, but Mariana asks her to dance. It's the feeling of two like substances sliding into contact. Even in her noisy windpants and shapeless Antarctic-issue black fleece, Mariana is graceful, and knows how to make Colson look like a better dancer than she is.

Colson wonders about the wisdom of trying to kiss her, and Mariana takes the guesswork out of it for her. At the end of a twirl, she comes fully into her arms, chest and stomach and thighs pressing into her. Mariana is tall, Colson realizes dreamily, taller than she is.

Mariana kisses her.

Colson gives in; lets the swirl of the alcohol and the moment swallow her up.

"So," Mariana says, into her mouth. There's a small, inviting smile on her face. "What now?"

"Um." *Great response*, she thinks. "Back to your place?"

"Oh, I don't think you want that. Unless you're the kind of woman who likes an audience."

"Well, when you put it that way… I have no roommates."

They kiss again, leisurely this time. This is, Colson muses, the best part about being older, and with older women. There's much less getting mind-blasted on alcohol and falling into bed together. Consent is clear and unambiguous. Which means there's no real need to rush.

"Shall we grab a bottle for the road?" Mariana says. "Since we can do that here, you know. Just pay cash and get alcohol."

"You've been at Mac how long? You're already grumbling like one of the locals."

She grins at her. "I'm very adaptable, Jackie. You'll learn that about me."

Colson has had more to drink than she has; Mariana insists on driving the snowmobile. She shrieks with exhilaration as she whips it around the first of several corners. She drives it like a natural; Colson's tired operator brain files away that she must have grown up in Minnesota or Wisconsin or Idaho, someplace you'd have reason to handle a snowmobile at a young age.

"Hold on to me!" she yells back at her. "I'm gonna take this jump!"

Colson grips her waist tightly; the snowmobile leaves the ground, her senses going airborne with it. She's never driven the snowmobile like this. She drives it like practical transport. She's from California, born and raised in sunny San Diego. Life with DEVGRU and the Agency has taken her many cold places, but she's still a sun-and-sand gal at heart.

Back at McMurdo, in her dorm room, they cuddle in her narrow twin-size bed and have a drink, then another. Colson's eyes suddenly feel heavy. It's been a bone-weary few days of enforcing round-the-clock quarantine, and it's almost over. She closes her eyes. Just for a moment.

Mariana watches her fall asleep. She waits, motionless, for almost thirty minutes, until Colson's breathing takes on the rhythmic exhalations of an alcohol-induced deep sleep.

Then she slides out of the small twin bed, and methodically searches her room.

The room itself is Spartan. Inside a computer bag, she finds a token card, USB reader, and RSA fob on a keychain. Mariana has been a national security reporter for most of her career; she recognizes the logo of the intelligence agency embedded on the front of the token card. She also knows the card and fob are useless unless they are combined with a secure password.

She takes a picture of the fob and the card with her cell phone. Proof that shadowy three-letter agencies have established themselves at McMurdo Station. Then she gets into the narrow bed with Colson and curls around her strong frame, like a pair of commas. She closes her eyes, and tries to go to sleep. Sometimes, it's nice to have someone to hold, especially when it's cold outside.

Chapter Twenty-Eight

October 14.

The wooden Chalet is built around a central meeting space, bracketed by cathedral windows that cast light down onto a small podium, the NSF Office of Polar Programs flag, and a roll-up projector screen. Normally, due to shift work and general apathy, maybe ten percent of Mactowners attend all-hands meetings. For this meeting, however, people begin arriving as soon as the lockdown is released at 11:00 AM. By 11:45, the building is packed. Chairs are stacked in rows of eight to the very back of the room, but it still isn't enough to house over four-hundred people. The second floor overlooks the first, like balcony seating in a church, and the conference table there gets pushed to the side to create a standing-room only space.

Marshal Anne has the firefighters on standby, but has decided not to enforce the fire code regulations. Anyone who wants to listen should be able to. She shuffles through the crowd, directing people where to stand. Packing them in like sardines in a can.

The noise of people making small talk is a dull roar in the small building.

At 12:10 PM, Winston steps in front of the podium. He taps the microphone and it squeals. "Settle down," he grunts into it.

He stares out at a sea of faces, some curious, but most drawn tight in hostility or ire. "All right, then," he says. "First, the thing on everyone's mind. The lockdown."

Winston draws a long pause, then bends down and speaks right into the mike. "Quit your whining, it's over. And, because of the blizzard coming in, the Station will stand down for the next two days. Everyone's off."

The crowd cheers. "This ain't Guantanamo, Winny!" someone yells above the noise.

Marshal Anne steps forward. "I heard that, Bateman," she bellows, pointing at him. "He ain't Winny to you, and you shut your clamhole until he's done, you hear me?"

"Yeah, Bateman, you twat!" someone else hollers. A ripple of chuckles runs through the room, defusing the tension.

"Now for some exciting news," Winston continues.

He looks around, waiting for the room to quiet.

"Just before sunrise three days ago, a Basler took off from Willy airfield, headed to Pole. If the weather stays clear, the winter crew from Pole will be here later today."

A murmur starts to race through the building; they've all heard that Pole has been out of contact, status unknown, for several months. A hand shoots up in one of the front rows. Winston looks a little affronted, but decides to take the question. "Yeah. Wayne."

"They all coming home on that plane? The whole crew?"

Winston nods. "That's right."

"Well, a winterized Basler don't fit more than 20 people," Wayne Weiss says. "What happened to the rest of that crew?"

Suddenly the whole lodge is deathly silent.

The manager is quiet for a long moment, as if stalled by the weight of several seasons of memory. His hands grip the podium like a squeeze-toy.

"Mactowners," Winston says, and his voice is grave. "We all know life on the ice is hard. It takes a lot to keep this port city going, and sometimes, we get short with one another. Right?" He clears his throat; no one moves. "I've seen the signs in the bathrooms for people who don't clear their hair out of the drain." This time there's a soft whisper of chuckles.

Winston gestures to Marshal Anne, who is still standing with hands on her hips, as if daring anyone to misbehave. "Anne is the law here, but I'm thankful she hasn't had much real trouble to report back. Now… damn it all. I wish I could say that was the case for Pole."

The projector flickers on. A picture begins to take form on the screen beside Winston; a mustached man with deep hazel eyes, shaggy greying hair, and a heavy, fleshy face. He's dressed in a Big Red jacket and is staring right into the camera. Below the picture, a name: WILLIAM GAUDIN.

Marshal Anne strides up to beneath the picture of Gaudin. When she speaks, her voice rings.

"Some of you in here know this man. Bill Gaudin was Manager of the South Pole crew this winter." Her green eyes scan faces, row by row. "Unfortunately, it appears Gaudin was not the most stable of Polies. He was carrying on an affair with a married woman on crew, his deputy manager, and had numerous documented violations of the alcohol ration policy. That's new here, but it's been the policy at Pole for a long time. This season, during the dead of winter, Gaudin… snapped."

The slide changes to show a picture of hand-scrawled notes from a diary. The writing is so heavy that it has cut through the page. Vengeful words spilling across and between the lines; the writing of a deeply disturbed man.

Weeks is soft – know it like its tattooed on his pasty forehead. Last century glasses – round chin – squashed nose – that fuckin chuckle when he don't know what to say – it all screams take me out back and pound the blood out of me. That bitch of a bitch didn't pick LUIS fuckin WEEKS because he's charming or has a footlong for a schlong. No way, Andrea picked him because out of anyone on Station she could fuck, Weeks would drive me the absolute. Craziest. Bitch saved it like a knife riding up her pantyhose. Last resort, but deadly if used correctly. I OUGHT TO KILL HER FOR THAT. SHE WOULD DESERVE IT.

"This perceived betrayal" – she gestures up to the screen – "triggered something inside him."

People unconsciously lean forward in their seats. A hush falls over the room.

Marshal Anne says it.

"Bill Gaudin killed his lover, and several other members of the crew he was there to lead."

The room erupts into bedlam, people shouting questions to her and to each other. Disbelief and shock races between people, catching like wildfire. There has never been a murder in Antarctica, let alone a series of murders. The name *Ben Jacobs* begins to carry on tongues – is this why he'd arrived at McMurdo so beat up, unable to talk? Winston lets it carry on for two whole minutes, then hammers the podium with his fist, repeatedly, until things quiet down.

"Gaudin destroyed a lot of equipment, including Pole's communications gear, before the remaining crewmembers were able to stop him. They've been hunkered down, waiting for rescue. Last week we were able to establish intermittent communications with them and get the whole story."

Marshal Anne looks over at Winston, who speaks into the heavy silence.

"There are only six survivors, five of whom will be on that plane today."

This time, the room is so quiet the proverbial pin could have been heard dropping.

Marshal Anne's eyes are solemn. "There has never been a murder in Antarctica before. The ramifications of this are going to shake the polar program for years to come." She looks around the room, and her tone hardens. "What none of us need is some asshole with a TikTok getting the world out there amped up on clickbait and false rumors. So until the Pole survivors are off the ice, and the families of those deceased have been properly notified, I've directed station management not to restore the Internet."

"Marshal Pabon!"

Anne looks up to the top floor to see Mariana pushing her way to the front of the balcony.

"Marshal, my name is Mariana Egan. I'm a reporter with the *Chicago Tribune*."

In the front row, Colson twists around in her seat, looking shocked and furious.

"As a law enforcement agent, you must know that the censorship you just described is a violation of the First Amendment." Mariana's voice is loud and projects into every corner. "This is an American station, under American law. You don't have the authority to censor us. In fact, neither–"

Marshal Anne starts to interrupt.

"And before you say national security, Marshal," Mariana says loudly, "May I remind you that you are not a member of the military, and that neither the free speech nor the free press clauses of the First Amendment make any differentiation between national security reporters like myself and, as you so eloquently put it, an asshole with a TikTok."

"Now, let me tell you something about–"

"Let's listen to the Marshal–"

Winston and Anne both start talking, Colson is on her feet, but Mariana only gets louder. She's practically shouting now, refusing to cede. "And so if anyone, if anyone here – *if anyone here* would like to talk about how this censorship affects your work, or your ability to express yourself, please find me after this meeting, and *get your objection on the record*!"

The room explodes with sound. Upstairs, Mariana is mobbed by people tapping her shoulder, shouting in her ear. Marshal Anne has an expression like a kid in a play that has heard the wrong line, and now just stands on stage in baffled limbo. Colson grabs the Station Manager.

"How the hell is there a reporter down here?" she yells at Winston over the cacophony of the chalet.

"Like I've always said," Winston says. "There are too many damn people at this station!"

BOOK THREE

CITIZENS OF CRARY

OCTOBER 14 – OCTOBER 29

There will be no rest day or night
for those who worship the beast and its image,
or for anyone who receives the mark of its name.
And the smoke of their torment will rise for ever and ever.
Then I heard a voice from heaven say, Write this:
Blessed are the dead who die in the Lord from now on.

Revelations 14:11 – 13

Chapter Twenty-Nine

URGENT – WINTER WEATHER MESSAGE – SEVERE WEATHER ALERT

National Weather Service Denver CO for McMurdo Station Antarctica
Issued 331 AM CST Sat Oct 13 2028

CONDITION 1 CONDITION 1 CONDITION 1
McMurdo Sound Ross Island
Including the Stations of McMurdo, Scott
CONDITION 1 CONDITION 1 CONDITION 1

BLIZZARD WARNING IN EFFECT FROM 5 AM NZDT OCT 15 TO 6 PM NZDT OCT 16

* WHAT...Blizzard conditions expected across the entire Ross Dependency due to a low-pressure system dropping into the Ross Sea from the north, moving northwest to southeast. Total snow accumulations of 16 to 21 inches. Sustained winds of 40-55 knots, peak gusts exceeding 80 knots possible. Minimum central pressures below 950 millibars, driving unseasonable low temperatures of -35 F with windchill to exceed -75 F.
* WHERE...Ross Ice Shelf, Ross Island, Ross Dependency; some impacts at reduced intensity levels to Victoria Land and Oates Land.
* WHEN...0500 New Zealand Daylight Time (NZDT) October 15 to 1800 NZDT October 16 (CONDITION 2)

with peak impacts from 1400-2000 October 15 (CONDITION 1).

* IMPACTS...Travel should be restricted to emergencies only. Rope-line travel with winter survival kit. Standard Condition 1 and Condition 2 restrictions as applicable.

URGENT – WINTER WEATHER MESSAGE – SEVERE WEATHER ALERT

END END END

Chapter Thirty

October 14.

Screaming down the slopes, sheets of icy high-altitude wind throw themselves against the vehicles clustered at the edge of the meagre Chinese encampment, half a kilometer from the deserted Dome-A Station. The preparations have been made. Engines rumble into the thick cold, spewing columns of smoke. Three hand-picked men and one woman are inside their cabs, huddled uncomfortably in plastic seats, bracing themselves for another cruel journey, with an uncertain outcome at its long end.

Outside the caterpillar vehicle, the wind buffets fiercely. Jiuyin Mei kneels down in the snow beside Colonel Zhou Su, and the two men look over the assortment of tiny cameras and wires arranged inside a Pelican case. They've found ten, in total, though there may be more. Constant surveillance is a reality of life in Communist China, so neither of them can discount the idea that the cameras might have been placed there by the State. Jiuyin has a feeling that they will all trace back to domestic Chinese manufacturers, but the footage exfiltrates to a satellite antenna, and there aren't any Chinese satellites that have coverage this far south.

Zhou Su closes up the Pelican case. It will return to China with him for investigation.

They stand, and Jiuyin extends his hand. Instead, Zhou steps forward and puts his arms around the younger man. Jiuyin stands there, surprised and touched.

"I wish you luck on your journey," Zhou says.

Jiuyin bows deeply. "I'm sincerely thankful for your understanding, Colonel."

"I only wish there were an easier way to find the answers you seek."

Both men are headed in opposite directions. Most of the expedition will return to Zhongshan, then the icebreaker ship, under Zhou Su's command. But Jiuyin and four hand-picked shipmates have another destination.

There are secrets behind the deaths of the crew of Dome-A, and only one place in Antarctica to uncover them.

Jiuyin Mei steps up into the Caterpillar snow vehicle. With a lurch, it sets off, following the ground penetrating radar lead vehicle.

He's going deeper into the continent for answers.

Chapter Thirty-One

The days are already getting long at McMurdo; it's 8:00 PM on October 14, but the sun hovers well above the horizon. With the blizzard approaching, temperatures will drop rapidly, but for now Mac sits in a weather lull.

Colson is walking toward a vehicle when a Ford E350 van on snow tracks drives by. She stares after it in disbelief; it looks stuffed with people. She looks up toward Ob Hill and sees a line of snow vehicles, like ants, headed up and over the hill toward Willy airfield.

"What the fuck," she says to herself, furiously.

As their vehicle crests the hill, heading down toward the long flat expanse of the airfield, Colson can see dozens of vehicles already gathered out on the ice. The small snow-street between the containers of the Willy shanty town has turned into an impromptu tailgate party. The quarantine has been released, Mac Station is off work ahead of the storm, and people are clustered around vehicles, waiting for the inbound plane from South Pole. Twittering with laughter and mingled conversation, frosted breaths pluming and coalescing around them into ephemeral clouds.

"Is that the fucking bartender from Southern Exposure?" Colson says, disbelieving. A makeshift alcohol station is being set up out the back of a massive red bus on six-foot tires. The bus is a well-known local staple that bears the words IVAN THE TERRA BUS along its side.

Colson steps out of her vehicle to booming music from Ivan the Bus. She looks around and sees Marshal Anne, who spreads her arms as if to say, *nothing we can do about this.*

Outside the terminal building, in the center of a small crowd, is Mariana Egan. Asking questions, and recording answers with her phone. Mariana abruptly looks up, and makes eye contact with her. Smiles and waves casually. Right at her face.

Colson gives a grimace that could pass for a smile in response. She'll have to make sure the reporter finds herself on the very next plane leaving the continent.

Apparently, the Basler pilots have heard about the impromptu gathering, because Tristan Hyatt and Maui Hathaway decide to do a low flyby. The flat *thwap* of the propellers thrum through the clear sky like a rocket through an echoing alley, and an acknowledging cheer goes up from the crowd. As the plane loops around for its final approach, Colson wanders between Mactowners, listening.

Dude, can't wait to see them.

Told ya Pole was a weird fuckin place.

I knew three people on crew down there this season. I'm worried they didn't make it.

The ski plane touches down, its propellers loud in the snowy silence. It backtaxis through columns of airborne puffy snow. The engines shut down, the doors open and a raucous cheer goes up.

"Welcome back!" people shout. "Welcome back!"

Five Polies trickle down the stairs, followed by Dr. Mason, Lansdown and Sal. They all look surprised and shocked at the strength of the welcome. Despite herself, Colson feels a little buoyed by the vigor of Mac's hospitality. It reminds her of whole squadrons showing up to the airport to welcome deployed military members back. Camaraderie is a rare thing at Mac… even if she plans to nip it in the bud by quietly spiriting the Polies away to the hospital and not letting them leave.

Right on cue, Mackie drives a van out onto the snow. Colson's men are loaded into it, to scoop the newcomers up.

Suddenly, Siri splits away from the airplane stairs. She breaks into a jog, making a beeline right for the crowd. She waves as she runs, and the waiting crowd cheers loudly in response.

She comes to a stop in front of the terminal building, and rips off her hood. "Hi everyone!" she shouts, waving with both her hands. "We're so happy to be back at Mac. Safe and alive! Thank you for welcoming us!"

A woman thrusts herself forward. "Can I get a picture with you?"

"Definitely!" Siri waves her forward. "Anybody else want one?"

Just like that, the crowd swells past the edge of the terminal, spilling onto the snow. Penny and Bethany are also surrounded by eagerly chatting people.

"Oh fuck me," Colson groans.

Jonah and Rajan hang back in a small island of relative quiet in the shadow of the plane. "I can't believe it." Jonah shakes his head in subdued wonder. "We made it out of Pole alive."

Rajan looks like he's about to choke, then speaks. "Thanks for going along with this."

Jonah turns to him. "I'm not a cruel man, Rajan," he says. "I was a realist three months ago and I'm a realist now. This was my only way out of that station alive."

"Better stick to the story." Rajan squints into the low and powerless sunset. "See these guys coming up? I'm betting they're from the Agency."

Dr. Mason and the CIA boys say their hellos to each other with fist bumps and muted exchanges. None of them have a visible weapon. Doc Kaushik taps Mason; gestures back toward the plane. "Is LoNigro on there?"

Dr. Mason nods heavily.

"I'll unload him once the crowd disperses."

In the crowd, Siri, Penny and Bethany have formed a sort of receiving line. People file by, expressing happiness for their survival, welcoming them. Penny has his brightest surfer boy smile on. A few inappropriately lancing questions fly past them – *why did Bill really do it? Can you tell us about how so-and-so died?* – but mostly, it's quite heartwarming. Siri, an old Antarctic hand of five seasons, exchanges tearful hugs with familiar faces.

Mariana Egan emerges from the crowd, and grasps Bethany's hand first. She looks over her shoulder, scanning for someone, then says: "Hi, I'm a reporter with the *Chicago Tribune*." She shakes Penny's hand next. "Mariana, *Tribune*. Let me know if you want to talk!"

Behind her, Barham emerges, broad-shouldering people out of his way.

Mariana hurriedly moves over to Siri and throws her arms around her. "I'm a reporter with the *Chicago Tribune*," she says in Siri's ear. "If you or any of the other Polies want to talk, come find me!"

Then she pulls away, disappearing into the crowd. Siri looks up to see a bearded, slope-shouldered man scowling, looking after her, craning his neck.

Siri reaches out and grabs a sleeve. "Heather, hey! Do you have a SnoCat here?"

"Sure do," Heather Heigele, the fire tech, responds. "You want a ride to the bar?"

"Just get me the hell out of here."

Back by the airplane, Colson makes her way over to Rajan and Jonah.

"Let's you and me go have a few words about our fuckin' deal," Colson says, her eyes icy.

Chapter Thirty-Two

Every building at Mac has long, handicap-friendly ramps leading up to their main doors; Colson stomps out of Mackie's van and climbs the ramp to the hospital. The reception area in the quarantined hospital is as close to an access-controlled building as Colson can get, so she decides they'll talk there.

Rajan is on her heels, then abruptly, he comes to a dead-stop.

Staring at the pink panels on the building like he can see through them.

There's a wordless, incomprehensible murmur inside. Like the malicious buzzing of a hornet's nest.

Thrumming in slow intensity.

Jonah is halfway up the ramp when Rajan calls his name, sharply. He pauses, looks back.

"Come on," Colson says impatiently, irritation making her eyes small and her mouth tight. "Let's talk inside."

"Is this where you're holding Ben Jacobs?" Rajan says.

She comes back down the ramp and squares off to him. "How do you know about Ben?"

"Oh hell no." Jonah steps off the ramp. "I'm not going in that building."

"Exactly. Me neither," says Rajan. "Not without a gun in my hand."

Colson rolls her eyes. "You wouldn't say that if you saw him. He's barely alive."

Rajan's eyes glitter. "You are making a colossal mistake to believe that."

"Look, let's just talk someplace else," Dr. Mason interjects. "I bet the Chalet is empty."

"Fine," Colson says. "Go get Dr. Kim, Mason. He'll want to hear this."

On the second floor of the Chalet, down the hall from the Station Manager and Marshal's office, is an office reserved for the Senior US Representative to Antarctica. Colson has appropriated this office, and it's where they crowd into.

Sitting knee-to-knee with Dr. Mason and Jonah, Rajan has a chance to study Dr. Jon Kim. The DARPA man is middle-aged, thick around the middle, with a face that has a calculating liveliness. He shows too many teeth when he smiles. A salesman, but a damn clever one. A dangerous man.

(*would nuke a nursery just to*)

"In here we all know the truth, so I'm gonna cut right to it," Rajan says. "Yes, Gaudin lost his shit down at Pole, but Ben Jacobs was responsible for most of the deaths at Pole Station. He was the original symbiote." He looks around. "And you have him smack in the middle of the most crowded station in Antarctica."

"Well, now, let's back up." Dr. Kim sits forward, showing his teeth. "First of all, what you're neglecting–"

"Shut the fuck up, Kim," Rajan says.

Dr. Kim freezes on hearing his name. Rajan turns his head with a stare that could flay layers from him.

"Yeah, you. Jon Kim. We were crewmates with Summer Kerce," he says. Every syllable bitten off. "She gave her *life* for us. Do you know what that means?"

Dr. Kim looks stricken.

"It means we know that you're the man whose actions have directly resulted in the deaths of over fifty people." Rajan's voice is a low hiss now. "If I hear a word that sounds like *justification* come out of your mouth… I'm going to hurt you."

(*the same goes for you Mason you did this too*)

"All right, let's dial the aggression back a notch," Colson says, a hint of amusement in her voice. "We can play a round of the blame game when we're off the ice. Let's talk about what happens next."

Rajan stares at her. "Ben Jacobs is what happens next. You're sitting on a ticking time bomb that's going to go off. It's just a matter of when."

"Ben hasn't so much as stirred since he first got here," Colson says.

"That doesn't mean anything," Rajan says. "Is he restrained?"

"Of course, he is. We know what we're dealing with, Major. Hazmat suits, restraints, running the heater in the building up to eighty-five degrees... we've taken all the precautions."

Jonah clears his throat, and speaks for the first time.

"Rajan has a point," he says. "I watched our station doctor scan every inch of Ben, from head to toe, for a microbe infection. He still infected everyone with the grey-generation."

Grey generation? Colson looks at Dr. Kim questioningly.

Dr. Kim explains hesitantly, with a flitting look at Rajan. "There appear to be three generations of microbes. The original generation lived in deep Antarctic lakes. Extremely adaptable, cold tolerant, native to water. That's what my Harvard research group found years ago. When I moved to DARPA, I funded work to re-engineer the original generation to multiply exponentially. This is what you might call the black-generation. I succeeded, but only at *extremely* low temperatures. You could get that low at Dome-A, or South Pole, but almost nowhere else on Earth. Not even McMurdo. I hit a block in trying to increase the activation temperature while maintaining the high cellular division rate. But the CIA decided that was enough to try a test."

He looks at Dr. Mason, who nods.

"At South Pole, the black-generation mutated into... your grey-generation," he continues. "Those are the symbiotes, and they are tolerant to higher temperatures. Winter in Siberia types of temperatures. Maybe parts of northern China."

Rajan throws a cutting look at Dr. Mason.

(*don't forget Minnesota Mason you son of a bitch*)

Rajan says curtly, "Did you follow the instructions I passed on to Mason?"

"Ah, yes." Kim looks at the floor as he talks, unable to face the contempt radiating at him. "Yes, Doc Kaushik and I did a liver and kidney biopsy on Ben, per your suggestion. We took several tissue samples. Again, I understand the concerns, but a biopsy is an incredibly painful procedure, and Ben didn't so much as twitch on the table. But anyway," he continues, hurriedly, "your information was correct. Ben's insides are indeed crawling with *different* microbes."

Jonah nods, gravely. "The grey-generation."

"We found something else under X-ray. Kaushik and I can't be sure without cutting him open, but in some places… it looks like the microbes have… the only word is *metastasized,* but it's more than that. They've fused together to create organs we don't even recognize. Some kind of extreme symbiosis."

Everyone in the room falls silent, contemplating the implications of this.

"It's killing him, though, which is why he hasn't stirred. With that much internal damage, I don't know that he ever will."

"But do you see the problem?" Jonah replies. "Anyone who has been near Ben Jacobs could have these interior microbes, and you'd never even know."

"Until they attack you," Rajan adds grimly.

"That's true for now," Dr. Kim admitted, "but I'm working with our lab back Stateside on a few theories."

(*ah yes your fucking lab*

you and your other monsters)

Dr. Mason winces and lowers his head into his hands, as if he has a headache.

Rajan keeps his eyes fixed on Colson. "What I hope we can both agree on is that Ben Jacobs cannot be on *any* flight off this continent until you find a way to be sure that you're not risking exposing these mutated microbes to billions of people out there."

"Except that risk includes you," Colson says coldly. "You've been near Ben too, haven't you?"

Rajan's nostrils flare wide. "In the way that I'm near you right now."

His threat drops like a boulder. There's a long moment of hostile silence, then Colson says, "I'll consider what you've said. Anything else?"

"That's everything."

"Okay. Get the fuck out of here."

"Gladly." Rajan stands, as does Jonah.

"One more thing," she says.

Rajan looks back.

"If anyone says a word to that reporter, on or off the record, our deal is off. You make sure the rest of the Polies understand that."

* * *

Rajan lingers outside the Chalet, his face slowly turning numb in the cold. He beams his thoughts outward–

(*don't fuck this up Mason*)

– and listens for what's happening upstairs.

Inside, Dr. Kim goes right back to arguing for Ben Jacobs to be on the first plane out. "I can't examine him fully here, that's a fantasy. We can just quarantine Ben on the mainland, I don't get why that's such a big deal."

"It's a big deal because of the massive collateral damage if we have a containment failure," Dr. Mason says immediately.

(*fuck yeah tell them they need to understand*)

"Ben is dangerous. A leaky weapon. Colson, *we have all that we came for in hand,*" Dr. Mason says. "We can take our time right here in Antarctica. Maybe even move Ben to a remote field camp and set up there."

"I've heard enough," Colson says. Her tone brooks no argument. "In four days, that quarantine airplane will be ready to fly from Christchurch to here. Dr. Kim, developing a test to clear the twenty-six civilians in the hospital of any microbe infection, by that time, is your only priority now."

Rajan walks away, up the slope toward the Mac dormitories.

Outside, the temperature begins to drop.

Headed down into microbe activation temperatures. The colder it gets… the more the symbiotes come alive and multiply.

Chapter Thirty-Three

October 15.

Daylight comes with a washed-out sky of pure white. The temperature drops thirty degrees overnight. By 5:00 AM the next day, the storm has arrived. It's negative 20 degrees F out, blowing 30 knots of wind off the ocean right into town, bringing a heavy stream of snow with it.

Rajan wakes up on a twin-bed next to Siri in a reasonably clean, if small, dorm room. Over a foot of snow has already collected on the windowsill. He pulls her lithe frame closer and nestles in to her. A smile twitches on Siri's face, but dies out quickly.

"You know what I was just thinking?" she says, half into her pillow.

(*unfortunately I do*)

"I'm sorry." She opens her eyes and turns, looking up at him. "Don't you agree?"

"Yeah," he says, heavily. "Yeah, it's grey-generation weather."

"If Ben is awake at any time–"

"Yeah." Rajan swings his legs out of bed, and reaches for his pants. "Yeah, it'll be soon."

Siri and Rajan hover by the double blue doors leading out of the dormitory. Outside, the wind has already picked up. There are flecks of ice in the snow now. Soon, it'll be too cold to actually snow; hospitably cold temperatures for the grey-generation microbes, while the wind turns the Station into a whiteout.

Siri pulls the hood up on her Big Red, eyes distant. He reaches out, touches her arm.

(*what's the matter Siri*)

Waves of unease tumble off of her.

(*i have a bad feeling I'm tired Rajan that's all*)

They clump carefully down the metal stairs and reach their gloved hands out for the safety lines that have been strung between buildings. The snow is already starting to eddy as it falls from the whitened sky. Buildings losing their color loom dimly on either side. Rajan can feel the dropping pressure in the swelling of the muscles in his jaw.

At the Chalet, Winston is in his office, but Marshal Anne is not. "She's probably got feet up in her room," he tells them. "I'm about to do the same, before the wind picks up too much more." He pauses, considering them with his sharp eyes. "Is this urgent?"

"I think so–" Rajan starts.

"Yes," Siri says flatly. "It's urgent."

Winston stands and reaches for his snow goggles. "All right then. Let's go get her."

They walk back the way they'd come, following each other with a hand on the safety lines. Their hands are bowed against the fiercely buffeting wind, building quickly to hurricane force, and they can barely see ten feet in front of them. Siri moves fast, down the safety rope hand-over-hand. But as they cross an intersection, she drifts to a stop. Her hood slips away from her face, snow collecting inside it.

Her hand comes loose from the safety line.

"Siri?" Rajan asks.

(*shhhh*)

Winston starts to speak, and Rajan throws up a hand. "Hang on," he says, "just hang on."

The hairs on his arm rise as he feels her mind scanning. She has an eerie grasp on how to steer the antenna of her thoughts. The amplitude of her search *picks up*.

Shit, Rajan thinks, she's powerful. *She's really something.*

Siri leaves. Off the line, right into the wind.

"Where's she going?" Winston calls.

"I don't know!" She's starting to disappear in the blowing snow. "Come on!"

Rajan breaks into a run after her. Winston hesitates for a moment, then takes off after them with a muttered, "Oh hell".

Siri is moving fast. Rajan tries to focus his thoughts at her back–

Abruptly she comes to a stop, right in the center of the path. Snow gusts around her in chaotic waves.

In front of her is the hospital.

She looks at him. Suddenly, he feels a massive thumping wave of fear spill all over him.

"I don't hear anything," Siri says.

Rajan turns to Winston as he runs up to them. "Get on the radio and tell the Marshal to meet us here!" he shouts, over the wind. "Tell her to bring her gun!"

Marshal Anne emerges from the snow like an apparition. Her wavy bangs are swept away from her high-boned face, pinned almost cruelly back. Under her hood, her green eyes are deep and serious.

She has her hand on her pistol.

"Talk to me," Marshal Anne says.

"I don't think there's anyone in there," Siri says blankly. Her eyes haven't moved from the hospital since she came to stand in front of it.

"And you think this why?"

"Marshal, please," Rajan interrupts. "Could we save the Jeopardy session for later?"

The Marshal pauses, then nods. "All right. Nobody follow me in. Somebody follows me in, they're likely to get shot. Cool?"

"We'll wait right here."

She shares a look with Winston. "Give me three minutes. If I'm not back, then call Colson."

"Colson?" Winston looks surprised.

"Yeah." Her voice has taken on that clipped intonation. "Three minutes flat."

* * *

Like any trained shooter, Marshal Anne believes in instinct. As she walks up the ramp to the main door, she removes her gun from its holster. It's the first time she has ever drawn it in Antarctica. Maybe it's something in the air, but she'd felt a massive rush of adrenalin as she'd looked at Siri. Like it was radiating off of her.

I'm not going to die here for want of caution, she thinks, and racks a bullet into the gun.

She slides one of the doors aside slowly. Most of the hospital is in darkness. Her heart begins beating fast.

It's too silent inside.

She steps forward, past the room of medical relics, following the yellow arrows. Her shadow moves strangely in the low light, like dark fingers trying to play hide-and-seek with her. She pushes through a set of swinging double door–

– and comes to a stop. A little *oof* comes out of her, like she has been slugged in the gut.

Marshal Anne puts her back to a wall, gun hand stiff-armed in front of her. Pointing into the gloom of the building. With her other hand, she pulls her radio from her belt. She dials a channel number from memory.

"Marshal Anne." Colson's voice through the radio sounds as close to relaxed as she's ever heard. "To what do I owe the pleasure?"

She looks down at the blood on the floor, pooling under her snow boots. "I've got some bad news."

Outside, the snow continues to build, the wind blowing into a gale now. Siri's eyes roll restlessly, like a horse in a storm.

Rajan looks toward the dorms to see another running figure, shadowed in the streaking snow. It's almost upon them before he recognizes Colson. She runs right past them.

Inside the hospital, Colson stands beside Marshal Anne, and looks down–

At the slumped body of Doc Kaushik.

The medic lies in a coagulating pool of blood, the needle from an IV bag stuck into the side of his chest. His throat has been slit from end to end, and Colson can see a long trail of blood leading back toward the outpatient rooms. Kaushik had staggered down the hallway, bleeding profusely, before collapsing here.

Colson crouches and carefully moves Doc Kaushik's bulky jacket.

"His gun is gone," she says, voice flat. "So is his radio. Have you–"

"Not yet," Marshal Anne replies.

Both of them point their guns at the adjacent trauma bay. They advance slowly. Colson nods sharply, and they *push* through the swinging doors, Colson going left, Anne going right. Both of them come to a stop.

There should have been twenty-six people inside. But they are alone.

Ben Jacobs, Doc Cait, and the others in quarantine, are all gone.

Chapter Thirty-Four

Colson organizes a search party, but the wind is now at hurricane force, enough to shove a grown man to his knees. It lifts the snow into an impenetrable curtain, and makes it hard to breathe. The cold is like a wall. The searchers have to clip themselves to the safety ropes. The temperature keeps dropping and by evening the search has been called off.

Wherever the twenty-six people are, they are not on the Station.

The wind moans outside, rattling the thick, double-paned windows of the cafeteria building. Siri and Rajan sit at a long table, cups of coffee between their cold hands.

First Jonah, then Bethany, trickle into the Mac dining hall in search of a meal. Siri waves them over. Jonah comes willingly enough. The edges of his beard are trimmed and his eyes look more alert. Bethany hesitates by the food buffet line, clearly contemplating ignoring them, but at last she trudges over. There Siri tells her, as she has just told Jonah, that Ben Jacobs has escaped.

Vanished into the snowy night.

The cold, negative 50 F and below, is when the symbiotes can strike.

It's the sense of something huge rising toward the surface of the ocean, like a whale about to break a fishing boat across its back.

The four Polies sit silently together. None of their thoughts are cheerful ones. They have lived through this before; they know what's coming. The experiences they've shared are like sand. Gritty. Abrasive. And bloody.

Very bloody.

Jonah speaks, at last. "What about Penny? Where is he?"

Bethany rolls her eyes. "Probably sound asleep in his room," she says. "That boy is fucking clueless, always."

Rajan looks up abruptly. "The grey-generation needs a catalyst."

"What?" Bethany glares at him.

"Ben Jacobs didn't escape alone. But as long as he hasn't been able to find any THC… I don't think he *can* create any more grey-generation symbiotes." He tries to smile around the table, hope breaking across his face like the dawn sun over rolling hills. "I think we stay together, lock ourselves in here, and wait this night out. Right here, in this building. Mac Station has a Marshal and plenty of CIA goons to take care of things out there."

He looks around at them.

"We just stay together."

Leaving the cafeteria, Siri lingers behind. She stands at a window, looking out into the darkness. It's one of the last sunsets for the season. In two days, the sun will remain continuously afloat in the white sky for the next four months. The Antarctic summer.

"Anything from Ben?" Rajan asks softly.

She shakes her head. "Not even a whisper."

Fear is a funny thing, Rajan thinks. It dominates the mind. Roars, with vast waves rushing down from the bottom of the throat and up from the shaky knees, to slam together in the middle, where it hurts. His stomach actually aches with dread, pinching on the inside. Like being hungry and thirsty at the same time. The feeling frightens Rajan. He has been scared before. But the familiarity of this fear, and the way it hurts, is almost paralyzing.

Siri looks back at him, and he knows that she has understood every part of what he's experiencing. What's more, he feels the resonance of the same brimming waves within her. They have no choice but to wait, and face their anxiety.

She turns and abruptly surges into his arms. He stumbles backward, caught by surprise. She's all over him, kissing him frantically, her body taut like a spring.

"Quickly," she breathes into his neck. She pulls him toward an empty office room. "Quickly, while we still can."

October 16.

The sun rises weakly above the horizon, just after 4:00 AM. There's nothing outside but a carpet of white, cracked by the buildings, and the moan of the dying wind.

The Crary Lab has sight lines into most major paths around Mac Station. It is four stories tall, with three interconnected buildings called pods. On the roof of the central Crary pod, Mackie and Barham have erected a white overhanging tent to keep the snow out of their eyes. They are buried deep in quilted sleeping bags that haven't done enough to keep the cold of the concrete roof from soaking into them. Mackie has a spotting scope, and scans the horizon to the south. Barham has his eye to a sniper rifle, doing the same to the north.

Scanning for the twenty-six missing people, and Ben Jacobs. Waiting for them to reappear, either in smaller numbers or as a whole.

Ready for them to show their teeth, and try to bite.

"All teams check in," Colson's voice comes across the radio. "Control."

"Overwatch west." Sal's voice.

"Overwatch east." Dr. Mason.

"Overwatch north." Lansdown.

Mackie lowers his mouth to his jacket. "Overwatch south."

"Lab," Dr. Jon Kim says.

Mackie snorts derisively. "Lab. Get the fuck outta here."

"Beakers, man," Barham replies. They've adopted the local slang, a curse word to refer to the scientists on crew.

"Keep your eyes up, everyone," Colson warns. "The symbiotes like to attack when it's cold, and it's about to start warming up. If they're coming, they're coming now."

* * *

From the Chalet, Marshal Anne looks up the slope of Mac station. Colson hasn't told her much, but the tension in her voice and the fact that she hasn't slept a wink tells Anne how worried she should be. In an armchair in the corner of the room, Winston's chest rises with a gentle rumbling snore, his hat on his face. Anne envies him his ability to fall asleep at a time like this.

In the lab, Dr. Kim pauses to take another gulp of cold coffee, then puts his eye back to the microscope, examining slides from Ben Jacobs's biopsies. Trying to pull together a symbiote detection test. He hasn't slept either.

In the computer room down the hall from the cafeteria, Siri and Rajan sit upright against a wall. They wait, like defendants for the jury. Listening, with their ears and their minds.

Bethany Hamidani paces, back and forth. Back and forth. Every now and then she looks out of the window set in the door, as if searching for something, then she returns to her pacing.

Mac Station stirs, slowly and ungently. The roads begin to fill with people, walking to and from their dorms to work, wherever that is. A Caterpillar with a plow bolted to its front starts up in a noisy whine, and kicks up hills of snow on either side of it as it carves out a walking path. Barham follows the driver in his scope, his finger flirts with the trigger for just a brief moment – "pow," he whispers – then he goes back to his scan. Person by person, street by street, until he hears Colson's voice on the radio.

"Everyone to the Movement Center," she says. "Top of the hour."

Mackie lets his sight tip over to the side and lets out a long groan. His breath clouds in front of him. "There must have been a more uncomfortable night in the Yukon, but fuck me if I can remember it."

In the Chalet, Marshal Anne reaches over and nudges Winston. "Hey." He doesn't move. "Hey," she says again.

"Yeah," Winston grunts from underneath his hat.

"Get up," she says. "It's time to buy a girl a drink."

* * *

"Look at them," Siri says, with wonder. "Not a clue."

The four of them – Jonah, Rajan, Siri and Bethany – are back at their table in the cafeteria. No sign of Penny; if he is in his dorm sleeping, it has been a peaceful night's rest for him. It's lunchtime, the weather has officially climbed above grey-generation activation temperatures of forty to fifty below zero, and Mac Station is in full swing. The wind is dying down; the Condition 1 weather alert has been lifted. The cafeteria bustles with activity; people filling plates, talking, trooping off to work. It's just another day to them.

But the battle-scarred Polies know danger lurks, somewhere in the snow.

They have been exhausted by suspicion and fear, with rescue impossible for months in the Antarctic winter. They have turned on each other, and resisted the siren call of a growing hive mind with Ben Jacobs at its center. Despite it all, they are somehow – improbably – alive.

More than anyone else, they are aware that any lull is just the symbiotic hive mind recomputing a new strategy for attack.

The symbiote is more than a disease. It is a biological weapon; one capable of exponential adaptation when combined with the devious human mind.

"People just want normalcy," Jonah's voice sounds dull. He pushes his chair back. "Maybe Penny had it right all along. I'm going back to my room to take a nap."

Rajan presses the palms of his hands against his eyes hard enough that tiny fireworks pop off behind his eyelids. "I don't know how you can sleep," he says. "Knowing Ben Jacobs is out there. Somewhere."

"If he's coming back," Jonah says, his face grim, "it'll be obvious."

Jonah closes the door of his dorm room, locks it, then puts his shoulder against the heavy wardrobe and pushes it in front of the door. He turns away, slightly out of breath, and pulls a short knife he's stolen from the cafeteria out of his pocket. It's just a steak knife, but it's sharp.

He climbs up onto the top bunk; then climbs down and rechecks the window latch. It's still locked.

He gets back into bed, and slips the knife under his pillow. Adjusts it until the handle pokes out, easy to grab. Then Jonah rolls over onto his side, and closes his eyes.

The internet is still down, so Mariana Egan takes herself to the cafeteria.

Some people avoid the reporter like the plague, not wanting to be seen talking to her, but most people are curious about what she's doing on the ice. She has a few interviews set up for today. Most will be unverifiable gossip, but it will keep her finger on the pulse of the Station until she can communicate back to the newsroom.

To her surprise, she sees three of the five Polie survivors at a table, talking in low voices. She starts to walk over to them–

Someone steps into her way.

It's Colson, smiling up at her.

"I don't think so," she says pleasantly.

"Free station, last I heard," Mariana replies. Waiting to see what she'll do.

"Come have breakfast with me," she says. "I'm much more interesting, I promise."

Mariana considers her. She still has that smile on her face, so Mariana decides to relent. It's a small station. She'll have other chances to talk to a Polie without Colson around.

They fold into chairs in another corner of the cafeteria. "So," Colson says, and now her smile is wolfish. "A reporter, huh?"

Mariana decides to go on the offensive. "So," she replies. "The CIA, huh?"

"You don't know that," Colson says.

She thinks back to the logo on the token card in Colson's room. *Oh, but I do.* "You seem upset about my being a reporter, Colson."

"It's Jackie. Just Jackie. Remember?"

Mariana chuckles ruefully.

"I'm sorry I fell asleep. I did enjoy our evening." Colson hesitates. "The evening surprised me. You being a reporter surprised me also."

She seems sincere. She's a trained liar, of course, but Mariana decides to be sincere as well. "I had a nice time with you the other night also, Jackie. And I'm sorry if I surprised you. But your job is to hide information. Mine is to expose it. One of us surprising the other was kind of inevitable, don't you think?"

Colson nods at her. Smiles, a little. "Any chance I can convince you to leave me and my boys out of whatever story you're writing?"

"Any chance I can get you to confirm who you work for, off the record?" Mariana says, eyes twinkling.

"Anything's possible between friends." She picks up a cup of yogurt. "What else are you good at, Mariana, other than sharking at pool and finding fine whisky in the middle of nowhere?"

Wayne Weiss takes a deep breath, fog tumbling out of his mouth. Jeez, he's out of shape. Too much drinking at Gallagher's and not enough exercise.

It's his third season in Antarctica, he's finally made it to electrician lead, an invite to return next summer all but assured, but he's well and truly fucking tired of Mactown. He'll be out on a plane in ten days, and he's resolved to never return to this wretched continent again.

So he might as well see the sights one last time. Wring every last drop out of this so-called adventure.

Fresh snow crunches under his boots. It's another half-kilometer to Discovery hut, a historic structure originally built by Robert Scott in the Heroic Age of Antarctic exploration.

Wayne rounds a corner, passing Ice Pier, and Mactown falls behind the terrain. He pauses for a moment, enjoying the scenery. The wind still tugs at his jacket, but the clouds are lifting. On this stretch of icy path, flagged on one side, he's quite alone.

It's nice to be alone. Life can get a little claustrophobic in Mactown.

He rounds another corner, and finds himself looking down at the ocean; except it's really just blocks of sea ice, mildly parted in jagged cracks. A few yards away, down an icy incline, a seal is sunning itself in the rising sun. Yeah, that's pretty cool.

Unlike the penguins. He knows people find penguins adorable, but he sure doesn't. *Those weird backward pointing needle-teeth are the stuff of nightmares,* Wayne thinks. And they fuckin' smell. They stink like rotten fish. *You are what you eat, I guess it's true.*

The seal makes a sudden sound and he turns in time to see it do a backflip, splashing through thin ice into the water below. It's gone in a heartbeat.

Wayne frowns. There's something else dark down there.

A form. A shadow. A dark leech on a pale sheet.

A man?

Can't be. It's moving almost on fours.

Then, suddenly, it's leaping up the side of the embankment, headed right toward him. Wayne just stands there, dumbly frozen. It looks…

Well, it kind of looks like Doc Cait, doesn't it? If she were galloping like a fucking deer instead of running.

He blinks. Sometimes, the ice gets so white, you can get blinded by it–

He opens his eyes and Caitlin Morris is standing right in front of him. Water from her hair drips onto his boots.

Her hair is soaking, plastered to the sides of her too-pale face. Already starting to crystallize and freeze.

Her eyes are jet black, shot through with a weird, glowing kind of blue.

Wayne starts to say–

He never gets the chance. Doc Cait opens her mouth. It opens wide – too wide, as if her jaw is on a hinge.

She vomits a cannon of ice-cold water right into his face.

Chapter Thirty-Five

October 16.

The Macallan single malt bottle sits between Marshal Anne and Winston, the amount of amber fluid in it significantly lower. Anne gives a delicate burp. She feels pleasantly buzzed, enough that she's relieved she's not wearing her gun anymore.

"Come on, old man," she says. "Out with it."

He raises an eyebrow.

"Don't silent cowboy me," she says. "You've been thinking and drinking. Only one's allowed from here on."

"I was just thinking twenty-six people have disappeared, in one fell swoop, and…" Winston looks into his glass. "What the hell happened to them is one question, but that's not even where my head's at."

"What are you worried about?"

"No one even noticed they're gone," he says, hollowly, voice coming from far down an echoing hallway. "Mac didn't used to be like that."

"It's odd circumstances. Those people were quarantined. Away from everyone."

Winston continues like he hasn't heard her. "Used to be this place was about something. Now it's just another place to work, shit and fuck. I'm not here to be a drone."

"Sure you are, boss."

He looks up sharply at her and Marshal Anne looks right back at him.

"You think I don't know you've been broken, back in the world?" she says. "Of course you have. So have I. *That's why we're here*. Truth is, we just idolized Antarctica. We turned it into what we needed it to be, and now we're mad that it's showing us we were wrong." She pauses for a long moment. "Where are you from, Winny?"

"Ohio. Dayton."

"Middle of nowhere. Nobody gives a shit."

"The fuck you say?"

"Come on." Marshal Anne throws him a smile that crinkles her eyes but makes them somehow brighter. "Nobody goes to Dayton thinking it's anything but Dayton. Now ask me where I'm from."

"I see where this is going. You're from San Diego or the Florida Keys or someplace nice like that."

"Hawaii," Marshal Anne nods. "People who vacation in Hawaii think it's all that, but for people *from* there, man, it's just another place. It's got the same human bullshit as Dayton." She spreads her arms. "If that disappoints me, that's not Hawaii's fault. It's my fault for making Hawaii into something it never was."

A slow smile comes to the grizzled Station Manager's face. "You got a real special way of making me feel like a fool, you know that, Marshal?"

She starts to reply–

The door to the bar bursts open, and Mariana Egan spills in.

The reporter's hair is askew, her eyes wild.

She looks around, neck moving jerkily, and catches sight of them.

"Come quick," she pants.

Siri slams up from her seat so fast that her chair goes flying away from her; smashes against the far wall of the cafeteria. Her hair whips into a storm around her face. A few eyes nearby turn, and the level of chatter from the forty-odd people inside dips momentarily.

Into that lull, she screams. Loud, toneless, shrill.

No one moves.

"Didn't you hear me?" Siri shouts, and this time her voice is a roar. "RUUUNNNNNN!"

* * *

Marshal Anne, with Winston right behind her, spills into the street outside Gallagher's. She blinks quickly in the sunlight.

Someone runs by her. Pounding away in a mad scramble.

A scream.

Marshal Anne whips around, looking downhill. About thirty yards away, the door to one of the dorms bursts open and a woman without a jacket stumbles out. She flies down the stairs, then trips, tumbling to the street in a puff of snow.

Behind her, a man smashes through the doors, crouched down on all fours.

He lets out an inhuman shriek–

Then leaps on the fallen woman and vomits what looks like seawater all over her face. Blasting her with it like a water cannon.

Marshal Anne's scalp swarms with a thousand ants. *What the hell–*

Winston shouts behind her. She turns just in time to see someone falling out of the top floor of the Crary lab. The next moment someone else comes launching out of the same window.

No jacket. No shirt. A bare chest.

A howl of pure rage that sets her teeth on edge.

Instinct steps in; brushes her slow baffled mind aside and simply *takes over*. She whirls. "Get to the Chalet, boss," Marshal Anne barks. "Sound the alarm, and lock the door!"

"Where are you–"

"To get my gun. *Go*!"

She breaks into a hard run, not stopping to see if Winston has followed her instructions. The cold bites into her lungs. She passes the Chapel of the Snows at a dead sprint. Pastor Taylor Kwanje is outside, unscrewing a display case, swapping the announcement sheet.

"Get inside!" she yells as she runs past him. "Get the fuck inside, lock the door!"

Anne bangs through the door of her dorm. She bounds up the stairs, taking them two at a time. Somewhere in the building, she hears a scream. The sound of breaking glass.

She runs around a corner and stops dead. Black spots dance in front of her eyes.

In the hallway, hair dripping with moisture, is Doc Cait.

Marshal Anne's palms break into a sweat.

She takes a step backward, and Cait's head *swivels*. Then the rest of her body turns under her neck, like a disjointed robot.

Cait lets out that same high inhuman scream.

Then races right at her.

Marshal Anne sways, turns and runs. She makes it into the stairwell, then Cait thuds into her back and she loses her footing, going down on the stairs. A step smacks her in the forehead. She manages to roll halfway over before Cait swarms on top of her. The doc is little but *dear God she's so strong,* and Anne can't shake her off.

"Cait–" she gasps. "Caitlin!"

The doctor looks down. Her eyes are flooded with stark, deep-water blue.

She unhinges her jaw. Marshal Anne hears bones snapping like twigs. The sound pins her in place. Pure, unfiltered horror at what is about to happen.

"Hey!" someone yells.

Cait's head snaps up, mouth inhumanly agape.

"Yeah, over here. Come get me. Come on!"

Cait bounds off Marshal Anne and across most of the landing in one leap. She goes down on all fours, springs up–

Jonah Mitchell ducks and leaps to the side.

Cait smashes into the wall and bounces off like she hasn't even noticed the impact–

Jonah pivots around, arm flashing, and drives a steak knife firmly into the side of her head.

The doctor lets out a gurgling scream.

A blast of icy water roars out of her mouth, dashing over the wall next to Jonah.

Then Cait sags, slowly, to her knees. She falls into the soaking carpet, knife sticking out of her temple.

Marshal Anne gathers to her feet, shaken. She feels like throwing up. "She didn't even recognize me," she pants.

Jonah looks at her, as if seeing her for the first time. "Marshal. You got your gun?"

Anne starts up the stairs. "Not yet."

* * *

A siren begins to blare, through every speaker on the station.

"Emergency lockdown," Winston shouts into the microphone, even as he pushes his desk forward, ripping the phone cord out of the wall, barricading the door to his office. "Everyone stay in your buildings! *Do not go outside!*"

Jonah stands in the doorway of Marshal Anne's room as she wrenches her safe open and whips out her gun belt. "Do you know what the hell is going on?" she says, over the sound of the siren.

"This is just like South Pole," he says. Voice tense. "This is what happened there."

"Wait, what?" Anne dumps the magazine out of her pistol, checks it, then slams it back in. "I was told Gaudin killed everyone on your crew."

Jonah shakes his head. "That was a lie. A microbe infestation killed most of us. And it started with Ben Jacobs."

"Colson, you fuck!" Marshal Anne hisses furiously. Somewhere, her mind is collecting the implications of what she's learning, what is happening across her station, but she's still moving on instinct, without planning or consideration. A shooter's mind: clean, tactical, focused. If you survive the next hour, then you think about the next day, but not before.

She hesitates, then reopens the safe and pulls out her spare gun. "You know how to shoot, Jonah?"

"I was raised on a small farm in Pennsylvania."

She raises an eyebrow.

"Yeah. I can shoot."

She hands him the revolver. "Watch my back. There's six shots in that."

"Five *useful* shots," he says. "Trust me. You want to save one for yourself."

Rajan and Siri race across the large cafeteria and burst into the outer hallway. People are running in confused pandemonium, or craning to peer through frosted windows. Rajan pauses and picks up a long metal food tray. It's not much of a weapon, but it's all he can lay hands on.

"This way." Siri points, and they run down the corridor.

(krrrrrghhh)

They round a corner and come to an abrupt halt.

In the hallway, two dripping wet Mactown women are pinning a man against the wall. His heels are off the ground, feet kicking frantically.

A hiss of scratchy furious noise explodes inside Rajan and Siri's head–

(krrrrrghhhHHHHHHHH)

Then the second woman *unhinges* her jaw and blasts the man in the face with a powerful deluge of water.

The man chokes, then his eyes roll into the back of his head. Ice covers his face like a glass top on a table. One of the women slops him over her back with careless ease, and takes off running away from them, her captive slung like a sack over her shoulder.

The second woman turns, looking at them.

Her head cocks to the side.

(*kkkkrrrrrr*)

Rajan bursts into motion.

Right at her.

(*siri run run run*)

The woman unhinges her jaw again, lower teeth dropping away–

(*what the FUCK*)

Rajan puts the tray up in front of his face just in time. Water slaps against it, then he slams into the woman. Pinning her against the wall. She bucks against the tray with a furious strength and he struggles to hold on. Shaking with a full-body effort. To let go is game over–

Then Siri runs up behind him. She slides to her knees, splashing in the water on the linoleum floor, and grabs the woman's leg.

She closes her eyes–

(*kkkkrrrghhh*NOOOOOOO)

– and the woman slumps against Rajan's tray.

* * *

Her name is Gisela Childers, and the last thing she remembers clearly is playing cards in a berthing room at Phoenix Airfield.

She remembers afterward only through a dreamlike curtain of blue. The hospital. Doc Cait. A tall man with a white gun walking around looking very serious.

Then, suddenly–

The gunman in the hospital hallway turns, but Ben Jacobs is fast, *so fast*. Gisela watches through the porthole of the trauma bay door as Ben springs *up*. The man's gun swivels, trying to track him up to the ceiling, then Ben drops down on top of him.

Stabs him in the chest with a needle still attached to an IV bag.

As the man sags, Ben curls his fingers around a scalpel held between his teeth.

He slices the gunman's throat.

Ben enters the room she is in. He has a serene smile on his emaciated face.

His jaw sags open and a grey stormcloud blows out of it and across her face.

(*one then two then three then all*)

She knows it's his voice in her head.

She says it with him. They say it with him. "One then two then three then all."

Gisela remembers walking out of the hospital. It is blowing snow powerfully, but the milky cold is no more than a sullen pump through her, like the burn of muscles after a punishing workout. There are others from the hospital with her, each of them clutching onto something beyond what their eyes can see.

The signal of their leader. Their Pied Piper.

(*one then two then three then all*)

They follow him through the whiteness and the wind. They stumble down inclines and through buffeting snow until there's nothing but wobbling ice beneath their feet. She looks up and she can see at least five more people, spread out on the glacial shore, all looking up into the sky as if listening for something.

(*go to him go go go*)

She doesn't hesitate. She dives off the ice, plunging into the water.

Gisela sinks, like a heavy rock. Deeper and deeper, until the water turns from snow-lit blue to deep black. It bubbles into her throat and she struggles instinctively.

(*don't fear we come from the water*)

(*this was our first home and it will be our new home*)

(*first one then two then three then –*)

The world closes in on her and Gisela understands she is dying, but she is powerless to fight it. The human part of her brain sparks and spasms, like a fly caught in a spider's web. She feels something flooding through her, strengthening in the icy water. Spreading, invading. It's hungry. Oh God, it's so hungry.

Then there is only the voice. His voice.

The voice of a man, bare-chested, floating with his back against a block of ice. His eyes are open in a nightmare of a fixed stare. His blonde hair spreads around him in the water, gently, every bone in his muscular frame evident. Gash marks like fingernails light up his cheek in the diffuse light of the water.

He is dead, she knows, drowned like she is drowning, and yet his mouth is opening. His dead lips.

"Come to us," the man gurgles.

She moves slowly, drugged by the cold, her human senses almost gone.

She sees something in the water between them.

A grey-blue river. Moving. It enters her mouth, pierces her ears.

Something turns on, sharpens.

Something else heaves a final breath and is extinguished.

You are the blue-generation now. Yes, you will do just fine.

She thinks: *what must I do*, but all that comes out is a scratchy painful mental blast of static.

(*find more of us us us*)

(*yes more we need more us us us*)

Rajan doesn't catch all of it – Siri is deep in Gisela's mind, rummaging, but he catches the second voice very clearly.

(*yes more we need more us us us*)

Siri releases Gisela and looks up at him, her eyes bleak.

(*did you*)

(*yeah*)

His lips are dry. "The man in the water was Penny," he says. "Dear God. Penny was one of the symbiotes all along. *How is that possible?*"

Four months ago. June 27, the night of death at South Pole. Jonah and Bethany had locked Rajan, Siri and Keyon out. The last band of microbe-infested symbiotes were closing on them and the Station. But at IceCube Laboratory, Greg "Lucky" Penny had been blissfully unaware of the life-or-death fight a mile away. The emergency radio was squawking, but he'd turned it way down so he could hear his music. Right before bed, Penny rolled himself a blunt with the last of the weed Clint had sold him.

Way overpriced, but it was the South Pole, after all.

He'd curled up on the hard cot in the corner of his lab space, earbuds in, head gently nodding. He didn't feel his eyes blinking black before they slipped closed.

A small sliver of microbe-infection. Just enough. Mutating with the THC coursing through his veins. A quiet throb as it tightened its grip. Starved itself in wait for *more more more* –

Four months later, the moment Penny touched down on the airplane from Pole, things began sharpening for Ben Jacobs. After his brutal trek across the continent, there was no more *him*. There was only *us*, and there were enough of us still left for one last forced evolution.

As the temperature dropped, Penny had begun to *wake up*.

The *we* inside Penny had been catalyzed months ago, but we didn't fully bond with him, because then the hated others–

(*fuckers siri rajan keyon fuckers*)

– would have been able to sense us. But *we* had remained a silent sliver of purpose inside him, and in the dropping temperatures of the McMurdo snowstorm, the right moment came. You know what denotes sentient intelligence? The ability to be sneaky. The desire for revenge. We began to multiply, and suddenly there was a voice in Penny's head.

A grid of white light, burned into his brain, that drew closer to him; spoke to him.

Penny went out in the cold. Like a homing beacon to a magnet, drawn to the hospital where Ben Jacobs was. Where the rest of *us* were.

Penny stood below the window of the McMurdo hospital and exhaled with all his strength. We flowed out of him, an unending river of death, over the hospital and into it.

Finding our way to Ben Jacobs.

Strengthening him. Freeing him. Giving him the quiver of another heartbeat in his body.

(*thank you Penny you have served us well*)

Penny sagged to the snow. His voice in return was almost too weak. But our Ben voice was warm, reassuring. Strengthening.

(*I will make you the leader of a new generation*)

(*come to me come to us come to the water*)

Bethany Hamidani sits in a chair wedged against the door of her dorm room, looking out of the window. There's commotion in the hallway outside, screaming, and she hears the sound of a crashing window.

Then a thump against her door.

Bethany goes absolutely still. Down below her, there's something moving in the snow. Worming.

It pokes its head up, and softly hisses her name.

Chapter Thirty-Six

The moment the alarm goes off, and Colson hears Winston's voice across the loudspeaker, she knows she has lost the Station.

It happened so fast, she thinks wonderingly, even as she jumps to her feet in the Movement Center and starts wriggling into her haz suit.

She'd been prepared for the missing infected to strike when the conditions were favorable to them. During the cold, with the blowing snow restricting visibility.

But now? When the sun is shining, and the temperature is *rising*?

Except she should have known better. You always strike when the adversary least expects. When they are tired from being wound up and on watch.

This is not just biology, she thinks. *This is intelligence. Sentient biology.*

Colson looks around at her men. They are tired from their long cold night, but they know the score. Operators, ready to operate. *Hoo-fucking-yah.*

"We don't know who is infected and who is not," she says. "We will not risk our lives trying to guess. Weapons free. Questions?"

There are no questions.

"I can tell you right now that we're not punching our ticket off this ice without a way to prove we're not one of the infected, and there's no infection test without Dr. Kim. So, our first priority is to go get him."

Colson surges out of the Movement Building, Heckler and Koch MP5N out in front of her. Behind her and offset, but clamped to her side, is Sal. The rest of the men spread automatically out into fire team formation. Mackie and Barham have left flank, the rifleman position. Dr. Mason is on the right, the grenadier position. Lansdown brings up the tail.

Colson's eyes scan the tops of buildings, down side streets, moving her head to widen her field of view past the restrictive haz-suit helmet. The movement building is uphill, which means they can roll down into town with superior eyelines.

"Contact right," Dr. Mason barks.

Down a side street they see two men in nothing but long-sleeved thermal shirts and pants. They are each carrying someone over their shoulders. Running away from them.

"Fire," Colson says coldly.

Sal and Dr. Mason squeeze their triggers, keeping their shots low. The legs blow out from both runners and they sag to the ground. Screaming in no language Colson can discern. Just raw animal pain and maybe–

Maybe hunger.

The fire team rotates smoothly, Dr. Mason taking point, and they move down the unplowed street. Boots crunching through snow. Blood spots thicken as they come up on the jacketless men. They are squirming furiously, trying to get to their feet. The two people they'd been carrying are thumped into the snow next to them, faces up. A thick sheen of solid splatted ice covers their faces.

Colson stares at them like one might stare at a grisly car accident, almost mesmerized.

One of the jacketless men rolls over and his jaw opens wide, stomach bunching–

Sal shoots him in the neck. A small fountain of water bubbles out from his lips, mixed with bright frothy blood. Colson blinks twice. She steps up next to him and shoots the other man in the back of the head.

"What about these two–" Dr. Mason starts.

Colson fires once, then again. Blood spatters over the snow.

"It passes by touch," she says, without any emotion in her voice. "Pivot."

Despite Winston's broadcast, there are dozens of people in the streets, most running like they have a destination in mind.

Colson pulls her team in tight and they flow past anyone that ignores them. Sal kicks the door of the first pod in the Crary building open. There's chaos inside, and Colson squeezes a shot off into the ceiling.

"Clear the hallway!" she shouts.

People disappear, diving into rooms off the side. The team moves quickly, up the stairs to the third floor. Dr. Kim appears in a doorway, behind a pane of glass. "There was something happening next door," he says with a grimace.

"Mackie, Barham, with me," Sal says.

"Everyone else, to the roof." Colson is already moving.

The three of them move down the hallway, poking their heads cautiously into the next lab. They see nothing except a smashed window. Sal goes up to it. The wind ruffles his Hazmat suit. Three stories below is the clear imprint of a man landed in the snowbank, but there's no man there.

"Let's back the fuck out of here," Sal says tightly.

On the roof of the Crary Lab, Colson and Dr. Mason watch a row of people stream down the hill, out of firing range, just specks against white ice. Most of them carry two people over their shoulders. Like hunting hounds, returning to their master with their catch.

The original twenty-six infected have found more prey.

(*they are taking people lifting them away somewhere*)

Siri's voice comes clearly to Dr. Mason.

(*they are building their numbers. stay safe mason*)

Mackie and Barham are on the roofs of the other two Crary pods, sweeping anything they can see in the streets below. "Firing," Colson hears, in the radio in her ear. She looks to the right, scanning with her binoculars.

By Gallagher's bar, someone moving rapidly on all fours sags to the ground, blood spurting into the snow next to them.

Colson looks back toward the frozen ocean. The last of the infected have made it down the slope. She watches them dive into slim crevices of water between glacial ice. Down beneath the frozen surface. They do not reappear.

"That's not a good sign at all," Dr. Mason says from next to her. His voice is full of cotton.

"Another forced mutation," Dr. Kim breathes, almost in awe.

"Explain that," Colson barks.

"The temperature of that water is maybe 40 degrees Fahrenheit. Above freezing." Dr. Mason says heavily. "If the infected can multiply in such a warm temperature, we're going to get overrun."

Chapter Thirty Seven

Colson and her fire team head down toward the Chalet. The slantwise bolt of the late sun above her is shrouded in high clouds that create a refracted circle of rainbow colors. The circle grows, occupying most of the sky, highlighting its emptiness. No contrails, no pollution, but no life, either–

Colson catches motion out of the corner of her eye and pivots, gun coming up. She sees Rajan and Siri approaching them from the cafeteria, hands up. Colson lowers her gun and waves at them impatiently. They break into a run over to them.

"Colson," Siri pants. "This is what happened at Pole."

"I gathered," she says grimly. "The symbiotes appear to have withdrawn, they're hiding beneath the ice, but we've got to consolidate the crew into a safe zone before they come back, or we're going to get picked off."

"I thought you'd say that, but that's exactly how Ben Jacobs got most of the crew at Pole. When everyone was gathered in one place." Siri's clear eyes fix hers. "Anyone could have the microbes on them now. If a single person in our safe zone is infected, we'll all become infected."

"I'm open to ideas. Dr. Kim was working on a test, but he's not there yet–"

"She can do it," Rajan interrupts.

"What?"

Behind Colson, Dr. Mason's eyes are wide.

(*hope you know what you're doing*)

(*it's life or death now*)

"Siri can tell if the microbes are on someone," Rajan says.

Siri raises her hand to her head. "I can hear them. It sounds like screaming embedded into radio static."

Colson gives her a penetrating look that draws and pins Siri up for inspection; a bug beneath the microscope. She's about to reply when Barham says, "Contact right!"

The group pivots, guns coming up, then Colson says, "Stand down."

From the dorms, walking up the hill toward them, are Marshal Anne and Jonah.

In the Chalet, they regroup with Winston. The Station Manager listens to their dilemma, and suggests the cafeteria as a safe zone. Colson shakes her head.

"I don't like it."

"People will need food, Colson," Winston says. "That's the limiting–"

"What I need more than food are eyelines." She jerks her chin at Barham, who is carrying his sniper rifle. "I've seen these new sea creatures jump out of four-story windows and survive, but I bet you they can't jump *up* four stories."

"Then we clear every floor of the three Crary pods," Winston says. "That building is four stories tall. We can gather everyone on the top two floors."

Colson nods, liking this suggestion. "If we barricade ourselves in, and disable the elevators, that gives my guys control of the roof, and a kill box in the stairways. We've got plenty of ammunition in the Movement Center that we can stockpile at Crary."

"But what about food?" Marshal Anne asks. "What's the long-term plan?"

"Escort teams." Colson looks at Rajan, hesitates. "Major. Have you deployed? Been on a movement squad?"

"Yes," Rajan says shortly.

"Then with you, Marshal, that's eight trained guns, enough for two fire teams. We can escort cooks back and forth with food from the cafeteria. Winston?"

"Seems all right to me," Winston grunts.

"Sal, take a team to clear Crary." She looks at Siri, hesitates, then continues. "Take her with you to determine who gets to stay in. Shoot anyone she says to shoot. Lansdown, you're with me, Dr. Mason and the Marshal. We start up at Ob Hill, clear each building and send anyone we find down to Crary."

She looks around. Gets nods from everyone.

Dr. Mason looks at Siri. "How much time do you think we have?"

Siri's head tilts to one side. "It takes them a while to regroup mentally. From what I could hear, this new strain isn't as coherent as the symbiotes were. It's not much more than *kill, grow, eat–"*

(*one then two then three–*)

"Tell me what that means," Colson says.

"It means we have a little time, but not much."

Colson's men have fought in the partisan street wars in Taiwan; they have real-world experience in urban combat. Moving quickly but efficiently, they clear building after building, floor after floor. Winston goes with them. His eyes are large with suppressed dread, but he is the keeper of the keys to every building and room at Mac. They go through tunnels, storage rooms, trade shops and warehouses; room by room, corner by corner. They encounter almost no resistance. Ben Jacobs and his twenty-six have swept through town, caught who they can catch, and appear to have left.

Conserving their strength for their next strike. It's also what she would do.

In the dark ice tunnels underneath the Mac power plant, Lansdown opens a door to find three men, huddled together in a corner. They look confused and terrified. He lets his gun drop to his side and steps forward to speak to them.

Suddenly Dr. Mason screams. "Fire fire fire!"

Lansdown snaps his gun up and both men pull their triggers. The small space fills with the echo of bullets.

"What the hell!" Marshal Anne yells, horrified. "They were just sitting there!"

Dr. Mason points. "Look, Marshal."

The bodies are leaking.

Water drips out of their ears, mouths, the sides of their eyes. Pooling around their heads.

"You don't want that to hit you," Dr. Mason says. "That's how they incapacitate you."

"They were just sitting here waiting for us?"

"Waiting for anyone," he replies grimly. "This is a numbers game now."

On the ground floor of Crary Lab, Rajan hesitates, as if squinting in his mind, then Siri hears it.

(*krrrr*)

He's replaying it from his memory. The sound Gisela Childers had heard in her head as she drowned under the ice, and the microbes moved their way through her. It's not quite right, but when Siri latches onto the sound, she finds she can sharpen it with her memory.

(krrrrrghhh)

In front of them, a woman with a red beanie coughs. She doesn't respond.

"She's okay," Siri says.

"Head to the top floor, red," Sal says. His face is unsmiling, one hand on the butt of his gun. "Next!"

Suddenly Rajan's eyes fly open. Siri looks up in time to see Bethany Hamidani join the line to gain access to Crary. Her eyes are downcast, but abruptly she looks up, as if aware she's being stared at. Rajan springs to his feet and walks past Siri, right toward her.

"Did you know?" he shouts.

Bethany's eyes flicker. "Did I know what?"

He comes to a stop right in front of her. "Don't play coy with me."

"Get the fuck out of my face, Rajan." Bethany's face is tight and pinched.

Siri appears next to them. "What's happening here?"

"Are you one of them?"

"Rajan!"

"It's a fair question. None of us spent time with Penny except *her*." He leans closer to her. "Are you the last symbiote?"

"Fuck you, man." Bethany stares back at him with brittle defiance.

Suddenly Sal looms behind them, his hand inside the trigger guard of his weapon. Siri grabs Rajan's arm, roughly.

(*rajan please not like this*)

"Do we have a problem with this one?" Sal asks.

Bethany throws a panicked look at Sal. Rajan hesitates, then Siri's hand finds his.

(*let's look we know what to look for*)

(*we can't hear the grey only the blue she could still be infected*)

(*just shhh and listen with me*)

By nightfall, 192 Mactowners are gathered on the top floors of the three pods of Crary, including Bethany. People are reorganizing furniture, staking out corners amidst crowded spaces. Marshal Anne walks up to Winston as he stares out of a window, watching the sun refuse to set from the sky.

"What is it, boss?" Marshal Anne asks.

"192. That's the count." He looks at her, his eyes bleak. "We're missing over *two hundred and thirty Mactowners.* Gone, beneath the ice. People I'm responsible for."

She puts her hand on his shoulder. "There may be more to come, boss," she says, her voice gentle. "It's not time to mourn. Not yet."

In a corner office of Crary, Colson faces Dr. Mason and Dr. Kim. Her voice is calm, but her agitation is clear in every suppressed movement her hands make.

"Boys, I talked to Langley on the sat-phone." she says. "With Evil Bill himself."

Both men's faces go rigid. People don't call him "Evil" because of his caring nature.

"CIA isn't sending the quarantine aircraft anymore," she says grimly. "Not for Ben, not for anybody. We have orders to regain control of Mac Station, and contain the outbreak. The airplane won't take off until we can show Langley convincing evidence that *none* of us are infected."

"So..." Dr. Kim's voice is a gas-balloon tethered to concrete, climbing but refusing to float free. "So we're all trapped here?"

Colson grimaces, then simply nods. "Until you punch us a ticket out."

She opens her mouth to say more, then stops, seeing an unexpected face outside in the hallway.

"Your work is all the more critical now, Dr. Kim. Let's regroup in the morning," she says. "Call on my radio if you need anything."

Colson walks out of the office. "Well, hi," she says. "This is unexpected."

Mariana Egan faces her with an intensity in her eyes Colson hasn't seen before. "I know something most people in here don't," the reporter says, each word bitten off but somehow breathless. "This is the *third* Antarctic Station to go offline in the last few months."

Colson sighs. "What do you want me to say, Mariana?"

"I want you to tell me you understand that we may not leave here alive."

"I understand that," Colson says, with quiet strength. "I'm not ready to accept that as the final outcome."

Mariana nods forcefully at that. "Good. *Good.*"

She takes a step closer.

"If that's the case…"

In that sunlit instant, the air between them thickens into a pressure that's almost physical.

"Come with me before I change my mind," Mariana whispers.

Chapter Thirty-Eight

Even under thermal infrared scopes, nothing comes crawling back out of the icy ocean over the short, cold night. As daylight stretches over McMurdo Station, the barometer reluctantly rises. Zero degrees Fahrenheit. Practically balmy, compared to the stormy weather of the last two days.

Nothing stirs out on the ice.

The body can become used to being tired. Can acclimate to long hours of sunlight; even to physical pain. And yet, Dr. Jon Kim thinks, *fear* is something he hasn't become inured to. Up to now, his rivalry with Dr. Mason has been based on professional jostling for primacy; nothing unusual, really. But in the last forty-eight hours, Kim has realized that he actively hates his CIA counterpart.

Because fucking Mason is also a soldier. A former special operator. He's *trained* to deal with this fear, to compartmentalize and be calm in the face of danger, and Kim is not. Not equipped at all, in fact, and once you know that about yourself, you cannot unlearn it.

That weight lies heavy when their path off the ice runs through him.

In the morning, there is a knock on the closed door of his third-floor Crary lab. Standing outside is someone he hadn't expected.

"Hi," Jonah says. "Do you know who I am?"

"Uh…" Dr. Kim's eyes move rapidly. "You're one of the Pole survivors. You're…"

"I'm Jonah Mitchell," he says. "I've got twenty-eight years of practical experience running experiments on behalf of scientists from all around the world. If we survive the next wave of attacks, what you're doing will be our only ticket out of here, so I want to help."

Dr. Kim doesn't ask Jonah how he has figured this out. His mind is heavy with exhaustion, he has a lot of work to do, and he can use the extra hands. In that moment, however, his mind turns to Siri and Rajan.

What they seem to be able to do.

Dr. Mason is now more shooter than scientist. But that doesn't mean Dr. Kim is lesser. He may be *just* a scientist, but he's one of the world's *best* scientists, and he senses that a huge scientific discovery lurks behind Rajan and Siri. Something that may make being here, in the middle of this chaos, worth it.

If Rajan and Siri really can *sense* the microbes...

Then it's possible they can communicate with them.

And the microbes can communicate back.

A person who knows Siri and Rajan can be a very useful source of information.

"Come in, Jonah," Dr. Kim says. "Let me show you what I've been experimenting with."

People have to eat, even if just one meal a day. After a short nap, Winston assembles a dining crew of six cooks and bakers. The first fire team, led by Colson, pushes out of Crary and hustles the short distance to the blue cafeteria building, watched like hawks by Lansdown and Sal from their overwatch point.

They sweep every room within the cafeteria building and Colson finds herself glad she won't have to defend this place – there are too many low windows, each an easy access point.

Colson and Dr. Mason set up in sniper positions on the sloped blue roof of the cafeteria, creating a crossing line of fire. The day is sunny, clear skies, a cold but low wind whistling through the empty streets of Mactown. An almost perfect ice day.

The dining team preps food, then places large food trays and deep pots onto wheeled carts. Everyone egresses together, across the snowy road, clustering tightly like scared chickens, eyes darting everywhere at once.

At Crary, the trays and pots are relocated to the second floor. The fire teams eat first, then take up gunner positions by the windows. Jumpable, Rajan has told Colson. He has seen them jump that high at Pole.

In groups of ten, they bring people down to the second floor to eat. Keeping things controllable. Rationed.

Night falls late, and thinly. The Station tries to sleep. It is the last nightfall for the next several months.

It takes four more days for Mac Station to break.

Colson isn't sure if it's the limited food, the lack of visible danger, or that things are warming up outside with the round-the-clock sunshine, to the point where the snow is turning into slush for part of the afternoon. Two days later, October 20, she is stopped with several questions about this pandemic, how it's transmitted, and what the risk really is. Three days in, cooped up with not much else to talk about, the questions are the same, but more aggressive. The word *bitch* starts to pick up an echo.

On day four, October 22, Aaron Bateman stands up and declares loudly that he's not coming back.

Bateman is an assistant baker, with two years at Mac and one year cooking at Palmer Station. "There's plenty of food and beds right out that window, and we're sleeping on the floor hungry," he declares. His arms gesticulate somewhat madly. "I'm going to head over and cook. But I ain't coming back. And I'll be there cooking tomorrow if anyone wants to join me and sleep in a real bed."

There's a lot of affirmative-sounding noise, but Aaron and his friend Stuart Crowe, a fuelie, are the only two who don't return. As the escort fire-team trickles back into Crary without them, Colson can feel the pressure of the Station's regard. Everyone watches her, waiting for her reaction.

Unexpectedly, she defers to Winston. "My men are staying here and will protect anyone who stays here," she says. "But I'm not going to stop anyone from leaving."

Winston reminds everyone that they need to be smart. It's hard to be crowded into one space, but while Penny and Ben and two hundred blue-generation infected are lurking beneath the ice, it isn't safe outside. They'll figure something out, he promises.

In private, he tells Colson, "I wish you hadn't let Bateman go."

"So I can be the unreasonable bitch?" Colson says testily.

"Yeah," Winston says heavily. "At least that way they don't do the dumbest thing possible."

Marshal Anne stares at Colson as she walks away, beautiful green eyes narrowed. "I don't buy it," she tells Winston later. "Colson doesn't give a shit about being liked. Why would she agree to let people wander around out there?"

Dr. Mason slips into the small room in the third Crary pod. It's now sunlight at all hours, but the hands on his watch tell him it's 8:00 in the morning. Pastor Kwanje is enclosed by people holding hands, leading them through prayers. His room has become the unofficial new church of the Station. Dr. Mason stands against the wall, watching quietly. To his surprise, he sees Rajan in the group, gun laid in front of him. Rajan's eyes are closed, but Mason senses his suddenly wary regard. Watching Mason through his own eyes.

Pastor Kwanje looks up, lips continuing to move. Gently, he moves his head, beckoning him over.

At first Dr. Mason doesn't move. Then, slowly, he takes his gun off its strap, lays it at his feet, and kneels down next to Rajan.

Rajan opens his eyes and looks at him with an inscrutable expression. Mason is aware of both of them standing at some vital line; like they are travelers about to cross over into a new country. Things are changing. Factions realigning. Survival, and the hope to survive, is all that remains.

Both men close their eyes, and murmur the prayer along with the others gathered there.

Please God, Dr. Mason allows himself to ask, in his mind. *If you're up there, if you can hear a son of a bitch like me. I want to see my wife again. Please let me see my wife again.*

And he hears Rajan's prayer in response. *Please God,* Rajan is asking. *Please forgive me for the lives I have to take to protect those I love. If there is forgiveness for that, please forgive me.*

* * *

Half-huddled inside her sleeping bag, Mariana sits with her back to a wall, laptop plugged in beside her. She is working in a bit of a daze, numbed by cold and not enough food. She is transcribing her latest interviews, and adding metadata to the accompanying pictures.

A shadow falls over her.

She looks up to see Siri crouch down. The two women consider each other for a lingering moment.

"If I talk to you," Siri says, "how will you get the word back to the mainland?"

Mariana feels a ripple of excitement. The thrill of the fisherman with a bite on their line.

"That's exactly why you have to talk to me, Siri," she replies. "In case it's all that gets left behind."

The truth of her words rings between them like a hammer pounded into a bell.

"Tonight." Siri says. "Third floor bathroom. I'll give you the story you came here for."

Chapter Thirty-Nine

EXCERPT from *In the Wake of War: A First-hand Account of Humanity's Deadliest Struggle,*
Winner of the Pulitzer Prize for Explanatory Reporting (posthumously awarded)
Assembled from the diaries of Mariana Egan, War Correspondent, *Chicago Tribune*
As presented at the Fifth Global Conference for Armament Limitation, Geneva, 2043 AD.
Edited by Jane Bradshaw.

Siri and I huddled together in the bathroom on the third floor of Crary. We whispered, but she put her lips near my phone, so it could pick up every word. It was perhaps the most extraordinary story I'd ever heard, made all the more potent by the reality beyond the door we'd locked ourselves behind. This was not Siri's first, but second time at a ravaged Antarctic station. Over nearly two hours, her voice often hitching with fear or sadness, she told me about the microbe pandemic that had ravaged South Pole Station. About the symbiotes killing her crewmembers off, one by one, over a shocking long winter night.

And she told me about Benjamin Jacobs. Once a NOAA Lieutenant, then a frozen desiccated corpse, now the leader of a tribe that has been picking us off. The source of our sea sentient infestation.

Toward the end of our whispered conversation, I pulled up a photo of the redacted communication I had been sent. The document that mentioned HAVE VIKING, an infection, and perished crewmembers.

The document that had started my journey here.

I pushed on to the questions that would blow this from a human-interest pandemic story into a national security exposé.

"Was this sent from South Pole?" I asked.

Siri zoomed in on my phone screen, inhaling every word. A myriad of emotions flitted across her wan face. Then she handed it back to me. Something like a sigh escaped her.

"I was there when that was typed," Siri said. Right into my phone's voice memo. "I won't tell you who typed it, but yes, I can vouch for that communique being sent from South Pole."

I was now certain that the author of the communique was Rajan Chariya. Siri and Rajan were close; she would want to protect him.

Siri pointed to my phone. "When you first saw this, did you think it came from South Pole?"

I nodded.

"Then why…" She waves her hand toward the door, meaning everything beyond it. "Why would you come to Antarctica? To harm's way?"

It was a question that caught me by surprise. The desire to chase the story wherever it led, and know the truth, was something so fundamental to my nature that I'd never thought to question it. Even when other reporters had asked me why I'd risked all my contacts to write my story on General Rason, my answer had been simply that it had never occurred to me to do otherwise.

The truth mattered, but the truth was dangerous. To expose it was to inherently invite danger.

Instead of answering her question, I asked one of my own. "What's HAVE VIKING, Siri?"

She looked away. "I don't know," she said, and it was clear to me that she was lying.

"Siri." Here I did push her. "Did the CIA have something to do with this pandemic? Did they start this nightmare we're all trapped in?"

Her face tightened.

I went still with anticipation.

"What I know for sure is that HAVE VIKING is the name of a classified program that deliberately sought to implant the microbes at Dome-A. If any of the South Pole survivors don't make it back to the mainland… if Keyon Geerts doesn't make it out of South Pole alive," —and now Siri leaned closer to my phone— "the CIA is where people should start asking questions. That's all I want to say."

October 23.

"I think I have something," Dr. Kim says.

Colson listens carefully. "Let's get Mason in here," she says at the end of his explanation.

Kim keeps a pleasant smile on his face. He doesn't object.

Minutes later, Dr. Mason enters, hand resting on the butt of the gun around his neck. Like Colson, his eyes are bloodshot red. His skin is tight at the edges and droopy around his eyes and mouth. None of the eight people on the two armed fire teams have been sleeping much, while it seems like the rest of the Station does nothing but sleep.

"Start at the beginning, Dr. Kim," Colson says. "Tell Mason what you told me."

"All right. We know the grey-generation microbes live inside humans, and somehow form a bond with their hosts. Ben Jacobs was the first symbiote, and according to the Polies, he infected everyone else. And yet… the twenty-six Mactowners that Ben Jacobs escaped with did *not* become the grey-generation. During the storm, the temperature was right for the grey-generation to spread, but it didn't."

Colson interjects. "You're sure it didn't?"

"I've talked extensively with Jonah Mitchell, one of the Pole survivors, and he's sure, too," Kim says, nodding. "The symbiotes work together, like a hive mind. They would have continued to spread quietly. The attacks we're seeing are *sentient,* but not symbiotic. Sort of like, uh, the difference between a child taking orders from a parent, and pro-athlete teammates problem-solving together. I don't fully understand how, but I suspect there's a catalyst of some kind involved."

"You're saying Ben and Penny didn't have whatever catalyst they had at Pole," Colson says.

"Yeah. Maybe it's something endemic to that site. Do you have any idea what it might be, Mason?"

"None," Dr. Mason says calmly.

"Are you sure?"

"Get to the point, Dr. Kim."

"Well… the grey can't spread. And so what happens? Another forced mutation that *can* spread. This is what I theorized would happen at Dome-A, in fact." He throws a smug look at Dr. Mason. "All this organism needs is a high diversity gene pool to access, and a catalyst. Don't you see?"

Dr. Kim's eyes widen; there's a sickly shine to them, like the reflection of something venomous. "The *water* was the catalyst for the sentients; the blue-generation! Cold water, like the water the *original* generation thrived in. Somewhere in their DNA, these microbes preserve the genetic memory of their water-based origin, which triggered an almost immediate mutation. A smart play, really, by Ben Jacobs. Perhaps the only one that ensured the survival of his kind."

"But they aren't his kind," Dr. Mason interjects. "Right?"

"The blue-generation aren't symbiotes." Dr. Kim nods. "They can take over our motor control, but the pairing between human and microbe in the blue-generation is imperfect. Parasitic. Unlike the grey-generation. They are the perfect specimen."

He clears his throat as Colson stares at him. "Anyway. Let me show you what I've found."

Colson and Dr. Mason stand in Dr. Kim's third-floor lab, now enclosed in their haz suits. Strapped to a table, behind a locking metal door, is the blue-generation sentient Gisela Childers. She had been found in the cafeteria building, unconscious, days ago. IVs stream into her body. She appears thin and lifeless.

"I've kept her constantly drugged, don't worry," Dr. Kim says. "A bag an hour. She's barely alive."

Dr. Mason looks hard at him.

"Yeah, yeah," Dr. Kim says, impatiently, "but Ben Jacobs was literally a different species. The sentients are more malleable than the symbiotes."

Colson winds her hand around an invisible circle: keep it moving.

"Okay, right. Ten minutes ago, I pumped her full of warm water. I've also delivered a 3-cc shot of apomorphine, which will irritate the lining of her stomach. She'll want to throw up when she regains consciousness."

"She's awake," Dr. Mason says.

"It should be a few more minutes, she's been kept heavily sedated–"

Dr. Mason lunges closer to the table and slaps its side.

Gisela's eyes fly open, flooded with iceberg blue.

In the quiet lab, they hear the bones in her jaw break cleanly to let her open her mouth wide, almost to her chest. A gout of water bursts out of her throat, blasting Mason's haz-suit in the face, a torrential and sudden discharge. It starts to freeze on his facemask almost immediately.

Dr. Kim scrambles forward and jabs Gisela in the wrist with a needle. She screams, head tossing, and blasts him in the side of his mask as well, hard enough to make him stumble.

Then her eyes roll into the back of her head, and she slumps.

"Well, there you have it," Dr. Kim says, with a runny little laugh. "She turns the water cold, somehow, inside her. I'll have to study how she does that. But, anyway, that's how you test for sentients. If you give someone ipecac or apomorphine, and there are microbes in the vomit… voila. Blue-generation found."

"And that won't work for the grey-generation?" Dr. Mason thumps his faceshield, trying to break the ice away.

"Perhaps not." Dr. Kim sounds reluctant. "The vomiting is involuntary, you see. Uncontrollable. Jonah thinks the symbiotes have learned to control their involuntary responses. They don't feel a response to cold or pain. But there is one involuntary response every generation of microbes has."

"Of course. *Heat*!" Dr. Mason exclaims.

"Precisely. If we can interfere with the body's thermoregulation system–"

"What does that mean?" Colson asks.

"We cause it to be much hotter inside the body than the microbes can bear, while creating a cooler environment outside the body. That's how I think we can not just detect the grey-generation microbes, but force them out of anyone that's infected with them. A… cure. Maybe."

Colson looks at Dr. Mason, who is munching his lip inside his chem-suit thoughtfully.

"It could work," Dr. Mason says at last. "Our bodies have autonomous nervous systems with a heat adjustment mechanism. That's why we sweat: to keep the internal temperature of the body constant and bearable. If you mess with that system…"

"Bingo," Dr. Kim replies. "I've been talking with some experts back home. We're thinking maybe a cocktail of oxybutynin or glycopyrrolate to suppress sweating. Then anticholinergic medications like benztropine or dinitrophenol to prevent cell receptors from binding to their neurotransmitter – essentially it makes the brain forget to kick on the body's cooling mechanisms. Together, they'll spike the body's internal temperature like a fever."

Dr. Mason nods again. "If you make a symbiote uncomfortable enough… they may give up their microbes. But it's dangerous, Kim. There's a reason people die of high fevers."

"It's either that, or give every person here a biopsy, and I'm not a fucking surgeon," Dr. Kim says, his bone-deep fatigue visibly baring its fangs. "The risk of post-op infection alone…"

Colson nods, jerkily. "We have to do it." She looks at both men. "People will have to choose whether they're willing to take the risk, or get left behind."

"Is that why you let that idiot Aaron Bateman go back to his bed?" Dr. Mason asks.

"No." Colson's eyes are grey steel. "To secure the Station, I need to smoke Ben Jacobs out. If we're buttoned up tight, he'll stay down under the ice, wherever he's hiding. But to increase his numbers? Yeah, I think he'll poke his head back up."

Over the next four days, six more people drift away from the group. On the morning of October 26, when the cooks go across to the cafeteria, the group of mutineers are playing cribbage and laughing amongst themselves. A bottle of booze is mostly empty on their table. Bateman is at the center of the group.

Winston heads back with the next escort group to let them know that even though they aren't with the others, Station rules still apply, and that includes drinking anywhere that isn't the bar. The next evening, as the sun blazes brightly in the midnight sky, there are lights on in Gallagher's, and the sound of music wafts down the street to Crary.

The next morning, day nine of the Crary lockdown, ten more people leave.

A Sno-Cat rumbles down main street, Stuart Crowe at the wheel, shoveling mushy snow to the side. It's a sunny day that pokes above twenty Fahrenheit. He waves cheerily as he goes by.

Day ten, a herd of twenty-eight more people leave Crary.

October 29

It's night eleven of the lockdown, although it's night only by the clock. Mackie and Barham are back on their perch, scanning the ocean through their scopes. It's another bone-chilling, uncomfortable watch. Mackie can hear loud music and laughter carrying over the breeze from Gallagher's. His attention has waned plenty, but he can't miss the blobs that start rising from the ice, because there are so many of them. He doesn't catch the first, or even the third, but by the tenth he's wide awake.

"Barham," he says roughly. "Pivot over here, man."

Barham, pointed the other direction to look up Ob Hill, comes out of his sleeping bag as he pulls his sniper rifle around. He places his eye against his thermal scope, aiming down at the ocean, and sucks in a sharp breath.

A stream of dots is emerging from the ocean, clambering onto the ice. Their surface temperatures are just above freezing, but against the five-degree Fahrenheit night, they stand out like fires.

Ten… two dozen… four dozen. Fifty. A hundred.

A small army, rising out of the water.

BOOK FOUR

IVAN THE TERRA BUS

OCTOBER 29 – NOVEMBER 3

In nineteen ninety-four
We bought him off the factory floor
He had a ladder built into the door
And cost three-hundred grand or more
But he means much more to us...
He's Ivan the Terra Bus!

He's Ivan the Terra Bus
He's bringing our friends to us
He took some friends away
Took them down to the Ice Runway
Someday he'll come for us...
He's Ivan the Terra Bus!

lyrics to "Ivan the Terra Bus" by
Bill Jirsa and Allison 'Sandwich' Barden

Chapter Forty

October 29.

Both fire teams, Siri, and Winston stand on the roof of the Crary Lab. The CIA shooters lie prone, eyes to rifle scopes, ammunition lined up beside them, as ready as they can be for the fight to come to them.

The sound of foot-tapping music from Gallaghers, floating across the day glare, is satirically incongruent.

Rajan bends to Siri, whose eyes are closed. "Anything?" he asks.

"Just a murmur," she says. "Like the ocean on rocks."

Mackie does a second head count: 161 sentients milling on the glacial ice. But they haven't come onto shore yet.

Winston walks over to Colson. "Should we head over to Gallagher's?" he says urgently. "Get the boys back into Crary before those creatures make it up here?"

Colson puts her hand on the older man's shoulder. Her eyes are kind, but her voice brooks no argument. "Sorry, Winston," she says. "They're the goats that staked themselves in the front yard, and the maneater isn't here yet."

"Chief," Barham says sharply. "Check out the rise to the east."

Colson snaps her binoculars to her face. Then, wordlessly, she hands them to Rajan.

A single shadowy form stands on top of the promontory. Rajan immediately knows who that is. Senses it in his gut.

Colson knows it too. "Please tell me Ben Jacobs is in range," she says to Barham, who shakes his head.

"Colson," Rajan says. Ben is atop a ridgeline that he knows looks in the direction of–

"Maybe if we get in a Sno-Cat and drive a little–"

"Colson!"

"What?"

Rajan's eyes are wide. "They're moving."

Colson takes the binoculars back. The sentient herd from the ice is rumbling forward as a collective. Loping furiously over the snow, most of them on fours; a bloodthirsty tiger unsheathing its claws. Heading off the ice…

But not toward them.

"They're going for Scott Base," Rajan's voice is dull with horror. "That's what's over the horizon in that direction. And the Kiwis have no idea what's coming for them."

Chapter Forty-One

The herd is maybe two miles away, but they are already moving fast, breaking into a run. The path to Scott Base, not paved or packed down since the storm, is eight miles around Ross Island.

Frantic discussion breaks out, but Colson closes her eyes, fingertips pressed into her temples. Not hurrying into a decision.

Then she turns, and the orders come fast.

"There are eighty-five people at Scott. Every person we save is someone we don't have to fight later. So we're going to move in force for the Kiwis." Her eyes turn to Siri. "You were a driver, right?"

"That's right."

"Can you drive Ivan?"

Ivan the Terra Bus is a Mac institution, the first and last thing most Antarcticans see on the continent. Beefy, bright red, and elevated on six-foot-tall snow tires, the massive bus normally ferries people and luggage between airfields, McMurdo and Scott Stations. Ivan even has its own song, known well to most Mactowners.

By the FEMC building, Siri fires up the bus and it groans ominously. She revs it in low gear, trying to build up heat in the engine case. Behind her, five CIA operatives are spread out; Barham and Mackie on the roof, lashed to the luggage rack with tie-down straps; Dr. Mason and Lansdown in firing positions at open windows on the left and right sides of the bus, and Colson standing rigidly next to her. In the center of the bus, armed and ready, are Rajan and Marshal Anne.

Siri looks up at Colson. Breath puffing in gentle clouds at her lips. "Are you sure this is a good idea?"

"No," she says.

"Okay then. Here we go."

Ivan lurches forward. The top of the bus picks up a shimmy almost immediately; a fairly noticeable and unpleasant one. They are high off the snow and top-heavy.

Ivan's tires crush through uncompacted snow, winding around the McMurdo Sound on a path that would normally be well-plowed by this time in the season. As they round a corner, something glints–

A man, airborne, arms extended, long blond hair trailing behind him.

Leaping off the panic-white snow toward her, trying to grab onto something.

Abruptly he's snatched to the side, as if by a hook. Siri catches a glimpse of a dark red hole in his chest, then he's gone, falling toward the wheels.

Siri instinctively lets up on the gas, and Colson immediately lunges forward. "Don't stop for anything," she grates. "You keep on driving or this becomes the end of all of us."

Siri nods, grimly. She increases speed toward Scott Base.

Ivan rounds another corner, too fast, throwing everyone to one side, large tires grasping for purchase. Three blue-generation sentients are on the snow road.

Arms by their side, ice matted and thick in their hair and on their wet jackets. Waiting.

Into her radio, Colson shouts: "All shooters, weapons free!"

More sentients leap off the snow, scrambling down the snow hill on their right, trying to lunge at the windows or grab onto the front grille. Siri holds her foot flat to the floor, but Ivan the Bus is big and heavy and doesn't have much more speed to give. Dr. Mason and Lansdown open fire from the sides of the bus. Bodies tumble off. The bus bumps as it drives over one body, then a second.

Scott Base, home of the New Zealand Antarctic Program, is now dead ahead.

She drives down the main street of the base. As she downshifts, Siri hears a blaring alarm. Most of the green-colored buildings are connected by underground tunnels, but too many doors hang open, the alarm pouring through them.

"Stop there," Colson points. "The radio tower."

Barham and Mackie leap off the bus as it slows, and immediately begin climbing. Siri pulls Ivan around in a snow-spraying turn, leaning on the horn. Hoping to find someone – anyone.

From Scott's movement center, a door opens, and a head pokes out.

Dr. Mason waves and yells through the window. "Come on!" he shouts. "Get onboard!"

"Large pod moving back to the ocean," Mackie says dispassionately into their radios. Like he's talking about the weather. "They're carrying people on their backs. Firing."

A barrage of shots ring out from the radio tower, flying over their heads, first ones and twos, then fully automatic fire. A group of people in the bright orange jackets of the Kiwi program break out of a nearby green container, running toward Ivan.

"Dismount," Colson says, pulling out her gun.

Siri opens the bus door. They pour out as Scott people clamber desperately into the interior. She lays on the horn again, engine rumbling.

Abruptly, something crosses her windshield.

It's a sentient, charging straight at Colson's back–

A shot rings out from the tower. The sentient drops dead within touching distance of her.

Another sentient lunging out of a green building veers away. Lansdown fires from the hip, as does Rajan, but both of them miss. The sentient moves fast, low to the ground, running back down the hill. Back toward the ocean. Scott Base is closer to the water; penguins and seals are usually visible from the main dining facility.

"We're going to clear the buildings and tunnels," Colson says. "One by one, slowly and methodically. Okay? Everyone on me. *Let's move.*"

Siri clutches the wheel of the big bus, staring out into the snow-lit day. They are going to war against their teammates. Scott or Mac or Pole, they are all Antarcticans. Like her, they have made a choice that has brought them to the bottom of the world, away from creature comforts and technology. It seems unfair that it should end for them like this.

Above her, more shots sing out.

"They're hungry," Siri whispers to herself. Her voice is hollow. "They're so hungry."

It's a slow, quiet drive from Scott back to McMurdo. Ivan's bench seats hold the shooters, and nineteen stunned New Zealanders.

The nineteen are all that remains of Scott's crew.

The floor of the big red bus is littered with ejected shells from the short but vicious firefight coming into Scott. The sea sentients are gone, disappeared with their new prey into the depths of the icy water that birthed them. They have left behind a deserted station.

As Ivan crests Ob Hill, back into McMurdo, there are more bodies in the snow. Four outside Gallagher's bar. The area around Crary has also been the scene of a firefight.

Siri slows, then stops the bus, staring out to the white and grey horizon. It's cold. It's daylight, but above all, it's cold.

Sal comes down the ramp of Crary. Blood is spattered over his haz suit. "What happened?" Colson asks.

"The sentients came hard, right after you guys left," Sal says grimly. "We lost all the mutineers except Bateman; that cockroach somehow made it back to Crary. A few guys decided to hole up inside Gallagher and that didn't work out too well for them. The sentients retreated about twenty minutes ago."

"Right as we left Scott Base." For the first time, Colson looks overwhelmed. She blinks slowly, breath puffing in ungentle clouds at her lips.

It's their continent now. The ice belongs to the sentients.

Just before midnight, Aaron Bateman gets in a heated argument with the surviving members of the dining team. The junior cook had been the first to loudly proclaim his desire to leave the safety of Crary, and everyone that had followed him out is now dead.

"Hey, no one forced 'em to do it!" Bateman yells, and that's when mild-mannered conservator Ramon Garcia decides to let loose and punch him. Or, at least, he tries; Bateman has a hundred pounds on him and swats him away. Perhaps it might have ended there, if Bateman hadn't chosen to then step forward and punch Garcia hard enough to lay him flat.

That's when Michelle Ajuria, the only surviving mobility technician, picks up a metal folding chair, snaps it closed, and with a loud scream that pierces the room, swings it into the side of Bateman's head.

Marshal Anne wrestles them off of each other, and tells Bateman to get his ass downstairs to the third floor.

"Keep your fucking mouth shut if you know what's good for you," she snarls at him.

Bateman slinks off, blood dripping down his collar, an angry glint in his eye.

Sal pulls the dining team together – there's only three of them left now – to move across the open ice to the cafeteria. People still have to eat, and their position may not improve the next day.

That's when Dr. Kim rushes up to him. "I've got the final formula," he says, breathlessly.

"Doc, I'm in the middle of something right now."

"You want to get out of here or what?" Dr. Kim says, impatiently. "Jonah and I need an escort to the hospital. I'm ready to make a production run for microbe tests, and I need supplies."

Sal is too tired to argue any further. "All right, doc. The hospital, then the cafeteria."

From the roof, beneath the formless dazzle of the sun, Mackie watches a band of sentients emerge from the ocean through his thermal spotter scope. They spread out like a fan, seeping in toward McMurdo from every compass direction. Empty buildings provide cover at the Station's edge, but the sentients will have to run across snow streets to get closer, and that will be their moment.

"Two targets," he says. "In the shadows, east side. Four hundred meters."

"Acquired," Barham replies.

"Fire."

The rifle barks, and a body slumps out of the shadows near the helipad. As Barham fires again, Mackie's sharp eyes catch more sentients lunging up the hill toward the Chalet.

"Contact left. Moving fast," he says sharply. "Group of two."

Barham squeezes off two shots, both lethal, and pauses to reload.

"Four now, coming hard down main street! Spotter is shooting."

Mackie throws himself down beside Barham and pulls up his rifle. He exhales slowly; fires twice. One of the sentients is stopped dead in her tracks. The other evades, moving sinuously, charging hard for the Crary building.

Mackie's scope jitters over him but he can't steady the shot– – then the man's head dissolves in a spray of red mist. Barham has nailed him.

"They're so fucking fast!" Mackie pants.

The swell fades. But Mackie now sees movement all the way up to Ob Hill, and as far down as the Movement Control Center. The sentients have them surrounded.

Slowly seeping closer to them.

"I'm seeing more, coming out of the ocean," Barham says, tightly.

In the cafeteria, six carts of food are ready, each member of the dining team pulling and pushing a cart. Beside them are Dr. Kim and Jonah, each clutching large refrigerated bags. Everyone looks scared, eyes wide.

"Whatever you do, don't rush. Don't trip," Sal warns, as Lansdown opens the door and peers outside. "Steady as she goes, and stay together. Move. Move now."

Downstairs on the second floor of Crary, another fight is happening, but this one is non-verbal. Siri and Rajan are staring each other down from opposite ends of a table by the food line, minds working furiously at each other.

(*i can't believe you talked to the reporter*)

Siri flinches as another shot rings out overhead, but her eyes remain stony.

(*those thugs you're running with will cut us loose if they have to–*)

(*i KNOW that siri but colson said that if we talked to mariana our deal is off–*)

(*– and this is all their fault THIS IS ALL THEIR FAULT*)

Rajan breaks off his thought as Bethany Hamidani walks down the stairs in the direction of food.

Bethany stops in her tracks, seeing him.

He stares at her, a fixed look on his face.

She throws a look over at the food line, then spins on her heel and leaves. Above them, two more gunshots pierce the day and echo dully in the building.

"I know, Siri," he says, not needing to hear her voice in his head to know what she's thinking. "But Penny surprised us once. Who's to say it won't happen again while we're looking the other way?"

As the clock strikes 6:00 AM over the Ross Island dependency, a scream pierces the third-floor hallway.

Aaron Bateman has been found dead, strangled in his sleeping bag.

Lansdown and Sal relieve Mackie and Barham on sniper duty. The Station is now ringed by sea sentients. In some quadrants, Lansdown has to let them charge forward while beating them back elsewhere. Then he pivots Sal's shots, as they break out en masse, and Sal gets three or four before the others find new cover.

But the noose is tightening. There are just too many of them.

Some of the sentients turn away from Mac Station. Headed the long way around, back down the hill toward the ocean. As some sentients leave, more arrive. But they have to regain the ground previously ceded, and that allows the snipers another crack at them.

"Is it the cold? Why don't they just hold their position?" Lansdown wonders aloud.

Sal has been noticing something strange. He tracks one woman as she jumps from ice block to ice block, then dives into the water and disappears underneath it. "Blue fleece," he says aloud.

An hour later, he spots a woman emerging from the water. Blue fleece. The same woman, he's almost positive. He can see ice forming in her hair as she rushes up the hill back toward Mac Station, galloping on all fours. It's spooky to watch her move like a gazelle, while no breath expels from her. She's a drowned corpse running.

Blue fleece woman makes it to the helipad, then starts roving closer, up the hill. She waits in the shadow of the water treatment plant. She pokes her head out, but Sal doesn't take aim at her. He wants to see what she does.

She prowls around for a while, but there's no cover until she reaches the church, and she has to run straight uphill. He puts a shot in the snow in front of her, and she starts withdrawing. Back down the hill, across the ice, into the water.

An hour later she's back, running between buildings. This time she makes a break for the church, and Sal shoots her right in the head.

He bends to his radio. "Dr. Kim, Dr. Mason. Do these sentients have some kind of time limit on how long they can stay out of the water?"

Inside Crary, the mood is somber. Frightened people go down to the second floor to eat, then scurry back to spots they've staked out on the third and fourth floors. Grumbles about the cramped quarters are gone now. Occasionally, a rifle bang echoes through the building.

In their corner room on the top floor, Colson and Dr. Mason are on the satellite phone.

"We tested that formula for Dr. Kim," Evil Bill is saying. "It's a twelve-hour recovery period, but the body's temperature spikes to almost 105 degrees Fahrenheit. It's going to feel like you're boiling alive."

"Summer in Antarctica, just what I was hoping for," Colson sighs.

"The thing we can't test here is whether it actually expels the microbes. All we can tell you is that it won't kill you. Probably."

Colson puts her head in her hands.

Evil Bill won't allow aircraft to land at Mac, but he has mounted thermal pods onto LC-130s for overhead recon. They are mapping sentient movements under the ice in high-definition imagery, up and down the coastline.

"We can confirm your observation," Bill continues. "The sentients seem to need to return to the water, maybe every two hours or so. They stay down for an hour, then come back up–"

"Hang on, Bill," Colson interrupts.

She points at the door. Dr. Mason opens it to reveal Marshal Anne, standing there trying not to look like she'd been eavesdropping.

Colson hesitates, then puts a finger over her lips and waves her in. "Again, how many sentients off the coast at any time?" she says into the sat-phone.

"Between 100 and 110. About fifty spread out around you, rotating in and out. Oh, one more piece of news."

"I'm almost afraid to ask."

"We detected a contingent of about twenty souls, clustered together inside Shackleton's Hut at Cape Royds. Maybe twenty clicks from you? Their thermal signatures read different."

Marshal Anne's face tightens. So does Colson's.

"Different like… like warmer?"

"Yeah." Evil Bill sounds grim.

"Ben Jacobs is saving a subset of people for the grey-generation, whenever he finds his catalyst again," Dr. Mason realizes. "Kim was right. The catalyst that creates symbiotes isn't here, but God help those people if Ben finds it."

"Any chance I can get a MOAB?" Colson interrupts.

"You keep asking for a boom and I keep telling you no booms," Evil Bill says. "Go find yourself a symbiote, and test Dr. Kim's formula. And bring that symbiote back to me while you're at it. No negative test, no ride home."

Colson flips the finger at the phone with almost violent intent, but her voice comes out calm and even when she replies. "Copy that. Colson out."

She looks up to find Marshal Anne studying her with cool eyes. "What's a MOAB?"

She sits back in her chair. "It stands for Mother of all Bombs," Colson says. Whatever agitation she'd felt is now pressed down and packed back as tightly as a cake of tea. "An LC-130 with a roll-out MOAB will create a pressure wave under the water so large that it'll smash most of the sentients in their nest in one swoop. Reverse the odds. The problem is… the second we bomb Antarctica, the situation here goes public, and my people won't do that."

"So we're on our own."

"Essentially."

"Both fire teams are exhausted, Colson." Marshal Anne runs her hand through her oily hair in frustration. "We can't keep this up forever."

"Don't I fuckin' know it."

"What do you mean?"

Colson sighs. "I've been counting shots and kills," she says. "There were 426 people at Mac and 81 at Scott base. That's 507 souls, 146 of whom are with us in this building. My boys have taken out 78 sentients, at last count."

"I can't do math in public."

"That means there are 263 sentients out there. Plus the twenty prisoners at Shackleton's Hut. They have the numbers to hold ground even as they rotate in and out of the water. Pretty soon everything downhill of Crary will belong to them."

As if to highlight her point, three more shots ring out overhead, in rapid succession.

"And there's no airplane coming for us," Marshal Anne's jaw is tight.

"Not until everyone tests negative for symbiote infection. Dr. Kim is producing a big batch of some gnarly stuff right now, but there's a problem."

"Which is?"

Colson widens her arms. "How do we know it works if we have no positive tests?"

Marshal Anne stares at her.

"Yeah," Dr. Mason says, heavily. "We need Ben, or Penny, to prove Dr. Kim's drugs actually can detect the grey-generation, and maybe even expel them from the body. We need a grey-generation symbiote."

A floor beneath them, a chill slinks into the room and coils around Rajan and Siri as they listen to the scene through Dr. Mason.

They stare at each other, eyes large and lambent.

(*capture penny or ben there's no way that happens there's NO WAY*)

(*we need a new plan*)

(*i wonder if…*)

"You're hung up on Bethany just like you were hung up on Jonah," Siri interrupts. "Jonah did the right thing, when push came to shove. He burned TC's body."

(*but bethany was going to tell them where*)

"And Bethany will do the right thing when the time comes too," Siri continues firmly. "I believe that. I have to believe that."

She looks up at him with an approximation of a smile. It is lovely and tired and desperate and saddened. Rajan starts to respond, but there's something raw in his face; something bruised and anxious. They put their arms around each other; she pulls his head down onto her shoulder. He lets a long shuddering breath out into her neck.

She closes her eyes, inhaling his scent. Trying to center herself. Trying to think.

"We need a new plan," he says, muffled. "Or we'll be stuck here until we get picked off."

Siri covers Rajan's hand with hers. "I may have an idea."

At noon, Mackie and Barham rotate back into the sniper's nest. Most of the buildings have sentients lurking behind them now. But Ob Hill, uphill and behind them, remains clear thanks to the air growing warmer. It's too long a walk to circle miles around the Station, only to boomerang back to the water.

A stalemate.

Rajan lies down with the night sun shining right in his eyes, but he falls asleep out of sheer exhaustion. The next morning, when he wakes up, he can see his breath, pooling in the sleeping bag around him.

"Shit," he says.

They've lost the power and the heat.

Chapter Forty-Two

November 1.

Losing the heat could have been catastrophic, but it appears luck is finally on their side. It is fifteen degrees Fahrenheit, and forecast to warm up to almost thirty degrees. A sign of the seasons changing; the promise of something new.

The weather is a reprieve that sprouts quickly into a glimmer of hope for a crew living under the gun. The wind is still, and the Crary refugees hold their breath. By noon, the warming weather results in all the sentients, even those closer to the ocean, retreating. A sat-phone call back to Langley confirms it: not one sentient remains within the boundaries of the Station. They have all withdrawn beneath the ice, to recharge in the chilly waters.

Word spreads quickly, and in consultation with Colson, Winston lets people out of Crary. He warns them not to go out of audible range, so they hear the alarm if the sentients are detected coming back. But they can be outside. Bring things over from their dorm rooms. Or simply get a drink at the bar.

And it will only get warmer in the days to come. In a month, there will be barely any snow in the streets to speak of.

Lansdown leads a fire team to escort Facilities workers to the power substation. Mactowners and Kiwis make circles, or mobile walking picnics, that keep Crary at their locus. Every window is thrown open, to collect fresh air into the stagnant depths of the crowded building. Colson and Marshal Anne opt to sit on Adirondack chairs on the back deck of the Chalet, beside the statue of Admiral Byrd, looking out to the horizon and the slowly calving icebergs.

Colson turns up her volume as Lansdown radios back. “Power plant is clear. Three sentients down, 234 to go. Some amateur sabotage, shouldn’t be too hard to fix,” comes the reply. “Somebody’s thinking, though. Next time may not be so easy.”

Marshal Anne looks up to see Bethany Hamidani coming up the wooden steps, arms crossed across her chest. Her eyes are large and haunted, occupying too much of her face. She looks pinched and somehow diminished; like the imprisonment within Crary has been eating her from the inside out.

“Well, isn’t this nice,” she says. “Just a couple of Mac kids on a summer day.”

“Better than the alternative,” Marshal Anne replies.

“For the record, this is exactly why Jonah and I locked the others out,” Bethany says, through gritted teeth. “We watched this happen. You let up for one second, and it becomes a war zone. *You* could become a war zone.”

“It gets tiring, holding on that hard.” Colson lets out a long sigh. “Sometimes you have to let what’s coming come, and take your beatings.”

Bethany looks like Colson’s words have slapped her.

Above them, Sal leans out of a window on the second floor of the Chalet. “Look at that!”

Marshal Anne straightens to see a group of three penguins shuffling by, flappers wiggling. Just casually strolling through Mac like they own the place. She lets out a little hiccup of a laugh.

“Wow,” she says. “Take away all the machinery and the noise, and nature walks back in like nothing happened.”

Abruptly, Bethany stands up and leaves. Just as abruptly, Colson stiffens. “Hey. Where the fuck is Ivan the Terra Bus going?”

Chapter Forty-Three

EXCERPT from *In the Wake of War: A First-hand Account of Humanity's Deadliest Struggle,*
Winner of the Pulitzer Prize for Explanatory Reporting (posthumously awarded)
Assembled from the diaries of Mariana Egan, War Correspondent, *Chicago Tribune*
As presented at the Fifth Global Conference for Armament Limitation, Geneva, 2043 AD.
Edited by Jane Bradshaw.

The fact that I was stuck in the middle of the first Antarctic war zone wasn't a bad thing. A journalist, especially a War Correspondent, belongs in the middle of events as they unfold.

What was bad was being in the middle of things with no way to get information out.

It made dying stupidly and pointlessly a severe possibility.

As I stood by a window and watched the citizens of Crary – because that's all we were now; not a Station, just a building – dissipate outward to wander the streets under the open cold sky, I came the closest I've ever come to despair.

This was a parole period. A respite from the maelstrom. Soon, our war of attrition would reimpose itself on us. More sabotage. More things falling apart. Survival becoming more and more in doubt–

[timestamp interrupted]

[next entry is ninety minutes later]

Holy shit. Typing fast, lots has happened.

Siri and Rajan came to find me. And they proposed a crazy idea.

"Don't ask how we know this," Siri began. "But the CIA has airplanes in the air around McMurdo. They know the location of the sentients under the ice. They could bomb them from the sky and help us regain control of this Station. But they won't do it."

It made sense, of course. An air-delivered bomb would never get missed, and would violate the Antarctic Treaty.

"We've seen this scenario play out with Ben Jacobs at South Pole." Rajan spoke quickly, as if he wanted the conversation to be over with. "He knows how to bide his time. We're concerned that…"

"If we wait, Ben will get us all, in the end," Siri said. "Sabotaging the power is just his opening move."

"If there's a time to do something," Rajan said, "it's right now. The CIA boys are distracted, everyone's outside, and it's warm enough that the sentients will stay under the water."

The gates were open. We could indeed run through them. But to what end?

"We think it will change the CIA's calculus if what's happening down here becomes publicly known." Siri and Rajan looked at each other. It was clear to me that they disagreed about this statement, but Rajan said nothing out loud.

"Obviously I'd love to get the word out, but McMurdo's internet is being blocked," I said. "Your turn not to ask me how I know this, but the only way to communicate with the world is via Colson's sat-phone. It's keyed to an RSA fob that works with a password only the CIA crew knows."

"We know that password," Rajan said. Before I could ask him how, he pressed on. "But Colson or Kim carry that phone on their person, and we'll never get near it. We have a different idea."

"I'm listening."

"Mac's internet has been blocked for a while. But we've asked around, and Scott Base's internet has been working just fine in that time."

My mouth fell open.

Colson hadn't extended her satellite blockage to Scott. Why would she? It would raise international red flags.

Siri grabbed my hand. Her eyes were urgent. "But if we go, we have to take Ivan and go *now*. Before it gets cold again."

No time to type more. Sending this to you, Jane, in case I get this out and don't make it back. The CIA boys here will know I've sent this. I suspect they'll do whatever they can to prevent this coming to light. Publish as soon as you can.

Good luck to us both.

--mariana

[last entry]

Chapter Forty-Four

November 1.

Scott Base.

The Kiwi Station is deserted. Mariana doesn't hurry, but she doesn't linger, either. The fear of dying, particularly this far beyond the sanctuary of Crary, is bright and potent.

She has extracted two login IDs and passwords from the Scott refugees, and (*yes!*) the first one lets her log in to a networked computer. With trembling fingers, she pulls up a browser and types in the website of the *Chicago Tribune*.

The browser hesitates, starts to load, then freezes. Her heart collapses.

Then the screen lights up. *Taiwanese partisans claim bombing of Chinese garrison occupying Chiashan Air Force Base.* The day's international headline.

She's online!

Mariana has used the cramped, fear-filled days to gather dozens of first-person accounts of the horrors at McMurdo. She has interviewed survivors from Scott Base, meticulously documenting their sunlit night of horror, when over a hundred sentients had poured out of the ocean and decimated their crew. She has pictures of what can only be described as the Crary refugee camp; 200 people crammed together in a series of offices and labs; huddled in sleeping bags; lining up for food; living on top of one another.

Two snapshots, in particular, stand out.

The first, taken with her phone, but shockingly clear nonetheless: the cooks leaving the blue cafeteria building, huddled together, surrounded by men with guns. And in the corner of the frame, recoiling from a gunshot, a sentient, caught in the middle of springing toward them.

The second: Jackie Colson, gun in the snow next to her feet, stepping into her Hazmat suit right in the middle of Main Street, McMurdo.

The Station is under attack, and she has the exclusive, live from the scene.

But the interview with Siri is the direct proof her editor had asked her to find. Not just a deadly symbiotic and sentient pandemic ravaging Antarctic stations, but the fact of its source being an act of secret military aggression. Siri's quote on HAVE VIKING makes the redacted communique she'd received months ago publishable.

If she can get the news out.

Mariana logs into the backend of the *Tribune* server with her employee credentials. She has boiled it all into one zip file, ready to send. She plugs her USB drive into the computer and watches anxiously as the file uploads. She keeps her ears peeled for the rough but comforting cough of Ivan's engine; they've kept the bus engine running in case they have to leave abruptly.

As it uploads, Mariana hesitates.

There is a second zip file on the USB drive.

While waiting in Denver and Christchurch, Mariana had begun organizing recollections of her war coverage. She'd used it once already, to get her seat on the C-17.

In the file, she'd recounted personal conversations with General Rason, once the Supreme Commander of the Allied war effort against China. It included her knowledge of the political pressure from the White House to avoid war with Russia, even in the face of intelligence that Russia was actively assisting China. Plus, details of the impact on her career from reporting on Rason's refusal to cave to the White House, and the new avenues that had opened up once she'd found herself on the outside of the Pentagon looking in. There were also new whistleblower sources, who now trusted her to report on shady wartime acts within the military and intelligence communities.

One of those new sources had given her the Antarctic communique she was now sure had originated from Major Rajan Chariya.

Halfway through, however, her aggregation turned into a narrative of her struggles to stay alive and sane in Antarctica. Writing it had been oddly cathartic. She'd been typing right up to when Rajan and Siri had walked in.

Now her mouse hovers over that file. *In the Wake of War: A First-hand Account.* Normally, Mariana wouldn't dream of sending such a manuscript out before it had been edited and scrupulously referenced. But she is in a war zone, the population of the Station decreasing at every turn. It's enough to make anyone think about legacy, and Mariana has found herself writing hers.

Before she can think about it, she hits the upload button.

Just in case.

Right as the second file is done uploading, Siri pokes her head in. "Have you sent your stuff?" She sounds anxious. "I want to get back before it gets cold outside."

Mariana stands and smiles. A nervous witchy feeling of exhilaration sweeps through her. "I've sent everything I have back to Chicago."

"Let's hope it goes public, and the CIA is forced to help us."

They walk through the building, headed to the door closest to Ivan. Abruptly Siri stops; grabs Rajan's sleeve. "Do you hear that?" she says.

Mariana freezes. Her heart starts to pound.

"I don't hear anything." Rajan dips his head to one side and moves his jaw, clicking and unclicking it like there's water in his ear. "All I hear is this buzzing, I can barely–"

"It's getting louder." Her voice rises as if to match it.

Still shaking his head, Rajan reaches for the door, opens it, and stops short.

"Um," he says.

Mariana looks around him. There are dozens… no, *hundreds* of penguins. All waddling around each other, their flippers making soft swishing noises in the snow. Loosely circling the building and Ivan.

Blocking their way into Ivan.

Just then, Ivan's engine coughs, sputters, and dies.

* * *

"Man," Colson says, "they really stink, don't they?"

Marshal Anne wrinkles her nose and nods. She wraps herself up tighter in her jacket. The smell emanating thickly from the visiting penguins is like guano on the floor of a bat cave. A few waddle up onto the deck of the Chalet. When she looks up the snowy street, it's dotted with the black of penguins. One of them lies down in the middle of a street, rolling around in the snow like a pig trying to get dirty. Out on the ice, by the ocean, she can see hundreds of them, gathering, sunning just like them. Some of them are actively molting, like it's too hot for them.

Anne draws her feet up into her chair, away from them, a little nauseated by the growing smell of rotting fish. Colson seems less bothered. She kicks out lazily at one of them. "Go on," she says. "Get outta here."

The penguins waddle off, trickling away–

Then, abruptly, they turn.

They charge at Colson.

They are on her surprisingly quickly. Two of them launch themselves off the ground, trying to climb up her feet. Colson kicks out, her windpant leg rides up–

– and a third penguin leaps across the snow and sinks its sharp papillae into her leg.

Colson yells out in surprise and kicks out, and the penguin rakes its mouth backward. Blood spurts onto the snow.

Marshal Anne jerks away as a penguin takes a bite at her leg. It gets nothing but air and snaps angrily, opening its beak wide, revealing a mouth stuffed with bouquets of backward-curving spikes, on its tongue and the roof of its mouth.

It lets out a strange abrasive growl, like a dog barking.

There are two penguins on Colson's leg now. The penguin with its papillae sunk into the meat of her leg looks right back at her.

It is covered with patches of diseased-looking tarry feathers.

Its eyes are completely blue.

As she watches, noisome dark microbes spill out of its eyes and run up her leg. Into her wound.

"Fuck!" Jackie Colson screams. "Fuck!"

* * *

The heroic age of Antarctic expedition had left behind a surprising wealth of historic objects important to the discovery of the continent. Robert Scott's *Terra Nova* expedition, fated to end with the British explorer's death in 1912, had brought three Wolseley tractors with them, at the time the height of technology. One was lost to the sea ice four days after being unloaded from Scott's ship, and was just as abruptly rediscovered in 2021, submerged in McMurdo Sound. Battered and full of salty sea water, prolonged exposure to air would have sacrified the artifact to rusting, and so a desalination tank had been set up in an outhouse at the edge of Mac Station for its long-term treatment.

Antarctic conservator Dr. Ramon Garcia has been away from his tank for a long time. Immersed in checking the temperamental salinity levels of the water, it takes him a while to register that what he smells is different from the usual salty metallic tang in the outhouse.

He hears a squawk, and looks down to see a small penguin looking up at him. It bleeps in a friendly way.

"Why hello, little guy." A smile comes to Ramon's creased face. "What brings you in here? Too cold out there for you?"

It extends its flippers and waddles closer. It gives another little squawk, this one more of a bark.

That's when he notices that the outhouse is full of penguins.

Pouring in through the open door.

The back door to the Crary lab pushes open. Bethany Hamidani stands to the side, then holds the door. Past her, one penguin enters.

Then ten.

Then a stream of hundreds.

Chapter Forty-Five

McMurdo runs on the same time zone as Christchurch, which means it's just after 1:00 PM on November 1 when Mariana Egan uploads her files to the *Tribune*. That's 6:00 PM on October 31 in Chicago. Jane Bradshaw's national security editor, Penelope Fung, bursts into her office less than half an hour later.

"You've got to see what Mariana just sent us."

"Mariana?" Bradshaw blinks for a moment.

Penelope nods emphatically, tangled brown bangs bouncing around her face. "I think it's front-page stuff."

As soon as Bradshaw sees the picture of the person getting shot while running at a group of scared-looking Antarcticans, she calls her husband and tells him she won't make it home for trick-or-treating with their daughter. She stands up on the nearest table and claps.

The newsroom comes to a halt, looking at her.

"Everyone, listen up. If you're not working a feature, get in the conference room."

Mariana has been admirably thorough. In addition to a summary feature, the veteran reporter has written up a series of stories, heightened by a wealth of pictures. Audio files of her interviews create enough visceral human-interest material for a whole podcast series. It's a story too big to be told in a single front page, and they have the exclusive.

Bradshaw and her staff work furiously to pin down the arc of storytelling. By 8:00 PM, they have narrowed in on the next day's headline and initial copy. This will be the story they can unambiguously report on, courtesy of their reporter on the scene: there is an active biological threat at McMurdo Station, and it has spread from South Pole Station. There are over two hundred deaths on a continent that has never seen a single murder to date, and humans are going crazy on each other at that very moment. To fully report on the sentients living in the ice will take commentary from expert biologists, and Bradshaw briskly assigns teams to begin chasing down leads for the next day's headline.

The biggest story, however, will be the allegation that the United States might have had something to do with the origin of this threat.

"We need to think about how to tread," Penelope Fung cautions. "That accusation could have wartime implications."

The conference room falls silent. Mariana herself had written: "There's a thin line between using the First Amendment to expose government malfeasance, and publishing secrets that benefit the enemy. During a time of war, that thin line gets so bony it can almost disappear."

Bradshaw steps back, chewing on the stem of her glasses. *If any of the South Pole survivors don't make it back to the mainland, the CIA is where people should start asking questions.* That's the quote from Siri. Together with the redacted communique, both of which reference `HAVE VIKING`, it's a bomb waiting to drop.

The hell with it, she thinks. She is not willing to ignore what Siri's quote implies.

Not while she has a reporter in harm's way.

She looks at the clock. It's 9:00 PM in Langley.

"Fowler, start emailing any DoD agency press officer we've had contact with in the last two years," Bradshaw says. "Otto, same thing with CIA. Kim, you take the Defense Intelligence Agency and the National Reconnaissance Office. Let's mention this program name, `HAVE VIKING`, say we're going to press in the morning, and see who calls us back."

Chapter Forty-Six

November 1, 4:00 PM local time

McMurdo Station

The sound of a scream pierces the fourth floor of Crary.

Mason opens a bleary eye.

He's lying in his sleeping bag in a corner spot. He's tired, down to his bones, and he's decided to catch up on sleep rather than spend time in the sun. There's an atonal ringing in his ears. If it's more drama, he'll just–

Another scream, and Mason shoots upright. In time to see a sight he'll never forget.

Through the open doors stream a wall of penguins, so many that they are stacked back to front. They diffuse into the room like a speckled white-and-black flood, and suddenly the room is filled with their hoarse cries, like dogs barking. Four of them belly-flop onto Mackie, who is lying on the floor near the door. Mason sees a flash of beak, then Mackie is hit in the face by freezing water from multiple angles.

Mason struggles to his feet, legs still trapped, and his pistol falls to his feet inside his sleeping bag. He is about to bend and grab it when a penguin lunges at him, opening its beak wide.

The penguin is joined by a second, a fifth, a tenth. Their combined weight pushes his back against the wall. He yells aloud, briefly panicked, but they are only snapping at his sleeping bag. Little fibers fly off, exposing the inner lining.

Behind them, another row of penguins stare at him.

Hungrily.

He watches their eyes flush with blue, like a spinning toilet bowl.

The room around him is pure chaos. People scramble away from the biting birds. A row of penguins stacks itself, like a series of malevolent dominoes, in the way of Barham as he tries to vault over them. His arms flail, and down he goes in their midst.

Dr. Mason sees blood spurt into the air, and the croak of water splashing. He screams again inside his mind.

(*siri rajan WHERE ARE YOU*)

The penguins push against Mason, hoarsely barking as if they can hear his mental cries. Freezing water dashes against the bag. His shoulders slalom off and on the wall. He's wedged into the corner.

The penguins rush at him. There's too many of them. A strange feeling of disbelief slips over Mason, like a comforting blanket. He's being attacked by penguins. It's too unreal to be anything but a dream. If he just closes his eyes, maybe it will all go away…

That's when he becomes aware of the mental buzz of all of them. It itches like a cloud of gnats vibrating between his ears. Like a dog muttering to itself in its sleep – but hundreds of dogs.

No, thousands.

His toe knocks into his pistol, uselessly buried down in the sleeping bag.

He pushes forward before he can think about it, levering his hips, kicking his legs out like he's trying to jump his knees into his own chin. The four penguins at his feet, each of them weighing no more than ten pounds, are skittered aside like bowling pins. He feels a flash of hysteria at how ridiculous this would be if it might not end with his death.

He almost slips, but manages to hold his balance inside the sleeping bag as he slumps back against the wall. The penguins come for him immediately and he times his response; uses the wall to push off and lashes his legs out. This time his booted feet, inside the sleeping bag, smash through a penguin's skull.

The growling in his head spikes to a short shriek.

The penguins hesitate. One of them vomits water at him but it trickles against his knees.

Mason grunts harshly. He clutches the lip of the bag at his chest, and like it's a gunny sack race, takes a hop-step forward. He feels briefly ridiculous, but then bones crunch under his feet. He lashes his feet out again.

This time the penguins shrink backward–

And it's just enough time. Mason takes a big hop backward, shoulders thumping into the wall, and drops to his knees, plunging his arm into the depths of the bag.

The penguins shriek and rush forward–

Mason stands up and fires into the penguin horde. Feathers shoot violently across the room. He pushes into the gap, keeping a shoulder along the wall, ignoring their snapping beaks. Fires again, then lunges for the door handle. He almost falls into the hallway as he pulls the door shut behind him.

He stays in his sleeping bag, bunny-hopping his way to the end of the hallway, then the roof.

Chapter Forty-Seven

October 31, 10:30 PM, Eastern Standard Time

Langley, Virginia

There's always a fire about to burn down a Central Intelligence Agency operation somewhere in the world, but Pamela Marshall has developed a finely tuned sense for the type of fuck-up news her boss will want to know about immediately. As in, *right fucking now.*

When she gets a red phone call from a Directorate of Operations Program Security Officer, and hears that the *Chicago Tribune* plans to publish an intercepted communique that bears the name of `HAVE VIKING`, she knows she'll have to interrupt Bill's schedule.

She dials the `HAVE VIKING` operations center. "When is the next satellite pass over McMurdo Station?"

"Forty minutes, ma'am."

"Okay. Tell the crew to expect Bill."

She can almost hear the voice on the other end of the line tighten. "Yes, ma'am."

Pamela badges herself into Evil Bill's office. The CIA Deputy Director for Operations is on a secure teleconference with the Chief of Station for Chinese-occupied Taiwan, and looks around. Annoyance flickers on Bill's face, but only for a moment. He mutes his call.

Pamela hands him a printed copy of the email from the *Tribune*. "They plan to publish online at midnight. The press officer asked for details, and these pictures were in the response."

Evil Bill sucks air in through his teeth. In the first picture, an infected human lunges at men he recognizes, right as it catches a bullet. The second picture is his cleanup lead, Jackie Colson, standing in the center of a snowy street, a gun beside her, stepping into a Hazmat suit.

He feels a stab of annoyance mixed with regret. Like Bill himself, Jackie Colson has a unique story. Bill had once been a Colonel, an elite pararescue specialist with Air Force Special Operations. But he had been the war-scarred veteran at a time when the administration had wanted to pretend it wasn't at war anymore, and so he hadn't been promoted to General. The CIA, with its unique nose for talent, had found him and renewed his purpose. Bill considered it something of a sacred duty to do the same. To look for the hidden talent and snatch it up before it was wasted.

Jackie Colson had completed the Navy's 37-week SWCC course, the first woman to ever graduate, and yet, she hadn't received a contract from an operational unit. She'd stuck it out, fought to get to DEVGRU, but there again, she'd encountered a glass ceiling. Bill had several uses for a trained operator who could slip into places a bearded man couldn't, and fight her way out. He'd pulled Jackie Colson into the shadows, where she'd excelled. She'd been a natural pick to lead the response team to McMurdo. But if this picture made it to a newspaper, her face would be known, painted, and therefore, of no more use to the covert operator community.

"The *Tribune* also sent this." Pamela shows him the redacted communique. "They say their reporter has a source who can validate it."

Now Bill is breathing heavily through both his nostrils. But he doesn't respond immediately. He is a chess player, above all else.

At last, he gives the documents back to her. "We'll give them a formal response, but not if they print tonight," he grates. "Tell them the Agency needs to determine if it's willing to be quoted or go on background, and the right people to make that decision won't be around until tomorrow morning. Let me know if they don't bite."

"I imagine they will." Pamela sounds calm.

"When is our next satellite or airplane overflight of McMurdo? I need to know what the hell is going on down there."

Pamela tries not to smile. "Next satellite pass is in thirty-four minutes."

Bill nods. A little curtly, perhaps because he has detected a touch of smugness in her response, but he won't hold it against her. He values competence, above all else.

"Has Navarro left for the day?"

Pamela always knows the CIA director's schedule. "He's at the British embassy tonight."

Evil Bill grimaces. The lines around his mouth drawn and tight. "America goes to the polls to vote for its next President in *four days,* Pam. It's not the time for this shit."

"No, sir."

"I want to be sure about one thing. We haven't told Navarro, or any of his staff, that we developed `HAVE VIKING` for use against Russia, right?"

"None of the politicals know," Pamela says steadily. "Given the administration's close ties to Russia, it seemed prudent to leave that out."

"Let's keep it that way. Get me a car to head to the embassy right after the satellite pass. We might need an emergency audience with the President."

"Yes, sir."

"*Fuck.*"

"Yes, sir."

Chapter Forty-Eight

November 1, 7:30 PM, New Zealand Standard Time

The sun is low on the horizon, hidden behind cirrus clouds that cast the ice into shadow. Atop Crary Lab, Dr. Mason can feel the cold thickening in the air. He hears a low growl in his head–

(*krrrrgrrr*)

– and walks to the edge of the roof beside Lansdown. He draws his pistol. The two men look down.

The slushy roads beneath him are thick with penguins, their honking and barking and stink filling the air. Thousands of them. More penguins that he ever knew could exist in one place. Penguins waddle up and down handicap-accessible ramps from every building he can see. The snow is flecked black with their molted feathers.

Abruptly, the penguins beneath him part like the Red Sea, and a sentient dashes from the building, headed for cover across the slushy street.

Dr. Mason aims and fires.

The sentient half-spins around, but keeps going, bent over in half. Mason's second bullet thumps into the man's neck. He skids to his knees in the snow, scattering penguins. They wash over and around him.

Mason looks at Lansdown and both men abruptly release disbelieving laughs. They'd grown up with *Pingu,* nature documentaries like *March of the Penguins,* visits to the zoo to see penguins waddle around on fake ice. Like most people, they'd shared the perception of penguins being overwhelmingly cute. Lovably awkward. Even dorky.

Except penguins are really tough marine predators. Well-adapted to one of the harshest climates on Earth. They hunt for fish and consume them by the millions.

They are the top of the evolutionary pyramid in this environment.

The penguins have a new source of food now.

Mason and Lansdown and every other resident of Mactown are the prey.

Mason's lips thin to no more than a scar beneath his nose. Against a finite number of human-sentients, it would have been a grim sniper-fight of attrition, but one they could have won.

There simply aren't enough bullets to push thousands of penguin-sentients out.

They have lost the Station.

Behind him, the trapdoor thumps. The iron bar wedged into it doesn't yield. They are safe, up here. But it also means they can't get off this roof.

Dr. Mason straightens, looking into the sun. A voice echoes in his head–

(*one then two then three NOW ALL)*

– and is then gone. It leaves behind a sound, as if the rasp of the ocean is a low growling.

Dr. Mason feels the first stab of hunger.

In the Chalet, Marshal Anne rocks back and forth on her heels gently. She has her pistol out, held between her legs.

In front of her, Colson is stretched out on the sofa in Winston's office. Her face is pale; too pale. Her leg is elevated, and Anne can see the nasty bite mark in the flesh of her calves. Blue lines like nerves radiate outward from the wound. They have moved up her leg, and there's the start of lines pulsing under the skin of her neck. No longer whispering but shouting of infection; the promise of icy vengeance.

"It's cold. I'm so cold," Colson mutters. Her jaw is shaking so hard her words come out in a trembling rush. Her eyes turn to Marshal Anne, filled with a deep fear.

Not of death.

Of something worse.

"I can feel myself being erased," she whispers.

Anne can smell her: sour eggs, baked into her skin like it's a dusty and spoiling oven. "Dr. Kim can sweat this out of you," the Marshal whispers.

"Except the lab and Crary are gone," Colson says.

"Sal is working on a way to get us over to Crary. We're going to retake that building and get Kim's formula. Just hang in there."

Colson closes her eyes in response, as if tired by the prospect of hope itself.

"The first time I killed someone, I understood my life would also end in violence." Her voice is a knowing sigh. "But fuck me... death by flightless bird isn't nearly as fiery an end as I hoped for."

Marshal Anne doesn't dare leave her, but she needs to check on Sal's progress. She leans forward and brushes Colson's jacket aside, reaching for her radio.

Colson's hand shoots across her, squeezing Marshal Anne's arm so hard it feels like she's trying to snap it in two.

Her eyes stare at Marshal Anne, an unyielding blue.

Anne has no time to think. Her gun pops up and she shoots Colson in the chest.

The bullet thumps through Colson, through the sofa, into the wooden floor beneath her. She sags, frothy blood beginning to pump out through a hole in her chest.

"Oh fuck oh *fuck* –" Marshal Anne says in a trembling rush.

"Good girl." Colson's strained whisper grinds through her like the half-stripped transmission of an old truck. Her eyes meet Anne's.

"Now finish it."

Anne brings her gun up. Her arm trembles, as though every muscle in it has been turned inside-out. Colson puts a half-smile on her face.

Marshal Anne closes her eyes and fires into Colson's chest again.

The room falls still around the echoing gunshot.

She stands, slowly, like a puppet cut loose from its strings.

She looks down at Colson, who had known what was happening to her. Had taken the soldier's way out. She remembers Jonah's words to her: *keep one bullet for yourself.*

She lifts Colson's radio. "This is Marshal Anne," she says into it. "Anyone out there?"

"Lansdown is here, with Dr. Mason," comes a reply.

"How's Crary?" she asks.

"Gone," Lansdown replies flatly. "Where's Colson?"

She sucks in a breath. "Colson is dead. I'm sorry."

There's silence on the frequency as they all absorb that. Tight shudders wrack Marshal Anne, each one tugging darts of pain out of her mind. She tenses like a spring as she resists the tears that come with those darts.

Sal comes on the radio, and his next words surprise her. "What's the plan, Chief?"

She's in charge now – there's no one else. She lowers the radio, trying to think. There has to be a way out. There has to be.

And then, to her shock, another voice comes on the radio.

"Hello, Marshal," it hisses, seeping into the eldritch light of the room.

This voice is rasping, clotted, like each syllable is forced through some viscous liquid.

"We'll be waiting for you," Ben Jacobs says.

Chapter Forty-Nine

November 1, 1:00 AM, Eastern Standard Time (8:00 PM New Zealand Standard Time)

The President of the United States is furious.

"You did what?" he roars. "And why the fuck?"

Evil Bill doesn't flinch. Beside him, neither does CIA Director Oliver Navarro.

They are seated in the Oval Office. The President is in a polo shirt and loose pants that do not hide his bulk. He paces up and down in front of the Resolute Desk, hands scarred from constant medical treatments clamped to his hips. He has just been briefed on `HAVE VIKING`, and the goals of the program. They've walked him through the Senate Intelligence Committee approvals, and the goals of airdropping a DARPA-modified microbe onto the Chinese Antarctic Station at Dome-A, in the hope of finding a mutation path toward tolerance for warmer temperatures. Bill doesn't connect those warmer temperatures to Russia. He focuses on China at every opportunity he can, even as he winds past the American deaths at South Pole, and the sentient takeover of Mac Station and Scott Base.

The President stops pacing. "Why wasn't I briefed on any of this?"

Director Navarro's voice is calm water over cool stones. "Sir, there was honestly no need to trouble you with what was at the time a very minor experimental operation."

The President looks mollified at this. Then his face scrunches up tightly again, perhaps remembering the next morning's headline. Three days before Election Day, this news could upend the election.

"Mr. President, there's still room to pivot," Navarro says quickly. "We have timestamped satellite imagery of the Chinese traverse that went from Dome-A to South Pole Station six months ago. If we give it to the *Tribune* for their story, we can lay blame for all the deaths on the Chinese. That would lessen the credibility of any rumors that the CIA was at fault."

The President narrows his eyes. "And does that provide us cover to clean this mess up?"

Director Navarro hesitates, unwilling to say the words out loud. Always a politician.

"A full clean-up of McMurdo is not a bad idea, Mr. President," Evil Bill speaks up. "If we call the Station a loss, and bomb it out of existence, we contain the infection to Antarctica, and leave no proof left for anyone to find."

Perhaps another President would have asked how many Americans could be killed, but not this one. Deaths at a small station in Antarctica is only on his radar so much as the press reports may sway undecided voters before they go to the polls. November 4, 2028 will bring an unprecedented election in more ways than one. This President is a wartime President, standing for election a fourth time, for a third term; backed by a Supreme Court and weak Congress that owe him allegiance.

But the scales of power are still sensitive. Victory is not a done deal.

The wrong story at the right time can have unpredictable effects.

"How do we expect the Russians to respond?" the President asks.

Before Evil Bill can reply that the Russian response has nothing to do with anything, Navarro steps back in, smoothly. "Both the Russians and the Chinese have a presence on the Antarctic continent, but far away from McMurdo. However, you raise an excellent point about other countries, sir. An inspired idea. If we brief the New Zealand government on their situation at Scott Base, and pressure them to approve us bombing *their* base too, then our action can be spun as a multilateral medical response, not military activity in violation of the Antarctic Treaty. We can have our friendly news outlets spin it so we look like the good guys who saved the day."

Most of this President's cabinet were picked not for their policy expertise or deep resume, but their expertise in appearing on news shows. They know how to spin a story.

"Go do it. Don't fuck it up." The President stifles a yawn. "I'm heading back to bed."

Both men stand. "Goodnight, Mr. President."

Once the President walks out, Navarro looks at Bill and puffs up his face. "That went about as well as it could have. What's next?"

"You call the Australian Minister of Defence," Bill says at once. "We'll need her support for the bombing operation. First thing tomorrow, we need to cue up a conversation between the President and the Kiwi Prime Minister about Scott Base."

"Done. How long can you stiff the *Tribune* for?"

"Tomorrow, I'll give them the imagery of the Chinese headed to South Pole, and talk them through our cover story. They'll delay press by at least another day to get us on record. By the time the story goes live, McMurdo Station and these sentients will be gone once and for all."

Navarro nods. "And what about the reporter down there who started all of this?"

"Mac Station is overrun," Evil Bill says, eyes blank. "I don't expect anyone except our people to make it."

Chapter Fifty

November 2.

South Pole Station is quiet.

Nothing moves in the pale winter daylight.

The wind occasionally blows hard enough to fan the tarp and plastic layered over the fire-warped Destination Alpha entrance. Ice in the tunnels occasionally drips, then catches and freezes, adding to large stalactites drawing down from the ceilings. The hallways are an empty tomb, despite the twenty-four-hour sun outside.

Keyon Geerts moves like a shadow through the Station, barely heard, all alone.

The silence allows him to contemplate a life driven by something other than the desire to be a farmer of pain; sowing the hurt that he has lived with all his life into others.

Time has grown soft and strange in the silence. Keyon reads his Bible, walks the cold halls in his Big Red and thinks about the emptiness hovering at the center of him. Wondering what, if not pulling strings, his life *would* be about.

There are tough realizations waiting to spear him behind that question. Not just his suppressed childhood pain, but wrestling with how natural that pain has made it for him to wound others. So many others. At first, the guilt is towering and extreme. Insurmountable.

The words in the Bible help soothe that twisting lance. Allow him to contemplate, if not give himself, forgiveness.

But first, he has to bolt the hard stripe voice down into a jailed corner of his mind from where it can never again run his decisions for him.

If Katie's death left him with one thing, by God, it would be that.

Repent, then, and turn to God. So that times of refreshing may come from the Lord. Keyon wakes up on the second morning in November with that line from the Book of Acts in his head, and so it seems like fate when he goes to the rooftop of the Station with his morning coffee and sees smoke on the horizon. His sharp eyes pick out four dots on the white horizon, preceded by long columns of blown exhaust smoke.

I have repented, and behold, my salvation is at hand, he thinks, and with a rush of joy, Keyon realizes that he's ready to leave.

He's ready to move on and imprint new meaning to his life.

He reaches out with his mind.

(*siri? rajan?*)

No response.

(*are you there?*)

Keyon goes back inside, and finds binoculars in the Science Lab. He stands at the lab's tall windows and looks toward the incoming traverse.

That's when he realizes that the markings on the side do not read *National Science Foundation*. In fact, he can't read them at all.

The markings are Chinese.

Jiuyin Mei, brother of Lingling Mei, has arrived at South Pole.

Chapter Fifty-One

6:00 AM New Zealand Standard Time

Dr. Mason awakes on the roof of Crary, after the coldest night he can remember.

Even with his Big Red on, huddled against Lansdown for warmth, the unrelenting sunlight, the cold, and the squawking of thousands of penguins mean he has slept in only stolen snatches. This morning, his stomach is decidedly growling.

He gathers himself to his feet like an old rubber band stretched one too many times. Pale yellow clouds streak the clear sky like banners. Together with Lansdown, they look out over McMurdo Station with haunted eyes. The penguins have clustered in two groups around Crary and the Chalet, in rows of black and white like concert ticket-holders.

Shuffling restlessly. Waiting.

Lansdown's face is stone. He points.

Atop Ob Hill, just out of rifle range and silhouetted against the horizon, stands a lone figure. Mason can't see a face, but he knows exactly who it is.

Ben Jacobs speaks into his mind.

(*come to us now*)

(*Resisssst us and you will DIIIIIIIIIIIIE*)

Chapter Fifty-Two

November 2.

Bethany Hamidani surveys Crary with what can only be described as terrified ennui.

Every floor of Crary is filled with penguins, but they flow around her like they don't even see her. Her numb feet glide between dozens of empty sleeping bags covered in penguin shit. The nearly two-hundred people who had once found refuge here are all gone. Spirited away to the water to become sentients, or held as prisoners for Ben to pour the grey-generation into. A fate worse than death.

A fate that is now hers, she knows.

Behind her, a step. A rustle of feathers as the penguins scuttle and flatfoot out of the way of someone approaching.

Someone that smells like rot and decay and watery death; a smell that dominates the fishy stink of the penguins.

The penguins turn and face her as one. They fall silent and still.

She feels a drop of cold water on her neck.

"Beth*anyyyyyyyyy*," a voice whispers. Right into her ear. A low deep rattle, like a viper drawing its fangs back. Inflating lungs that don't breathe anymore.

Her heartbeat spikes. Her lips tighten and disappear into her bloodless face.

The penguins shuffle closer, tightening the circle.

"Fa*ccccccccccce* me," the voice commands her.

She forces her knees to bend, her lead legs to move. She half-turns to face her former lover.

Penny's eyes are the first thing she notices. They are watery, flooded with the brightest pellucid blue. Emotion or mercy own no real-estate in those eyes. His shirtless chest and stomach are stained with purpling bruises. Melting ice flecks coat his body; his hair is frozen down onto his forehead. His mouth is hitched up, revealing unnaturally white teeth beneath. His skin is slowly rotting on his bones; he is dead, a dead man walking, unnaturally still when he isn't talking, because he doesn't breathe.

She hears him, though.

Some strain within her, buried deep, hears Penny on a frequency she doesn't understand.

Some part of her would welcome him if he devoured her.

When the sentients had begun to surge out of the icy ocean, and as she had huddled in Crary with the other terrified survivors, she had felt the thin strain of the grey-generation inside her come alive. The catalyst of marijuana-borne THC, held only within her hair follicles, creating a whisper only she could hear. She hates Penny, hates him fiercely for what he has infected her with, but she's also afraid of him, because she doesn't know how deep the strain has penetrated her.

Whether she's herself only because he is allowing it to be so.

"You've done we*lllllll*," Penny rattles. A long tear drips out of his nose. His edges seem to blur with water. It bubbles under his skin, in the corner of his eyes, seeps out of his ears. The surfer boy is now a man of the waves.

She tries to be nonchalant in her shrug. Like she hadn't resisted the voice in her head.

Like the microbes inside her hadn't then *hurt* her. Punished her.

Now Penny's finger points, in slow motion, like a balloon falling toward the floor. Noise explodes into her head. Blood wells in her nose and scratches in her throat. Her skin crawls.

She understands what he wants.

(*one of us*)

The words rasp out of his throat. "One of *ussssssss*." Then: "Go."

Sometimes you have to let what's coming come, and take your beatings, Colson had said.

One of them–

(*us*)

– is downstairs, and once more, she is to let them in.

Bethany walks stiffly down the stairs to the third floor. Outside, the streets of McMurdo are flooded with penguins, all of them following orders. She's no more than a penguin, following orders.

The realization comes to her in a sure, hot flood.

I should kill myself. Before it gets worse. While I'm still myself.

She looks over her shoulder, up at the fourth-floor hallway. There is a window at the end. Her scalp feels like it's tightening down on her skull.

She could run at it, hurl herself through it and down to the ice below.

Hope to snap her neck on landing.

Bethany shudders. To end up half-alive, and infected, would be a fate worse than death. Hope is not a strategy. She has to be sure.

She walks slowly down to the third-floor. The penguins part in front of a door on the right. She sidles up the hallway, flattening her shoulders against the wall, then peeks through the window set in the door.

In a back room, Dr. Jonny Kim and another person stand with backs turned to her. Some recognition of that other person sparks in her tired mind, but she refuses to pursue it. Knowing who the person is will be just another thing in a long line of things to feel guilty about, once she is the last woman standing in a station full of sentients.

A survivor, she thinks dully. *You've always been a survivor.*

Dr. Kim is bent over a lab table. All she can see is bare feet, but somehow, she *knows* those feet belong to Gisela Childers. A sea sentient, longing to return to the water, but trapped away from it and withering into a husk.

(*i hate you Penny*)

And suddenly, in her head, the words clear as a bell:

(*i always liked you bethany don't make me hurt you*)

Her lip trembles. There's no getting out, when she can't even be safe inside her own head.

She reaches her hand out, and touches the door handle.

It's locked.

She raises her Judas fist, and knocks on the door. Asking to be let in.

Chapter Fifty-Three

In the Chalet, Sal steps back, and tosses the roll of duct tape aside. "Can you move?"

Marshal Anne takes a lurching step forward. Around her stomach and thighs and calves, thick bulky cushions from the sofa chairs upstairs are duct-taped around her; hiding her skin. She can move, but like the marshmallow woman. She nods.

She pulls her ski mask up, careful to tuck it into her collar in case she gets vomited on.

It's time to try and retake their old fortress of Crary and consolidate forces with anyone else left alive in there. But that means facing an enemy that knows they are coming.

Beside her, Winston looks grey with fear. Like her, his lower half is also wrapped up with duct-taped cushions. "If you want to stay here, Winny, you should," she says.

He shakes his head. From behind his mask, he says, "I think it's safer if I'm with you two."

Marshal Anne looks between Sal and Winston.

"All right, then. Whoever is in front has the count. We only step, and step together, when that person calls. Those fucking penguins are just upright birds. If we stick together, we can punch a hole through them."

"And if someone goes down?" Sal's voice is toneless.

Marshal Anne's pistol is strapped in a holster around her chest, and she taps it. "They get two in the head and one in the chest," she says. "Just like we learned in school."

"Let's get this fucking done." Sal reaches for the door. "On my count."

Anne hefts a tall staff in her hand, ripped from the wooden paneling of the chalet and strapped together with duct tape. Winston does the same. The two of them stand at slightly more than right angles to Sal, forming an awkward cushion-encased triangle.

Her adrenalin spikes.

Sal throws open the door.

She smells them before she sees them. The penguins have been waiting. They are set upon immediately, rocked backward by the mass of bobbing birds squawking and barking loudly, papillae flashing.

"Ready to step!" Sal roars. "Step!"

He pushes forward into the biting, snapping, clawing mass. Winston and Anne move with him. A block of penguins are broom-shoved out of the way.

"Step!"

Marshal Anne pushes against Sal, who pushes forward, and they are suddenly outside, on the deck of the Chalet, in the latent sun.

Anne stares at the penguins. The contrast between the fuzzy benevolence with which she'd previously considered them, and their current situation, strikes her like a thunderbolt. After all she has done and seen with law enforcement and the Marshals, these tiny flightless birds, standing three feet tall, might be the ones to end her life.

Sal calls a step. They push again. The penguins are piling up against each other, sharp papillae jabbing into the cushions. Bursts and flashes of freezing water dash against her waist, her boots. She's suddenly terrified by how many microbes are all over her clothes. But they aren't on her skin, and so she keeps stepping to Sal's count.

Down the stairs. They are in the street. She sees waving arms on top of Crary. "Just keep coming," Mason shouts into his radio. "Don't stop!"

They push forward. The penguins squawk, furiously, spilling against each other in a frenzy. The noise is overwhelming. It's like walking through molasses. "Step!"

Beside her, she can feel Winston hesitating. Flagging in strength. Cords of strain stand out on his neck.

"Keep it with me, Winny!" she screams. "This is not how you're ending this season!"

"Aye aye, Marshal," he grunts. His staff swings, knocking a penguin off its clawed feet.

"Step!" Sal grunts. She hears the tiredness in his voice.

"Let's pivot, Sal. I've got the lead."

They rotate, so that Marshal Anne is facing forward, the cushions around her lower body their leading shield. They are halfway to Crary, but the penguin mass in front of her is manic. "Step!" she screams hoarsely.

She keeps her staff swinging – back and forth, back and forth. Every inch forward is a struggle. She looks out and all she can see are more penguins. Crary is far away – perhaps too far. Her arms are toast. Her legs are rubber.

A penguin falls down in front of her. She steps into it, its skull crunching under her boot.

Another penguin falls down. The penguin behind it drops, then a third on top of the other two, crushing them. It creates a small ramp – and a fourth penguin races up it, flippers waving wildly. Its beak opens, it launches, and hurls a blast of microbe-laden water right at her.

She screams, involuntarily. The water hits her in the chest, but droplets spatter against her flimsy faceshield and ski-mask. Her boots knock against the three penguins prone in the snow in front of her. A calf-high obstacle.

"Pivot right!" she screams, pumped up on the wine of adrenalin. "Go around!"

They step together. There's so much mass bobbing and heaving against them. Beaks snap constantly at their cushioned knees and calves. The smell is eye-watering.

Then Anne looks up toward Crary.

"Hold!" she calls.

In front of her is an unbelievable sight.

The penguins are falling down on top of each other. Stacking up like dominoes fallen against a wall. No – creating a wall. Crushing and suffocating each other. The blue-shot eyes of the penguins on the bottom are oozing microbes, bugging out as they are crushed under the weight rapidly accumulating above them.

Closer to Crary, the penguin ramps grow almost chest-high. Hundreds of piled-up birds, stacking like bricks with low thudding sounds that have a liquid quality to them. One emperor penguin stands atop each pile, like a sullen sentinel.

Waiting.

"Shit, Anne," Winston pants. "They're killing each other to stop us."

In front of them, a ramp of penguins starts to grow. High enough to blast them in the face repeatedly. High enough to knock her onto her back. Fear bunches like an overloaded circuit breaker in her solar plexus, spreading with terrifying speed to the rest of her body. Anne pulls her gun out, and Sal does the same. Her face is streaming with sweat.

"It was a good plan, Marshal," Sal says.

A burble of absurdist, shocked laughter escapes Anne. *Of all the ways to go out…*

Then, suddenly, the squawk of the birds is drowned out by a long, sustained airhorn blast.

Anne's head snaps over her shoulder. A headlight blazes around the corner of the snow road from Ice Pier.

It's Ivan the Terra Bus.

The big red bus is nearly twenty feet tall. It zigzags forward, crushing penguins effortlessly beneath its massive snow tires. It bears down toward them, engine roaring, and its horn is the most beautiful sound Marshal Anne has ever heard.

Ivan sweeps by them and blows through the first wall of penguins without even slowing, leaving a massive arc of blood and feathers behind it in the snow. Penguin skulls squash and implode under the wheels like chestnuts bursting in a hot fire.

Then comes the angry scream of airbrakes, and the chuff of deep-tread tires digging in for grip on loose ice. Ivan comes to a stop, and Mariana and Rajan lean out of the window.

"Get on the bus!" Rajan shouts.

"Fuck yeah!" Anne screams deliriously. "Let's go, boys! To Crary!"

Crary is filled with penguins, biting and snapping at them. But in the narrow hallway, they can stand three abreast in an armored line. Anne, Winston and Sal protect Mariana and Rajan behind them and advance, step by step, like Roman legionaries behind the shields of their sofa cushions, swinging their staffs for blood. Penguins spill away from them, flowing into other pods or out of the building. As they advance, they close and lock doors propped open, shutting them out.

Outside, under Siri's control, Ivan roars around the building in huge circles, horn vengefully blaring. Mowing down any sentient, bird or human, in its path.

On the third floor, only sleeping bags are left behind in a long library room that had once held over forty people. Sal shines his flashlight in through glass windows set in doors, looking for survivors. Behind one door, something shifts in the shadows.

"Guns up," he says sharply.

He kicks open the door and steps back.

Nothing moves–

Then a woman emerges. Every step a disjointed lurch. She looks emaciated, the bones on her face poking through. Her hair has almost completely fallen out. But her eyes are as blue as the sea. She smells of salt and sour sweat.

Her head cocks to the side, then her chin drops toward her chest–

Sal shoots her in the head. Gisela Childers falls down amongst the retreating penguins.

They push into Kim's lab. Winston closes the door behind them and sags against it, breathing hard. A series of hypodermic needles and IV bags lie on their side on the floor, spilt. Restraints on the patient table in the back lie open.

In the corner lies a man in a Hazmat suit. The plexiglass on the faceshield is caved inward, smashed by blunt force, and the face inside is a bloody pulp. Dr. Kim has a hypodermic needle sticking out of his eye, a grisly *coup de gras*. Gisela had gotten free and gotten her revenge, somehow.

"Not a pleasant way to die," Marshal Anne says, and shudders.

"That's what you get when you play God." From behind her, Rajan speaks through his teeth. There's diamond-edged disdain in every line on his drawn face.

Mariana just looks ill. *They've had a fight of their own to get back here,* Marshal Anne thinks. The reporter is starting to slip into shock.

The Marshal advances around the corner of the lab table, and stops short.

In the corner, slumped on the floor, is another woman.

Bethany Hamidani.

A hypodermic needle protrudes from her belly. The plunger all the way down.

Bethany is alive but unconscious, narrow chest fluttering up and down, breathing shallowly and rapidly. Her skin is flushed, reddened despite her brown skin. Anne bends closer to her, cautiously, and can feel heat radiating from her.

"If she's alive, Marshal, we should–" Rajan starts.

Anne throws up a hand, then covers her lips with one finger. *Shhh.*

They wait, in the deathly silence. Anne's eyes flick between Dr. Kim's smashed faceshield, the empty restraints, and the needle stabbed into Bethany. Who is breathing like she has a heavy fever.

Then they hear it. A thump, then a second.

Sal snaps his gun up, pointing it at a tall cabinet in the corner, as its handle starts to turn.

"Take the others outside, Marshal." His voice is all ice. "Quickly."

Anne puts herself in front of Winston, her gun pointed, and they back up.

The cabinet thumps again. "I'm a friendly," a muffled voice says from inside. "I'm not infected."

Sal cocks his gun.

"Wait. The sentients don't talk," Marshal Anne says.

She steps back into the room.

"Who's in there?" she shouts.

"Hello, Marshal," Jonah Mitchell says from inside the cabinet. "It's good to hear your voice."

Chapter Fifty-Four

November 2.

Ivan the Terra Bus sits in the center of Mac Station, engine on, internal heat blasting as hard as it can go. It's just before nine in the evening. The bus is surrounded by penguins who squawk, shit and occasionally throw themselves against the tires with barely-suppressed fury.

Sal crouches with Lansdown and Dr. Mason; the three of them are all that's left of the CIA crew. Marshal Anne, Winston and Mariana huddle beside them. Behind there are three of the four remaining South Pole survivors – Siri, Rajan and Jonah.

After a short argument between Rajan and Siri, they've decided to leave the unconscious, feverish Bethany locked in the third-floor Crary lab. The incubation time for Dr. Kim's drugs, according to Dr. Mason, is twelve hours. None of them are exactly sure what happens after that time.

From over five-hundred people, they are now only nine. They are all tired, exhausted, hungry. But, at least for now, alive.

Mariana points through the steamed-up window. "Look!" she whispers.

She wipes the glass in time for them to see shadows running between the Mac dorms.

Sentients. Waiting behind their shield of penguins for the moment to strike.

This is their station now.

Dr. Mason tries to stretch his long legs and a groan escapes him. The cold from his long sunlit night on the roof has gotten inside him. Devouring like a hungry beast. *Frostbite,* he thinks dully. At least in his toes, maybe elsewhere.

Rajan looks at him across the bus.

(*what now mason*)

(*willy*)

"I think we should go to Willy Airfield," Dr. Mason says aloud. "The penguins may not have gotten to the pilots and ground crew there yet."

"Why are the pilots and ground crew out there and not here?" Winston asks, and there's an edge in his voice.

"You CIA bastards were going to leave us behind," Mariana says. Her voice trembles somewhere between fear and rage.

Dr. Mason shakes his head. "Colson had them on warm standby in case we got the green light to evacuate. She was going to pile everyone she could into a Basler and try to head home, as soon as Dr. Kim had cleared us with his fever formula."

"And that's why there's reason for hope." Jonah's voice fills the bus suddenly. Unlike their hoarse whispers, his voice is loud, booming, filled with energy. All eyes in the bus turn to him like moths to a flame.

"Yeah?" Sal says. "You wanna explain that one to us?"

Jonah whirls on Sal. Rajan recognizes this spark, this immovable *certainty.* It had been in his eyes when he had locked Rajan out of the Station. A consuming, almost religious fire that refuses to acknowledge any outcome except the one Jonah desires – to *survive.*

"*Bethany had the grey microbes in her,*" Jonah says. "And I saw her give them up."

Dr. Mason sits forward. "I'm sorry. What did you say?"

"I'm telling you that Dr. Kim's formula worked!"

Siri reaches up and touches his sleeve. "Start at the beginning, Jonah."

"As soon as Bethany came into the lab and brought the penguins with her, I knew she was a symbiote." His eyes are lit coals, flickering with the memory of fear. "So, I... grabbed one of Kim's loaded needles and I went at her with it."

"Holy shit," Rajan breathes. "That was gutsy."

"No. I just thought I was dead for sure. I had nothing to lose. I shouldn't have made it." Now his face is puzzled. "She just stood there and watched me come at her. She *let* me get near her, I think."

Siri and Rajan exchange a look. A wan *I told you so* smile appears on Siri's face.

"I injected her with the syringe, and she collapsed," Jonah continues. "Then I locked myself in the cabinet to get away from Gisela. I watched her beat Dr. Kim to a pulp through a crack in the door, but I also saw what happened to Bethany."

Jonah looks at Dr. Mason. "Dr. Kim couldn't prove his drugs worked, because he didn't have a grey-generation symbiote to test on. Well… now it's proven."

The whole bus is silent now. Listening.

"It took a few hours to work. Bethany had been almost comatose since I jabbed her, but she came awake and started screaming. Gisela was suddenly right beside her, as if summoned. Bethany screamed… she vomited… and a stream of grey microbes came out of her and went into Gisela." He looks at Siri and Rajan. "I've seen something like that once before. When Summer Kerce got infected in the lower gym at Pole."

"Holy shit," Siri breathes. "So it's possible to beat it."

"This is not just a cure. This is *hope*. More hope than any of us Polies have had in the last year." Jonah's voice fills the bus with conviction. "*We can beat this thing*!"

Dr. Mason puts his face to the window glass; turns his eyes up Ob Hill. Ben and Penny are out there somewhere, and have an army of sentients under the ice. Ivan being mobile means they're not sitting ducks, but they don't have infinite fuel onboard.

(*it's now or never*)

"Colson had a sat-phone in her office in the Chalet," he says, still facing out. "I can give Langley this report and ask for an evac." He turns to them, his eyes bleak. "I've got to tell you: I don't know if we'll get one. But we can try."

Exhaustion is drawn into every line of Marshal Anne's face, but she rises. "Let's fucking do it." She slaps Siri on the back. "Ready to plow the roads?"

Siri stands. Now there's something like energy in her voice. "Better believe it, Marshal."

"Anne, wait." Winston's eyes are bleak and despairing. "Shouldn't we – can't we search the buildings for any other survivors? People might have locked themselves away, like Jonah did."

She puts her hand on his shoulder. "Of course, boss. We'll drop Mason off at the Chalet, and then head right out again. Start clearing buildings."

"Thank you," the Station Manager whispers. He sinks back down, and seems to shrivel into his seat. "Thank you."

In the back of the bus, Marshal Anne, Dr. Mason, Sal and Lansdown pull themselves into the last Hazmat suits, retrieved from the room in which Dr. Kim had died. They turn their oxygen on behind face shields. Then Siri gets behind the wheel of Ivan.

She jams down the accelerator.

The bus leaps forward, smashing a path through the penguins clustered around them. The bus picks up its unpleasant shimmy. As they drive through the Station, sentients openly stare from the snowy side-streets, ice on their faces and damp jackets. Lansdown rolls down a window and points his gun, and they disappear, like ethereal shadows.

Outside the Chalet, the four armed crewmembers in Hazmat suits step down to the ice.

A sudden chuff of snow–

A cloud of penguins launch themselves from the overhang on the second floor, beaks looming open. Dr. Mason ducks to the side, and Marshal Anne swings her staff where his head had just been, connecting with a penguin and cracking its skull.

"Fuck me, they're getting bolder," Mason pants.

"Get inside, quickly," Anne says.

Dr. Mason hurries up the stairs. Into the Station Manager's office. A sharp breath sucks through his lips as he sees Colson's body and the two bullet holes in it. Water has dripped out of her ear and frozen in a reflective pool by her limp fingers.

"Ah, fuck," Marshal Anne says behind him, softly.

Dr. Mason finds Colson's sat-phone on the desk. In a notebook beside it are a list of satellite contact times. "One hour to the next pass. I'll have a connection to Langley then," he says. "Is that all right?"

Marshal Anne nods. "We'll sweep the other buildings, and get some canned food out of the cafeteria for everyone. You gonna be okay here?"

Mason lifts his pistol. "I'll be fine."

When they're gone, Mason double-checks that the windows are locked, then drags the heavy desk chair across the room and wedges it under the door. He sags down to the carpet.

He's in here with a dead body, but dear Lord, he's so cold, so tired–

Dr. Mason wakes to the sound of his watch beeping. He sits up blearily, somehow even more tired than before he closed his eyes. He can't feel anything beneath his waist; the cold numbness has spread up from his boots while he was resting. He's afraid to investigate further. He has a bad feeling about what he'll find.

He shuffles to his feet and opens the sat-phone. Dials a number he knows by heart: the number to the ops room for HAVE VIKING.

"Operator," says the voice.

"I need the pit boss."

"Please authenticate."

"Sign, Canary."

"Countersign, Canary is blue, what is your action?"

"Canary is blue, action is skate."

"You are connected."

"This is Mason," he says. "Colson is dead. The Station has been completely taken over by the sentients. There are nine survivors, including myself, and our situation is hour to hour. But..." Dr. Mason takes a deep breath. "One of the South Pole survivors was a grey-generation lurker, and we were able to test Kim's fever formula. It looks like it worked."

Dr. Mason spends the next ten minutes debriefing. At the end of it, even from a planet away, he recognizes Evil Bill's voice. "Is Dr. Kim alive?"

"No, sir." For better or worse, he's back in charge of the op now. "He was killed by a sentient he was experimenting on."

"Our latest overflight shows almost three hundred sentients roosting beneath that ice. Colson asked me for something, before she died," Evil Bill says. "She wanted me to roll out a MOAB. She wanted us to come in hot."

"That would be public, sir." He closes his eyes. "I get that."

"Must be your lucky day, Mason."

The Agency man stares at the sat-phone. "Are you saying what I think you're saying?"

"The President has authorized an overt strike action," Bill confirms. "Four LC-130s loaded with MOABs just took off from Australia. We're about four hours away from turning McMurdo into a smoking hole in the ground."

"Holy shit, yeah!" Mason springs up, and his voice has fire in it. He has forced himself not to think about his wife, but now she bursts into his mind like a ripening flower. There might just be a chance he can see her again, and for that, he'll do anything. *Anything.*

"Don't thank me yet. This is all going to get spun as the fault of the Chinese, and I need no one left around who can contradict that. Do you understand what I'm saying, Mason?"

"I do. The survivors from South Pole have already gone along with one story," Dr. Mason says. "I'm certain they'll back up another."

"But the reporter won't."

Mason falls silent.

The pieces fall into place quickly for him. Evil Bill knows Mariana is here because he's had to know it. The President hasn't made an overt action to save their lives. He has done it because the story can't be contained; perhaps has blown out to the public already.

It's almost election day. A cold hand grips him as he glimpses the politics lurking behind the scenes. Forces too strong to row against.

"I can't let your plane set wheels down in New Zealand until I hear from you, or any of our Agency boys left alive, that stories are straight, loose ends are tied off, and you have that fever test administered to every single person there including yourself. If none of you make it onto that plane, sorry, but that plane won't make it to New Zealand. Simple as that."

"Yes, sir." Dr. Mason says.

"This is way above me now. If I don't get that confirmation, Mason, *we'll shoot the plane down*. Make no mistake."

"Yes, sir."

"Then get the fuck out of McMurdo. That station is about to be a smoking crater."

Dr. Mason hangs up the phone and sits in the silence of the Station Manager's room.

Evil Bill doesn't know what he's done.

Dr. Mason senses that Rajan and Siri have not been mentally tuned in to his conversation. Searching sentient-infested buildings for survivors is taking all their attention. But the second he gets back onto Ivan, they'll smell it on him. They'll tap right into his brain and unravel the whole conversation.

And he knows something else, too.

He has learned that he can *intuit* things that aren't solid thoughts; a swirling instinct that floats beneath the fast-moving current of the mental net he shares with Rajan and Siri. He doesn't understand how it works, but he knows to trust it.

Siri will *never* go along with Mariana being murdered.

He doesn't know why – not yet – but he's sure of it.

Mason starts humming to himself, thinking about song lyrics, thinking about his wife, anything but his conversation with Bill. The sat-phone is still connected, and it has a slow dial-up internet function. Mason types in the website of the *Chicago Tribune*.

It takes five minutes to load, but there it is. *Tragedy and over 100 deaths: Mysterious Biological Pandemic Raging at three Antarctic Stations.*

The byline is attributed to Mariana Egan and Jane Bradshaw.

Mariana had come to rescue them, in Ivan the Bus, from Scott Base. And now he knows why she'd taken the bus there in the first place. To use the Internet. She'd broken through the cone of silence they'd imposed on Antarctica. A clever move. She had forced the CIA's hand, possibly saved his life by doing so, but she would pay with her own life for it.

He sings, louder, trying to drown out his clamoring thoughts. He scans the article quickly. It suggests that more news is forthcoming about the origin of the pandemic.

Except he knows the origin begins with the Central Intelligence Agency.

With his black program, `HAVE VIKING`.

Dr. Mason thinks about the buzz of the penguins. The weird mental growl of the sentients.

(*krrrrrrgggg*)

He replays it in his mind and it fills his thoughts surprisingly well. He keeps reading.

The *Tribune* promises an exclusive interview, in tomorrow's issue, with one of the survivors of the pandemic. Stunning revelations to follow about its origin, it says.

It's Siri. Dr. Mason just knows, with no need to question the finding. And now he understands the instinct he'd felt with cold certainty.

Siri is Mariana's source. And Siri will know he has been ordered to kill Mariana.

In making that order, Evil Bill has forced his hand.

If Siri reads that order on him, like lipstick on his collar, he'll be exposed. She will go to the US Marshal with that information.

And without Mariana dead, there will be no ride for any of them off this continent.

Dr. Mason pulls out his pistol; checks the load. He doesn't agonize about what needs to be done. He knows he needs to do it.

The Marshal first.

The Polies who live rent-free in his head second.

Then Mariana.

He picks up his radio and jabs the button. "Hey," he pants into it. "Hey, you guys, I need some help in here, I need some help in the Chalet!"

Chapter Fifty-Five

The thing Mason doesn't realize is that the microbes are also on the microbe net.

The penguins don't understand what they are picking up, but they can relay. From bird to bird, meaningless words get passed along with the noise of the penguin collective. Indecipherable to most, but not Penny. And not Ben Jacobs.

Through the radio he'd taken off Doc Kaushik's corpse, Ben hears Dr. Mason's cry for help. But through the microbe net, his mind *hears* the intent behind it.

(*that station is about to be a smoking crater*)

Beside him, Penny is covered in ice, just emerged back from the water. He is just a husk of who he could have been. He has given up too much of the grey within him to birth the blue-generation. Greg Penny is dead. The man beside Ben Jacobs, icicles hanging off his hair and arms, is Greg Penny's sentient shell.

Ben listens to Penny roar in the strange noises of the dead and understands, coldly, that the sentients are not the future. They are foot soldiers, living on the edge of survival. They can roam the Antarctic oceans, an apex predator in the cold water, but they can never spread to the warm shores of New Zealand or Australia. They will feed on every penguin and fish and skua adjacent to the ice, but ultimately, they will die out.

The grey-generation is their species' future. Combined with the humans, their adaptation potential is endless. But to harness that, he needs the THC that bridges the microbes with the human mind. A catalyst he doesn't have.

Ben Jacobs has kept his sentient army underneath the ice. He has been a wartime general, directing the penguins to take the lead with their greater numbers. But he has also been a cunning fox in the shadows, waiting for the right moment to pounce.

When Ben hears Mason's thoughts, he knows that wait is over.

It is time to summon his army. Make one last push. Overwhelm the last threads of resistance to *us us u–*

(*my children all of you rise from the ocean come to us come COME COME*)

Chapter Fifty-Six

November 3. Just after 1:00 AM, local time.

The occupants of Ivan the Terra Bus greedily open cans of tuna, pineapple, spam. Fingers dip past serrated edges and scoop hydrogenated oils and meat and fruit into their mouths. The first smiles flicker as the canned food hits their empty cold bellies.

Ivan has six new occupants now, who had managed to barricade themselves away from the penguins in the dorm, including Pastor Kwanje. Siri has assured Marshal Anne that all of them are clear of the water-based microbial strain.

Then the radio bursts into life.

"Hey, you guys." Dr. Mason sounds panicked. "I need some help in the Chalet!"

Marshal Anne jumps to her feet; checks her weapon. Beside her, Sal does the same. Siri gets behind the wheel of Ivan and jerks the large vehicle out of park. They rumble forward, away from the cafeteria.

As Siri drives, she reaches back to Rajan.

(*i haven't been listening for mason*)

(*mason mason are you all right*)

(*krrrrrrggggHHHHH*)

Dr. Mason's thoughts dimly echo to them as if from the back of a loud tunnel, but when they reach out to him, all they get is the low growl of the sentients.

(*we're coming mason we're coming hold on*)

The bus squeals to a stop outside the Chalet. Marshal Anne and Sal pull their Hazmat helmets on and charge out of the bus. They push through the penguin herd; they don't have far to go. Sal charges up the ramp to the chalet first.

(*krrrggggkrrr shhh shhh more noise krrgggg*)

Siri turns in her seat, frowning at Rajan.

(*it doesn't sound right–*)

Then, suddenly, the sentient noise drops away like it has been sliced with a knife.

(*got to do it I'm sorry no choice she has to go*)

Siri's body clenches so tightly that her muscles spasm.

"Anne, NO!" she screams through the half-open window of the bus.

That's when she sees the herd of sentients. No – it's a mob.

Running flat-out, halfway across the Sound. Right toward them.

Sal charges through the main door of the Chalet, ready to fire, but there's no one inside except Dr. Mason, standing by the door, pistol by his side.

"What happened?" Sal is already looking past him, into the building's shadows.

Marshal Anne walks in, gun slung across her Hazmat suit. She sees Dr. Mason, raises her head to say something, and Mason shoots her in the chest.

Sal whirls, gun coming up to his shoulder. "Don't shoot!" Mason shouts. He raises his pistol toward the roof. "Friendly, don't shoot."

"You shot her, man, you shot the Marshal!"

"I know!" Dr. Mason pulls his earpiece out, lets it dangle from his ear. "Listen to me, Sal."

Sal lowers his gun, his face puzzled. He pulls his earpiece out as well. "Why the fuck would you–"

"She's the only shooter not on our team. Bill wants the reporter–"

From the ground, Marshal Anne coughs. A bubble of blood grows and spills across her lips. Dr. Mason looks down, and her pistol is pointing at him.

He opens his mouth, and she fires.

Chapter Fifty-Seven

The bullet strikes Dr. Mason high in the shoulder, half-spins him around. He sinks to one knee, yelling out in shock and pain. Sal points his gun at Marshal Anne, but he can't bring himself to pull the trigger.

Anne's left hand scrabbles for purchase on the wooden floor and her next shot goes high, punching up into the rafters. Blood spills between her teeth and reddens her mouth.

Mason pinwheels, finger tightening. He pumps two bullets into her.

Her body jumps.

Then splays gently, like a deflating tire.

Dr. Mason struggles to his feet, grabbing his left arm with his gun hand. Blood spills through his fingers, a frothy, dark carmine pumping in time with his racing heartbeat.

"What the fuck, man?" Sal yells.

"No time, Sal," Dr. Mason gasps. His voice is like dry bones clattering. "Orders from home station. I need you – need you to get Rajan and Siri off the bus and bring them here. At gunpoint if you have to." Mason looks up, then shouts. "Get moving, now!"

Sal takes one last look at the bullet-ridden Marshal, breath fogging his Hazmat suit facemask.

That's when machine gun fire breaks out from the bus in the snow outside.

"Contact!" Lansdown yells into his radio from his perch on top of Ivan the Terra bus.

The herd of sentients is swarming down the main street of Mac Station. Running toward the bus. Dozens of bodies. Maybe hundreds.

"Ah, shit," Lansdown's voice is bleak.

He flicks his gun to full auto.

He gets down onto one knee and opens fire.

Sentients in the front row stumble and fall, knock back into others. But the herd flows around them. Keeps coming.

Running right into his line of fire like a colonial army.

Lansdown screams, deliriously. He rakes the charging crowd, pouring bullets into them, then his gun clicks dry.

"Where the fuck are you guys?" he shouts into his radio as he reloads.

The first sentients reach Ivan and throw themselves on it. The van rocks nastily. A man in an orange Kiwi Antarctic jacket crouches, then leaps straight up from the snow toward Lansdown. Arms outstretched in claws, face dropped open in a grotesque scream–

Lansdown racks a bullet into the chamber of his gun and fires from the hip; the sentient's body thumps down onto the windshield of Ivan, cracking it. He stands, sending bursts of gunfire straight down into the crowd around the bus, but there are too many, smashing Ivan's windows with their heads and their fists. Trying to worm through broken glass. Grabbing onto the windshield. One person, then two, are pulled bodily out of the van through a broken window, to thump down into the snow.

His gun clicks empty again, right as Lansdown sees–

(*Oh fuck*)

– a face he recognizes. One of the Pole survivors.

Greg Penny. In the street, facing down the big red bus.

Naked to the chest, a sheen of ice covering his muscled body.

Penny reaches down and picks up a penguin by the scruff of its neck.

Hurls it right at him.

The penguin smashes into Lansdown, already biting and snapping. His finger tightens on the trigger as he goes down like a kid socked by a baseball. He clambers to his feet–

Sam Eske, one of the ground crew who had first found Ben Jacobs, is standing on the roof of the bus right in front of him. Close enough to kiss him. Eyes flooded with blue.

Lansdown pulls his gun up, and Eske leaps into him.

Somewhere to Rajan's right, a scream. The unmistakable sound of someone being dragged through a window.

Rajan whirls, in time to meet Mariana Egan's terrified eyes –

The reporter is yanked through the broken bus window, clamoring hands seizing her jacket, tugging her hair. Then she's gone, her scream cut-off like smoke against a dash of water.

Gunfire from above the bus. Rajan pulls himself up the aisle of Ivan toward Siri, then suddenly stops short.

A sentient spills through a broken window and into a seat. A woman.

She straightens with sinuous fluidity and looks at him. Her body tenses–

(*krrrrghhhhhh*)

A shot rings out.

A neat hole the size of a quarter appears in her head.

Rajan looks back, temporarily deafened. Behind him, Jonah looks shaken, but his hand is steady, and so is the smoking pistol it clutches.

"You have a gun?" is all Rajan can think to say.

"The Marshal gave it to me," Jonah says. Then his face tightens. Rajan ducks, and Jonah fires at a second sentient that has its head and shoulders through another window.

Rajan runs up the aisle, hands over his head. Somewhere, Jonah fires again. A penguin smashes into the windshield as if hurled out of a cannon.

(*siri go drive please go*)

The engine is running. Siri is at the wheel, but the bus doesn't move. Rajan makes it to her, looks forward, and sees why she has frozen.

Penny is in front of the bus, staring right at them. His skin is yellow. His lip is pulled up to reveal his snarling teeth.

(*KRRRRRGHHHHHHHRAJANNNNNNN*)

Rajan looks down at Siri; clutches her shoulder.

(*rajan what about mason what about bethany*)

(*i'm sorry siri but you have to drive now NOW DRIVE DRIVE*)

Siri plants her foot on the gas, and Ivan the Terra Bus lurches forward.

* * *

Sal watches in shock from the back deck of the Chalet as a half-naked man in the snow hurls a penguin right at Lansdown. Watches a sentient leap up from the ground, rip Lansdown's Hazmat faceshield off, and blast his fellow SEAL in the face with frigid water. Lansdown slumps, his gun tumbling off the van.

Sal lifts his gun to his chest, and is knocked to his knees from behind. His faceshield slams into the snowy deck of the Chalet.

There's a sentient on top of him. It's immensely strong, pinning his arms down. Its jaw hinges open and it blasts the back of his Hazmat suit with ice-cold water. Sal looks over his shoulder, and sees it bare its teeth. A vision of Dr. Kim's body flashes before his eyes, and Sal heaves, shifting his weight. The sentient spills over the side of him, thumping into the snow.

Sal rolls over, pinning his attacker down with his knee. Fumbling for his gun. He fires twice into it, then raises himself to a crouch. The bus is moving. It thumps into two, then a clump of sentients running at it. Sal sprays fire into the crowd surrounding the van. Bodies fall to the side. Then the bus is through the herd, driving downhill and away, toward the ice runways.

Sal takes a deep, shaky breath. Stands up–

Then whirls and fires.

Penny stands behind him. No shirt on.

Sal's bullet catches Penny in the shoulder. Then the gun clicks dry.

Penny doesn't move. Viscous blood oozes down his shoulder, then stops.

His teeth bare in an awful grin.

Sal feels something catch in his throat. In every death scenario he has imagined – and he has imagined several – he'd always had a chance.

Penny tackles him low, knocking him down to the deck. Sal has time to let his eyes roll back and see Marshal Anne's motionless form on the floor, through the door of the Chalet. He experiences a brief but evanescent stab of regret, then Penny rips his Hazmat helmet off and vomits a deluge of water over him and Sal feels nothing anymore.

Chapter Fifty-Eight

November 3.

Mac Station feels empty.

The penguins are withdrawing to the water. Several of them are trailing blood, missing flippers, awkwardly gimping. Dozens of them just fall down on the walk, and don't get up again. The smell of fire and gunpowder lingers in the air; the very snow on the ground seems to have a blood-like clumpy wetness. The streets are littered with dead penguins and the tire-crushed or bullet-ridden bodies of Antarctic crewmembers, the breeze gently stirring the exposed down filling in their shot-up jackets.

The Chalet is lit by the sick pallid light that sometimes falls over the tundra before a ruinous storm. Inside, seven dead bodies drip water onto the administration building's floor.

Beyond them, four sentients crowd Dr. Mason against a wall. They are dripping wet, icicles shadowing their snowy bodies, staring at him with singular intent. He faces them with an empty gun in his hand, the pain in his shot arm a deep ache that lances with the beat of his heart.

Dr. Mason lets the gun slip to his feet. He can hear them snarling in his mind, ready to burst into motion and rip him apart. But they hold, unnaturally still, waiting for something.

For someone.

The door handle turns, slowly.

Ben Jacobs walks in.

A smile sits on Ben's sagging, loose lips. A terrible quickening of interest stretches his mouth like a rubberband, revealing gapped, tombstone teeth.

"Richard Mason," the former Polie speaks. His voice is raspy, as if his vocal cords are full of insects. "We have been looking forward to meeting you."

Dr. Mason remains silent. Letting Ben draw closer with every step. There's a knife on his belt underneath his jacket. All it will take is one fast decisive move–

Ben Jacobs takes one more step and Dr. Mason moves, faster than he thought he could. His hand is a blur. The knife drives in a deadly arc, Mason's whole body bent behind its lethal purpose.

The knife stops, the tip of its blade quivering inches from Ben's grinning jaw.

Ben has moved just as fast. Holds his arm in an immovable cinch.

Ben stares at him, eyes grey and lashing.

(*of course we knew mason*)

Dr. Mason's eyes widen.

(*we know everything you're thinking. this is our gift. you're just borrowing it*)

Ben's grip tightens, grinding his bones together. Dr. Mason lets out a gasp of strangled pain. The knife tumbles out of his nerveless fingers. The force increases until Mason can't even scream in pain anymore. He buckles to his knees, body twisted like a comma around his crushed hand.

Ben stares down at him. His lips come off his teeth. Dr. Mason hears the bones in his dominant hand snap like dry twigs. One, two, three. The blood loss from his gunshot wound wells up, and he welcomes the darkness rushing in.

"No," Ben snarls, and suddenly the twist on his arm changes. His eyes fly wide open like he has been electrocuted. "No release for you, Dr. Mason," Ben buzzes in his broken voice. "We have business together."

The pain releases, fractionally, although he's still hanging by his broken hand. "What do you want?" Dr. Mason gasps.

"We… want… the plane."

(*and we know you can make sure it lands safely in New Zealand*)

Ben Jacobs draws closer, until their foreheads are almost touching. "We want you to lie for us. Will you do that, Dr. Mason?"

As if anticipating his answer, the pain in his hand suddenly turns *up*. Dr. Mason howls in agony. A bone splint drives up through his hand, puncturing his skin. Blood spills down his arm. The pain is so bright he feels blinded by it.

(*I can't I can't I can't*)

Then his head fills with noise. A wild shrieking that crawls behind his eyes and between his ears and suddenly he can't bear it–

"Yes!" Dr. Mason screams, voice high and panicky. "Yes, I'll do it, I'll do whatever you want!"

The pain backs off. Slowly, so that he doesn't pass out. Dr. Mason clutches his broken right hand with his shot left arm. He looks down, and sees his knife on the floor by Ben's shoes.

He tries to summon the will to grab it. Somehow clutch it in a ruined arm and swing it.

But that will finds no way to bubble up and into the outside world. In an agony of humiliation, that's when Mason understands he has been beaten. His destiny is no longer his.

(*very good*)

Ben's voice is now a smooth purr in his head.

(*now look at us*)

Dr. Mason looks up.

"You're going to get *ussssss* off the ice in the Basler," Ben says. Every word out of his throat comes to Dr. Mason from across some great distance; harmonics of Ben's power echoing in his mind. "You'll tell them you have us drugged. You'll swear that you've tested the pilots and yourself and no one shows signs of infection. You will keep your mouth shut when we land, and you will let them take us away."

Mason scrapes together his courage. He can't do it; he can't release his terrible infection onto the whole world–

(*you will tell them exactly that or you will never see your wife again*)

Dr. Mason looks up at Ben, skin white and blanched as new snow. The symbiote bends down, until they are eye to eye again.

(*we see through you doctor mason*
we know who you are)

Mason can't look away. Ben's voice drowns everything else out of his head.

(we have heard you as you've said your prayers. but for a man of blood like you all you can hope for is to hold those dear to you one last time. that we can give to you)

Around him, the sentients crowd closer. Ready to punish. Ready to rip him apart at a moment's notice.

(*we are the vengeance you asked for*

and we will wreak it in your name across the cold plains of the world)

"You're going to do it, Dr. Mason," There's glee in Ben Jacobs's voice. "You're a survivor. You don't know any other way to be."

Chapter Fifty-Nine

November 3.

Royal Australian Air Force Base Richmond,
New South Wales

The C-5 Galaxy touches down on Australian soil just after sunrise. Its large cargo bay is loaded with six MOAB bombs. Each sits in its own cradle, which in turn rests on an airdrop platform. The ground crews move with urgency, transferring and tethering the platforms to airdrop rails in the bellies of nearby LC-130s. Each MOAB, or GBU-43/B Massive Ordnance Air Blast weapon, carries 18,700 pounds of high explosive.

Just one MOAB will rip up most of the sea ice around McMurdo Station; chew up anything underneath.

Six will destroy McMurdo and Scott completely.

As the bombs are being loaded, a frenzied high-level discussion is occurring between the United States Secretary of Defense and the New Zealand Minister of Defence. Within the FIVE EYES intelligence-sharing apparatus, the US has released top-secret satellite infrared images showing that Scott Base is now abandoned. Hundreds of penguins in the streets. Gaping open doors. No uninfected human thermal signatures.

The New Zealand government has been told that their Station has been decimated by a microbial pandemic, stemming from illegal biological experimentation by the Chinese at their Dome-A station. There are no survivors.

The question is whether New Zealand will allow the sentients roosting in their base to remain there, or be obliterated with Mac Station.

It's a time of war and urgent decision-making. No committees, no endless debating of courses of action. Yes or no, that's all. In the end, the fact that the Americans have chosen drastic action for their station sways the Kiwis. Let the purge be complete, and then the consequences for China and their plague will have to follow.

Four LC-130s take off an hour after the C-5 lands in Australia. Three aircraft are loaded with two bombs each. The fourth LC-130 is under the command of Major Austin Baker; his last flight above the ice continent before new active-duty orders pull him to a Taiwan Straits deployment. His aircraft carries a thermal and hyperspectral pod that can map underneath the sea ice. It will count bodies – before and after.

As Rajan and the ragged survivors within Ivan the Terra Bus close on Willy Airfield, the weapons-laden LC-130s are less than twenty minutes away.

Chapter Sixty

Hope is a fragile thing, Rajan thinks. Difficult to weave, and so easily shattered.

Siri takes her foot off the gas, and Ivan the Terra Bus slowly squeaks to a stop. Exhaust popping. Its engine rumbles in the cold. Behind them, anxious eyes peer through the windshield.

The flat icy plateau past the Willy shanty town is flecked with dark spots. Some short, some tall. Ahead of them, standing in the middle of a dazzling sea of white snow, plugged into external air and power, the midnight sun sparkles off the red-tipped Basler aircraft. It is surrounded by multiple rings of penguins, studded with the occasional loping human-sentient.

Waiting.

One of the Willy containers cracks open. Maui Hathaway, the Basler's military co-pilot, pokes his head out cautiously.

Siri opens the door of Ivan. "Quickly," Rajan beckons at him. "Get inside."

Maui, Basler pilot Tristan Hyatt, and the last surviving mobility technician, Michelle Ajuria, pile down the stairs of the terminal building. Rajan is already starting the replay of the sentient noise–

(*krrrrrghhh*)

– and Siri picks it up in her mind as they climb aboard. None of them react and she nods in relief as she closes the door.

"What happened here?" Rajan asks.

Hyatt starts to reply, then throws up his hands. "I don't even know how to describe it."

"We woke up and our building was surrounded," Maui starts. "Hundreds of penguins. A few of the crew members with ice on their faces." He looks baffled by the words coming out of his mouth. "Then a few minutes ago, they just left. Went down to the airplane."

(*Ben is sparing them saving them*)

Rajan nods grimly. "Ben Jacobs needs all three of you alive. Without you, he can't de-ice and fly out of here. To take his infection to the rest of the world."

(*one then two then three THEN ALL*)

There are now eight people on the bus, and the tension inside is thick. Pastor Kwanje huddles in the back with Winston, and Michelle Ajuria drifts aimlessly down the aisle toward them. The pilots and three Polies – Rajan, Siri and Jonah – stare ahead at the besieged Basler.

The plane is their only chance to get off the continent and save their own lives.

Siri snaps out of her inertia. She sits down at the wheel of the bus, and looks back with a wild and bitter smile. "Hold on, everyone."

She drops her foot like an anchor onto the gas pedal, and Ivan leaps forward. Driving right at the aircraft.

Ivan the Terra Bus smashes into the first ring of penguins and sentients surrounding the Basler.

A few fall under her wheels. The majority of the penguins, however, flow out of her way like the Red Sea parting, and then reform the ring behind Ivan. Siri keeps the tall vehicle moving, as close to the airplane as she dares, but the ring around the Basler remains dense with penguins. The bus is too tall; she would have to ram the airplane itself to attack them.

She sweeps past the plane, a few dead penguins staining the ice behind her. The rings around the plane reform, tighter into the underbelly of the taildragger aircraft, clustering under its nose pointed into the sky. Watching her silently.

The message is clear.

The blunt hammer of Ivan the Terra Bus won't help them board the Basler.

Then, into Siri and Rajan's heads, comes another voice.

Both of them turn their heads as one, drawn with the helpless fascination of moths to a flame. At the edge of the hill, a snowmobile is coming toward them. Racing fast.

Winston rises from his seat, staring. "Is that–"

"It's Dr. Mason." Rajan's voice is brittle as a vase about to shatter. "And he's with Ben."

On the flat plateau of ice that is Williams Airfield, the large red Antarctic bus with the last eight survivors of two stations faces down a black snowmobile with two people on it. Behind the vehicles, the Basler sits on its large skis, surrounded by clustering penguins and sentients.

Everything is still.

Except Siri and Rajan can hear Dr. Mason in their heads. His pain, both physical and mental. Everything he knows and has experienced spills out to them limply. Mariana's death warrant from CIA headquarters, now ironically fulfilled. Planes with bombs, inbound from the mainland, due any minute.

And what Ben Jacobs wants: the airplane headed north to fertile hunting ground.

They have the pilots. But without word from Dr. Mason, who is now the last surviving CIA team member, the plane won't be allowed to land. The Basler will be shot down before it gets to New Zealand.

It's a standoff.

Ben Jacobs steps off the snowmobile. He stands with his hands on his hips and thrusts his jaw into the air, as if drawing a deep breath. Behind him, Mason slumps over the seat of the snowmobile.

Ben's voice comes into their minds.

(*come to us come come*)

At first, Rajan thinks Ben is talking to them. He starts to formulate a response, then Pastor Kwanje shouts from behind him.

"Drive, drive, they're coming this way!"

Rajan and Siri's heads jerk like they've been caught on the end of a fishing line. The sentients are running away from the airplane, right at them.

Siri presses the accelerator. The bus draws away from Ben.

(*STOP*)

The sentients pause. They stand in the snow, halfway between the airplane and the bus, like sullen statues.

(*rajannnnnn*)

(*siriiiiiiiiiii*)

(*come make a deal with us*)

The sentients take a step back, as if to signify good intentions. The wind rips through shards of broken glass, moaning between the bus's gaping windows.

Siri stands up from behind the driver's seat.

She looks at Rajan. A deep ocean of feelings passes between them, unspoken.

She extends her hand, and he takes it. Gently kisses it.

"The odds have never been all that good," Rajan whispers.

Jonah comes up to them. "What's going on?"

"Ben wants to talk," Siri says.

"You know he doesn't want to *talk*," Jonah says sharply.

"We know." Her voice comes out calmer than she expects.

Their heads turn, looking through the windshield. Ben is waiting for them, horridly jaunty. Dr. Mason is sagged across the snowmobile. His voice in their heads is a soft river flowing past them; regretful and wounded. He doesn't have much fight left in him.

"Come on!" Jonah hisses. "We've got to think of something!"

Rajan puts his hand on Jonah's shoulder. "I'm sorry," he says. "I think… this is checkmate."

"I don't see how that's the case," Jonah says, a stubborn tone in his voice.

Siri touches her hand to her head. "It's a long story, Jonah, but they can hear us," she says. "Both Ben and Dr. Mason can hear what Rajan and I are thinking. So they know we don't have guns, or Hazmat suits. They know we've got just an eighth of a tank of gas left in Ivan. And in less than an hour, this whole plateau is going to be turned into ash. Ben can survive without a station to go home to, but we can't. If we don't get on that plane, we're all dead anyway."

Something spasms across Jonah's face, then it hardens. Like he has made some kind of decision, slotted neatly into an answer like a coin in a vending machine. "He can't read my mind," Jonah says. "Right?"

They nod. "That's right."

Jonah looks at Rajan, and suddenly–

(*oh my wait wait you're going to–*)

(*krrrrrghhh*)

"What the hell?" Siri looks at him.

Rajan shakes his head, almost violently. He spins on his heel and walks away from them. He holds his hands over his ears. He sits down on a bench seat at the end of the bus and puts his head between his legs. Sending nothing out in his mind except for the sentient roar.

(*krrrrrghhhHHHHHHHH*)

Jonah reaches over, and pulls the handle that opens the bus doors.

He steps down onto the fresh snow.

Jonah takes his time walking over to the snowmobile. It gives him a savage pleasure to see the smile on his former protégé's face falter as he closes the distance to them.

Jonah comes to a stop right beside Dr. Mason. An unkempt pool of bright blood drips gently into the snow beside the CIA scientist.

Once, what seems like a million years ago, Jonah Mitchell and Ben Jacobs had been co-caretakers of the Atmospheric Research Observatory, at the South Pole. And now here they are. Staring at each other on another snowy plateau, but this time, only one of them is still human.

"We told Siri and Rajan we wanted them to come talk to us," Ben rasps.

"Fuck what you want, Benjamin," Jonah says pleasantly.

Ben stares at him. The smile drops off his face. His agitation swells like the quiver of a snake about to strike.

"You want to deal?" Jonah says. "You deal with me."

"Let us all get on the plane together," Ben wheezes. "Everyone gets to go home. We know you want to go home, Jonah."

Jonah doesn't reply.

"We know what you did at South Pole," he whispers.

Jonah grimaces. It's the feeling of a knife slid gently into his heart.

"You locked your friends out because you wanted to survive." Ben takes another step forward. His voice is a whisper. "We are offering you survival, Jonah. You let us live, and we will let you live. Peacefully. Your time isn't destined to end here."

Jonah shifts his feet in the ice. "I remember when I looked at Rajan through the door of South Pole Station," he says. His eyes are far away. "He was trying to get me to let him in, and I said something to him that's been haunting me ever since."

He looks at Ben Jacobs and lets out a sigh that's more like a whimper.

"I told him that *I've spent too much time here to want to die here."*

A rubber band smile pops onto Ben's face. Stretching from ear to ear.

Then they hear a muted roar. An engine.

Both of them instinctively snap their necks up, looking into the bright blue sky. Their time is almost up; the bombs will be dropping any minute now.

The roar is steady. From the ground, not the air.

Ben turns over his shoulder to see a red snowmobile speeding toward them from the Willy shanty town. Jonah can't see the person, encased in a Big Red and huddled behind the meager windscreen, but he suddenly *knows* who it is. He laughs, harshly.

Peals of laughter split his face.

Ben's head turns back toward him, and Jonah's hand has come out of his pocket.

In it, he holds Marshal Anne's backup sidearm.

Ben's eyes widen, but he's already moving away–

Jonah fires.

Dr. Mason tumbles into the snow between them. A neat quarter-sized hole in his head. Jonah's gun clicks empty, the hammer locking back.

(*NOOOOOOOOO*)

There's a massive rumble behind Jonah. Sentients breaking into motion, rushing right toward him, but he doesn't turn. He looks Ben right in the eye.

"You know, I was saving that last bullet for myself," he says calmly. A sense of dreamlike acceptance burnishes his voice. "Perhaps I am ready to die here, after all."

Ben's face splits in a savage snarl. Suddenly, he is standing right in front of Jonah. So close that the older man can feel his rotting breath cascading in hot waves over his face.

"Do you know what you've done," Ben hisses.

Ever the realist, even at the cost of lives, Jonah says his last words.

"I know exactly."

Ben's hand flashes out, in a claw, and rips Jonah's Adam's apple out of his neck.

That's when Ivan the Terra Bus lurches into motion, and barrels right at him.

Chapter Sixty-One

One hour ago.

In the lab on the third floor of the Crary building, Bethany Hamidani struggles to her feet and plucks the needle out of her skin, feeling like a truck has run over her.

She takes one look at the body of Dr. Kim in the corner and lurches forward, trying to get away as quickly as possible. The door of the third-floor lab is locked, but even amidst what feels like the worst fever-driven fugue she has ever been in, she knows the window set in the door doesn't stand a chance against the fire extinguisher in the corner.

The third-floor hallway is covered with molted penguin feathers, and stinks like rotten fish, but is completely empty. She stumbles past Gisela Childers' body, bleary-eyed, expecting at any moment to hear Penny's watery whisper, but she makes it to the ground floor without encountering anyone or anything.

Crary is deserted.

Outside, the snowy path is covered with blood. She almost throws up as she sees a human face squashed into red chili, a brutal tire mark having crushed its way into the man's neck and popped his skull. More bodies, more feathers. More gristle and carnage. McMurdo is a fucking warzone.

Then, suddenly, she hears a voice. Wait, it says. Slow down, it says.

A groan, carried over the wind.

She unhinges her knees and sags quickly to the snow. She lets her head slip down to the cold snow. Playing dead. Just one body amidst so many others.

The voices grow louder.

She sees them. Walking up toward the FEMC building. Dr. Mason and *Ben Jacobs.*

Her heart plummets. Ben is going to sense her. The microbes inside her will draw him like a magnet...

Ben walks right by, followed by a stumbling Mason, leaving nothing but a few scattered drops of blood from the bullet hole in Mason's arm in their wake.

Lying there, the wind sharp in her face, watching their receding forms, she realizes that something is missing.

Something that was once inside her.

Bethany rises up to her knees, then runs down a snowy side path as quietly as she can.

Bethany slides cautiously up the wooden stairs of the Chalet, soft snow crunching under her boots. She steps over the outline of a body imprinted in the snow, and a gun, but no body. The Adirondack chairs still sit outside, one of them in a pool of blood.

Inside, her breath tightens in her chest. She has seen bodies before, during the microbe attacks at South Pole. That was death. This is *war.*

Sentients riddled with gunshots lie splayed across the floor, freezing water leaking out of their bodies, faces contorted in snarls. These people hadn't started as her crew, but she recognizes them all from their cramped days together within Crary. Their brutal end sticks in her throat.

A cough.

Bethany whirls.

A very soft moan comes from the floor.

Bethany runs across the Chalet, crashing down to her knees beside Marshal Anne Pabon. Anne lies in a pool of blood. She's pale; too pale. High red spots are fading from her cheeks. The gaping hole in her chest seems to be breathing, rattling every time she sucks air through her mouth.

"Oh my God," Bethany gasps.

Marshal Anne grabs her with a surprising strength.

"You have to stop them," the dying woman whispers.

Bethany's eyes fill with regret. "I don't know that Ben can be stopped, Marshal."

"Willy," she says. Every word costs her; is dragged out of her. "They... are... leaving."

Bethany hears the rasp of a motor and raises herself to her knees. Just enough to peek out of the window and see a snowmobile race out of FEMC. Mason and Ben.

She looks down to see Anne pressing her pistol into her hand.

"You have to try," Marshal Anne whispers.

Then her green eyes close. Her chest settles. The Chalet goes quiet. Bethany is left all alone, the cold metal of the gun pressing into her palm.

Now.

Bethany slams on the brakes of the snowmobile, stopping on what is usually Willy's ice runway, beside Ivan the Terra bus and Dr. Mason's body.

Ben's black snowmobile is rapidly shrinking into the horizon. He's much faster than the bus, and fleeing.

Bethany pulls the long-barreled Heckler and Koch MP5N off her back. On her way up to FEMC to find a snowmobile, she'd stumbled across a gun, lying in the snow next to the tire-crushed sentient.

It had once been Lansdown's gun, and it's fully loaded.

She squints down the barrel, trying to steady the crosshairs on Ben's back. He's driving fast, smashing through small icy wind-hills, away into the whiteness of the Sound.

She fires a three-shot semi-automatic burst.

The gun bucks wildly. It hits her in the shoulder like it's alive, rears its barrel halfway into the sky like a spooked horse. When it steadies, she sees Ben is still going.

Rajan spills out of Ivan the bus. He runs over to her.

"Bethany," he says. "Give me the gun."

She stares daggers at him. "Hell no."

"Bethany, please," he says. "You have no reason to, but please trust me now."

There is no give in her eyes. No trust. Rajan's hand starts to drop–

Then she extends it to him, roughly, like she's shoving it at him.

"Don't make me regret this," she says, and she sounds afraid, like a balloon losing air.

Rajan takes it from her immediately. He snaps out the retractable shoulder stock and fits it into the nook of his shoulder. Snaps the weapon from semi-auto to single shot. He looks down the sights. The barrel moves slowly.

Nothing happens.

He breathes out gently.

Then he pulls the trigger, fires, then fires again.

Bethany's eyes jerk up to the horizon. For a beat, everything is still.

Then, like the snowmobile has run into a wall, it pitches nose down. She sees a human form fly into the air, a flash of light, a crack of thunder, and the snowmobile explodes.

And just then, a grey LC-130 aircraft flies over their heads. Its fearsome sound thrums down into their chests.

"He's not dead," Bethany says, pointing at the flames licking at the white horizon. "You know he's not dead."

"I know," Rajan says, looking up at the aircraft, "but if we don't get airborne *right now*, we'll die with him."

Rajan breaks into a run, around to the back of Ivan. Bethany hesitates, then revs the snowmobile, and takes off with a spray of snow. Rajan slings the rifle across his back, and climbs up on top of the bus. He throws himself down, hooking his legs under the luggage rack. He sets the rifle out in front of him.

"Go, Siri, go!" he shouts, and the bus accelerates into motion after Bethany.

In front of her, the symbiotes are milling, confused. Ben is gone. Penny is gone. They are like sheep without a leader. Bethany lets out a hoarse shout and accelerates, pulling ahead of Ivan.

Something glints in the snowy sunlight. Bethany sees –

(*no WAY*)

– Mariana.

The reporter is airborne, arms extended toward her snowmobile, blue eyes sparking with malevolence.

Abruptly Mariana goes limp. Blood spurts from her head. Bethany catches a glimpse of a dark red hole in the side of her face from Rajan's shot, then she's crashing into the snow and Bethany is past her, skis spraying snow over her body.

Ivan's tires crush through uncompacted snow, barreling toward the Basler. The front of the bus sways, jigs, then begins to aim, like it's a weapon.

More shots ring out on top, faster now. A body goes under the big wheels, then the bus swings wide. It's too big to fit under the aircraft, but Bethany's snowmobile is not. She ducks behind the windscreen, screams aloud, and runs right at the penguins.

Through them.

Her snowmobile is fast, and heavy on horsepower. Smashing into them scatters them like misshapen dominoes. She shoots out under the other side of the Basler's wheels and drags around in a tight arc, leg thrust out for balance, then she accelerates right back in.

Without Penny or Ben, these are just birds, and they flock away from the loud whine and deadly speed of her snowmobile. Scattering like grains in the wind, squawking, moving almost comically slowly outward from the plane. Ivan roars in from the back, flattening some of them, then it squeals to a stop.

Rajan fires, gun swiveling fast, searching for sentients. The penguins keep on fleeing.

In the bus, Siri turns and points at Hyatt and Maui.

"Get up there," she says, urgently, "and for all our sakes, get this airplane going!"

Chapter Sixty-Two

Silence. Only the sound of cold wind.

Ben Jacobs sits in the snow, dazed. Our senses are ringing, stretched too thin, distressingly spotty and unreliable. Somewhere, we smell burning flesh, searing Ben to his bones, but our eyes are fixed straight up.

We can hear the airplanes overhead.

And then–

The horizon lights up with a crack of pure light.

We feel the air around us grow packed with heat, then Ben is knocked flat to the snow by the shock wave. We try to turn his head and it's suddenly too heavy to lift. Somewhere within us, a host of sea sentients scream, and are then silenced. Cut off, like a severed phone line.

We turn Ben's head to see the sky burning.

A gigantic plume of ash and fire rises from the ocean in a mushroom cloud.

Just like that, hundreds of the blue-generation *us* have been wiped out.

In the cockpit, Maui Hathaway and Tristan Hyatt, look out and see hundreds of penguins regrouping, a few scattered loping humans between them.

"We're going to have to run right through them," Maui says grimly.

"Yeah, well." Hyatt reaches up for the DC generator. "Let's see if she'll start, first."

The voltage spikes. The propellers don't turn. Not enough heat built up in the engines.

Hyatt sticks his head out of the window and catches Michelle Ajuria's eye. "Hook up the ground cart!" He looks up, and the herd is swarming toward them. "Hurry!"

Over the horizon, the sky lights up. In the direction of Scott Base. Our mind and our world turn into a blinding white shriek of pain. We throw Ben's hands up in front of his eyes, our horror imprinted on his face in a silent scream.

Another shock wave blasts into our back, ice dust sandblasting us. The cafeteria, the Church of the Snows, Crary Lab, Gallaghers, and the center of McMurdo Station detonate and wither in a wall of unrelenting flame.

We stumble to our feet right as another LC-130 flies overhead. It banks across Cape Royds, out over the sea with its deadly payload–

– toward Shackleton's Hut *and our prisoners.*

We let out a scream of pure frustration through Ben's tortured throat.

Another white flash. We sense when our prisoners, held far from the Station in waiting for the gift of the grey-generation, are wiped out.

"How are they doing this?" we scream through Ben's raw throat at no one. Except we know. It floats to us through Mason's memory, once stamped onto the network, now erased. Thermal pods. The aircraft sense body heat, anything above the temperature of the snow.

We start digging a hole in the snow. Frantically.

Behind us, the red Basler rises into the air, climbing unsteadily away from Willy Airfield. The last of the human survivors, leaving – leaving for the mainland without us.

Ben's eyes bulge in their sockets. Our thoughts are huge and moist and warm and terrified. But it's not over, not yet, because we have one more trick. One last hidden ace in the hole.

We cast our hive mind out to find Bethany–

All that comes back is deafening silence.

(*NOOOOOOO*)

Except it isn't total silence.

There is an imprint in the darkness. A hollow shape where once there had been a presence. Bethany is alive, but she is – somehow – no longer one of us.

The Basler banks into the sky overhead, pointed the wrong way.

Pointed south.

Dr. Mason is dead, and without him, there is no way for either the survivors, or us, to leave this continent.

Jonah had known that, when he'd pulled the trigger. If he'd aimed his last bullet at us, we would have evaded it easily, but not the CIA scientist.

Now no one would leave. Not them, not us. No chance of spread.

Tears of silent rage roll down Ben's face. We feel a tide of sorrow and hopelessness, flecked with hard pits of pure suffocating frustration.

We turn Ben's eyes south, back to Pole. Back to where it all began.

That way lies the only chance of survival.

It's a long walk, we think.

But we've done it before.

Chapter Sixty-Three

November 3.

South Pole Station.

The Basler circles South Pole Station, wings waggling. It begins a short, unstable approach at the minimum practical airspeed. Tristan Hyatt sets the big ski aircraft down as gently as he can. The skis catch in the blown snow of the barely-curated runway; the nose of the old plane tips down dangerously. Hyatt fights the yoke, lips drawn back over his teeth in a canine snarl, and somehow the nose stays out of the snow.

They keep rolling, then come to a slow stop, yards from the bottom of the world.

In the jump seat of the cockpit, Rajan looks up the snow hill toward Amundsen-Scott South Pole Station, where he had started his tumultuous ice season. He sags against the icy window. A cold flicker runs over his skin, like the touch of ghost fingers. "Never thought I'd see this place again," he says, and his voice is an empty chasm.

He turns and looks down the aisle of the Basler. Pastor Kwanje and Winston. The two pilots, Hyatt and Maui. Siri, Bethany and Michelle Ajuria.

The eight of them are all that's left.

Hyatt reaches up to the mixture cut-off lever. "Once I kill this, it's done," he warns. "It'll be too cold for the engine to restart. We'll be here until we're rescued."

"This is the only place we can go," Rajan says heavily.

Silence settles over the South Pole as the propellers whisper to a halt, then arrest. Rajan looks up to see Siri crouching next to him.

Her face is tight as she points through the Basler window, toward a cluster of three snow vehicles outside the Station.

"Those vehicles aren't ours," she says. "Who is that?"

Twenty-four hours ago.

The dark dot of South Pole Station, where the sun meets the snow on the horizon, should have been a relief. It means the end of a long and brutal trek for Jiuyin Mei and his handpicked crew of four – from the port in Qingdao, through the sea ice to Zhongshan, across the Antarctic crevasses to Dome-A, and finally, the American station is in sight.

But Jiuyin knows it is here the danger really begins. Following the footsteps of the last members of the Dome-A crew. All the answers lie here, at the very bottom of the world, and they may not be easily revealed.

His radio crackles. "Sir. On the roof of the station."

Jiuyin is in the second of three snow vehicles, staring through the scratched, ice-flecked windshield. He pans his binoculars in time to see a tall black man, wrapped in a bright red jacket, on top of the building. Incongruously, the man appears to have a coffee cup in his hand.

Then he disappears.

Jiuyin smiles grimly, and checks the load on the machine gun between his legs.

So. They have now seen each other.

The three vehicles spread out, circling the station independently. Jiuyin's sharp eye notices the scorch marks at the entry to the arches, the barely plowed runway, and finally, the burned front entrance to the Station. The outer of two doors blown clean off its hinges. If they have to fight, it will not be the first fight this station has seen.

He can practically feel the adrenalin radiating from the driver of his SnoCat. Zhang Minghao is ready for a firefight, after what he has seen at Dome-A. "Stop," Jiuyin says.

The two men look up at the station. Their engine rumbles in the cold. Spewing clouds of smoke. Nothing stirs inside.

"There are many places a clever person could hide in there," Jiuyin murmurs.

He carefully wriggles into his Hazmat suit. Minghao buttons him up, then he picks up the radio in the cab. "Everyone hold position. But be ready."

Jiuyin steps down onto the snow.

"Sir, your gun!" Minghao exclaims. It's on the floor of the cab.

Jiuyin almost changes his mind. But all he can think about is Lingling, spread on that kitchen sink. Eyes half-closed and rolled back toward him. *Can you see what killed me, brother?*

And he prays that she can hear his answer, wherever she is now. *Not yet, mèimei. But I will look until I can't anymore.*

He is a man well-trained in violence; perhaps his default state. Especially when it comes to matters of the motherland. But he owes it to his sister to try another way first.

He closes the door of the cab. He walks toward the broad, flat steps of South Pole Station. Climbs them, moving slowly. He comes to a stop on the landing, several steps away from the warped Destination Alpha inner door.

He should be afraid. But he just waits, mind blank.

Exposed and unarmed, on the doorstep of his enemy.

The tarp moves. Jiuyin thinks he recognizes the frame of the man he'd seen atop the station before. He is not dressed in any protective gear except a Big Red jacket. And he wears a snow-white submachine gun; slung across him, muzzle pointed at the ground, but his hand is on the stock.

"You speak English?" the man shouts. Puffs of cold air drift from his mouth.

"Yes." Jiuyin says.

"Tell me why you're here."

"Lingling Mei was on Jiang Cheng's crew at Dome-A. She died there." Suddenly it's difficult to speak, and there are tears in his eyes. "She was my sister."

They stare at each other for a long moment.

Then the man steps out onto the landing, and pulls down his ski mask.

"We've got a lot to talk about," Keyon says. "I guess you'd better come inside."

Now.

Rajan looks out of the window of the Basler aircraft. Standing by the side of the shipping container that doubles as South Pole Terminal is a man in a red jacket with a thick black-colored stripe at the waist, flanked by three men. A woman stands apart from them, enclosed in a Hazmat suit.

She holds a glass container, split open like a flower.

Rajan knows there will be black dots all over it. Heat-scarred microbes.

(*rajan*)

His heart leaps as the Chinese men part, and Keyon steps forward. Rajan puts his hand on the glass, spreads his fingers wide. From down on the snow, Keyon opens his arms. Both men basking in the other's affection and relief.

They are both still here.

"I'm so happy to see you, Rajan," Keyon mouths the words, even as they echo in his mind. His face splits into a grin that quickly shadows away.

(*but you're back here and not on an island in the Caribbean so something is wrong*)

Seeing the Chinese markings on the vehicles by Pole Station, Rajan feels a bit like a loose bolt knocking around a jet engine. After his own government had been willing to accept their deaths as collateral damage, could their enemy actually turn out to be their savior?

Rajan thinks about Mason, who had slyly offered him a way to come to Antarctica. The man who had started this whole nightmare is now slumped over a snowmobile somewhere on the McMurdo sound, but there's an imprint of his thoughts, left behind–

(*this is all going to get spun as the fault of the Chinese and I need no one left around who can contradict that. do you understand what i'm saying mason*)

"They came without an airplane, Raj," Siri says softly, from beside him. Sensing everything that's racing through his mind. "They could be our way out of here. Even..."

(*our way off this continent*)

Except the stakes have changed. Everything is different now. The Americans have bombed McMurdo, bombed Scott. The Pacific Rim war has come to Antarctica; intersected with the microbes.

The ice plague wars have begun.

"Dropping munitions is a big, overt statement. That means the CIA will have figured out a way to blame China for this on the world stage." Rajan looks up, eyes empty, then past her at the Chinese snow vehicles. "What do you think the orders of those people will become, when they hear from their superiors?"

Siri takes his hand in hers. She looks into his eyes.

"Let's go find out."

Epilogue

Off the coast of Antarctica.

North and east of Zhongshan Station, the Chinese Vitus Bering Class icebreaker ship, *MV Xue Long 2,* sails gently at three knots, encased in bright daylight even though the ship's clock shows midnight. Colonel Zhou Su is awake and on the bridge when the watch officer shouts, "Sighting ahoy! Man in the water!"

The crew bursts into motion, spotlights blazing across the lit deck. A zodiac boat is lowered down to the ice-speckled waves. The men aboard it gently pull a body, face down and floating, out of the water. They bring him up to the deck.

The corpse wears an American Big Red jacket. His fine blond hair clings to the icicles on his face like seaweed draped over a drowned man. There's an unhealed gash in his face. What look like fingermarks claw down his cheek.

They roll him over and Penny's eyes blink black, then flush with blue.

About the Author

Mikey (Michael Nayak) has worked as a planetary scientist, pilot and skydiving instructor, and most recently as a Program Manager with the Defense Advanced Research Projects Agency (DARPA). He is a US Air Force Test Pilot School graduate, former NASA Space Shuttle engineer, and a former Principal Investigator with the US Antarctic Program. He has deployed to both McMurdo and South Pole Stations. Mikey invites you to connect with him on Instagram at @AuthorMichaelNayak; more about his writing is available at www.michaelnayak.com.

Author's Note

Sometimes, truth is just as strange as fiction.

In February 2025, *Symbiote* was released, portraying a fragmenting winter crew in an isolated environment already at the extremes of the human condition. In March 2025, the Sanae IV research station in Antarctica (South Africa) was racked by allegations of inappropriate behavior, physical assault, sexual harassment, "an environment of fear", and crew members "plead[ing] to be rescued" during a winter deployment (BBC, www.bbc.com/news/articles/cgkm0k2j6edo).

From the BBC article: "Working in such close proximity to a small group of colleagues [has] risks. You know exactly how they put their coffee cup down; you know that they scratch their nose three times before they sit down; you know everything about them. And in the bad circumstances, it can start to irritate you. Because there's nothing else. There's no other stimulus and you're with [these] people 24/7."

Antarctica is not for the faint of heart.

A few years ago, I had the opportunity of a lifetime: to deploy to Amundsen-Scott South Pole Station, for the summer season, as a National Science Foundation (NSF) and Air Force Office of Scientific Research (AFOSR) Principal Investigator. I wrote most of the prequel to this book, *Symbiote,* while a crewmember at South Pole Station.

I'm not alone in thinking my time on the ice was life-changing. I received this note through my website, www.michaelnayak.com, and it touched me deeply.

Hi Fellow Polie,

I do not offer that lightly. I have been to the Ice twice: 26 months in total at the South Pole. I have wintered over twice. Every time I see another article on the Pole, I grit my teeth and wonder what inane bullshit will be trotted about the most amazing, hard, brutal and beautiful place on earth, by some asshat who went down for 4 months and spent 3.5 of them drunk in the Slump.

You, Michael, get it.

You not only get it, you have been able to express such admiration and understanding about a place that is hard to understand. How do you explain the way your skin feels working outside at 60 below zero, the way the ice builds up on your eyelashes, the way you breathe while shoveling out the 12th triwall of the day? How do you wrap your head around the the fierce protectiveness that you have for people who, in all honesty, you would probably not even speak to off Ice. How indeed?

Yet, you did. And you did it so well, that I sit here in Dubai and feel tears in my eyes. God, I miss the South Pole. Congrats. And thank you. Truly thank you for being a true OAE.

Thanks to Lynnette Harper (winter-over 2006/2011), and the hundreds of Old Antarctic Explorers (OAEs) like her. They really are a unique breed of human. The fragility that Sanae IV revealed make that even more potent. I'll be eternally grateful to have been a Polie, for however evanescent a time.

Now, to bring it a little closer to home: I wrote *Sentient* while working long days as a Program Manager (PM) at the Defense Advanced Research Projects Agency, or DARPA. I was affiliated with three of the agency's six technical offices – the Strategic Technology Office, the Defense Sciences Office – and oh yes, briefly, the Biological Technologies Office.

Like Dr. Kim, I am a DARPA PM. And that, too, has been a life-changing experience.

DARPA is a strange place[1]. It's a government agency whose only mission is to change what's possible. It created the first networked computers, which grew into the sprawling web of the Internet. It created the first miniaturized position navigation and timing devices, and today, GPS is used for everything from Google Maps to syncing ATM machines. It funded mRNA research, and today the world has used mRNA vaccines to move past a global pandemic. Walking through the doors of the agency's headquarters, you feel that legacy. But being a DARPA PM means you don't really pay any attention to all that.

It's already history. And the job of a DARPA PM is to make the future.

Perhaps that's what makes DARPA such a strange place. It's not just imagining a future that doesn't exist. It's grabbing that future and dragging it into the present. In many ways, DARPA and being a hard science-fiction author have a lot in common. You imagine a future. You try to ground it in reality. And it's a bit of a trust fall:

You have to believe in the vision so much that it becomes true.

In the Ice Plague Wars series, as several authors have before me, I've made DARPA the bad guy. Being a place of legend and secrecy, it's almost too easy. In truth, DARPA is so much more than that. The agency is, above all else, thoughtful and deliberate. *How are you going to change the world? How do we make this idea bigger? Will we change the course of technology, or create a new field, with this idea?*

These are not just casual questions.

These are pointed queries asked of a PM as they defend their ideas.

As an author, however, I find myself imagining a dark side to such an enterprise. Especially in a time of war: what if that autonomy and genius were turned toward more nefarious goals? *We're locked in a conflict with a near-peer adversary: how does this idea help break us out of the stalemate we find ourselves in?*

---

1 Partly adapted from Chapter 3 of *The Commercial Lunar Economy Field Guide: A Vision for Industry on the Moon in the Next Decade*, edited by Michael Nayak, Air University Press (2025). Used with permission from the author.

I believe DARPA is a force for good in an uncertain world. Should it ever lose that vision, you might just get Dr. Kim, and his callous mad-scientist mentality of experiment-at-all-costs. Let's hope that never happens.

As always, I owe sincere thanks to my agent, Lindsay Guzzardo of Martin Literary Management, who has been the wind in my sails to get this book into your hands. A huge thanks to editor Gemma Creffield, who made sure this book lived up to its potential. My thanks to Caroline Lambe, Desola Coker, Amy Portsmouth, April Northall, Simon Spanton Walker, Dan Hanks, Raeesa Saint, and the rest of the Angry Robot crew: their energy and hard work made *Sentient* a reality!

Ariel O'Connor was a cheerful supporter and fan of my writing, but also helped me better understand the unique intersection of art and science that is the job of a conservator, and what their role in the Antarctic ecosystem might be.

I'd like to thank my friends for their support: Gisela Munoz, Andrea Luethi, Robin Despins, Anne Cheever, Ashley Gonzales, Sarah Johnson, Anna Sheppard, Bogdan Udrea, Stan Straight, Christina Doolittle-Straight, Brooke Hayden, Alissa Vigil, Evelyn "11" Kent, Kyle "Maui" Hathaway, Melissa Staley-Hathaway, Andrew "Doc" Emery, Rachael "Duck" Bradshaw, and Jillian Hannah. Thanks to Sarah Kerce for being my first social media manager. Now I do it myself, to connect directly with you, dear reader. Please share your thoughts with me on Instagram: @authormichaelnayak.

Back to DARPA for a moment. Nothing is forever: key to the agency's model of innovation is the idea that every program manager has a limited term. By the time this book comes out, I'll be on my way to whatever is next. This author acknowledgement is also my farewell thank-you. For all my inspiring coworkers: thank you for letting me share DARPA with you. I hope to be back one day and breathe this rarefied air with you again!

I'd like to thank my incredible team at DARPA, who have allowed me to maximize the impact I've made, while also doing my dream job of being an author. Thanks for walking the tightrope of bandwidth with me and for continuing to opt in, every day: Lee Pele, Christie White, Anna Hall, Kaushik Iyer, Ken Hyatt, Santanu Basu, Erin Fowler, David Ott, and Jane

Kim. Thanks also to former team members Kevin Reed, Colleen Reiche, Matthew Julian, Hunter Gabbard and Ashley Batjer.

There's a small army of incredible, hard-working support staff that keep every technical office at DARPA running. No fast-moving company could ask for better Chief Operating Officers. At the Defense Sciences Office: thank you to Heather Heigele, Julie Evans and Karen McMullen. At the Strategic Technology Office: thank you to Linda Marshall, Jasmine Mack, Marybeth "MB" Barham, Michelle Ajuria, Joe Amalfitano, Rob Newton (let's fucking go!), Jess "Head Executioner" Marsh, Nick Haeuptle, Calvin Wakeman, Justin Voithofer, Jack Weiss, Becky McClure, Jess "JC" Chambal and Dave Jakubek. At the Biological Technologies Office: thank you to Ryann Glaccum, Andrew Younger and Lenny Tender. Like Pokemon, I'm collecting all the amazing DARPA security reps: Nick Pellegra, Ashley Jung, Jacob Fortner, Casey Murphy, Philip Jones, Brian Flavin, Jamie Bugett, Jackie Croat, Mark Bryant, Corey Mahoney, Amy Gutierrez. Additional and sincere thanks to Sara van Gorder, Whitney Mason, Simon Klink, Filza Hall, James "Mac" Ritch, Laura Younger, Oscar Cerna, Lindsay Heil, Allyson O'Brien, Vince Urick (rest in peace, Vince), Rob McHenry and Steve Gribschaw.

I owe a special shout out to my fellow Program Managers. They come into work every day and they don't just try to make a difference. They *make* a difference. I have no idea what I'll do after DARPA, but if it involves working with any of you again, I'd count it as a win.

A special thank you to Philip Root and Stefanie Tompkins, who took a risk on me, and gave me the opportunity to come to DARPA. I hope I've done well by you.

I haven't gotten everyone. Not even close. To everyone whom I crossed paths with during my time there: thank you for what you do. Here's to *your* DARPA adventure. Keep innovating, and defining the future. I'm proud to have been one of you.

And thank you, dear reader. Thanks for coming with me on this journey. You are why I write. Stay tuned for what's next:

@authormichaelnayak on Instagram, and
www.michaelnayak.com.